The
Nightingale's
Castle

The Nightingale's Castle

A Novel of Erzsébet Báthory, the Blood Countess

Sonia Velton

HARPER ● PERENNIAL

NEW YORK ● LONDON ● TORONTO ● SYDNEY ● NEW DELHI ● AUCKLAND

HARPER ● PERENNIAL

HarperCollins books may be purchased for educational, business, or sales promotional use. For information, please email the Special Markets Department at SPsales@harpercollins.com.

FIRST U.S. EDITION

Designed by Jen Overstreet

Library of Congress Cataloging-in-Publication Data

Names: Velton, Sonia, author.
Title: The nightingale's castle : a novel of Erzabeth Báthory / Sonia
   Velton.
Description: First edition. | New York, NY : HarperPerennial, 2024. |
Identifiers: LCCN 2023033358 (print) | LCCN 2023033359 (ebook) | ISBN
   9780063351462 (paperback) | ISBN 9780063351486 (ebook)
Subjects: LCSH: Báthory, Erzsébet, 1560-1614—Fiction. |
   Countesses—Hungary—Fiction. | Hungary—History—Turkish occupation,
   1526-1699—Fiction. | LCGFT: Historical fiction. | Novels.
Classification: LCC PR6122.E48 B53 2019 (print) | LCC PR6122.E48 (ebook)
   | DDC 823/.92—dc23/eng/20231019
LC record available at https://lccn.loc.gov/2023033358
LC ebook record available at https://lccn.loc.gov/2023033359

ISBN 978-0-06-335146-2 (pbk.)

24 25 26 27 28 LBC 5 4 3 2 1

For my mother, Sandra

Contents

Historical Note ix
Prologue 1

Part I: Summer . . . 3

Chapter 1: The Girl Catchers 5
Chapter 2: The Castle on the Hill 11
Chapter 3: The Changeling 20
Chapter 4: The Lady of Čachtice 29
Chapter 5: Keys, Clocks, and Pearls 36
Chapter 6: The Gynaeceum 46
Chapter 7: The Sun Is Still Beautiful,
 Though Ready to Set 55
Chapter 8: The Bald Coachman's Wife 59
Chapter 9: Innocence Lost 66
Chapter 10: The Goose 72
Chapter 11: *Sprezzatura* 80
Chapter 12: Antimony 86

Part II: Autumn . . . 97

Chapter 13: Songs for the Dead 99
Chapter 14: Ephemera 108
Chapter 15: Melancholia 120
Chapter 16: Dorka 131
Chapter 17: Kata 138
Chapter 18: Rose Honey 143
Chapter 19: *Káröröm* 147

CONTENTS

CHAPTER 20: Dutiful Love 156
CHAPTER 21: Winter's Witch 159

Part III: Winter . . . 173

CHAPTER 22: The One to Whom the Herbs
            and Flowers Talk. 175
CHAPTER 23: Unknown and Mysterious Causes. 179
CHAPTER 24: Paper Flowers 188
CHAPTER 25: Plumes and Swagger. 193
CHAPTER 26: Between Stones. 201
CHAPTER 27: A Better Man. 209
CHAPTER 28: Phantoms. 214
CHAPTER 29: *Et Tortura* 217
CHAPTER 30: Eleven Questions 220
CHAPTER 31: Let the Master Answer 228
CHAPTER 32: Paragon of Evil 234
CHAPTER 33: Bridle Thy Tongue, Woman 239
CHAPTER 34: Protector of the Goodly
            and the Innocent 247
CHAPTER 35: The Tenth Witness. 253
CHAPTER 36: Privy and Purposeful Accomplices 258

Part IV: Spring . . . 263

CHAPTER 37: Sundry Witches 265
CHAPTER 38: The Palatine's Wife. 272
CHAPTER 39: Homecoming. 278
CHAPTER 40: The Ideal Courtier 286

            Author's Note 293
            Use of Translated Text 297
            Acknowledgments. 299

Historical Note

In 1573, when she was thirteen years old, Countess Erzsébet Báthory reputedly gave birth to an illegitimate child. The infant, a girl, was swiftly bundled up and handed to a villager to be brought up in one of the hamlets surrounding the castle.

History has not recorded what became of the child after that.

When Báthory, the so-called Blood Countess, was arrested in Hungary on December 29, 1610, for allegedly murdering numerous young girls, her four "accomplices" were arrested alongside her. They were János Ficzkó Újváry, a young lad and *johannes factotum* (jack-of-all-trades); Ilona Jó Nagy, former wet nurse to the countess's children; Dorottya Szentes, a senior servant; and Katalin Beneczky, a washerwoman.

The
Nightingale's
Castle

I will not allow myself to be dominated by men for long.

—Countess Erzsébet Báthory,
letter to György Bánffy, February 3, 1606

He saw the sun's dimmed visage disappear,
And spied forth issuing from a cavern hoar
A monster, which a woman's likeness wore.

—*Orlando Furioso, canto 42* 1532

Prologue

In this topsy-turvy world a serving girl can be a queen. She can sit on a wooden throne and, all around her, men will bow their heads and listen. Her word will be law.

"Tell us about this book," says the prosecutor. He is the queen-maker, the one who has elevated this keeper of animals, this sewer of stitches, to such an exalted place.

"It belonged to the countess," she says. "It was in a rosewood box in her library."

The prosecutor doesn't ask how a serving girl came to be in the privy chambers of a countess. Details are as unwelcome in a courtroom as children; merely troublesome and unnecessary.

"You opened it?"

She shrugs. "The key was always kept in the lock."

"What was inside?"

"A book, a kind of ledger."

Remembering the book makes the girl nervous. It was such a sinister thing; an inventory of death, a catalog of misfortune. In her hand she holds a little wooden goose, her poor man's orb. Someone told her once to rub its neck if she felt worried or sad, and she does so now, working her thumb into the worn groove.

"Well, what was in it?" The prosecutor tries to keep the impatience from his voice, but he senses that this girl has important evidence to give. She is different from the other witnesses, with their tales of corpses and burn marks, welts and pincered flesh. She has a connection to the countess that the other girls didn't. He needs to pry her open like an oyster, pluck out the pearl within.

"A list of girls' names, and alongside each one was how she died."

"She cannot even read!"

A voice from the gallery, shrill as a whistle.

"I could see it was a list of names plain enough," insists the girl.

"Who wrote this list?"

"It was in the countess's own hand, a record of all the girls she murdered, and how she did it."

The courtroom erupts, but the prosecutor is momentarily silent. He looks to the jury, the twenty good men who, in this topsy-turvy world, now sit in judgment on a countess. He sees himself reflected in the fine cut of their clothes, the fat that pads their cheeks, the moral certainty of their gaze; and in that moment, he knows that this will be easy.

"How many names were there?" he asks.

The girl-queen shifts on her temporary throne. The trouble with a new woolen petticoat is that it itches. The trouble with good leather slippers is that they pinch. It is odd that, of all the girls who died, this one survived. Of all the girls who had their mouths sewn shut, this one has managed to open hers.

"Hundreds," she replies.

Part I

Summer

Hungary,
1610

Chapter 1

THE GIRL CATCHERS

They are coming up the dirt track that threads past the cottage before it disappears up a mountainside thick with pine trees. She doesn't see them, just notices that the geese clustered at her feet have stopped their incessant snapping at the grass and tilted their sleek heads toward the path, pupils black dots of indignation in their ice-blue eyes.

She turns and clicks her tongue. "Who are these two, my little friends?" she whispers to the birds, resting the basket of grain on her hip.

They make a strange pair, the couple walking up the hill in the late afternoon. A woman, breathless and flushed from the summer warmth, and a young man striding alongside her in patterned leather boots up to his knees, a self-important feather bobbing from his kolpak hat.

"*Apa*, we have visitors," the girl says to the old man sitting in a chair up against the cottage's whitewashed wall, dozing in the shade of its thick thatch roof.

The old man stirs only when the geese scatter, honking outrage at the patterned boots whipping through the grass. He blinks for a moment at the westering sun, then gets up.

"We have come from Čachtice Castle," the booted man says grandly. Up close, she sees that he is more boy than man, his skin still smooth over bones yet to take on the set of manhood. The older woman joins him, shooing at a goose still nipping the grass. She smiles while she catches her breath, but her eyes are fixed steady on the girl.

"I am Dorottya Szentes," she says, after a moment, "and this is János Ficzkó Újváry. We have walked up from the town because we heard the girl needs work."

"Then you heard wrong."

The girl flinches. The old man's words are unexpected, and they have an edge to them, sharp and steely as a blade.

"Come now, sir," says Dorottya Szentes, "what girl would not want to better herself at the court of the Countess Erzsébet Báthory? Why, every girl in the town wants to come back to Čachtice with us."

"So take them and leave us be."

The woman draws in a deliberate breath, then turns to the girl, smiling again. It is an outside smile, thinks the girl, not an inside smile. It merely rests on her face, pretty as sunlight, but it would be gone with a passing cloud.

"You may call me Dorka, child. Everybody does. And what is your name?"

"Boróka. It's short for Borbála."

"And your family name?"

"They call me Boróka Libalány."

The boy snorts. "Boróka goose-girl!"

"Yes," the girl says evenly, "just like they call you János, the lad from Újváry. That's the way it is for people who come from nowhere and belong to no one."

The boy's face darkens, but he says nothing. She notices the feather in his kolpak is from an eagle: white at the base, darkening to an almost black tip. A fine flourish indeed for the lad from Újváry.

"Well, Boróka goose-girl," says Dorka, "we have work for you at Čachtice. My lady needs maids and seamstresses. Can you sew? Cook? Even if you know little more than how to pluck a goose, it matters not. We will teach you how to better yourself."

"The girl is fine as she is," says the old man.

"Is she?" Dorka looks Boróka up and down, taking in the rough linen of her coif and the blousy sleeves of her chemise, a little too short now for her slender arms, a little too grubby at the wrists. Her eyes linger on the girl's face, on the twist of hair falling over her shoulder, dark and shiny as polished wood, until the end where it curls and lightens to gold. "This girl is well favored," she says. "Do you not want a husband for her? Or should she spend her life here, picking those dainty feet through the goose droppings?"

The boy, Ficzkó, laughs. "She can be the Lady of Five Apple Trees," he says, throwing his arm wide to gesture to the orchard stretching behind the cottage, then folding into an elaborate bow.

"Better that than dead," replies the old man.

"What do you mean?" asks Dorka.

"You know what I mean. I've heard that the girls who go to Čachtice Castle never return."

Dorka tuts and sighs. "You must not listen to gossip. My lady cannot offer a position to every girl. These stories are nonsense, spread by the half-witted doxies she discards."

The man laughs. "I would not call András of Keresztúr a half-witted doxy. He is the chief notary, and many witnesses have come forward already."

Dorka cannot conceal her impatience. "Ask yourself this," she says. "What can a serf from Újhely possibly know about my lady's court?"

"What are these people saying, *Apa*?" the girl asks.

Before he can answer, Dorka interrupts. "You call him *Apa*, yet this man is not your father, is he?" Her voice has changed; its pitch is lower, the cadence slower. It sounds slippery in the girl's ears, as if the woman's meaning is impossible to grasp.

"He is father to me," she says.

"Of course," says Dorka, "and how wonderful it would be if the world were that simple, but it isn't, my dear. How old are you?"

"Fifteen."

"A woman, then." Dorka studies her hard. "Do you know what they do to women who live with men who are neither husband nor father to them?"

"Enough," the man warns, but Dorka ignores him.

"They slit their noses," she says, "so that all will know them for the whores they are."

"I am an old man!"

Dorka's eyes flick over him. "You have not yet threescore years, so young enough to trouble the local scolds. We have been in Trenčín only a day, and already I have heard what they say about you two."

"Now who is listening to gossip?"

Dorka's smile is wide. "Indeed, you are right. Perhaps neither of us should be judging the other? Still, you must not worry about these rumors. So long as you let us have the girl, I will tell the gossipmongers that I have seen you with my own eyes and you are a good father to this girl, nothing more."

"Why does that sound like a threat?" says the man.

"It is not a threat, sir, it is a plea: Allow Boróka to come with us to serve the countess. This girl is too good for the geese, or some brutish blacksmith's son."

Inside the cottage, József sits at the kitchen table, scraping at the piece of wood in his hand with a whittling knife. Thick curls of wood drop onto the floor around him as he slides the knife up with a slow, deliberate fury.

Boróka laughs as she sets a plate of salted pork and beans down in front of him. "What is that you're making?" she asks, sitting down opposite him. "Dorka's head?"

József chuckles in spite of himself and puts the carved wood down on the table with a sigh. The shape of a skull is already emerging, and is that a nose? Monstrously long, beaklike, with two eyes above, just vacant holes made with a gouging knife pressed deep into the wood by a vengeful hand.

"No, it is not," says József, wiping his hands on his shirt and picking up a chunk of barley bread. "I would not waste my time making an image of Dorka or her little puppet boy."

The beans are stewed, cooked over an open hearth in a stew pot flavored with caraway and fennel. He jabs the coarse bread into the sauce, then yanks at it with his teeth.

"Why so angry, *Apa*?"

József puts the bread down on his plate, chewing slowly, his appetite fading. Then he rests his forehead on his fingertips, staring down at the table. He stays like that for some moments until the girl wonders whether she should rise and go to him.

When he looks up, József reaches his hand out across the table to her, opening his palm to request her hand in return. "Oh, Boróka," he whispers when she gives it to him, "I'm angry because I know she's right."

A chill runs through Boróka despite the warm evening, despite the cooking fire settling in the grate. She tenses, as if to withdraw her hand, but he holds it tight. "You cannot stay here any longer," he says to her. "You know that."

"But you made a promise," she whispers.

"And I have kept it." József grips her hand more firmly, as if to reinforce the truth of what he is saying. "I told her I would keep you safe, and I have. Now I have to ask myself: Will I be breaking my promise if I let you go, or if I keep you here?"

Slowly Boróka withdraws her hand, and this time he lets her. She sits back in her chair and looks at the food, untouched, on her plate.

A few moments pass before József speaks again. "It is no life for you," he says, "hidden away up here on a hillside."

The sun is setting, and the window above the table is a palette of color: fiery shades through to deepest indigo as the sky darkens and begins to merge with the Carpathian Mountains. They will soon need to light a candle, but neither of them moves. Then Boróka says: "I have never missed other children. I have made friends with the geese and the squirrels that come to steal their grain. I have not lacked for learning, because you have taught me everything. I do not need any more than this."

"You heard what Dorka said." József's voice is gruff, catching round the edges like the half-whittled wood lying next to him. "She will make trouble for us in the town, and we do not need any more of that."

"So is that my choice?" asks Boróka, watching him as he picks up his fork and stabs at a piece of pork. "Go with them to Čachtice or stay here and have my nose slit?"

"No," he replies, "your choice is to go to Čachtice or end up dead like your mother."

Chapter 2

The Castle on the Hill

With every jolt of the carriage Boróka's heart seems to rattle in her chest. They are creaking up a hill, the horses snorting and panting as the wheels crunch over loose stones and catch in grooves baked hard by the summer sun. She grips the wooden figure in her hand, running her thumb over its surface, as if there is reassurance to be found in its smooth curves. *Remember you are loved*, József had told her when he pressed it into her hands.

The carriage lurches suddenly, and Boróka gasps and clutches at her seat.

"For shame," exclaims Dorka opposite her. "What a nervous little bird you are!"

Boróka steadies herself, mumbles an apology. She feels as if they are riding in a huge iron ball being ratcheted slowly up the hill, and that when they get to the top they will hurtle down into something unknown. She bites down on her lower lip and stares at her lap. Although she is concentrating on the coarse weave of her kirtle, she becomes aware of someone's gaze. She looks up and sees that the girl sitting next to Dorka is smiling at her. Boróka's eyes dart to Dorka, but she is busy looking out the window, her brow knitted in concentration as if important matters lie hidden among the stones and sparse shrubs that litter the hillside. The girl puffs out her chest. *For shame!* she mouths silently, mimicking the way Dorka pressed her knuckles into her hip when she said it.

Boróka suppresses a giggle. The girl grins back at her with dimpled cheeks and blows a plume of air up toward her forehead where strands of hair, wispy as the tips of wheat ears, stick to her skin. Her name is Suzanna—Dorka had said as much when she climbed into the carriage—and Boróka is trying to remember whether she has ever seen her in the town, ever stood behind her waiting for the baker to open his doors in the morning, or jostled for space with her at the market when the merchant came with bolts of cloth dyed striking shades of madder and woad. She doesn't think so. She knows most of those girls by sight, at least, but they are the only two in the carriage. So much for every girl in the town wanting to come to Čachtice.

Boróka looks out of the window. She can see the tip of Ficzkó's feather waving beyond the roof of the carriage from where he sits up front next to the coachman. She studies it for lack of anything else to look at, until the carriage turns a corner and a new vista opens up, the likes of which she has never seen before.

Boróka is well used to beauty on a vast scale. She grew up in the mountains and no longer gasps to see the rocky contours of the Carpathians emerge from the black pines that blanket the mountainside, snow-tipped in winter, dense as wolves' fur in summer. But this is not nature's accidental magnificence; it is a cultivated grandeur, built from the very rocks on which it stands. Smooth walls of stone stretch high and wide, so polished by time that the grays shift with the light, like a winter's sky. Beyond the ramparts rise towers and turrets, capped with roofs like pointed hats, colored the same red shades as the parched earth beneath them.

Dorka sees her staring and allows herself a satisfied smile. "Better than your tumbledown cottage, eh?" she says, pressing herself back against the seat so that Suzanna can lean over and look as well. "So, now are you glad you came?"

That is the question Boróka silently asks the castle, but its walls are inscrutable, its windows dark and shuttered, blind to the outside world, keeping its secrets safe.

❋

Suzanna is trailing her fingers along the wall, walking its full circumference. "I have never lived in a circular room before," she says, thrilled. The turret is so small it doesn't take long before she is standing next to Boróka again. "Have you?"

Boróka shakes her head. She has lived in only two places: József's whitewashed cottage and another place. One that she sometimes tries to remember but cannot grasp, as if the memory is a phantom, prone to making shadowy appearances, then disappearing as soon as she tries to fix her eyes upon it.

It is evening, and the tallow candle is turning the air acrid. Boróka walks over to the window and stares out into an empty black landscape that swallows her gaze. Somewhere out there József will be standing at the door of the cottage, whistling into the night, calling the dogs. Then he will shut them all safely inside and set about dampening the fire and filling the jug with water ready for the morning.

"Are you all right?"

Suzanna is behind her, and though she almost whispers the words, they make Boróka's body tense.

"I miss my *apa*," she says, turning around.

"Try not to think about it," says Suzanna, pinching the candle flame between her fingers. "Come," she says, taking hold of Boróka's hand, "let's get into bed."

On the floor is a straw pallet for both of them to sleep on. It is almost as big as the room, which is little more than an old weapons store, a lookout at the top of a staircase that winds up from the tower below. Once they are under the coverlet Boróka studies her bedfellow, the planes of her face in the darkness, the spiky outline of her hair. "Why did you come here?" she asks.

Suzanna's eyes are expressionless, but Boróka hears the resigned draw of her breath.

"My mother sold me," Suzanna says.

"Sold you? How could she do that?"

"Oh, easily." Suzanna rolls over and stares up at the ceiling. "*You useless creature!*" she says, in a voice made so shrill and waspish it makes Boróka want to laugh. "*Haven't you brought the water in yet, lazy girl? Look at these stitches! Did the pigs sew them with their trotters? Who made this bread? Shall I use it to chop the firewood?*"

Boróka snorts. "Was it that bad?"

"Worse. I couldn't do a thing right, and she didn't need me anyway. I have three older sisters all far more likely to make a good marriage than me. I wasn't any use to her, so she was pleased enough to get rid of me."

"I'm sorry," says Boróka.

"Don't be. I haven't had a bed almost to myself since the day I was born!"

Suzanna stretches out, a starfish on the straw mattress. It feels strange to Boróka to have her there. She has always slept alone, save for the dogs who sometimes came to lie next to her, leaning their weight against her and nudging their noses into her neck. She doesn't know whether to shrink from the press of Suzanna's outstretched limbs or embrace her as she did the dogs, seeking warmth, a kind of solid companionship.

"Do you feel scared?" whispers Boróka.

Suzanna turns her head toward her. In the moonlight the whites of her eyes become luminous as pearls. "Of what?"

"Of the countess. People say that many girls come here but few ever return."

Suzanna shifts around to face Boróka again. "I'm scared of hunger," she says after a moment, "and I'm scared of the cold. I'm scared of the wolves that come down to the village in the winter and drag the sick from their beds. What is there to be frightened of here, where our bellies will be full and our feet warm?" Then she stealthily slides her foot across the bed and runs her toes up Boróka's calf, making her jump.

Suzanna laughs. "Dorka was right, you are a nervous little bird!"

"We should sleep," says Boróka, a little testily. "It's getting late."

"As you wish," says Suzanna, propping herself up on one elbow and pulling down the sack of chaff at the top of the mattress so they can rest their heads on it. "What's this?" she says, taking something out from underneath.

"It's nothing," says Boróka, "just a keepsake József made for me."

"But what *is* it?" Suzanna holds it up, inspecting the fluid lines of the wood, squinting in the dark at the delicately carved wings, the webbed feet.

Boróka reaches up, closes her hand around it.

"It's a goose, silly," she says.

It's not yet light, but they are both standing in the castle's vast kitchen, slippered feet chill on the floor, cheeks aglow from the fire. The kitchen—with its vaulted stone ceiling lit all around with oil lamps—is like a crypt. Boróka has her eyes downcast, studying the edge of a wooden table, the wicker baskets filled with vegetables beneath it and the numerous redware pots and bowls laid out on top.

They are waiting to be told what to do, how to make themselves useful, but at the moment they just seem to be in the way. Near the hearth, with its powerful fire, a sweating cook is kneading dough, while another takes out loaves already baked and slides them onto the table: fresh, golden, and smelling of home. The threat of tears begins with a prickle in Boróka's nose. She tilts back her head, as if she could simply drain them away, squeezes her eyes shut, then blinks them open, searching for something to focus on. Above her, the domed ceiling is celestial. Shadowy objects are suspended from chains fixed to the stone: a circle of iron hung with pots and pans, like orbiting planets, and a wooden rack fixed with bunches of herbs and strings of garlic. A dead pheasant looks set to take flight through this strange sky, were it not for the hook riven into its iridescent plumage.

"There you are."

The girls startle and spin around.

"My lady will be up soon," announces Dorka, bustling past them. "The countess takes cinnamon water upon waking, or sometimes a potage of honey and brandied figs."

Dorka gestures to a maidservant, who immediately fetches a basin and begins to fill it with hot water from above the hearth.

"My lady never breaks her fast with meat. Instead, she prefers pitted damson plums with slices of lemon and ginger."

Boróka swallows hard. Is she meant to be learning all this? It's just that she already cannot remember if plums or figs are in the potage and whether the water is flavored with cinnamon or ginger. The maidservant drapes a linen towel over Dorka's arm, then hands her the bowl of water. Dorka turns back to Boróka and Suzanna, eyeing them expectantly.

Boróka holds out her hands, horrified to see that they are trembling. "Do—" She tries to speak, but the words seem caught in a throat swollen with fear. She coughs, takes a breath. "Do you wish me to take that to my lady countess?"

"You?" Dorka laughs so loud the cook looks up from his incessant rolling and shaping of the dough. "You're not fit to have the mistress's eyes upon you! No, I shall take it to her; you're to stay here. Sweep the floor and scrub the table. When the sun comes up, take the slops out to the pigs."

Outside the kitchen is a cobbled courtyard strewn with straw. Close to the castle walls, crude enclosures of wood, hide, and thatch shelter pigs and goats from the sun. Chickens squawk and scatter as Suzanna throws the slops into the pen.

"It feels like home already," mutters Suzanna as a rotten cauliflower head lands flatly in the mud and a large hog grunts and wrestles with the remains of a haunch of venison.

"What will we have to do next, do you think?" asks Boróka, picking out a squishy fig that hadn't passed muster for the mistress's potage and hand-feeding it to a piglet.

"Oh, I don't know, shovel out the midden?"

Boróka blanches. "Do you really thi—" Then she is silent, looking up toward the castle's high turrets. Suzanna empties the rest of the bucket, then follows Boróka's gaze.

The courtyard gives way to an orchard filled with cherry, plum, and apple trees. Overlooking the orchard is a row of elegant casements, diamond-paned leadlights surrounded by pointed stone arches, set into an upper floor jettying out beyond the castle walls. Something has caught Boróka's eye—the curtains being drawn—and beyond them is a woman, looking out over a world laid at her feet.

"Do you think it's her?" Boróka whispers, as if the woman might somehow catch her words, carried on a tattletale breeze.

Suzanna shrugs, but Boróka cannot stop staring at the figure, slim as reeds, as she fades from view.

"Beautiful, isn't she?" Ficzkó has come to stand beside them, dressed in a dark blue dolman with pleated sleeves, exposing a white shirt beneath. "But be careful who you stare at, goose-girl. Even the pigs know to keep their snouts to the ground."

Boróka flushes and lowers her eyes. She knows he's still looking at her. His gaze feels intense, like the glare of the sun, something she might both seek and want to shield herself from.

"I have work to do," she mumbles, bending to pick up the pail.

"Indeed you do," replies Ficzkó, "and that is why I'm here. You are both to go to the east room, next to the buttery. Ilona Jó Nagy is waiting for you there."

The east room is so called because it catches the morning sun, and eight girls are sitting around a table in front of its large window, heads bent, concentrating on the sewing in their hands as if their lives depended on it. In the center of the table is a pile of garments: shirts and chemises, ruffs, collars and cuffs, smelling faintly of tallow soap and stiff from drying in the sun.

Ilona Jó leans over the table and presses her knuckles firmly on its smooth walnut surface. It is as if she has become one with the furniture: fixed and rigid, the tendons on the backs of her hands flexed and taut.

"Can you sew?" she asks Suzanna.

Suzanna suppresses a smile. "My mother used to say that I couldn't sew worse if I had trotters for hands."

The needle of the girl opposite stills. She raises her head a fraction to stare at Suzanna, eyes wide, lips parted in a silent exclamation.

"What did you say?" Ilona's voice pricks like the pins in a box in front of her.

Suzanna glances at the girl, who immediately returns her attention to the petticoat she is darning, pulling the thread so tightly she gives it pleats.

"I'll do my best," she says, chastened.

"Indeed you will." Ilona reaches into the pile of clothes and pulls out a stocking. "Begin with this," she says, dropping it in front of Suzanna. "And mind I can't see the stitches."

Suzanna picks up the stocking. It is made of a material she has never touched before, gossamer in her hands, delicate as a moth's wing. To Suzanna's dismay, even the finest thread seems to drag through it like a cart horse pulling a plow. She glances at Boróka, who has been given a white linen headdress, starched and embellished with beads at the front. Boróka's fingers are impossibly nimble, and she soon reattaches the loose tie of the *pacsa*. Ilona nods, satisfied, and hands her a shift with a pulled hem. "Look to your own work," she snaps at Suzanna as she passes.

In years, Ilona Jó is about the same as Dorka: that is, an old crone well past her fiftieth year. But while age has attached itself to Dorka in layers, pressing out her bodice and settling round her neck in folds, it has stripped Ilona bare. She stands at the head of the table like a silver birch in winter: a thin, pale column, all knots and skeletal limbs.

Suzanna has finished her darning. She lays the stocking on the table, smoothing it out with her fingers. While she is looking at the pile of clothes, wondering what to take next, the stocking slides out from in front of her, pincered between Ilona's finger and thumb.

"Do you mean to mock me?"

Ilona's voice is quiet, but the girls all look up, their eyes inevitably drawn to the stocking dangling from her fingers.

"No, mistress."

"Then why have you done this?"

"Done what, mistress?"

"This!" Ilona shakes the stocking so that it jerks like a hooked fish. "This stocking is made of the finest silk, imported from Lyon, and you have *ruined* it. The holes are all . . . *puckered*. My lady countess's legs will look like she has a pox!"

One of the girls sniggers but it is hard to tell which one, as a moment later all their faces wear the same expressionless mask.

"Do you understand why you're here?" asks Ilona, but Suzanna shakes her head miserably. "You are here to show me what skills you have. The girls who can sew will be seamstresses, perhaps even join the lace school. The girls who can tell goose fat from lard will work in the kitchen. But the girls who can do neither . . ." Ilona pauses. She lays the stocking carefully back down in front of Suzanna, as if submitting evidence. "Well, they must go to the laundry house to help with the great wash."

"It wasn't her fault."

Ilona's eyes slide from Suzanna to Boróka, reluctantly, as if dragged away by something even more troublesome.

"No one could darn silk neatly with thread of flax," says Boróka, her voice barely louder than the rustling from the other six girls, all shifting nervously in their seats.

For a moment Ilona stares at her, then she does something extraordinary. She crouches down next to Boróka and takes hold of her hand, gently running her thumb over the girl's skin. "What a shame," she whispers. "I had thought these fingers as deft as any I had ever seen, but now they will be ruined, stripped to the bone by a week submerged in potash and hot chamber lye."

Chapter 3

The Changeling

He has been watching her for a while now. From the low wall separating the courtyard from the orchard, where he sits, he has a clear line of sight to the washhouse. The great wash is well underway. Baskets of bedsheets, pillowcases, towels, and linens are being brought forth from chests in the garrets where they have been accumulating over the months that the countess has been in residence. Every time a girl appears, the washerwoman, Katalin Beneczky, takes the basket from her, then sends her back for more.

The door of the washhouse has been left open and steam escapes, like smoke, into the summer air. He has a long piece of grass in his mouth and its tip, heavy with seeds and bushy as a squirrel's tail, bobs up and down as he absently chews on the other end. He watches her take her skirts in her hands and lift them up past her ankles before stepping her bare feet upon a wooden stool. The wash pail is deep, and she gathers her petticoats higher, tucking them up into the fastenings of the apron tied round her waist. Then she climbs into the soapy water, cautious, flinching as the warmth creeps up thighs the color of hawthorn honey.

The cuff comes out of nowhere, catching him unawares across his brow. He cries out and spits the grass stem onto the cobblestones.

"I'll have none of that," says Dorka, glaring at him.

"None of what?" says Ficzkó, sulky, rubbing above his eye.

"There's plenty more needs your attention than that girl," she says, nodding toward the washhouse. "We need more ashes for the lye. Look to it that you bring some to the outhouse, and don't dally."

Ficzkó waits until Dorka's back is turned before he scowls properly, defiantly staying put until she walks away and the door of the kitchen closes behind her. He has on a new saffron kaftan, its color as intense as the marsh marigolds that blanket the Váh Valley. He is no ash-mule, he grumbles to himself, while he gets it anyway.

The inside of the outhouse is dark and cool. His eyes adjust from the squint that shielded him from the summer sun to a wide-eyed gaze looking for somewhere to put down his sack of wood ash. The outhouse is like the landscape; it changes with the seasons, becoming washhouse, brewhouse, or apple store depending on the rhythms of the castle. Today it is full of washing bats hung on hooks behind huge barrels mounted on blocks, dripping lye into buckets. He drops the sack against the wall and stands there a moment, brushing stray ashes from the shoulder of his kaftan.

A movement at the outhouse door makes him turn. He recognizes, not her face—which is just a silhouette with the sun behind her—but the shape of her. Her waist, the twist of her hair, her legs under bunched skirts, bare feet, still damp and soapy, picking up dust and straw as she steps inside.

He is motionless while she looks at the utensils hanging on the wall, picking up first bat, then board, inspecting, then replacing them. He knows she has seen him when she gasps and tugs at her skirts, pulling them down to cover her legs, as exposed as the skin of a plucked chicken.

"No need to cover yourself on my account."

She blinks at him, a sun god in his saffron kaftan, emerging from the darkness.

"Is that you, Ficzkó?" she says.

Before Ficzkó was Ficzkó, he was János.

His mother birthed him in the same unremarkable way she had all her children: squatting in the croft where she was working when the time came, then bundling her newborn up in a shawl and pulling him back to their dwelling in a handcart along with the rest of the day's harvest. At first—when she had used the corner of her apron to wipe the remains of her own self from the crevices and folds of his face— there was nothing to suggest that this child was any different from any other, so she set about rubbing his skin as though she was polishing the windowpanes, as the child had not yet taken a single breath. Just when she had begun to wonder whether the child would even live, he opened his mouth and let out a wail lusty enough to startle the crows. "Good boy," she whispered to him.

And that was when he first opened his eyes.

The day before his birth she had gone to the market. She took with her five fine cabbages to exchange for barley and rye. There was a man, someone she had never seen before, selling vegetables, and he called her over. "Mistress," he said, "you are the most beautiful woman in Újvár. Your eyes! They are like water meadows in the sunlight. What color do you say they are?"

Of course, she should have chided him for his impertinence, but she didn't. The baby was weighing heavy in her belly, and it had been a long time since a man had paid her any attention at all. She did not want to go back to her cabbages, with their stink bugs and flea beetles, so she answered him: "Either green or blue, sir, as you prefer."

This delighted the hawker. "I say green," he replied, "for it is the color of love," which just made her blush. Then—to keep her with him a moment longer—he said, "Mistress, buy something, please. What about this?"

To her astonishment he held up a carrot so comically grotesque, so malformed, that she laughed out loud and took it from him, as she had never seen the likes of it before. It appeared to be a gnarled hand, the fingers twisted round each other in a tight spiral, all knobbles and tendrils. But rather than fling this misshapen thing from her, she simply gave him a coy smile and said, "I think not, sir."

"Keep it," the man replied. "No one else will buy it, and it will remind you of me: ugly, but full of goodness."

Fool that she was, she was flattered. She was so consumed by her own vanity that she dropped the carrot into her cart and took it home. Then, later, with the hands that had touched it, she rubbed her swollen belly, murmuring soothing words to the ripple of limbs under her skin.

It was only now—looking down at her baby's strange eyes—that she remembered. Green is not only the color of love, it is the color of demons. The hawker, with his devilish flattery and deformed produce, had cursed her. Blue or green, he had asked her? And now, there it was: the evidence of her flirtatious indecision set forever on the face of her very own child.

Ficzkó moves slowly around Boróka. She watches him, still as a hare observing a fox. He stops when he is between her and the door.

"Don't call me Ficzkó," he says.

It was both fortunate and unfortunate that the cobbler paid little attention to his new son, János. Fortunate because, if he had, he might have seen those ambiguous eyes for himself and forbidden his wife from even putting the infant to her breast, and that would have ended him in quick time. Unfortunate because that may well have been preferable to what followed.

As it was, the boy had a chance to live because it didn't occur to his father to look closely at his fourth son any more than he was inclined to inspect his wife's cabbages. It was her work to tend to them both, and hers alone, so for the first weeks of his life János survived, carefully swaddled in his mother's shawl.

But babies grow and throw off their swaddles, especially this one, who had an apparently insatiable appetite. Even after he had been put to the breast he still screamed in frustration, his fists bunched tight and his face turning red with rage. She knew not what she was doing wrong, having fed all this child's brothers quite well. It was not long before the cobbler, frustrated by the child's constant noise, strode over to János and fixed him with a furious stare.

Even János was obliged to take a breath between wails at some point, and when he did, he opened his eyes and returned the look his father was giving him with his own, distinctly equivocal, gaze.

Cobblers, unlike butchers and blacksmiths, are not known for their temper, but when János's father caught sight of his son's inexplicable eyes, he flew into a rage. He had known all along that there was something strange about this fractious child, and now he had proof of it. He caught his wife by her wrist. "What manner of child has one eye that is blue and one that is green?" he demanded.

"It was my own doing," she sobbed, sinking down to the floor, her skirts puddled all around her.

"How so?" asked the cobbler, standing over her, still gripping her wrist. But she couldn't tell him. She could not explain to her husband that her virtue had been tested. Temptation had been put in her way in the form of a flirtatious stranger, and instead of turning away from him, as she ought, she had been so taken in by his flattery that she had allowed him to taint her own child. That carrot was a sure sign of misfortune, of nature gone awry, but instead of fleeing she had simply turned up her palms to accept it.

"How so?" he said again, but his wife hung her head.

The cobbler nodded slowly, then released her wrist. "It is as I thought," he said. "The boy is a changeling. You must have turned your face away from him as you slept and allowed the fairies to take him."

And she nodded, because even this shameful negligence was preferable to the truth.

The girl is backing away from him. In a few moments she is against the wall, jutting tools pressing into her skin. He doesn't feel sorry for her, doesn't think that he might be frightening her. Instead, her fear makes him angry. Beautiful things have always flinched from him, when all he wants to do is touch them, stroke them, love them. It was the same with the cat that used to sit in the sun on the orchard wall, years ago:

smoke-gray with fur almost as long as his young fingers and paws so white it looked like it had walked through a sack of flour. Every time he tried to grab it, it clawed its way up into a fruit tree and sat there among the bare branches, or the blossoms, or the pears, eyeing him with infuriating disdain. One day it had been asleep, and he had managed, for a moment, to stroke that fur, soft as clouds, before it had swiped at him and drawn beads of blood from the back of his hand.

The next time the cook put fish scraps in a bowl and set it on the cobbles behind the kitchen door, the cat wasn't there. Nor the next day, or the one after that. When they asked him if he had seen it, he told them what he knew for certain to be true: that Stefan had taken it.

He is inches away from her, so close he can almost feel her. Her aura is as warm and scented as a summer meadow, something he wants to step into, get lost in. He sees the girl's hand twitch, as if about to move. He keeps looking at her face, but out of the corner of his eye he is watching her hand as it hovers at her side, uncertain. He braces himself, almost wanting her to strike him, knowing that the sting of the slap will be as vicious—and as fateful—as the scratch of that beautiful cat.

The cobbler, though he was a modest man of leather and laces and tacks, was by no means stupid: He was well aware what had to be done in order to rid them of the changeling and have their own child returned. He knew that changelings need human milk to survive, so first he had his wife feed the babe nothing but pap through a cow's horn for a full month. This seemed to enrage the changeling even more and the crying worsened. The cobbler was at his wits' end. János was his fourth son; he already had boys aplenty to plow the croft and apprentice his trade. He had hoped, this time, for a daughter to look after him in his later years. Instead, not only did he have another mouth to feed but one that was perpetually open in a piercing, insistent scream, so he took the child to a midden and set about whipping him with a birch stick, while his wife stood by and wept.

Months passed, and the fairies seemed to care not a jot that their changeling was as miserable as it was possible to be. No amount of starving or whipping seemed to make them feel sorry enough for their own child to take him back and return the cobbler's rightful son. Stranger still, the changeling grew strong despite his mistreatment, almost as if someone had been feeding the boy bacon scraps and wholesome cabbage soup behind the cobbler's back.

Then one day, when the child was in his third year, he wandered into his father's shop while the cobbler was at his workbench hammering wooden pegs into the heel of one of the baker's shoes. The cobbler didn't see him, but the baker's wife did.

"What an uncommonly beautiful child," she exclaimed, before the cobbler had had a chance to shoo János away. The baker's wife was fond of children and immediately dug about in her pockets for a packet of candied lemon she was sure she had. János could not believe his good fortune when the baker's wife offered him such a treat, and he took it from her with a grateful smile.

The very next week not a single person brought their shoes to be mended by the cobbler. This was no surprise to the cobbler himself. The baker's wife was known to be a gossip and she had surely told the good people of Újvár that his child had eyes like no other. A changeling was bad luck and he was certain he would do no business until he was rid of it. After all, who wants to walk in an unlucky man's shoes?

The shovel was old but made of wrought iron and was still sound and perfectly serviceable. If you had asked the cobbler where it had come from, he wouldn't have been able to tell you. It had been his father's, and his father's before him, used to dig a path through the winter snows so that customers could reach three generations of cobblers. This time the task was different, but the shovel was wide and flat, and just what the cobbler needed.

It took a minute or so to heat up. In that time even the cobbler himself wondered if it could really be true that a changeling sat upon it would be unable to stand the heat and disappear up the chimney, never to return. But he pushed aside his misgivings, set his jaw, and gripped the wooden handle tight, holding the shovel steady above the fire.

Surely, even the fairies would not stand by and watch their kin burn.

❄

When her hand makes contact with his skin, it is more shocking than Ficzkó could ever have imagined. The gentleness of it blindsides him and he almost rears back, repelled by her fingertips on his jaw, their water-soaked softness and lavender-soap smell. His astonishment keeps him rigid as she brushes away a trace of wood ash.

"What happened to you, Ficzkó?" she whispers.

The reason that János's mother liked cabbages so much was that they were predictable. They grew in the same way, at the same time, year upon year, and, provided she watered them and picked the caterpillars off their leaves, they gave her no trouble.

Not so her husband.

She was in the croft when she heard her son's screams. She put down her trowel, picked up her skirts, and ran back into the house.

Now, every wife knows not to gainsay her husband and—through almost ten years and four children—she had bitten her tongue on more occasions than she could remember, but the sight of her little boy above the fire, like a suckling pig, was too much for her. She grabbed the shovel and swung it with such force that János flew off his blistering perch and landed, with much relief, on the cool flagstones.

If the story could have ended there, then János might have stayed János forever, but his mother had grown up near the forest, with its pack dogs and brown bears, and she knew that once an animal has a mind to kill its young it will not rest until it is done.

As fate would have it, a traveling troupe were performing in the town square; a raggle-taggle band of puppeteers, acrobats, minstrels, and jugglers. Early the next morning, as the troupe rolled up their tents and filled their wagons with trunks, she took little János to the puppeteer and abandoned him to a life she hoped could be lived unseen, hidden away in a puppet booth, seeing the world through the painted eyes of a dancing marionette.

It wasn't long before the puppeteer forgot what the boy's full name was, and so he became János Ficzkó Újváry: János, the fellow from Újvár; then, later, just Ficzkó.

For Ficzkó's part he did not much care what he was called because, unbeknownst to his father, the cobbler's plan had worked. As soon as Ficzkó felt the shovel's searing embrace he had cleaved apart, separating himself into two different people. He was both Ficzkó and . . . someone else entirely, and from that moment on, this other person was responsible for every wicked thing he did.

Ficzkó is adept at protecting himself from everything except a gentle touch. He knows what to do with aggression, but concern leaves him floundering. He catches hold of her wrist, twists her arm away from his face. She starts to struggle, tries to pull free, but he holds her tight. In the gloom her eyes are wide and fearful. She will know better than to assault him with her kindness again, he thinks.

The outhouse darkens. The washerwoman is standing in the doorway. She has come to find Boróka, wondering what has happened to the washing dolly she asked her to fetch. "What's going on here?" she says, her voice sharp.

Ficzkó lets go of Boróka's wrist but doesn't step back. He makes her squeeze past him, enjoys the press of her against him, the brush of her skirts. When Boróka emerges, the washerwoman sees that her face is pale with shock.

"What did you do to frighten her so?" she demands.

Ficzkó shrugs. "It wasn't me," he says, "it was Stefan."

Ficzkó stays in the cool outhouse a moment to collect himself. He puts out an arm, leans against the wall while his breath slows. As he looks down, he notices something lying on the floor. He bends to pick it up, inspects it with a smile. It must have fallen out of the girl's apron in the tussle, he thinks. No one but a goose-girl would own such a thing.

Chapter 4

The Lady of Čachtice

The thunderous menace of the sky is matched only by the look of absolute fury on the washerwoman's face.

"The last days of summer are clean taken from us!" Katalin Beneczky says to Boróka, glaring at the leaden clouds, edged silver by the retreating sun.

Every spare inch of space has been covered with sheets laid out to dry. The grass has become a patchwork quilt, made only with squares of white. Trees cling to pillowcases caught in their branches, fluttering in a breeze threatening rain from the west. The great wash is so close to being dry, so almost ready to be put away, that this sudden change to the weather has brought Kata storming out into the courtyard where she now stands like a sentinel, hands on hips, face tilted up to the heavens, as if just the fierceness of her countenance could keep the rain away.

Undeterred, the first raindrop lands on the sleeve of her chemise. Kata grips the washing bat as if she were going to war and begins to bang it against the stone wall.

"In!" she screams. "In!"

A moment later girls scurry out of the kitchen door. They spread through the courtyard like mice invading a grain store. Two a sheet, they draw it end to end, then pick up the corners before they step toward each other in a perfectly choreographed dance. Boróka looks for

Suzanna so she can help with the sheets, but Suzanna didn't come out of the kitchen with the other girls, so Boróka runs along the hedges, plucking small linens from the bushes like berries.

It's pouring now. Rain splinters against the castle walls and begins to pool in the cracks between the cobblestones. Kata wipes her brow with the back of her hand. "We'll do the wash a month earlier next year," she says, laughing.

The girls run back to the washhouse, laundry piled so high in their arms they can barely see over it. Emptied of its barrels of lye and buckets of soapy water, there is space for rush matting, and the girls put down the sheets, then catch their breath, plucking at the damp sleeves of their chemises, lifting the material from where it's sticking to their skin.

Boróka looks to see if Suzanna is inside the washhouse, but she still can't see her. Now that she thinks of it, she hasn't seen Suzanna since the early morning when she'd left her in their turret because they were late for work and Suzanna couldn't find her shoe. Or was it her coif?

"How are your hands?"

Boróka holds them up, showing front then back to Kata. "Not too bad."

"It's always like this for the first wash."

Kata walks over to a wooden shelf on the washhouse wall. She reaches up and takes down a small bottle of the kind that József keeps in his workroom, dark green glass with a narrow neck and stopper.

"Here," she says, beckoning Boróka toward her, "this will help."

Kata pours some liquid into her own palm, then holds out her hands. Boróka hesitates. It seems intimate somehow for a woman she met only a week ago, albeit that they have spent every day together since, to touch her like this. But Kata takes her hands and begins to work the oil into her skin. Boróka can smell almonds and something else—rose water, perhaps? Kata's hands are warm and gentle in a way that József's never were. It wasn't that he was unkind, he just cared for her in a different way. He taught her the things she needed to know, protected her, fed and clothed her, but he barely ever touched her.

She can remember sitting on his knee as a small child, learning her letters with his arms around her and the bristle of his beard against her cheek, but in the last few years she was with him he had done little more than pat her hair, or clasp her in a brief, awkward embrace. Kata's touch is like a mother's: instinctive, as natural as a smile.

"There," she says, letting go of Boróka's hands, "all will be well in a day or two."

Boróka looks down at her hands, the redness now shiny with oil. "Mistress Ilona Jó told me the lye would strip my fingers to the bone."

Kata frowns. "She was just trying to frighten you. Pay her no heed next time." Then Kata turns away, giving her attention to another girl who has seen the almond oil and rolled up her sleeve to show Kata some ailment that requires her ministrations.

The great wash is done. Though the downpour has eased, it's still raining lightly, and even when it stops they won't be able to put the sheets out again until the grass is dry. Boróka slips out of the wash-house. It's odd, she thinks, not to have seen Suzanna all morning.

She hurries back to the courtyard and peers in the kitchen door. No one but the cook hacking at meat with a cleaver and a scullery maid scraping dirt from a pile of vegetables. Surely Suzanna and her clumsy fingers are not with Ilona? She must have been given a job somewhere else.

The rain is so light now it is little more than a fine mist. Boróka wanders through an archway at the far end of the courtyard. She has had little time to explore—standing in buckets and up to her elbows in tallow soap—so she has not yet seen the stables that lie beyond the archway.

In a few steps she is in a smaller courtyard with a row of barn stalls on either side. Straight ahead are two huge wooden doors shot through with metal bolts and bars, a sturdy barrier between the castle and the outside world. A stable boy is feeding fistfuls of hay to a horse, larger than any she has ever seen before, while stroking its neck, whispering into its ear like a lover. He eyes her, curious, as she wanders past the barn stalls. There is no reason for Suzanna to be here among these beasts with their tack of honeyed leather and burnished brass. She is about to go when a great rumbling wells up in the distance. It must be thunder, another downpour, but when she looks up, the sky is the same inscrutable gray. Then the stable boy drops the hay and runs to the doors. He slides across bolts and pulls up battens from where they are secured into the cobbles until, with all the creaking and groaning of an old man getting to his feet, the vast doors swing open.

Havoc. The dogs of war let slip. Horses, so black their flanks shine like spinel stone, bearing down on her. Nostrils flaring, breath hot and damp in air already steamy with rain. And the noise; the hooves clattering against the cobbles, the stable hand grabbing for the reins, shouting, "Whoa!" and "Back, back!" while a stallion rears and nickers. Boróka didn't step into this moil; it engulfed her suddenly, as if the doors had opened out on a storm of powerful muscle, panting muzzles, and white, rolling eyes.

There must be five horses in the stable yard now. She needs to get out of the way before they trample her. She steps backward but the cobbles are slippery with rain and muck. The back of her hem catches under her heel and she stumbles, her feet slipping out in front of her. Her hands slap against the cobbles as she tries to break her fall. Then, sitting helpless on the stable-yard floor, she looks up.

If she were to look no farther than the skirts draped crimson over the stallion's heaving flank, the riding jacket buttoned up to the neck, the cuffs studded with a row of pearls, Boróka would think that it was a woman mounted on the horse that now advances toward her. But this, surely, can be no woman. It is an aberration, a freak. No face, just a flat, black oval devoid of expression. But yet, it *is* looking at her, gazing down with eyes that are no more than slits. The horse paws the cobbles and tosses its head above her. Boróka tries to push herself back with heels that slide on the slick floor, but it is futile. This headless—no, *faceless*—horseman is almost upon her, come straight from the most terrifying of her childhood stories. She cannot get away. Her back is against the wooden post of a barn stall. The creature descends from the horse, graceful, as if assisted by unseen creatures, servants of the underworld. Boróka's nails scrape hard against the stone, clutching at nothing but straw and horse dung.

A voice, lyrical, almost amused: "You do not like horses?"

Then that fixed and lifeless visage is gone, loosened away by a tug on black Florentine ribbon. Boróka tries to speak, but this woman, with her jeweled bodice and embroidered blackwork collar, is every bit as terrifying as any headless horseman.

Dorka hurries into the stable yard, come to meet her mistress after a ride cut short by the rain. She gasps when she sees Boróka.

"Get up," she hisses, "you look like a warthog wallowing."

But her mistress smiles and hands her the riding vizard, which Dorka takes with a deep curtsy.

"Come," the jeweled woman says, extending a hand gloved in perfumed leather to Boróka. "I do not care to see my girls sitting in the mud."

When Boróka throws open the door of the turret room she is thrilled to see that Suzanna is there.

"You will not believe what happened," she says, already pulling off her muddy overskirt. "I was at the stables when the countess herself rode in!"

Suzanna takes in Boróka's disheveled appearance. "Did she trample you?" she says, aghast. "Oh, Boróka, are you badly hurt?"

Boróka laughs. "No, I fell over in the mud. She helped me up."

Suzanna's eyes narrow. "Are you sure it was the countess?"

"Of course. She was covered in jewels, and when she got down from her horse the stable smelled of violets. She was . . . exquisite."

Suzanna steps back, looks Boróka up and down as if to check that she is, indeed, all in one piece. "It must have been a visiting noble," she says, a little dismissively.

Boróka doesn't have time to argue. She needs to get back to Kata, see what she can help with now that the rain has stopped. "Shall we go?" she asks, securing her clean skirt with a bow.

"Go where?" says Suzanna flatly.

"Back to the laundry house."

Suzanna lets out a despondent breath. "I won't be helping with the laundry anymore."

"Why not?"

"Because Kata won't let me after I put too much lye in the wash and it turned the countess's pillowcases yellow."

"Oh dear," says Boróka. "What will you do, then? Help in the kitchen?"

Suzanna shakes her head. "Dorka chases me away whenever she sees me after I peeled the wrong root and the countess got turnip for breakfast instead of ginger. No, I have to go back to the sewing room."

"To be a seamstress?" says Boróka, surprised. "That doesn't seem"—Boróka chooses her words carefully—"a good use of your talents."

"It isn't! But Mistress Ilona said she *had* to have me back because I will cause 'less havoc' in the east room, where she can keep an eye on me." Suzanna's voice becomes tremulous. "I don't think that's the reason, though. She *wants* me to get it wrong, Boróka, I know she does. She's hoping I'll make a mistake so she can punish me. That's why I'm still here. I cannot go down there, I cannot!"

"But you must, Suzanna, it will be worse for you if you don't."

Suzanna squeezes her eyes closed, shakes her head. Tears begin to seep into the creases of skin.

Boróka puts her arms around her, strokes her hair. "I will ask Kata if I can be released after the wash is dry. It will not be so bad if we are there together, do you not think?"

Boróka feels Suzanna nod, so she takes hold of her shoulders, looks at her again. "I have something that will bring you comfort," she says, then bends down to her discarded skirt, slots her hand into the folds of fabric. "I keep it with me always," she says, "but you may have it for a while."

Boróka rises, perplexed, then goes over to yesterday's apron and searches in the pocket sewn into the front. "I cannot find it," she says, her voice pitched high with alarm.

"Find what?" asks Suzanna.

"My goose," she replies. "My little wooden goose."

"Oh," says Suzanna, not sounding very concerned.

"You don't understand," says Boróka. "That goose is all I have to remind me of my *apa*. I stroke its neck whenever I feel anxious or alone. I *need* to find it, Suzanna!"

"We will find it, don't worry," says Suzanna, now the one to offer comfort. "I'll help you look for it later. But listen, Boróka; neither of us really needs a goose." Suzanna steps toward her, takes Boróka's hands in her own. "We have each other, don't we?"

Boróka tries to smile, squeezes Suzanna's hands in return, but her mind is racing, thinking of all the places her precious goose could be.

Chapter 5

Keys, Clocks,
and Pearls

Almost every girl in the castle is lined up in the great hall. A man with small black eyes and a mustache waxed into fine points struts back and forth in front of them. He studies the color of their hair and how it falls over their shoulders. He considers their limbs, the length of their necks, the width of their waists. Occasionally, he pauses and picks up a hand by the wrist, checking the smoothness of the skin, the slenderness of the fingers. Most often he finds them lacking and drops the wrist as if discarding a used handkerchief.

Dorka accompanies him on this inspection. She glares at each girl passed over as if her ruddy complexion or thickset ankles were acts of deliberate defiance. Then the man suddenly stops. He goes back a pace and stares hard at the girl in front of him.

"This one," he says.

The painter, Valentino, has come to paint the countess. He is from Padua, but it has been years since he was last in Italy. Instead, he travels from town to town, court to court, manor to manor, in a wagon loaded with almost finished canvases. Men astride horses—awaiting features but already furnished with impressively wide calves and curlicued beards—and ladies, as yet no more than shoulders, small hands folded in laps.

36

The countess, however, has insisted that she be painted from scratch, and this will take time. A girl is needed. Someone to stand in the countess's place through the long hours spent filling in the voluminous sleeves of her chemise or perfecting the elegant drape of her damask skirts.

Thus far, only the scene has been set and the first drawing done. The countess is an outline, a chimera waiting to be realized. Valentino is no Holbein, but he is a perfectionist at heart and if the girl is wrong—if she bears no resemblance to the countess at all—then the light will not fall just so. He needs a girl who is almost the countess herself. She should, at least, have the same slender form. Ideally, the same dark hair and long, delicate fingers. Of course, no serving girl could possibly share the countess's haughty demeanor, that certain imperiousness in her gaze, but if the girl is graced with a high, round forehead, long nose, and large eyes, then all the better.

The painter did not expect to actually find her. He thought the image he saw as he passed along the row of homespun girls was as much his own creation as one of his paintings—simply, the girl he would most like to find—until he stepped back and stared at her again.

Boróka has been scrubbed, plucked, and dressed like a feast-day partridge. She stands in the countess's private library, a starched lace collar scratching her neck and a boned corset digging into her skin. For all her attributes, she is still far too short, so they have made her stand in velvet chopines at least six inches high, which are pinching her toes and giving her vertigo. Who knew that luxury was so uncomfortable, that wealth came at such a cost?

She can't help but wilt under the layers of privilege. Linens, petticoats, brocaded overskirts, and a white apron edged with delicate lace. "Stand up straight," snaps Dorka, who is standing on a wooden stool behind her, adjusting the headdress that covers her maiden hair, transforming her from an unwed girl into a woman of rank and status.

"There, Master Valentino, sir, is she ready now?" asks Dorka, clambering down and whisking the stool out of the carefully engineered scene: a polished table on a Turkey rug, possessions artfully arranged, shades of red, brown, and gold expertly blended.

Valentino takes a step forward to appraise Boróka. Unused to her finery, she is awkward as a bride revealed to her betrothed. She lowers her eyes, worried that, despite the illusion of wealth and womanhood, she will still be found lacking.

"Not quite," says the painter. He picks up a ring from the table and takes her left hand. "To signify your generosity," he says, with a twitch of his lips, as he slips it on her little finger. Into her other hand he presses a large key, saying, "Because you are the perfect mistress of your household." Then he reaches for a necklace and hangs it around her neck. "Pearls," he explains, "to represent your nobility of character as well as your great material wealth."

Boróka lifts her gaze and sees that one waxed tip of the painter's mustache is lifted in a quirk, so she returns his surreptitious smile with one of her own.

"Don't be smirking like that for the painting," snipes Dorka.

Four hours later and the painter has drawn Boróka's hand at least ten times. He has drawn it fingers outstretched and as an almost closed fist, resting on the wood. He has taken off the ring and put it on her other hand, then taken it off that hand and placed it on the table in front of her. *No, no, no,* he muttered to himself, tilting Boróka's head this way and that. *La luce!* he exclaimed, then half closed the shutters before throwing them wide open again with an anguished cry. After the first two hours, Dorka had grown tired of her role as chaperone and announced that she had best get her mending as there was precious little else to do sitting there. As she left she threw a pointed, almost accusatory glance at the painter's work in progress, which sent him scrambling for the dust sheet to cover it. Not ten minutes ago, he discarded the first drawing and, since then, has been sitting staring miserably at his blank canvas, rolling the end of his mustache between his fingers.

Boróka daren't move. The painter's creativity is almost palpable; it stretches like a gossamer thread between them, and she worries that even the ebb and flow of her breath might disturb it. A shift in position to ease her aching back or a shuffle of her feet to stop her knees from trembling—perched as she is on her lofty chopines—might sever it completely.

In only a few more minutes, the light saves them both. The library is part of the countess's privy chambers, which face south and over-look the orchards. As the afternoon wears on, the sun is pinched from the sky by the towers and turrets of the west wall. When the room falls into shadow, the painter's furrowed features unfold in relief, like a moonflower opening to the darkening sky.

"Enough," he says, rising swiftly from his chair, "we will begin again in the morning." Then he throws the dust cover over the easel and, without telling her what to do with the symbols of her generosity and nobility of character, he stalks from the room.

Dorka seems in no hurry to return with her mending, so Boróka stands there for a moment, still clutching the key and wondering how to take off the chopines without falling over. The trick, she discovers, is to ease her foot out, without bending to undo them. They are too big for her anyway, and soon she is standing in her stockinged feet on the Turkey carpet, wiggling her toes in its soft pile, rolling back her shoulders and circling her neck.

She puts the key down on the table and slips off the ring that the painter had soon returned to its first position on the little finger of her left hand. She should wait for Dorka so that she can give these precious items back. What if she leaves them on the table and they go missing? Dorka might think she had slipped the ring into the pocket hanging from her kirtle. Now that she thinks of it, where *are* her own clothes? She stands and waits. Her eyes are drawn to all the things she was not allowed to look at while she posed for the painter, staring at a distant copy of Machiavelli's *The Prince* and nothing else. The walls are lined with books. Row upon row of them, bound in red leather and tan vellum, with gold-tooled spines bearing names: Tyndale, Calvin, and Copernicus. She looks down at the table. Though she has spent hours with her hand resting on it, she could barely see what's on it. There is a polished rosewood box, inlaid with mother-of-pearl and set with an ironwork lock, and, sitting on top of it, something so intriguing that she crouches down to get a closer look.

It is a golden cylinder supported by feet in the shape of tiny winged gargoyles staring intently at the four corners of the room. The curved sides are engraved with vases and flowers, scrolls and leaves, circling with no beginning and no end. The top of the cylinder is a disk of silver inscribed with a circle of spaced letters she cannot read, which form no word, and beneath them numbers that seem to count nothing at all. An ornate black needle points directly toward her, as if identifying her: *There is the one who is looking at things she shouldn't be.* In the silence she hears a sound, as measured and constant as her own heart beating.

"*Memento mori,*" says a voice behind her.

Boróka spins around and falls into a curtsy so quickly that she barely straightens up. She stays like this, a cuckoo sitting in a nest of silken skirts that are not her own, until the lady is standing right beside her, looking down at her.

"Remember, you must die," she says.

Boróka's heart no longer beats a gentle rhythm; it hammers in her chest. Her lungs snatch at the air even though she is as still as she has ever tried to be in her life, as if she could turn herself into no more than furniture, simply blend into the ornate pattern of the Turkey rug or even disappear completely. Anything that might mean that the gaze that prickles her scalp and singes her cheeks would simply pass over her. She does not want to die.

"That is what the clock represents," the countess says, bidding her rise with a flick of her hand. "It reminds us of the relentless passage of time and our own mortality."

Boróka looks up and sees that the countess is looking at her intently. She thinks it insolent to actually meet her gaze, yet this great lady seems to want to look at her face. Boróka tilts up her chin and the countess's eyes sweep over her features, her hair, the length of her.

"So," the countess says, "you are me."

"My lady, I do not presume—" But the countess laughs.

"Worry not, you do me a service standing here. Has the painter done anything at all today?"

She walks over to the easel and lifts the dust sheet before sighing. "I see that I have disappeared completely. These itinerant painters are all the same, I shall send for someone from the court in Vienna next time." She drops the sheet and turns back to Boróka. "I'm afraid we shall need you until he gets it right."

"Of course, it is my honor," she says, but the countess is already walking toward her bookshelves.

"Now, where is my book?" she says, running a finger over their neatly aligned spines. "Dorka does insist on tidying everything away all the time."

"Which book do you seek, my lady?"

The countess turns to her with a quizzical look. "Surely, one book is much the same as another to a girl like you?"

"Is it this one," Boróka asks, reaching behind her and picking up the book Dorka had taken off the stool before she used it to stand on, "by Hans Sachs?"

"It is," she says, coming toward Boróka to take it from her.

"I love his verse."

"You have learned your letters?"

"My father taught me."

"And you spent your time reading verse together, did you?"

Boróka drops her gaze, feeling that she is being mocked.

"*Why art thou thus cast down, my love?*"

Boróka slowly lifts her eyes to the countess's. She is not smiling exactly, but there is something playful about her expression, as if they have begun a game, but one without any known rules and with the countess as the only arbiter. Boróka thinks hard, chasing down the words in her mind, picturing herself sitting by the fire with József and his books, hoping that the image will bring the words of the verse back with them.

"*Silver or gold or lands, But for a little time is given,*" she says, only hesitating a little. "*And helps us not to enter heaven.*"

The countess raises a perfectly arched eyebrow. "And who is your father, to be so educated himself?" she asks.

"He was the town doctor, but that was years ago. Now he lives in the hills, where we—" She corrects herself: "*He* keeps animals and makes things out of wood."

"A strange life for a doctor. No wonder you have not two florins to rub together."

Boróka says nothing. It is remarkable that she is even exchanging any words at all with this woman who is so exalted as to be almost a princess. She cannot presume to tell her what had forced József to live up in the hills like a wolf with his cub.

"And your mother?"

"She . . ." Boróka pauses. *If anyone asks,* József had told her, *tell them that she died. Young women die all the time. It could have been a plague, a pox, childbirth. No one will question it.* Boróka looks at the woman in front of her. Perhaps she is emboldened by the pearls at her own throat, by the trappings that suggest she is the countess's equal, but she feels no need to soften the edges of her past, like Valentino might gloss over the flaws of his subjects.

"She is dead, my lady."

"In childbed?"

"I know not. I was taken in as a foundling by the doctor. He could tell me nothing of my real father and only that my mother was dead."

She had half expected the countess to shrink from her as if she were tainted, as if tragedy were a trait passed from mother to daughter, but she just studies her more intently.

"Why would the doctor take you in? Was there not a woman who could give you a home?"

A child does not question why a parent cares for them. To her, it had seemed the most natural thing in the world to be living alone with József, until Dorka brought the town's poisonous thoughts up the hill with her.

"I know of no one, my lady. In truth, we had little to do with the townsfolk."

She hopes the countess will question her no further. Even she doesn't understand why József always told her to come straight back from the market; why he warned her not to speak to anyone more than was necessary to buy their bread or have her shoes mended.

The countess is distracted. The library door has opened, and Dorka is coming in. She stops suddenly when she sees Boróka standing not three feet away from her mistress's person, then hurries toward them. "My lady," she says, aghast, "I have been delayed in the kitchen and could not return sooner. I had no idea this girl was such a saucebox that she would dare address you."

"She was helping me find my book, Dorka, that is all."

"Your book?" Dorka's eyes fly to the book still in Boróka's hand. "She must have moved it, meddlesome child!" She plucks it from her, brushing it as if it had been dropped on a filthy floor, and offers it up to her mistress. Then she takes hold of Boróka's shoulders, twisting her around and propelling her off the Turkey rug. "I will tidy up here for you, my lady," she says, with the implication that it is only Boróka that needs to be cleared away.

"One moment, if you please." The countess's voice makes them both stop and turn around.

"Yes, my lady?" says Dorka.

"No," she says, "I was speaking to the girl."

Boróka feels Dorka's hand grip her arm above the elbow, a mean, resentful pinch. "Look at my lady countess when she's speaking to you," Dorka says.

"Tomorrow morning you will come to the gynaeceum," the countess informs Boróka. "Let the painter work on the background until the afternoon; it will do him good."

Dorka's hand tightens around Boróka's arm. "The gynaeceum, my lady? Are you sure? This girl is a servant, little more than a common serf."

"Do not question me, Dorka, I am quite sure. The gynaeceum will meet in my privy chambers to practice a ruelle. As it stands, I could have a better conversation about literature with my own half-finished portrait than any of those ignorant girls."

43

Then the lady is gone, retreating to her bedchamber in a rustle of damask the same indigo blue as the darkening sky. Boróka tries to pull her arm from Dorka's grasp, but she holds it tight.

"Do not think yourself favored," she tells her. "My lady's benevolence is like the sun: The warmth is always followed by darkness."

On the straw pallet inside their turret, Boróka tells Suzanna what has happened in a breathless rush. Suzanna is silent. She doesn't respond when Boróka describes the ornaments she wore, or the taut feel of the bodice, both firm and satiny to the touch. When she tells her she thought she would fall right off her velvet chopines and end up a silken heap on the floor, Suzanna does not gasp or laugh. When she gets to the end of the story—the golden clock, the countess resplendent in indigo damask—it is just as well that darkness has fallen so Boróka cannot see her pinched expression, the peevish set of her jaw.

"Then"—Boróka pauses, lowers her voice—"the countess told me I'm to attend the gynaeceum. I don't even know what the gynaeceum is, but Dorka was *most* put out, which can only bode well."

"How wonderful," says Suzanna, her voice flat.

"Suzanna?" Boróka is beginning to wish that she hadn't complained quite so much about how maddening the itch from a jeweled headdress is. "What did you do today?" she asks, to change the subject.

"Oh, nothing so hard as pretending to be a countess."

Boróka reaches out and strokes her friend's hair. "Don't be like that," she says.

"Like what, *my lady*?" Suzanna says, her voice cutting through the darkness.

Boróka snatches back her hand. She doesn't understand why Suzanna is being so sarcastic. "I just thought you'd be interested," she says.

"I am interested! Very interested to know how terribly hard it is to stand still and look rich and beautiful, while I'm bent over my sewing with that absolute *witch* looming over me, pulling my ear every time I drop a stitch, slapping my wrists when my lace isn't tight enough. Truly,

Ilona Jó is worse than my *mother*. Would that I could be released to do something better, like gutting fish or mucking out the pigpen."

"I did not think Ilona quite so cruel as you suggest."

Suzanna glares at her. "Did you not? You, with your perfect stitches and biddable needle that does just as you wish it to."

Boróka sighs. "I cannot help that I am able to sew."

"Of course you can't," says Suzanna. "Just like you cannot help that your hair is as long and lustrous at the countess's, your waist just as slender, and your eyes as fine and dark."

Tired, Boróka rolls over to face the wall. Suzanna has drained the excitement from her, absorbed it like weeds taking moisture from the parched earth. She slips her hand under the sack of chaff, instinctively searching for the little wooden goose even though she knows it's not there. She's looked everywhere for it, still cannot find it.

"You promised me you would come back to the east room." Suzanna's voice sounds splintered.

"I didn't promise, I said I would try. It's not my fault that I'm needed for the portrait."

"It will not be so bad if we are there together, you said."

"Good night, Suzanna," Boróka says wearily.

But Suzanna is not quite ready to sleep. She leans in close, until Boróka can feel her warm breath on her ear.

"I *do* know what the gynaeceum is," she whispers. "It's where she tortures the girls. They say that if you listen you can hear them crying, that their screams carry on the breeze like dust."

Chapter 6

The Gynaeceum

It is a common assumption of the lower classes that nobility and wealth are two sides of the same coin. A goatherd or a wool spinner might be forgiven for thinking that the daughter of a baron would not want for meat or wine, that she could stave off the winter cold with a fur-lined mantle and a fire in every grate, but war and profligacy are great levelers. Unmarried maids seem common as mice in the manors and towns. The men who might have wed them are lying dead on the battlefields, while their squire fathers are ensconced in alehouses, frittering away their dowries on gambling and tippling. Almost better to be a laundry maid than a daughter of the petty nobility, for even the most caustic lye smarts less than bitter disappointment.

When a man is in the market for a fine new mare he looks for a well-chiseled head on a long neck. High withers are important, along with long legs and a glossy coat of a deep, rich color. She should be graceful and agile, with a refined appearance. Stamina and good breeding potential are a must, but intelligence is also valued, though not at the expense of being too sensitive or, God forbid, too spirited.

Rare is the creature born with all these attributes, but what is not inherited can be learned. Even the rank and file of the lesser gentry know this, so they send their daughters to the countess's gynaeceum in the hope that a knowledge of literature, household management, lute playing, and rudimentary Latin will help them find a husband. If some additional instruction in the subtleties of wifehood—the need for obedience, fidelity, and silence, for example—will help them to keep him, then all the better.

The upset that Boróka's fine portrait clothes caused Suzanna is nothing compared to the consternation that her rough-hewn kirtle appears to be causing the young noble girls at the gynaeceum. Their disdain makes her worry that she has a whiff of the great wash still stuck in its fibers, or the pungent aroma of the breakfast herrings caught in her hair. Not one of them will stand next to her, and she has just overheard the tall girl behind her whisper that she must be there only to empty the countess's chamber pot.

They all fall silent when the countess arrives. She is dressed in teal velvet over a white chemise with cuffs embroidered in ocher and gray. A white panel of delicate material, edged all around with lace, descends from her waist to the floor. It is so ephemeral that Boróka imagines that, if she touched it, her fingers would go right through it, as if it were spray from a waterfall.

An ornate settee, upholstered in brocaded gold silk, dominates the center of the room. The countess sits down on it, reclining rather ostentatiously against its scrolled arms and plush cushions. Chairs have been set out in front of the settee and, one by one, the girls all take a seat. Boróka thinks it best to sit at the back but, when she puts her hand on a chair, the tall girl shoos her away and sits there herself.

There is only one seat left. A stool, placed right at the feet of the countess herself.

Boróka lowers herself onto it and stares at the pointed toes of the countess's pink satin shoes peeking out from under the layered hems of her petticoat and gown. The countess's pose is artful, both relaxed and engaged. The girls are doing their best, but most of them shift about on their wooden chairs, or sit on their hands to keep from fidgeting, scratching, picking, or any other nasty habit they know the countess abhors. Nonetheless, an approximation of the literary salons of Europe has been created, with the countess its erudite host.

"Today," she begins, "we will be discussing the nature of the ideal courtier. This is the theme of Castiglione's *The Book of the Courtier*. So, girls, what qualities would the perfect lady of the court have, do you think?"

No one seems sure of the answer. Some of the girls look out through the leaded diamond panes of the windows, others stare at the portraits hanging on the walls, for who better to give up the secrets of nobility than the countess's own ancestors?

"It is a birthright," the tall girl who took Boróka's seat says. "Nobility is granted by virtue of rank and the quality of the family you are born into."

The countess nods slowly. "Yes, Orsolya, you are right. A courtier is defined, first and foremost, by their noble rank. Come"—the countess beckons to Orsolya with her hand—"stand here at the front. We shall use you as an example."

Orsolya flushes with pride and stands up. She picks her way through the other girls, returning their glances, both envious and admiring, with a satisfied smile.

"And we need one other," continues the countess.

Her eyes sweep over the assembled girls, some desperate to be singled out by their mistress, others equally desperate to be passed over, until her gaze comes to rest on the girl sitting on a stool at her feet. "You," she says, "stand up."

For a moment Boróka freezes, like a mouse that still hopes the owl hasn't seen it, even though it has already begun its swooping descent. But the stretching silence forces her from her seat, wishing with every inch she rises that the countess would change her mind. There can be no reason for Boróka to be involved in this discussion of matters so far above her humble station.

Fear is a strange thing. Boróka has been taught to fear the wolves and the bears, and how they could tear her flesh. She would run from fire, or a man, to escape how either could devour her, but this fear is something else entirely. It comes from simply being looked at, and by a cluster of harmless maids her own age. Their eyes are not claws, she tells herself, their smirks have no bite, but still she sweats and trembles and hears only chaos in her head. To calm herself she thinks of József and the solid walls of their whitewashed cottage, of an ordinary world still turning.

This girl, Orsolya, is indeed tall, a full head above Boróka. As tall, in fact, as the countess herself, who has risen from her settee to join them. "What other attributes should a lady of the court have?" the countess asks the waiting girls. They all turn their heads toward Orsolya, as imposing as a marble Aphrodite. From her silk-stockinged ankles right up to her high cheekbones, generations of breeding seem built into her very bones.

"Grace and good bearing," says one girl, eyeing Orsolya a little begrudgingly.

"Fine clothes and jewels," says another, looking at Orsolya's necklace of Venetian glass beads and the velvet *pacsa* set high on her forehead.

At the mention of fine clothes, some of the girls shift their gaze to Boróka and look her up and down. It is then that Boróka understands her purpose. She is there to represent the common sort. She is the plodding donkey to Orsolya's thoroughbred. She is the sackcloth that makes the silk seem all the finer. There was no favor in the instruction to attend the gynaeceum; she was just the nearest serving girl to hand when the countess decided she needed one. Paraded in front of these girls, she is as devoid of her own self as when she poses for the painter.

"A court lady should also be beautiful, should she not?" says the girl who just spoke. "Or at least," she continues, looking directly at Boróka, "she should not look like a bumpkin."

The girls giggle. It even seems an effort for the countess to retain her perfectly neutral expression. In Boróka's head, the laughing does not subside, it only gets louder until it is a swarm of bees. And then, from somewhere, there is a voice. Not frightened, not tentative, but clear and emphatic.

"Kindness," it says.

It takes even Boróka a second to realize that the voice is her own.

And now that she has heard it, she cannot stop it. "The perfect courtier should be kind," she says.

Silence as the girls look to the countess to tell them how they should react to what the little scarecrow just said.

The countess steps in front of Boróka and circles slowly around her. "They tell me your name is Boróka Libalány," she says.

Boróka nods.

"So what does the-girl-who-tends-the-geese know of courtly ways?"

"Nothing at all, my lady. I only know about geese and their ways. People think them vicious, but that is not so. They only hiss and snap when they are scared or ill-treated. To the people who care for them, they are devoted. They are loyal and brave and will guard you better than any watchdog. If I were a queen, I would want my courtiers to have the warrior spirit of a goose."

No one is laughing now. They have seen their mistress's mood turn on slighter provocation than this. *Geese?* What was the girl thinking?

The countess stops circling Boróka. She stands still in front of her, then says, "Are you comparing the most illustrious houses of Hungary to a pebble-brained bird?"

Boróka pales. "Not at all, my lady. My only thought was that noble qualities can be found in all sorts of places."

"Can they, indeed? Then it is a shame Castiglione did not pay a visit to the farmyard before he wrote his book."

There is a slight pause, then the countess smiles at her own wit. It is as if she has snipped the thread of tension that held the girls silent. They laugh with relief, as much as amusement, and none so hard as Orsolya. The countess winces, presses her hands to her ears.

"Orsolya!" she exclaims. "You know that I cannot abide laughter. Hearty laughing is how the lower orders express their awful joy at silly things. There is little so ill-bred as raucous laughter, especially from a woman. Now, go and sit down."

At the end of the ruelle Boróka is left to clear away the chairs. She carries one in each hand and makes five trips back and forth to the great hall, where the chairs have been borrowed from either side of the huge table that spans almost its whole length. Only the little stool on which she sat is left. It must be the one Dorka used to help dress her for the portrait, she thinks, picking it up and taking it through to the countess's library.

The countess is sitting at a large writing desk with an exquisitely detailed marquetry top. She doesn't look up when Boróka enters, so Boróka steals past her and leaves the stool by the floor-to-ceiling bookshelves that line one wall. When she turns to leave, the countess says, as if to no one at all, "Did you know that I am well-versed in Hungarian, Latin, Greek, and German?"

When nothing but silence follows the question, the countess looks up from whatever it is she is writing. "Well, did you?"

There is no one else in the room, so she can be talking to only Boróka.

"I did not know that, my lady," she replies.

"And I am a patron of the arts, of libraries and universities."

Boróka watches her, searching her face to try to decipher the meaning behind her words.

"I have more knowledge of medicine than most surgeons," continues the countess, "and I'm better acquainted with the stars than most astronomers."

"Your wisdom and learning are known to all, my lady," says Boróka.

"But there was something missing from my education." The countess carefully sets down her pen. "I needed to grow up with other girls. Do you see?"

Boróka is not sure she does. If only she had not come back with the stool, she would be in the kitchen by now and the only question anyone would be asking her is whether she wants rye or barley bread with her dinner.

"There's no use knowing how to speak Latin if the language of friendship is beyond you," observes the countess. "And you cannot profess to understand poetry, or literature, if you have not experienced the emotions that inspired the words. Now do you see? It is all well and good knowing your letters, but can you stand in front of your peers without quaking? Do you know how to deal with a group of girls your own age, and all their pride and petty jealousy? You need to learn these things just as much as the verses of Hans Sachs."

Boróka nods slowly, although she is still sifting through the countess's words. It cannot be that the countess is at all concerned with the instruction of a servant, so she must have done something wrong, failed to measure up in some important way.

"Thank you, my lady," she says, not knowing what else to say.

"And please make sure you have a proper chair next time."

"My lady?"

"When you come back to the gynaeceum, please bring a proper chair to sit on. You cannot discuss Castiglione squatting on a stool like a milkmaid."

When Boróka finally gets down to dinner, Suzanna seems quite relieved to see her.

"There you are," she says, taking hold of Boróka's sleeve and guiding her away from the other girls. "I've been waiting for you."

"Have you?" asks Boróka, her voice not unpleasant, just wary. She was not expecting Suzanna to want to sit with her after their conversation last night.

"Of course. I needed to know you were all right."

"Oh, Suzanna," says Boróka with a sigh, taking her arm back. "You must stop all this nonsense about the countess. There is no torture in the gynaeceum, only books!"

"Books?" says Suzanna, a little wrong-footed. "But that cannot be so."

"It *is* so. We talked about literature and what makes a good courtier. The only torturous part of it was when I had to stand up in front of some noble girls and they made fun of me."

Suzanna looks surprised, then her face darkens. "Perhaps she doesn't kill girls *every* time the gynaeceum meets?"

Boróka lowers her voice. There are ears and eyes everywhere in a countess's household, and the perfect courtier certainly doesn't gossip about her mistress. "Where have you heard these things? For my part, I cannot see that they are true. The lady has been nothing but good to me."

"From the best possible source," says Suzanna, "the mouth of God himself."

"God? How can that be?"

"Ponikenus, the pastor at Čachtice, called her a Jezebel in his sermon, a paragon of evil." Suzanna lowers her voice, sidesteps closer to the wall, away from the other girls filing into the kitchen. "He talked of being asked to bury countless maidens secretly in the church at night, with singing and chanting, and their bodies were always marked by *torture*."

Boróka is silent. Around her the noise seems amplified. The clattering of platters and spoons, chair legs scraping over the stone floor, and girls chattering make it hard to process what she is hearing. Who would question what their pastor told them? His sermon is not only the word of God but moral instruction. It is news, disseminated to the people en masse. It is how word spreads from parish to parish. Yet still, she feels compelled to ask, "If you are murdering maids, then why would you ask a priest to bury them? And with burial rites?"

"Erzsébet Báthory is a countess and therefore she does as she pleases," says Suzanna, "but even she knows that she will still have to answer to God. Think on it, Boróka. Why would a priest lie?"

She is right, of course. Every pastor she has ever known has delivered his sermons with such conviction, such rectitude, such . . . flourish that the words must be true. She cannot contradict the preachings of a clergyman just because she has spent an hour being taken in by the countess's wit and learning, being seduced by her beautiful damask and satin slippers. There was a moment, as the countess circled around her, that Boróka had felt actual fear, that she had fancied she saw in the countess's eyes a glint of cruel enjoyment. Perhaps she has been too quick to think that a woman of such grace and sophistication could not possibly be what people say she is.

Suzanna takes Boróka's arm and draws her closer. "You should not believe that the countess is what she seems. If she really favors you, then you will be able to observe her, see how she behaves when no one is watching."

Boróka nods slowly.

"And will you tell me?" asks Suzanna, insistent. "Will you tell me what she says and what she does?"

"Yes," says Boróka.

"Good," says Suzanna, releasing her. "Then we shall find out who this woman really is."

Boróka catches the eye of another girl, who must have been listening to what they were saying.

"Watch your mouths," the girl says as she passes, "lest you find that they are sewn shut."

Chapter 7

The Sun Is Still Beautiful, Though Ready to Set

—Italian proverb

The painter, Valentino, has been waiting for the countess for over an hour. His feelings are mixed. On the one hand, he is annoyed and impatient—there is a lady in a nearby town who wishes to be painted with her beloved lapdog and he has promised to visit her with examples of his work. On the other, he is glad that, at least this time, the delay is not his fault. Indeed, far from being crippled by his own creativity, he has made some progress with the girl as his model. He finds her less intimidating than the countess. He does not bristle as much with her as he does under the lady's watchful eye, which still manages to be hawkish and impossibly demanding even when staring into the middle distance. But, most of all, he loves the girl's youth, her smooth, open face and sculpted limbs. It is not that he desires her, he is simply taken in by her, hoodwinked by her tender years.

He has to stop himself sketching the girl's features on the canvas. More than once he has snatched up his graphite to capture the look she gives him when he catches her eye, which seems to suggest that she finds the whole situation a little preposterous. He, the master painter; she, the countess. Both looking the part but fooling no one but themselves. In as much as she both calms and inspires him, she is more muse than model.

But this is not the portrait of a pretty servant, however much he would like it to be. It is the preserved image of a great lady, destined to hang over huge stone fireplaces or grace the wood paneling of a majestic hall. He must concentrate only on outlines when the girl poses for him, on incidentals: garments and tawdry jewels. It is just frustrating, that is all. Any man would find it so, let alone an artist. To him, it is like being presented with a rosebud and told to paint the vase.

Under the circumstances, he thought it best to have at least one session with the countess herself, to reconnect this portrait with its true subject. So he sits in the library waiting, dreaming of the works of art he would create if he were free to paint for love, instead of money.

He jumps when she finally enters. That imperious gaze of hers unnerves him. It is almost as if she can see right through his skull and read his thoughts.

"Ah," he says, performing an elaborate obeisance, "*la bella contessa.*"

She has one of her intimates with her. Not the fat one this time, but the tall one with the looks and charm of a whipping stick. He cannot understand why the richest noblewoman in Hungary spends so much of her time with lowborn people. He heard that this one was her children's wet nurse. She must have been good, because he fears they have sucked her dry.

"Madam, I was concerned that we would not have enough light today, but the radiance of your person is such that I need not have worried."

He gets nothing for his flattery save a quelling look from Ilona. The countess is already taking up her place on the Turkey rug, resting her hand on that clock of which she seems so fond.

"Make this quick, if you please, sir. I have much to do today."

"Of course, your grace," he says, snatching up his graphite, "but remember that capturing beauty on a canvas is like snaring a butterfly: It must be carefully and delicately done."

Did she roll her eyes? Already his hand is shaking. Already he doubts that he can perform. Does she not realize that when he paints her they need to connect, almost as if they were about to make love? Would she say to a lover, *Just get on with it, please*? No!

Still, she probably can't remember any of that. This summer the countess will reach her fiftieth year, and she has been a widow for the past six. He does not doubt that she was beautiful once. He can imagine that those fine, dark eyes—that look at him so scornfully—once held a softer gaze; that the lips, which seem so often pressed thin with dissatisfaction, once spoke a tender word. But now the most radiant thing about her is her jewels.

He does his best. He has had to change the angle of her head, for the tilt of her chin is higher than the girl's. He wishes she would lower it, as it does her no favors. She must think it makes her look superior, but it just draws out the stringy cords of her neck. He stays silent; brave is the man who would say that to a countess.

It takes him a mere three hours to sketch her face. He has to admit that, now the second drawing is complete, the portrait is looking quite impressive. Relief makes him feel better disposed toward his subject, more able to appreciate the fine set of her features and the undoubted grace of her bearing. He has drawn her as he sees her—a mature, yet still very handsome, woman. To make her look like a maid would be to insult her.

Il sole è ancora bello, anche se pronto a tramontare, he says to himself: The sun is still beautiful, though ready to set.

"He has made me look like a lizard!"

She didn't have to look. There is a pile of correspondence on her desk that needs to be dealt with and she could have simply sat down and attended to that. But no, she had to lift the dust sheet to see what an itinerant portrait painter considers a morning's work these days.

She turns to Ilona. "Do I really look like that?"

"Of course not, mistress. The man is a talentless fool. I will tell him to be gone by the morning."

The countess is silent, staring at the portrait. "My neck," she whispers, while she plucks at the skin under her chin with her fingers. "Bring me my looking glass, Ilona."

The countess stands in front of the window with the mirror held high, twisting her neck this way and that. "No, the wretched man is right. It *does* look like that."

"Calm yourself," says Ilona, gently taking the mirror from her. "You are of an age now when these things should not concern you."

"Not concern me? Oh, how I envy you, Ilona. It must be so easy to get old when you had not beauty to begin with."

Ilona stares hard at her mistress but says nothing. The countess turns back to her sketched likeness and looks at it again, as if giving it the opportunity to mollify her.

"I will take it away, mistress," says Ilona, reaching for the canvas.

"No"—the countess holds up a hand to stop her—"look here: He has captured the slenderness of my waist and the neatness of my hands perfectly. He must redo the head, of course, but with the rest I am satisfied."

Ilona nods. It must be satisfying indeed, she thinks, to have the figure and hands of a girl not yet sixteen.

Chapter 8

The Bald
Coachman's Wife

Silence, save for the clacking of bobbins. The little clicks and taps that mean the castle will be well stocked with pillowcases, tooth cloths, cuffs and ruffs, all edged with the finest lace. The girls handle the bone bobbins as if they were born to it, crossing and twisting each pair almost instinctively. Their stitches are neat and rhythmic, the tension on the linen thread is perfect, and their pins precisely placed. This is the lace school, attended by only the genuinely skilled, not the shabby creatures that mend and darn unseen and unmentionable garments.

Ilona Jó Nagy supervises the lace school with beady-eyed vigilance. She looks over the girls' shoulders as they work and runs her fingers over each finished piece. She holds it up to the light and tugs it to check how it holds together. It must not warp or twist. It should be tight, without being pulled or puckered. And, above all, it should follow the pricking exactly, without errors or baggy bits.

This is what she loves about lace: not its delicate beauty, but its order and symmetry. The exquisite predictability of the repeating pattern emerging from nothing but the placing of one thread over another: cross, twist, cross, cross, twist. In fact, in a life littered with nasty surprises, lace is the one thing she has found on which one can absolutely rely. If you follow the pricking with the correct sequence of stitches, then you know, with certainty, what you will get at the end. There are no broken promises, no cruel twists of fate; just expectations met in a dependable, if somewhat laborious, way.

Even from a young age Ilona knew all about the nature of a bald man. She had heard of the dangerous heat that lies within him, the hot sweat that pushes the hair out. To her, a completely bald, shiny head was something brazen and shameful. Baldness is the consequence of an indulgent lifestyle: copious food, late nights spent drinking and carousing, activities such as wrestling and, of course, an excess of sex. So when István Nagy, the bald coachman, set his cap at her, she immediately dismissed him. She would no more walk out with a bald man than she would go down to the village stocks and select a mate there. Besides, there could be no greater threat to her ordered world, her regular bedtimes and unmolested sleep, than a man of such . . . appetites.

Her father (who was neither rich nor well connected) thought his daughter (who was neither young nor pretty) foolish. Ilona had resisted the married state for quite some time due to her inherent reluctance to accommodate another person in any way, and he now began to regret that he had tolerated such independence. When Ilona's mother passed, it had suited him to keep Ilona living with him. Provided he ate when she prescribed, there had been no interruption to his meals appearing on the table. The floors remained swept clean, and when he had a hole in his shirt, Ilona mended it with a needle that was fast as a silver fish.

But a daughter is no wife and, after a respectable time had passed, he found himself someone to be both lover and housekeeper. Even though Ilona begged for a husband with a full head of hair, at least, it did no good. The bald coachman's offer was the only one on the table.

After marriage, Ilona discovered two astonishing things. The first was that she had been entirely wrong about István Nagy. As it turned out, a bald man is possessed of no more heightened passions than any other man, a fact she found almost disappointing. The second was that he owned a clock. He would not disclose how he had acquired such a remarkable object but, whether bought, inherited, or stolen, Ilona didn't care. She had finally found the perfect partner: time.

Nonetheless, the clock took almost as much getting used to as her new husband. Both were somewhat sensitive to the cold and worked best sitting in the kitchen near the fire; and both, though they appeared straightforward at first glance, concealed inner workings that were far more complex. However, having invested quite some time in trying to understand the clock, at least, Ilona learned what she needed to do each day to keep it going, and the startling information that it could disclose in return. She could now rise at six o'clock with a degree of certainty. She could *know* she was in bed by nine. She could eat her dinner at three, no matter that the seasons shifted around her, discombobulating her with days that lengthened and shortened like a concertina.

This life could have afforded Ilona a happiness of sorts, but in those days men were not left in peace to drive carriages, forge metal, or tan hides. There was always a war to be fought—if not against the Ottoman Turks to the east, then against the Catholic Habsburgs to the west. Those of an uncharitable mind might question whether Ilona's husband actually had to sign up for battle—the campaigning season was still some months away—or whether he just grew tired of playing second fiddle to a timepiece, and of marital relations tolerated only if they took place at a quarter past nine. Either way, within a year of marriage the bald coachman was dead on the battlefield.

She still had the clock, of course, but the problem was that her husband's spectacular lack of success in war was matched only by his ineptitude with money. Ilona uncovered debts sprouting like mushrooms from every dark corner of their lives. Even worse, she discovered she was with child as well.

Ilona was not the first woman to find herself both a widow and destitute, and nor will she be the last. Her father was more concerned with his new family than with helping her, so she was left unable to pay her husband's debts. With a newborn mouth to feed, Ilona had no obvious way to survive, so she did what women have been doing since the dawn of time: She sold her body.

And, really, she was perfect for it: tall, healthy, strong, and re-assuringly plain. When hiring Ilona, a mother could be confident that her infant would be nursed well, without having to allow a suspi-ciously pretty woman into her home. Ilona found a job almost imme-diately with the wife of a local landowner. She arrived on the first day (promptly, at eight in the morning) with her precious, rich milk and her own babe tucked under her shawl. However, it took only a single minute for her to discover the essential irony of being a wet nurse: Her milk was for her charge, and for him alone. Her own infant must be left at home, farmed out to a wet nurse himself or fed pap by whom-ever Ilona could find to do it.

She knew it would be impossible to fill the bellies of two new babies living in different places, so she had to put one first. They were both demanding little things. They both suckled ferociously and drained her in every conceivable way but, ultimately, she got paid to put up with one and not the other. Back home that night, Ilona covered her son with as many heavy blankets as she could find and weighed them down with stones at their four corners. Then she waited.

For thirty-two minutes precisely.

There was a revenge of sorts. Not exacted by her own ill-fated infant, of course, but by every other babe who sucked, pummeled, bit, squeezed, and screamed at Ilona from that day on. Indeed, it was hard to think of a woman less temperamentally suited to wet nursing than Ilona, for there is not a creature on earth who cares less for time than a baby.

That was when she turned to lace. She sat with one pillow for the baby and another for her bobbins. She passed the endless hours of tedious nursing by perfecting the art of keeping her elbows still while crossing and stitching with a flick of her wrists. And if the occasional pin found its way into the soft, chubby buttocks of one of her charges, made its eyes fly open in surprise and its face crease into a wail, then it did not much matter. She needed the lace because it was the only way she could turn the hideous chaos of constantly pandering to the unscheduled whims of another human being into something neat, or-dered, and predictable.

Fortunately for Ilona, wet nursing is one of the few professions where your taskmaster not only cannot tell tales, but also can be relied upon to wake up having completely forgotten the previous day's misdemeanors. Ilona's references and recommendations grew as steadily as her lace, given, as they were, by mothers who were delighted by her dependable punctuality and thrilled with the pretty lace trims that appeared on their baby's caps and gowns.

After a few years, it was the Countess Erzsébet Báthory herself who needed a wet nurse for her daughter, Anna. Who better than Ilona to nurse her, especially since not even she dared use the scion of Hungary's most noble bloodline as a pincushion? Ilona Jó stayed with the countess, nursing all the babies that followed, some of whom lived and some of whom didn't.

Something strange happened to Ilona during that time: She relaxed. Just a little. The terrible coil of tension that had existed within her, for as long as she could remember, began to unwind and continued to do so through every one of the countess's children she nursed. With each infant—first Anna, then Orsika, then Katalin—her position with the countess became more and more secure. She realized that she no longer had to fret, from one day to the next, about where her next meal would come from. She no longer had to worry about bad debts or marriage prospects, paying rent or hungry mouths to feed. She was respected, loved even, and her presence was essential to the well-being of the countess's growing family. Granted, no one would ever have described Ilona as a particularly affectionate nursemaid but, nevertheless, she was rather good at it, in an efficient, somewhat detached, kind of way. But it was a style that the ruthlessly organized countess seemed to appreciate, and they became close, often talking long after the necessary conversation about the children was finished.

Alongside this newfound feeling of relative security, something far more unwelcome appeared: bitter regret. For years she tried to suppress it; then, in 1598, she was handed the countess's firstborn son to put to her breast. All the babies she had nursed since the landowner's son had been girls, and when she looked down at Pál, with his velvety eyes and delicate swirl of hair, she did not see the countess's son, but her own. She tried not to look at him, ignored the warm, soft weight of him in her arms, but it was impossible. In the hours she nursed him, not even the lace could distract her from the awful thought that her life, and her son's, could have turned out differently. She was haunted by the notion that what she had done to her only child had not been the only choice open to her.

Watching Pál thrive and grow was like gazing upon Medusa: It turned her slowly to stone. By the time he left the countess's household to join his guardian, as all male heirs inevitably do, it was as if she were petrified completely. This hardened version of herself could not accept that other children were alive when her own son was not, and she could not help but punish them for it. Not the boys, though, never the boys. Just the girls.

No woman is a wet nurse for life. Ilona could not keep suckling children any more than the countess could keep bearing them, and eventually, the nurseries were empty. But the woman who has fed and nourished all your offspring does not get tossed aside once the children are weaned. She is given a place in the household, a position of respect, and it is only right that she should be kept and paid for until the day she dies. Besides, a bond forms between two women when they share the care of a child. Ilona had become part of the countess's children, she had given up some of herself to see them grow. She had listened to the countess's worries about the children's skin rashes and toothaches. She had comforted her when not all of them survived. Then the countess was made a widow herself and they became women of the same ilk: capable, resourceful, and independent out of necessity. Not to mention that strangest of things: a woman with no need of a man.

It is nine o'clock at night and there is an almost imperceptible quickening of the bobbins' clacking. One of the girls has noticed that she has made a mistake in the pattern, a good two inches back. A flush appears at the base of her neck, creeping upward, tingeing her cheeks. She will have to undo her lace, all the way back to where the mistake occurred. Her hands begin to tremble. She tries to remember the correct sequence of stitches in order to perform them in reverse, but her hands fumble, bobbins drop onto the pillow, linen threads tangle. The girl looks up—not at Ilona, who is watching her from the other side of the room, but at the clock placed squarely in the middle of the table. Ilona puts it there when the lace school begins its work for the day, set to chime at exactly ten o'clock that night. It serves as a reminder to them all. When Ilona looks at it, she remembers that no matter how bad things got, no matter what else she'd had to do to get by, she never had to sell her precious clock. To the girls—or, at least, to those of them who have not finished their lace or not completed it perfectly—the chime of that clock is like a death knell.

Chapter 9

INNOCENCE LOST

The countess is visiting the spa at Piešťany. Ilona and Dorka are down in the great hall preparing for a visit from a local dignitary. Boróka walks over to the window, silent in her stockinged feet. She can see Ficzkó in the courtyard below, hammering a new hide on a wooden frame, shirtsleeves rolled up his arms, dolman slung over the little stone wall. The hide won't quite reach all the way across the frame and keeps slipping out of his fingers before he can secure it with a nail. He is trying to hit it too hard, showing off the powerful flex of his muscles, and he keeps looking up to see if Orsolya is watching him. She is, though she pretends to only be interested in the friendly courtyard cat, which she has scooped up and is cuddling, hiding her coy glances behind fur mottled brown and cream like the inside of a nutmeg. Ficzkó is busy, Boróka thinks; he will not be prowling around inside the castle any time soon.

She pads back over to the little tableau she has walked away from: the Turkey rug and table, the golden clock and the mysterious box underneath. Her velvet chopines are left where she discarded them, empty, as if inviting her to step back into this make-believe world. The painter has left early today. Knowing that the countess is in Piešťany—and therefore unlikely to surprise him by sneaking up behind him and clicking her tongue, or sighing—had allowed him to paint with the kind of freedom he rarely experiences. The portrait's background is now shades of rust and burned orange, the colors hatched and feathered with confident, even masterful, strokes. The day's work complete, Valentino is away to the baron's wife and her little lapdog, and Boróka is left alone.

She would like to dig a little deeper into this countess's life, beat the bush and see what flies out. She looks around the room. So plush, so ornate. Like a sugar glaze on a cake, it's only the decorated outside she can see. Boróka stands by the table watching the clock's cogs and wheels turn inside their gilded case. These are the items the countess has chosen to represent her in the painting: her status, her personality, the understanding that even great wealth cannot protect her from the passage of time. But why is the rosewood box there? Boróka draws her finger along its polished side. It's so thickly varnished it feels almost sticky, clinging to the skin of her fingertip as if reluctant to let her go.

There is a bang and a clatter from the corridor outside. Boróka startles and snatches her hand away. She can feel the skip of her heart in her chest. She should leave—take off the ring, the pearls, the gown, and put her real life back on—but she doesn't want to. In this room, right at this moment, there is no one to tell her she is not a countess, that she shines only with a borrowed light, like the moon in the presence of the sun. She listens. A voice, snappy, irritable, and another in response. Now fading. No one coming near.

Carefully, as if she carries all of time in her hands, she lifts the clock off the box. The lid is inlaid with gold and mother-of-pearl and, in the center, is the Slavic rosette, a six-petaled rose inside a circle. She looks down at the ironwork lock. She almost wishes that the key had not been left inside. It is temptation objectified, the apple to her Eve. She turns it in the lock, hears its click of surrender. Before she lifts the lid she is innocent.

Inside the box is a small book, bound in oxblood vellum. It looks like a ledger, something that might contain household accounts or an inventory, perhaps. No harm, surely, in having a look at something like that. She opens the book, bends the creaking spine. No inventory, just words, densely written in a fluid, elegant hand. She cannot help but catch the first few lines and then, once she has started reading, the sin is already committed. She cannot unread what she has read, nor can her actions become more wrong with each word; at least, that is what she tells herself every time she turns the page.

I began life as I ended it: surrounded by water.

She told me it was a veiled birth, that I emerged from my mother still enclosed in the caul, which made sense because we always try to conceal the things we are ashamed of. She tried to keep me covered up even after I had forced my way out, and it was only the midwife, with her hook, that ripped me free. I was lucky, they said, because mermaid births are magical and a child born in water can never drown. That was the first of the lies.

Births are messy, foul things. Imagine how stale the air becomes once a woman takes to her chamber, the windows all closed and hung with tapestries, a fire in the grate warming the room to stifling. No wonder I preferred to stay in the water rather than take a gulp of that fetid air, panted and breathed a hundred times over. No wonder I squalled in alarm when first I opened my eyes to a world just as thick and dark as the one I had left behind.

Whom do they call when the sheets are stained with blood and fluid and ordure? Whose job is it to clean away the shameful marks and spots? The washerwoman's, of course. So that's who the midwife handed me to. The woman who takes your dirty blights and blemishes and makes them disappear.

She cleaned my mother's blood from my face, wiped the last traces of nobility from my eyes and nostrils, then wrapped me in fine linen edged with lace. A grand swaddle indeed, for the peasant I was about to become. I can imagine my last sight of my mother, a child herself, lying sweaty and spent on a bed strewn with amulets and prayer rolls. Sometimes I wonder: If I had been able to take one of those prayer rolls and unfurl it, what would have been written there? Would it have prayed for my safe delivery, or that I never lived to take a single breath?

I try not to think of her too often because my mother gave me nothing but life and her name. And she probably didn't even give me that. More likely, someone else—rather lacking in imagination—named me Erzsébet. For my second name I took the washerwoman's, and in that way I became a mix of both my mothers.

Even so, everyone knew that I wasn't the washerwoman's daughter, and when she refused to tell the townsfolk who I was, and where I had come from, they began to fill in the gaps themselves. It didn't help that I grew into a strange and skittish child, as if I already knew what their intentions were and guarded against them like a cat keeping low to the ground, all watchful eyes and slinking limbs. I suppose I could have tried to pretend that I was like them, but from the very beginning my hair gave me away. A shock of bright white grew from my temple all the way down my back, as stark and bold as a shooting star in the night sky. A witch's streak, they whispered to each other from behind their hands. Then someone remembered that a white stallion had been seen galloping high up in the Carpathians the summer before my birth. That stallion was my father, they said, and I had a lock of his white mane in my hair to prove it.

The truth was far more prosaic.

My father was a servant called Ladislav Bende. If he shared anything in common with the white stallion it was that he was unusually fair and, reputedly, had a fine, muscular physique and heroic bearing. He worked in a manor house in the walled town of Trnava, across the Danube from Sárvár Castle. Both the castle and the manor were owned by the illustrious Nádasdy family, and the manor had just become the new home of a thirteen-year-old girl called Erzsébet, the eighteen-year-old Nádasdy heir's betrothed.

This Erzsébet was a clever, willful thing. She received instruction in her future household duties with patience and forbearance, and she tolerated well enough her mother-in-law's pronouncements on the wifely arts she would need to employ in order to make a success of her future marriage to Ferenc Nádasdy. But the summer afternoons were long and the water meadows surrounding the town and castle called, with their lily pads, dragonflies, and blizzard of down-topped seeds. Some girls might have passed the tedious hours alone by sewing or in prayer, but Erzsébet loved climbing and exploring. She longed to be out riding and, in fact, there was no one to stop her. Her future husband was away at the garrisons on the border, learning the techniques of warfare and the brutal requirements of military discipline. If he ever gave a thought to his betrothed, it was surely not to imagine her galloping through the countryside like one of his own rough-hewn soldiers.

So Erzsébet was free to do largely as she pleased. Then came one evening that was so glorious, so long and light, that she couldn't bear to go home to the stuffy manor, with its stiff upholstered chairs and tart pickled herrings. The summer was so perfectly ripe, so intoxicating in its sultry bloom, that she tethered her horse and walked alone in the meadows, listening to the songbirds and catching bulrush seeds floating on the breeze.

After a while she reached the vineyards that encircled the town. An itinerant wine seller had set up his wagon at the end of a row of twisted vines, and now that it was getting late and work was finished for the day, people from the town had begun to join him. There were pipes and viols playing, music as free flowing and potent as the wine. People were dancing arm in arm, spinning, twirling, laughing; and there, in the middle of them all, was young Ladislav Bende. She knew him from the manor, of course, had stolen glances at him as he served the food or worked in the gardens, but she had never seen him quite like this: carefree, light on his feet, kicking his heels and tossing his head with its mane of hair, as gold as the wheat harvest to come.

There are two versions of what happened next. One tells of a headstrong girl, with a bright and curious mind, left unoccupied and unsupervised, and the terrible mischief that such a girl could make. The other is a sinister tale of innocence lost, of a child deliberately made giddy with wine and hempseed, then snatched away.

Whatever the truth of the matter, the family of the would-be groom preferred the latter version. Complaints were made in front of the priests at the cathedral chapter of Esztergom and church documents were prepared to allow the marriage to proceed. Then Ladislav—whether ardent lover or vile predator—was castrated and his offal thrown to the dogs.

But something remained that was less easy to resolve. A thickening of the girl's waist. A queasiness of her person when she dutifully chewed the pickled herrings, sitting rigid in her straight-backed chair, dreaming of bulrush seeds floating on the breeze.

Not a word more, only blank pages. Boróka closes the book and puts it back in the rosewood box, lowers the lid, and makes sure to lock it again. Then she arranges the painter's scene how it was before.

Chapter 10

The Goose

Suzanna sits at the east room table—head bent, brow furrowed—a silent disciple of cross-stitch and needlepoint. It's almost midday and all the other girls are sitting down to dinner, but Suzanna tries not to think about buttery pastry crumbling in her mouth, the warm weight of a pie in her belly.

Instead, she concentrates on the stitches in front of her, but she has been staring at them so long they are now like insects, seeming to crawl across the canvas on tiny tent-stitch legs. She blinks, shakes her head. She must keep track of them, count them precisely. The pattern she is following is of a horse, but she lost count of the brown stitches when the smell of the dinner wafted in through the open window, and now the horse looks more like a unicorn. Or is it blood? She scratches at the weave with her fingernail. It had taken Ilona two days to give her a blunt tapestry needle to use, and in the meantime, she had pricked her fingers so many times the beads of blood had turned her horse piebald.

She is not allowed to move until it is finished. No matter how many meals she misses, no matter how many sleepless nights she has to endure. This is what Ilona has told her, and she believes it.

She is beginning to unpick the brown stitches when the factotum comes in. She knows why he's here; it was her job to mend the seam of his leatherwork doublet. Her fingers still ache.

"About time," she tells him, barely looking up. "It was ready yesterday."

"I know," Ficzkó says, "but I wanted to come while you were here alone."

Suzanna's fingers stop plucking at the canvas. She is suddenly conscious of how thick the walls are, how empty the corridors at noontide.

Ficzkó's smile is as unexpected as it is reassuring. "You are always here," he says. "I wonder how anyone can love sewing so much."

Suzanna sets down her needlepoint. "I do *not* love sewing," she says emphatically. "I'm only here because my work takes me longer than everyone else." She looks pointedly at the door. "I suppose I had better get on with it."

Ficzkó nods. "Of course, but you must eat, no?"

"I *have* nothing to eat," she replies.

"No matter, I do." Ficzkó sits down beside her and pulls out a muslin, which he unwraps to reveal a slice of the cook's pie. "Take it," he says, pushing the muslin toward her. "Cook gave me two slices, and I've already eaten one."

Suzanna eyes the pie with some suspicion, and Ficzkó with even more, but, oh, the pie looks so good. It must still be warm to smell that rich, that meaty, that . . . "Thank you," she says, swiping it off the table and biting into it before he changes his mind.

Ficzkó picks up her needlepoint while she eats. "Hmm, a unicorn, nice."

"It's not a unicorn," says Suzanna through a mouthful of pie.

Ficzkó looks at it again, tugs at the canvas. "You need a blocking board," he tells her, "it will stop it warping like this."

"How do you know so much about needlepoint?"

"I used to sit with the countess while she embroidered when I was little. She always used a frame for her work. I'll put one on for you."

Ficzkó gets up and sorts through some sewing supplies on the sideboard while Suzanna eats her pie. When he sits back down, she stares at her needlepoint, taut and well shaped in a blocking frame. "Why are you being so kind to me?" she asks.

"It's not easy working for Ilona, is it?"

Suzanna shakes her head. She knows she shouldn't say anything bad about her mistress, but head shaking's not talking, is it?

"If there's one thing I've learned living here, it's to keep your head down and get on with your work. Don't notice anything, don't question anything, don't talk about anything."

"How long have you been here?"

"Since I was five."

Suzanna wonders how he has survived that long. "The countess," she says, "how do you find her?"

"She is a great and noble lady," says Ficzkó. "She has my absolute respect and devotion."

"Of course," says Suzanna, "but . . . what's she really like?"

Ficzkó tuts, shakes his head. "This is what I mean: See nothing, say nothing. It's the safest way, I promise you."

"Yes, but people are talking. You must have heard the things people say about her. Are they true?"

"I'd say it depends on who you are. If she likes you, then there's nothing she wouldn't do for you. But if she doesn't . . . Well, let's just say that my lady doesn't suffer fools gladly," he says carefully. "Nobody here does, which is why you would do well to heed my advice." He pauses, asks her, "What's your name?"

"Suzanna."

"Such a pretty name, it suits you. I've been watching you, *Suzanna*," he says, fixing her with a blue/green gaze, "you make me laugh."

Suzanna swallows down the last of the pie, brushes her lips in case there are any crumbs. It is almost inconceivable to her that anyone could find her pretty or funny. Her mother seemed not to be able to open her mouth without a complaint coming out. Suzanna tried not to be clumsy, ignorant, or cack-handed, but it was hard to do anything while listening to her mother's constant carping. Now that she thinks on it, the only time she can remember her mother truly laughing was when she asked her if she would be able to find a good husband for her.

"Do I?" she says.

He nods. Suzanna is finding it difficult to breathe. She looks from the green eye to the blue and back again, trying to decide which makes him look more handsome. It's an impossible task, like choosing between bluebells and cowslips, honey and strawberry jam. She already cannot wait to tell Boróka about this. She can keep her velvet chopines—the good-looking factotum likes *her*.

"Will you do something for me?" he asks.

Suzanna has little experience of boys, but she does know she has to be careful what she agrees to. She wonders, then, why she finds herself nodding quite so vigorously.

"You share a room with the goose-girl, don't you?"

Suddenly, Suzanna is perfectly still. She feels like she has been running through a summer meadow and tripped over a log.

"What of it?" she says.

"I want you to give her something." Ficzkó reaches into his pocket. "I would have given it to her myself, but I have not seen her since the great wash finished."

"There's no point looking for Boróka in the laundry house these days," says Suzanna rather bitterly.

Ficzkó places the wooden goose on the table. "She misplaced this, I believe."

"Where did you get that?"

"I found it."

"Where?"

"In the outhouse."

"What were you doing there?"

Ficzkó sets his jaw. He is trying hard to do the right thing, even though Stefan's voice is as loud in his head as Suzanna's mother's is in hers. Don't bother giving it back, Stefan tells him, just toss the goose into the fire. But Ficzkó is sorry now for what Stefan made him do in the outhouse. The bird is a crudely fashioned thing—of no value, clearly—but if she carries it about with her it must mean something to the girl. If he is the one to give it back to her, then maybe she will know that he is trying to be a better man.

"Will you give it to her?" He is insistent now, becoming impatient with this rather annoying girl. "And will you be sure to tell her I gave it to you, and that I'm . . ." He dredges up the word: "Sorry?"

Suzanna's look is reproachful, but she gives him a curt nod.

"Thank you," he says, rising and moving toward the door.

"Aren't you forgetting something?" Suzanna says flatly.

"What?"

"Your doublet."

"Oh, of course." He steps back, grabs it from the sideboard.

"You're most welcome," mutters Suzanna to his retreating back.

The painter has run out of Verona green. Without it, he cannot complete the underpainting for the countess's face and hands. He has returned to his lodgings to get some, and in the meantime, all Boróka can do is wait. It is the first week of August and her skin is moist under the thick layers of velvet. She tugs at the lace ruff, wishing she could take it off while she waits, take everything off and sit in her petticoats and chemise, but that would mean getting Dorka back to dress her again, and she would rather wilt than endure her rough hands and snide remarks.

She goes over to the bookshelves, pulls out the verses of Hans Sachs. No one will mind if she reads to pass the time, she thinks, as she sits down on the little stool. She is one verse in when the door opens and the countess, back from the spa at Piešt'any, walks in. Boróka is facing the bookshelves, with her back to the door, so she doesn't see her, and she is so engrossed in the book that she doesn't hear her either. For a moment the countess stares at the girl sitting, reading, in her library. She knows it cannot be, yet she cannot take her eyes off her. That hair that curls gold at the ends, those ears a little too prominent. She must be more tired from the journey than she thought for her eyes to play such tricks on her, but she so desperately wants to believe that it could be her.

It's foolish, but she cannot help but say her name: "Orsika?"

Boróka twists around. "My lady, I did not hear you come in," she says, rising, only to sink into an immediate curtsy.

"Of course, it is you, Boróka"—the countess's voice is a strange mix of relief and disappointment—"though I'll own that, for a moment, I imagined it was my dear daughter Orsika sitting there. It is uncanny how much you reminded me of her." The countess has recovered herself and is striding into the room, pulling off her gloves. "She also loved to read. I often found her here with her nose in a book."

"I did not know you had a daughter called Orsika, mistress."

The countess places her gloves carefully down on the walnut table. "That is because she died when she was about your age."

"I am sorry," says Boróka. "It is a tragedy to lose a child."

"You lose them all in the end. If not to sickness, then to marriage."

"Your children are destined for greatness, my lady."

The countess sighs. "Yes, but I almost wish that one of them *wasn't*. No mother should have a favorite child, but if I could have kept one of them with me it would have been Orsika. But I must not complain: I am blessed with three surviving children. Where is the painter?"

"Gone to fetch a pigment, my lady, to lend your skin the perfect hue."

The countess catches Boróka's eye and they both smile. "And you are to stand here in the heat waiting for him, I suppose?"

Boróka nods. "It is rather warm."

The countess tuts, walks over to a chest of drawers. She pulls one open and begins rifling through it. "Any lady wearing what you are on such a day would have one of these." She turns around. "Here."

Boróka puts down the book and walks over to the countess. "It's only a shabby thing," the countess continues, handing it to her, "but it will keep you cool while you wait."

Boróka has never held a fan like this one before. She turns it over in her hands, marvels at the ivory guards carved with chinoiserie figures. When she pulls them apart the silk leaf unfolds like a spreading wing. It is painted with tiny flowers, curled leaves, and butterflies. To Boróka, it is exquisite.

"My lady," she breathes, "I could not use such a beautiful thing."

The countess looks quite touched. "It is a child's fan," she says. "I think it belonged to my eldest daughter, Anna, but Orsika and Katalin loved it too." The countess watches Boróka trace the butterflies with her fingertips. "Why don't you keep it?" she says gently. "My girls have no use for it now."

Boróka is speechless. "I—" she begins, but can say no more.

"It's been a long time since either of my daughters were happy with a fan," the countess says ruefully. "These days Anna and Katalin want land and castles and money, not pretty fripperies—or at least their husbands do."

"But their husbands are already rich, powerful men," Boróka says.

The countess laughs, though the sound is hollow. "I have never known a rich man who did not want to be richer. And what is true of most men is doubly true of Counts Zrínyi and Drugeth. That is why they married into my family, after all. Yet I do not criticize them for it; they are good husbands to my daughters."

"Does your son not give you comfort?"

"It is not the job of a son to give his mother comfort, Boróka. Pál has been living at Sárvár Castle since he was six years old, learning horsemanship and swordplay with his tutor, Imre Megyeri."

"You must miss him?"

"Of course. A noblewoman might envy a peasant when it comes time to give up her son and heir to a guardian, but you have to accept it. It would have been easier, though, had he not gone the same year my beloved husband died. It is six years ago now that I lost both my men."

"Yet you are an example to us all, mistress. No one could run the castle as well as you."

"My husband was away at war for much of our marriage. I have had to manage our estates alone since I was not much older than you. When he died, I did not doubt that I could continue to do so."

"You are much admired, my lady," says Boróka.

The countess's expression is inscrutable.

"Am I?" she says.

Suzanna finally gets back to the turret at half past ten in the evening. Her back aches, and the skin on her fingers feels numb. Nevertheless, she grips the wooden goose in her hand to remind her to give it to Boróka before she falls asleep and dreams of cross-stitches. When she puts the candle down on the table, she sees something remarkable sitting in its pool of light. She picks it up, spreads it open, marveling at the silken landscape of flowers and butterflies that appears. It offers her a glimpse into a world of which she could never hope to be a part, and she can hardly bear to look at it. She closes the fan abruptly, puts it back down.

On the pallet, Boróka sleeps an untroubled sleep. This girl has everything, Suzanna thinks. What need has she for a wooden goose?

Chapter 11

SPREZZATURA

Orsolya is dreaming of going to her very first dance. She is wearing a yellow damask gown with diaphanous white sleeves that waft around her arms as she skips and twirls with her hands held aloft, clicking her fingers to the fluid sound of a lute. Then a fiddle starts and she begins to actually twitch on her little wooden chair because, in her dream, she is dancing as vivaciously as she possibly can. Over in the corner is a young man who looks like that factotum she sees around the courtyard sometimes, broad of shoulder and light of eye.

She dances in the sunlight, with his gaze upon her, until she senses a darkening, a shadow falling. He must be approaching her, taking a nervous breath and swallowing hard, steeling himself to dare to ask her to dance with him.

"Orsolya?"

She ignores him and keeps dancing. No need to make this too easy.

"Orsolya!"

The music stops abruptly, sucked into the same vortex as her beautiful gown and handsome admirer. She starts and clutches the edges of her chair, suddenly sitting bolt upright, eyes blinking, tasting the dryness of her own mouth.

"Were you sleeping?"

The countess is standing over her, blocking out the light. The faces of the other girls, like a field of sunflowers, are tilted toward her.

"No, my lady."

The countess folds her arms across her chest. "So, what is it, then?"

Orsolya's heart trips and stumbles in her chest. "What is what, my lady?" she asks, but her voice comes out croaky and weak.

"*Sprezzatura*, of course! What we have all been discussing this past while! I thought you were unusually quiet," mutters the countess, walking back to her settee and sitting down.

"I am so sorry," Orsolya says, tearful, "I don't know what happened. I just feel so tired."

The countess softens her pursed lips and disapproving stare, somewhat. "No matter," she says, "it is rather warm in here. So, now that Orsolya is back with us, who would like to try to define that most important quality of the perfect courtier, *sprezzatura*?" A beat, then: "Boróka, you try."

Boróka knows this is a test. Of all the noble qualities that may be within her grasp, *sprezzatura* is not yet one of them. Quite the opposite, in fact. She has felt as if she were clawing her way through each task ever since she first came to the castle, visibly nervous, worried about everything from speaking in front of the other girls to somehow managing to fall off her chopines. She never *has* fallen off, of course; she just *worries* about doing it. Always teetering on the edge of catastrophe, alert to everything that could possibly go wrong. If she can answer the countess without showing any of this, then she will have taken the first step toward mastering the elusive skill of *sprezzatura*. So she stands and looks at the other girls with a smile. Her hands are folded neatly in front of her, and her shoulders are back. They cannot see how her armpits prickle and her guts churn.

"I would describe it as a kind of studied carelessness," she says, her voice clear. "It's about making your actions appear without effort, even if that is not the case at all."

The countess nods, pleased. "Quite so, Boróka," she says. "It is nonchalance, is it not? Though not *so* nonchalant, *Orsolya*, that you literally fall asleep."

The girls giggle. Orsolya's cheeks are pink, but whether it's the warm room, the countess's teasing, or something else entirely, no one can tell.

As if to distract them all, the girl sitting next to Orsolya speaks: "But why do we need to know all this, my lady? I shall be married and have children, shall I not? I will not need to discuss books or know what *sprezzatura* is."

The countess tuts. That is precisely the kind of facile comment she would expect from Judit. "What if you are not blessed with children?"

Judit contemplates for a moment. "But I will be, surely. It is just what happens."

"Not always," replies the countess, rather sharply. "I myself had to wait ten years before I was able to give my husband a child."

The girls absorb this revelation.

"But you have three children, my lady. Their graces, Anna, Katalin, and Pál," replies Judit.

"Yes, I do"—the countess speaks as if she were explaining something to a small child—"but for many years I was barren."

The room is silent save for the rustling of girls shifting on their seats, feeling a little awkward. The countess is impossible to predict. Her moods are like opal stones constantly shifting their colors. She is at once caustic and kind. One minute dismissive and the next, like now, seeming to invite an intimacy that no one can accept for fear that, if they say the wrong thing, or presume too much, they might find themselves crushed like an insect under the countess's pointy, pink-satined toe.

So they stay quiet because that is much the safest way.

Then Orsolya coughs. It is a dry bark that seems to surprise even Orsolya herself. She tries to hide it by pretending she was merely clearing her throat. Now she must say something. Anything.

"Perhaps God only gives children when the time is right?" she ventures.

The countess's expression is suddenly wry. "Would that that were true, Orsolya," she says, "but, I assure you, it is not." She looks distant for a moment, then takes a deliberate breath and says, "No, sometimes you need help from a source more proximate than God."

The girls are mystified, expectant. The countess hesitates, but it is her job to instruct them. Not only in the arts and literature to inform their conversations and develop their characters but also in the more subtle challenges of married life. The difficulties they may have as wives and mothers. So she tells them: "Something happened when I was very young. For the ten years that followed my marriage, I felt that God was punishing me for it, denying me a child because I wasn't worthy. I had to turn to my lady steward, the Mistress of Myjava."

"The forest witch?" asks Judit, thrilled.

The countess nods. "Yes, Doricza Majorosné, the forest witch."

"What did she do?" Judit's eyes are wide. The other girls sit very still, not wanting a misplaced fidget to break the spell of the countess's confidence.

"Dori gave me incantations, special words to repeat after the new moon. She gave me powdered dove's heart to sprinkle into my wine. I bought emeralds from Georg Pech, the Viennese merchant, as she told me to, and I kept them with me because the color green strengthens the bonds of marriage and guards against infidelity and temptation."

"I cannot imagine that my lord Nádasdy was anything but devoted to you, my lady," says Orsolya shyly.

"He was devoted to me," replies the countess, "but the ardor of men wanes." The countess leans forward on her settee, lowers the pitch of her voice to a playful whisper. "In which case, Dori would recommend you spice his meals with red grass and mistletoe!"

The girls exchange glances, a little shocked, but Judit positively snorts. "I'm surprised that happened to Count Nádasdy," she says. "I thought they called him the Black Bey?"

It is hot in the privy chambers, stiflingly so, but the countess's voice, when it comes, feels chilling. "Whatever do you mean, Judit?" she says.

Judit is still sniggering, looking around her at the other girls. Her smirk slowly fades as she realizes that none of them will meet her gaze. Judit swallows. "Only that I would have expected him to be very, um . . ." Judit pauses. It is as if she already knows that the next thing she says could determine the path the rest of her life takes. The word that keeps coming to her is *virile*, but, as she glances up at the countess's fixed and humorless expression, she knows she cannot say that, so she tries to come up with something less . . . inflammatory.

"Manly?" she tries.

Some of the girls wince visibly. Orsolya has leaned so far away from her, in an attempt to distance herself, that it looks as if she might topple off her chair.

"Manly?" the countess repeats, carefully enunciating each syllable. The cozy intimacy of the ruelle seems to thicken around them, congeal into something sinister, oppressive. Judit's breath quickens, her forehead shines with moisture.

"I'm so sorry, my lady," whispers Judit. "I don't know what I'm saying."

"No," agrees the countess, "you do not, which makes me wonder why you say anything at all. The first rule of partaking in an intellectual discussion is that if you have nothing sensible to contribute then stay silent."

Judit nods miserably. "Yes, merciful lady," she says, trying not to cry.

The countess could leave it there, but the heat has shortened her temper. She has this ignorant girl between her teeth and is not inclined to let her go. The countess gets up, strides over to Judit. "Shall I tell you exactly how *manly* my husband was?" she asks her.

Judit tries to shrink into her seat as if it were a snail shell.

"It was the Ottomans who named my husband the Black Knight of Hungary. Do you know why?"

Judit is staring at the floor. She cannot speak, but she still has to respond to her mistress's question. She tries to shake her head, but it is more like a spasm, a terrified jerk.

The countess sinks down in front of her, tilts her head so that Judit cannot help but lift her eyes to meet those of her mistress. "It was because he celebrated defeating them by dancing with their corpses. He twirled them around, then tossed them into the air and caught them again. He played bowls with their severed heads." The countess has a strange smile on her lips, and her eyes glitter in the sunlight. She places a hand on Judit's knee, slides it slowly up her leg. Judit stares at it as if it were a viper, steals herself for its bite. "Now, Judit," she says, stilling her hand and digging her fingers into her leg, "if you ever dare disparage my husband's name again, I swear that I will do the same with you!"

Judit gasps and gulps down air, sobbing freely now. The countess pushes herself up from Judit's leg. "Why is it so hot today?" she mutters, walking over to her cabinet. She yanks open the top drawer and starts to claw though the contents. "Where's my fa—" She stops, shoots a furious glance at Boróka.

"Here, take mine," says Orsolya quickly, rising from her seat and holding out her fan.

The countess is about to dismiss the gesture with an impatient flick of her hand when something shocking happens. The fan falls from Orsolya's fingers. Her sculpted face is pale and there is a sheen to her skin. She staggers back against the chair, like a drunkard, and it slides away from her as she falls, its legs scraping across the floor with a screech of alarm.

For a moment everyone stares at Orsolya, collapsed on the floor, then the countess walks over and crouches down beside her. The girls start to cluster around, but the countess raises her hand sharply and stops them.

"Stay away," she says.

Chapter 12

ANTIMONY

Below the castle there exists another world entirely. It lies like a buried creature beneath them, with beating heart and twisted limbs that course through the limestone rock, ending in caves that gape like open wounds in the precipice. The caves are full of supplies: crates of wine and spices in sacks, Spanish olives and Pantelleria capers bottled in brine. Hidden away behind them is vast wealth locked into wooden chests: goblets and gilded silver bowls, tapestries and handfuls of florins that run through the fingers like sand. At the center of this underworld of tunnels and chambers are the dungeons. They are the leaden lungs of the castle, inhaling the pariahs, the rogues and miscreants, the sick and injured.

Orsolya lies on a wooden table in one of these cavernous cells. Her almost naked body is lit all around with candles, and Dorka is at work. On the table there are hooks and pliers. Tongs to tear into flesh and cautery irons to seal it back shut. Scalpels sharpened on whetstones and jagged-edged saws. Pincers to extract anything, from teeth to the truth.

Dorka picks out a fleam and studies it in the candlelight. Then she grips Orsolya's arm and draws its flinty blade across the tender, exposed skin inside her elbow. Blood, bright and shocking, spurts from where she has cut her, a steady river of life belying its pale, fragile source. A girl from the scullery squats in the shadows, basin cupped in her hands, catching the stream of blood like she were sculpted in stone beneath the plume of a garden fountain.

Orsolya wails, a tremulous cry that ends in a sigh, expired into the darkness.

"Stop the bloodletting."

Dorka looks up. It is the forest witch who has spoken, Dori Majorosné, summoned from Myjava. Dorka does nothing, just stands with Orsolya's arm still gripped in one hand, the fleam in the other, letting the blood flow.

"I only just cut her," she says, her voice as sharp as her blade.

"Do as she bade you." The countess is behind Dori. She approaches the table, close enough to observe Orsolya with a strange expression, something between concern and fascination.

Dorka ties a thin strip of material around the top of Orsolya's arm, yanking on it good and hard, before taking a rag and pressing down on the wound. Orsolya's lips part and she tries to speak, but the words are soundless, just air caught and released unformed.

"Does she sweat?" asks the witch.

Dorka nods. "She's warm as a plum dumpling, that one."

Dori takes a candle and holds it aloft over Orsolya's face, before she moves the light slowly down Orsolya's body, inspecting the skin, which takes on a reptilian sheen in the candle's glow. She pauses, holding the aureole over Orsolya's chest. The girl's ribs are like claws grasping at her stomach, jerking it down in time with breath that is rapid and shallow, as if somewhere behind her fluttering eyelids Orsolya is running, scared. Her skin is covered with red wounds. They pepper her torso and limbs but leave her face, hands, and feet oddly untouched.

Dori raises her inquisitorial candle to Dorka's face. "Did you make these marks?" she asks.

"For shame, I did not!" replies Dorka, indignant.

Dori turns to her mistress. "I recommend a purge," she says. "One pellet of antimony swallowed whole."

"A purge?" exclaims Dorka. "I think not! She has already rid herself of everything, top and bottom. It will do more mischief than good."

"Nonetheless," says Dori, her voice calm, "we must induce vomiting to release the bad humors before administering an infusion. Coriander for her fever, wormwood and mint to soothe her. If she coughs, give her comfrey."

Dorka scoffs. "We are not making a pie! The girl is suffering from a surfeit of blood, it is clear. Allow me to continue the bloodletting without delay." Under the table, the girl with the bowl shifts and rustles, readying herself to offer it up once more to a sky that rains blood.

"I will prepare an incantation to say three times tonight under the crescent moon." Dori's voice is low, but insistent.

"Useless words, my lady!" exclaims Dorka to the countess. "Bring me leeches so that I may treat these . . . pustules!"

"You forget yourself, Dorka. You shall have your leeches, but you must let Dori perform her spells."

Dorka presses her lips into a thin line. "As you wish, my lady," she says.

In the moment of silence that follows, Orsolya's lips part and her eyes crack open. She takes in the low ceiling, the same smooth stone as a sarcophagus, the candles, and the smell. Everything that should be inside her, now outside. Ripe, rusty, meaty. A smell to make dogs circle, vultures hover. She thinks herself lying in her own tomb, slowly decaying, turning to dust. Her eyes cast about, seeing only faces she doesn't recognize, gloomy angels fluttering around her like moths.

The countess steps forward, and Orsolya's eyes meet hers. "Merciful lady," Orsolya whispers, lifting her hand from the table. The countess moves as if to take it, but Dori stops her with a touch on her arm. "You must not," she says in hushed tones.

"We will help you," the countess says instead. "Tell us what ails you,"

"Everything hurts, my lady."

"Oh, Orsolya, you poor girl." The countess leans toward her, ignoring Dori's widening eyes, and strokes the girl's cheek, brushes the damp hair off her forehead. "The gynaeceum is most dull without you," she whispers into Orsolya's ear. "You must make sure you get better quickly so you can come back and rescue me from the tedium of it all."

ANTIMONY

Orsolya's lips twitch, but it is impossible to know whether it is a smile or a grimace, because a moment later she is lost again, fluttering back to the hinterlands of her mind where strange landscapes are stalked by cats the size of cows, with saucer eyes and nutmeg fur.

The countess straightens. "I am rather fond of this girl," she says, her eyes a little shiny in the candlelight. "It is my wish that we do all we can to help her. Dori, if you think the infusions and the purge will offer her some relief, please administer them. Only recommence the bloodletting if all else has failed," the countess adds, with a stern look at Dorka.

"She should not be alone after the purge," says Dori. "Is there someone who can be with her?"

The countess thinks for a moment, then suggests the girl she considers the most dispensable, the one that it would trouble her least to lose. "She shares a room with Judit," she says, "I will send her."

"Judit Vasváry?" says Dorka, aghast. "My lady, please, you cannot send a noble girl to tend her. What if she falls ill herself? Send someone of no consequence, I pray you. Little Marta here could do it." She gives the girl under the table a prod with her foot.

"It will give Orsolya some comfort if she knows the girl," says Dori.

"Do not worry, I will find someone," says the countess.

"You must away now, mistress," says Dori. "You have spent too long in this place of contagion as it is."

The countess looks again at the girl laid out on the table, the damp hair, the rash that bleeds across her skin, the strange way her body contracts with each breath, like a poked clam. "For the love of God, cover her, Dorka," she says in a harsh whisper. "We can give her back her dignity, if nothing else." Then she turns to Dori. "Do you have anything to protect me?"

The forest witch nods and takes a pendant on a metal chain from a leather pouch. "Put this around your neck while saying three Our Fathers," she says, holding it out to her mistress. "Inside is a prayer to keep you safe."

The countess covers Dori's outstretched hands with her own and brings them to her lips. She holds them there a moment, murmuring her thanks into the woman's rough hands, smelling of sweet bay and myrtle.

In the darkness, Dorka rolls her eyes, beseeching the damp, stony heavens to give her patience.

Orsolya's body convulses, retching nothing more than a thin dribble of frothy liquid into a bucket by the raised mattress on which they have laid her. She is clothed now in a soft, plain shift, with a coif to keep her hair from her face. When she has finished and rolled onto her back, the scullion creeps from the shadows and takes away the bucket. She does not flinch from its contents; the task is no more distasteful to her than pulling the tiny giblets from the larks and starlings that grace the countess's dinner table, or sweeping the dung from the courtyard cobbles. Whenever anything rank or soiled is deposited anywhere, she moves toward it as instinctively as a carrion crow, plucking it from view.

Boróka dips a cloth into a basin of clean water and dabs at Orsolya's lips. "Rest now, honey bee," she says, stroking her thumb over Orsolya's forehead. She never thought to be whispering sweet words to Orsolya, but the haughty girl who treated her with such disdain is gone—or, at least, lies dormant behind veiled eyes and a countenance as clammy as the walls that surround them.

The dungeons swallow everything, including time. Boróka doesn't know how long she has been sitting with Orsolya. There is no light, no noise, no rhythms of day and night. She has tried to pass the time when her patient is resting with the scullion girl. She has clay marbles in the pocket of her apron and suggested they see who can roll them farthest along the cracks between the huge stone flags, but she never so much as looked at Boróka, just shook her head in mute refusal. Yet the girl is not mute. She talks to herself all the time, a quiet, melodic chatter. Boróka sighs and puts down the cloth. When the purge is finished they will move Orsolya back up into the comfortable castle apartments, if she is well, but for now she lies sequestered, a thing apart.

The scullion squats down with the bucket, tips it this way and that, swills it around. "Not in this one," she says, putting it down.

"What are you doing, Marta?" asks Boróka, but Marta won't answer. She picks up a stick and shuffles over to Orsolya's chamber pot, then starts poking through the slops.

"Please, don't touch that," says Boróka, feeling perplexed, revolted.

The girl shakes her head. "Marta's job to find it," she mutters, swirling a figure of eight through the foul liquid over and over.

Little Marta, Dorka had called her, and Boróka can see why. Her limbs are thin and fragile, like sparrow bones, giving her the look of a girl even though, now that she studies her, she sees she has a woman's face. Marta is ageless somehow, both childish and careworn.

"There it be," says Marta, her eyes wide. She dips her fingers into the mess and pulls something out, which she drops into her apron and wipes dry. "Good girl, Marta," she says, satisfied. She drops the stick on the floor and gets to her feet. "Put antimony back for next time," she instructs herself, as she drops the expelled antimony pellet back into a glass jar standing next to Dorka's shiny, waiting fleam.

As if from far away, Boróka can hear the sound of heavy doors clanging open and closed, voices rolling down the stone corridors. The castle's subterranean guts are absorbing someone else, digesting them into its branches of tunnels and caverns. Marta squats on the floor, staring at the door. It is a marvel that her legs never seem to tire of this position. She could sit on the stone shelf that lines the walls, if she chose to, or perch on the edge of the examination table, but it is as if she has grown up without the privilege of a seat and has now become quite used to creeping around the floor, legs bent like a slender-limbed spider. "Will they let Marta out now?" she wonders aloud and, indeed, the door does open.

Katalin Beneczky steps inside. She holds a candle aloft, taking in Orsolya lying on her mattress and Boróka sitting beside her. As she sweeps the light around the room, Marta gives a gurgle of pleasure.

"Marta!" exclaims Kata. "Hello."

Marta looks at her from under her lashes and smiles back.

"I see you are nurse today, Marta. How is the patient?"

Marta pinches her nostrils between her finger and thumb.

Kata chuckles and nods. "Smelly, yes," she says, mirroring Marta's gesture, but Kata's smile quickly fades. She takes her candle to Orsolya's bedside and rests it on the stone shelf.

The washerwoman has a cloth bag with her. It must be to collect the laundry stained with blood and pus and shit, but the bottom sags with items weighty as metal or glass. Boróka watches as she lays her palm on Orsolya's forehead, then pushes up her sleeve and rests her fingertips on the smooth inside of her wrist at the point where her blood rises in blue branches to the surface of her skin. Kata frowns when she sees the bulk of a rag tied at her elbow and gently unties it, inspecting the fresh wound inflicted by Dorka's fleam. She replaces the rag with a piece of clean linen from her bag and pulls Orsolya's sleeve back down.

"Has the sickness passed?"

Boróka nods. "There is nothing left to purge," she says, "but she still coughs."

"What kind of cough?"

"A dry spasm, like a cat with something caught in its throat."

Kata looks solemn. "Like Judit," she says.

"Judit?"

"Yes, they just brought her down. She sickens in the same way."

A ripple of fear spreads down Boróka's spine as if a droplet of moisture had dripped from the dank ceiling and run down her back. Instinctively, she takes back her hand from where it rests on Orsolya's shoulder. "What ails them?" she asks.

"I know not," says Kata, "but we have seen this before. Not two years past, ten girls sickened and died."

"Will the purge cure her? The bloodletting?"

Kata laughs without mirth. "Perhaps," she says grimly, "if they don't kill her first." She reaches over and picks up a pendant that adorns Orsolya's neck, rotating the smooth bloodstone in her fingers. Orsolya has so many charms and amulets around her that she looks like an Egyptian priestess already bound for the afterlife.

"Who gave her these?"

"The forest witch," says Boróka.

"Dori Majorosné was here?"

Boróka nods.

"I will stay with Orsolya," says Kata firmly. "I have a salve for her rash."

Kata reaches into her bag and takes out a jar filled with something pale and waxy. When Kata begins to loosen the tie of Orsolya's shift, something about the movement at her neck rouses Orsolya and she opens her eyes.

Boróka takes her hand. "How do you feel, Orsolya?" she asks.

Orsolya studies her hard for a moment, as if her own gaze was something to be marshaled, caught, and fixed with effort on Boróka's worried face.

"Is that you, Boróka?"

"Yes, I am sent to sit with you until this sickness passes."

"You are kind," she breathes, squeezing Boróka's hand. "Thank you." Orsolya manages a slight lift of the corners of her mouth, but the smile quickly dissolves when the cough comes, contracting her body with a force that seems impossible for one so wan.

Kata places an arm around Orsolya's shoulders and tries to soothe her, but the amulets tangle and catch on her fingers. She tuts and lifts them from around Orsolya's neck.

"Is that wise, mistress?" asks Boróka, her voice a whisper lest she bring the washerwoman's audacity to the attention of the fairies, summoned by the witch's charms to watch over Orsolya.

"She will choke before she succumbs to any sickness," says Kata, matter-of-fact. She takes the jangling amulets over to the examination table and drops them into a wooden casket on the shelf. When she turns back, her eyes alight on Dorka's fleam, lying with the other instruments next to the table.

"There are some," she observes, picking it up by its bone handle, "who find more pleasure in the treating than the curing." She places the fleam in the casket along with the charms and closes the lid. "Go and rest, girls," she tells them. "Orsolya will be safe with me."

"Can Marta help Kata?"

Boróka had almost forgotten Marta, squatting in the shadows, her eyes solemn and owlish.

"If you wish, Marta, but you will need to wash your hands and change your apron first," Kata replies. "Boróka, you should sleep."

As soon as she speaks the words, Boróka feels awash with fatigue. She is grateful to go, desperate, now, to leave the stifling sickroom behind and return to a world of light and air, of color and sounds other than the rasp of sickness and suffering.

Kata walks her to the door. Before Boróka leaves, Kata grips her arm and says, "Stay away from the other girls. If you feel ill, come and find me first. Do you understand?"

Boróka swallows hard and nods. "Will Orsolya get better?"

"She *must* get better," Kata says, "and Judit as well. Not only for their own sakes, but for the countess's as well. If one of them dies, the rumors will begin again."

Boróka resurfaces into the courtyard and finds it is midmorning. An unconcerned world has simply carried on without her, turning the night she left behind into another day, as warm and glorious as the last. She must have sat with Orsolya all night. It feels both longer and like no time at all, as if her hours in the dungeons belonged to another life.

She tilts her face up to the sky, enjoying the warmth of the sun on her skin. When she opens her eyes she catches sight of the windows of the countess's privy chambers. Behind the leaded panes on the far left, a figure is sitting hunched behind his easel. With a rush of dismay she remembers that she is meant to be posing for the painter this morning.

When Boróka enters the countess's library, out of breath and flustered, Valentino doesn't look up. He studies his work in progress as if it hardly matters whether the girl is there or not.

"Forgive me, sir," she says. "I had forgotten I was to sit for you today."

Still he does not look up. It is one thing for the countess to be late, but a servant? He paints his displeasure on the canvas with petulant dabs of his brush.

"Did you prefer the pleasant weather to your work here?"

In truth, the painter is a little hurt. There is a tiny part of him that hopes—no, believes—that this girl enjoys their time together as much as he does. It does not sit well with him that she was so easily seduced by a summer's day. When she had not turned up he had stared out the window, watching some other girls talking and laughing in the courtyard, and he had realized how foolish was the thought that she might admire him. For a moment he saw himself through her eyes—a dull, old man—and it is this, not her tardiness, for which he resents her.

"No, sir. I have been in the dungeons tending to a girl who is sick."

Valentino shrinks from her, even though she is barely past the door. Dungeons, sickness? Is that why her face is so florid? Her breath so labored? This will not do. She is supposed to be vitality personified, this girl. When she poses for him she brings youth and beauty to the tableau in the same way that the pearls bring wealth and nobility. He cannot have her standing there wilting like a cut flower, her radiance fading before his very eyes. He might as well put a skull on the table and start painting that.

"A pestilence? Then away with you!" He dismisses her with a flick of his hand, tutting when droplets of umber-colored pigment spatter onto the dust sheet.

She drops a quick curtsy. "As you wish."

Her voice sounds so weary, so broken, that he cannot help but look at her again with more compassion. She has the hollow gauntness of a cadaver. She is either very ill or very tired. Either way, his heart softens. A little. She stirs so much in him that he thought was lost, including fatherly instincts he never knew he had.

"Rest, child," he says, more kindly. "I have plenty to be getting on with." He gestures to the coppery tones of the painting's background.

"Thank you," she says.

He is glad to see her smiling because, despite his apparent gruffness, he wishes her no ill at all. Now that she has caught her breath and the alarming color of her cheeks has settled, she looks more like herself. "I will see you again when you are able," he tells her.

"I look forward to it," she says, and he is mollified.

She is about to leave when she pauses. "Valentino, sir, may I ask you something?"

He looks up from his work. "You may."

"What is the purpose of the box in the painting?"

"The box?"

"Yes, the rosewood box with the six-petaled flower on its lid. What does it signify?"

"Does it have a flower on the lid?" he asks, laying down his brush and wiping his hands. "I had not noticed."

The painter walks over to the setting for his portrait. He lifts the clock and stares at the rosewood box underneath. "I don't think it represents anything," he says, setting the clock down on the table. "I used it only to raise the clock into my line of sight."

Boróka takes a step inside the room, edges closer toward the table. "Do you know what's inside?" she asks. Her voice is deliberately off-hand, a little forced.

"I have never thought to look," he says, but, of course, now that she has mentioned it, all he wants to do is look inside the box. And why not? The key is in the lock. If it were private it would have been hidden away, or the countess would have told him to remove it from the tableau. He unlocks the box, before he talks himself out of it, and lifts the lid.

Pah! He sets his jaw, a little annoyed with the girl now. She had made him think that there would be something to see, some secret of the countess's revealed.

"Enough of your nonsense," he says curtly, swiveling the box around to face her. "There is nothing inside, nothing at all."

Part II

Autumn

Chapter 13

Songs for the Dead

In almost all respects Marta prefers the dead to the living.

They do not scold her, or pull her hair. They do not kick her, like Dorka does, or call her *picsa*. They are beyond judging her or thinking her a *stupid woman*. With the dead she can stand tall, without fear of being slapped. She can look them in their filmy eyes and know that they will not notice when her words don't come out quite right. And if she detects even a hint of the disdain they showed her in life, then she simply draws down their lids and replaces their supercilious gaze with the blank stare of two round florins.

Marta washes the body with slow, deliberate sweeps across the skin. She takes a slender arm and draws the cloth down its entire length. "I will m-make you clean," she says. There, she said it almost perfectly. None of the words got stuck. It didn't take her many attempts to get past the first letter. With the dead she doesn't have to speak as if she were someone, anyone, other than herself to trick the words into coming out. And in return the dead talk to her too. They tell her who they were and what they did with the scabs and scars on their skin. A life of fetching and carrying is written into the calluses on this girl's hands and feet. She tries not to look at the wounds that cover her body. They tell only of her death, of her suffering at the end, and she doesn't want to know about that.

She turns the dead girl's hand palm up, bends the fingers—beginning to stiffen. The nails are broken, gray around the edges with ash. She brings the fingers to her nose and sniffs. You cannot get the smell of vinegar out of the skin, not when you are polishing all day. Marta gently replaces the arm by the girl's side and dips her linen back in the basin, swills it, squeezes it out.

When she has finished the girl's arms, she starts on the legs, washing from her ankles up to her thighs. The girl can only be about fourteen, but she has the knees of an old woman, puffy and swollen, the skin thick and rough as old leather. Every floor she has ever scrubbed is in those knees, every hearth cleaned, every floorboard polished. "By the time I've f-f-finished you will look like a lady," she tells her, although she knows this isn't really true. The girl's arms are pale from shoulder to elbow and tanned after that. Her face and neck are a different shade from her white breasts. The skin tells tales, and this could only be the body of a girl who has spent the summer outside in the sun, the sleeves of her chemise rolled halfway up her arms, tending herbs in the kitchen garden, collecting honey from the beehives, or elbow deep in soap suds, not two weeks ago, to clean the outside windowpanes before the weather changes.

She is not like that noble girl. Her skin was the same everywhere, as if she never did a day's work outside in all her life. Her cheeks were so soft—she stroked them—that the February winds surely never whipped around her face till her lips went numb. No, that girl was preserved like a plum in jam. Perfectly smooth and ripe.

Marta has been busy with bodies these past few weeks but, nonetheless, she cleans them all properly, whether common or noble. They will not go from her hands into the Lord's with dirt lurking anywhere. Even behind their ears. Or between their legs. She flushes to remember the noble girl. She shouldn't have done it, but she *had* to look. The girl was just lying there, offering answers to all the things about which she had ever wondered. It had almost surprised her to know that, under the fine gowns, the lace, the jewels, she was quite the same as any other girl.

When the servant girl is clean, Marta lays herbs on her chest, scatters chamomile and lavender around her limbs, then folds the shroud over the girl's face. "Farewell—" She realizes she doesn't know the girl's name, was never told it. Who does know her name, or where she came from? Who knows who her parents are? Who will remember her?

Marta gathers the ends of the shroud together at her head and feet and ties them with hemp string. She pulls the knots tight because this girl will not have a coffin and she cannot bear the thought of the shroud unwinding, exposing her, when she is tossed in the ground. And he is not always careful, that boy. She has watched him tip bodies into the grain store, like they were nothing but sacks of chaff. She dare not say anything. He lets her watch only because he thinks her dumb.

She didn't have to worry when they buried the noble girl. She was safe in a coffin of oak, with lemon balm in her hair. They took her to the churchyard at night, with hymns and prayers. Marta knows this because she watched the procession from a high-up window as it wound its way down to the village. She could see the torches they held aloft, hear their chanting and songs carried on the breeze. It was beautiful. She tries to see all the bodies safe into the ground. Once she has cleaned them, spent this time with them, she feels like she knows them. It's almost as if they belong to her.

No one will pay for the common girl to have prayers said over her body. No priest will chant her sins away in return for a handful of coins. So Marta begins to sing, clear and lilting. She sings for the dead girl's soul, and she sings for herself, for the sheer freedom of it, because the words always come easily when she sings.

The bodies, trussed in their white shrouds, remind him of insect larvae. This one, a bulging white oval, looks like one of the maggots it will soon become. He tries to lift it. If only it were soft like a maggot, not rigid as one of the new beams for the outhouse. It's demeaning, he thinks, lugging corpses around. He is the *johannes factotum*, a tradesman with skills, not a lumbering gravedigger.

So he simply *refuses* to bury the bodies. Instead, Stefan does it. Stefan doesn't mind this kind of task, doesn't balk at the smell, or the pain in his back after all the digging and heaving. In fact, Stefan does absolutely anything Ficzkó tells him to. He never asks questions or wonders what actually happened to all these dead girls. He never complains. Never tells.

Admittedly, he does sometimes get it wrong. Like now. The girl has landed on her face and is lying prone in the ground. Stefan shouldn't have rolled her into the pit, but this is the fifth body this week and he is getting tired. For a moment Ficzkó wonders whether to tell Stefan to fish her out. It's wrong to bury someone face down. It's humiliating, and the girl doesn't deserve to be punished for eternity in this way. Surely, she has been punished enough? But then, he has heard stories recently about bodies coming back to life. Their hair and fingernails keep growing beneath the shrouds and their bodies sigh and moan after death. He shudders. He doesn't want to leave her like this, but he also knows that the only way to make sure a body doesn't rise from the dead is to bury it face down.

It's Stefan who decides. He is iron-headed, this boy, as obstinate as it is possible to be. He doesn't care about the dignity of the dead; he picks up his shovel and drives it resolutely into the pile of displaced earth. Once the first spadeful has spattered onto the shroud, there is no turning back. She will stay staring at the fires of hell forever, with her soul trapped firmly in her mouth.

Ficzkó nods, satisfied. "Good work, Stefan," he says.

Back in his room, Ficzkó sheds Stefan like a skin. He peels off his soiled hose and shrugs out of his shirt, damp with the sweat of Stefan's toil. Once he has washed his face, scrubbed under his arms, he feels refreshed, like he has removed every last trace of Stefan and the awful things he does. He is plain Ficzkó again, in moss-green culottes and a matching dolman over a clean white shirt. He dampens his hair and sweeps it back from his face, peering into a small looking glass that the countess gave him. He tries so hard not to be Stefan, but he cannot get away from him. He is inside him, somehow. Every time Ficzkó looks in the mirror, Stefan stares back at him with a single green eye. He wonders that the countess has never cared about this strangeness, never even remarked upon it when, as a small child, she rescued him.

Or stole him.

When she was younger, the countess enjoyed going out without anyone knowing who she was. She would dress in a plain gown and *pacsa*, pull the many rings from her fingers, and unwind the pearls from her hair. In the summer of 1595 she heard that a traveling troupe was coming to town. There would be acrobats and minstrels, drums and viols playing. And something else, something she loved to watch more than anything else: a puppet show.

The puppets in this particular show were modest by any standards. Not the elegant marionettes she was used to, but crudely sewn glove puppets with garish painted faces. They bobbed along the flouncy trim of the booth's window acting out a biblical tale of human weakness, judgment, and deliverance. It was unremarkable, save for the fact that, every so often, the devil popped up on the stage. It was made of dark red cloth and had a large clay face with glaring white eyes and a huge hooked nose. It flapped its splayed clay hands and hopped up and down, surely intended to shock and thrill the audience, as its appearance was accompanied by a fizzing flash of silvery light. Except . . . this little devil was always late, arriving upon the stage quite some time after the chemical pop of the firework, then bumping blindly into the other characters as it blundered about the stage.

"Was Satan asleep?" heckled a man.

The crowd began to laugh and jeer. The puppet master's righteous tale was fast turning into a comedy, now that the glowering, menacing devil had become an object of such derision. Then someone threw something at the stage, a piece of rotten fruit that splatted wetly against the tatty black curtain behind the stage and rolled down into the hidden shadows of the booth. This was swiftly followed by a stale bread roll, which hit the wooden plinth and bounced back onto the cobbles of the market square.

Two puppets, impersonating a lord and lady, disappeared abruptly from the stage. A moment later the puppeteer appeared, holding up his fists still covered by Lord and Lady Temptation as if they were boxing gloves. The devil remained, bewildered, on the stage. It lifted its clay hands as if to shrug and say, *It wasn't my fault*, before it sank from view.

The crowd turned its attention to the puppeteer, who was now shouting at a man demanding his money back: far better sport than any puppet show. When the puppeteer shoved the man in the chest, the crowd closed around them, gleeful. All this for just a groat!

The countess, not interested in watching men brawl, walked around the back of the booth. The curtain was still open from where the outraged puppeteer had thrust it aside, and there, sitting on a stool, was a little boy with the devil on his arm.

The countess crouched down in front of him. "So you're Lucifer, are you?"

Ficzkó didn't answer. By that time he had had so many names he was struggling to keep up.

"I think he's meant to appear when the firework goes off," she explained, her voice kind.

The boy fixed her with pale eyes, both blue and green. "I know," he said.

"Then why didn't you do it?"

Ficzkó drew up his knees and wrapped his arms around his legs. The devil, pinned against his shin, hung its heavy clay head.

"Because I hate him."

"Who?"

In answer, Ficzkó turned his face toward the angry shouts of the puppeteer and the dull thud of his landing fists.

"Ah," said the countess, "you do not care for your puppet master, so you deliberately ruined his show?"

Ficzkó glowered at her, defiant.

"But now he will be angry with you."

The little boy's lip began to tremble. His stare softened and his eyes became wide and fearful. Before the countess could try to comfort him, the puppeteer appeared, panting and bloodied, his lip split and his puppets in tatters.

"You little shit," he said.

There wasn't much the countess could do when the man pulled off the broken puppets and grabbed Ficzkó by the ear. Ficzkó winced and pawed at the man's thick forearm, thumping it ineffectually with the devil, but his master dragged him out of the booth.

"Mistress Deak!" he roared. "Get thee here, Mistress Deak."

The boy began to squirm, but the puppeteer held him fast until a woman appeared, every bit as thickset and shapeless as Lady Temptation herself, with a face just as hard.

"What's he done now?" she asked, knuckles pressed into barely discernible hips.

"Making mischief again, Mistress Deak. If I didn't have a show to finish, I'd throttle the lad."

"Right, give him to me," said Mistress Deak, taking hold of Ficzkó's collar. "I'll put him away for you."

The puppet master released Ficzkó and brought his hand up to his damaged lip, pressing it and inspecting the blood transferred to the back of his hand. "I'll get you later," he muttered, glaring at the boy. Then he turned away and began rummaging in a box behind the booth. After a moment he straightened, took a deep breath, and stepped back into his booth to give the crowd their show, his swollen fists thrust inside a homespun Jonah and a gaping whale.

The countess, with little appetite now for music and entertainment, cinnamon buns and apple cakes, decided to follow Mistress Deak and her reluctant charge. They went to a wagon parked in an alley off the square. Inside was a wooden cage of the type that might house poultry on their way to market. Mistress Deak opened it, saying only, "In." And the boy did go in, meekly, and without protest. He circled around like a dog and sat down on the cage's floor as if he simply belonged there, crouched on an old blanket, crumpled and worn. The woman wedged a stick across the door and banged it in, good and firm. The boy pulled the puppet from his arm and held it in his lap, frowning at the devil's black-and-white eyes as if to say, *Look what you made me do.*

The rest of the fair was uneventful. The puppeteer managed to complete several productions of "Jonah and the Whale" without further incident, and Mistress Deak got some knitting done sitting on the steps of the wagon, guarding Ficzkó in his cage.

It was already evening, and the fair was almost over when something quite unexpected happened. The braziers had been lit and the air smelled of burning citrus peel and baking pies. The puppeteer was just weighing his takings in his hand and thinking of his supper when the local notary and his men clattered through the square on horseback. When the notary found the puppet booth, he dismounted and demanded to see the puppeteer's license to set off fireworks in a crowded public space. When the puppeteer could not produce one— claimed that it was unheard of, in all his twenty years of puppeteering, to even need one—the notary had him arrested.

A single night in the gaol at Bytča was enough for the puppeteer to miraculously recall the administrative requirements in relation to public performances utilizing dangerous pyrotechnics. In return for the fat pouch of groats in the puppeteer's pocket, the notary duly completed the necessary paperwork and the puppeteer was released. When he finally made it back to the market square, he found that there was little left save Mistress Deak and her knitting.

"What happened, Mistress Deak?" he asked her.

Mistress Deak shook her head, barely looking up from the rhythm of her stitches. "They took it, sir."

"Took what? My booth?"

"No, sir, that's in the wagon?"

"My puppets?" By now the man was distraught.

"No, sir."

"What, then, woman?"

Mistress Deak paused her clacking needles and looked up. "My very best chicken cage, sir, that's what they took, and with that useless boy still in it."

Ficzkó places his kolpak on his head, the one with the fancy eagle feather. Everything he has he owes to her. Since the age of five he has been her pet, a little monkey she dresses in velvet jackets and feather-plumed hats. Is it any wonder that he would do anything for her?

Literally anything.

Chapter 14

EPHEMERA

Despite the passing of the weeks, the portrait stands unfinished in the countess's library. The woman in the painting remains faceless, unknown. The tableau is without its real-life muse. No painter sits in front of the canvas ready to record every detail of this moment in time, before it is lost forever. It is into this apparent emptiness that Boróka steps to see if her job as sitter should resume; to see if, after weeks of death, they are once again permitted to think of trivial matters, like portraits and human vanity.

The library is as still as a painting itself. Through another door is the countess's chamber where, only four weeks ago, they all sat discussing *sprezzatura*, enjoying the thrill of the countess in an unguarded moment, disclosing the secrets of the married state; emeralds and infidelity, fireflies and desire. And they had all tried to remember what she told them because not one of them thought, sitting there in the sunlight on that perfect August day, that they might not live to ever need the knowledge. Not even Orsolya, though she was already the sickest.

Boróka realizes that there is no need for her to be here. Who knows where Valentino is? Perhaps he is sitting out the pestilence with the baroness and her lapdog. Before she goes, Boróka cannot help but do one thing. There is something that has been bothering her, something of which she cannot quite make sense, and it will take only a second to check. She goes over to the table. Her chopines are placed neatly underneath it, waiting for her to put them on and bring the tableau to life again. There is such stillness in the library, such silence from the corridors and anterooms, that she thinks herself completely alone, so she unlocks the rosewood box and lifts the lid.

The quick intake of her breath sounds ridiculously loud in her ears. She glances up, as if a gasp might be enough to bring Dorka bustling into the library, tutting and complaining. But there is no one in this room save herself, standing on the Turkey carpet reaching for a book bound in oxblood vellum.

She sits down on the little footstool by the bookshelves and puts the book in her lap. It falls open, as if by way of invitation. Why wasn't the book there when the painter looked? she wonders, as she leafs through the first few pages. Why is it back now? Suddenly, her hand stills. She has reached the end of the part she has already read, but now there is more, written in the same flowing script.

I called my new mother Ailing because when I was a small child that was all I could say of her name. We lived in her house on the town's main thoroughfare. We were happy enough, but the people's suspicions and rumors had settled over the town like a fog, and it caught in our lungs every day.

Over the years I grew up, their mistrust began to dissipate in the face of normality. No strange white stallion galloped through the town at night. The summers were warm and the winters mild enough. Harvests were good and the farmers prospered. Without famine or hardship, undue death or disease, the people did not have to find a reason for their misfortunes, and there was no need to turn their gaze toward the quiet, motherless child and the woman who looked after her.

Do you believe that history repeats itself? That we are fated to make the same mistakes as our mothers before us? I think Ailing did, because she kept me as close to her as she might a newborn lamb, pausing whatever she was doing to watch me if I so much as ventured onto the street. We kept ourselves to ourselves, growing what we could in our little garden and tending to the bees and the geese. Every so often someone would ask Ailing for a potion or a poultice, which she prepared for them without charge. For money we took in laundry, which we washed in the river.

I loved the river from the first moment I dipped my hand into it and felt it tug at my fingers, as if it were trying to take me even then. I couldn't believe that something with such force and movement was not alive itself; a serpent with a belly full of trailing reeds, continuously moving and sliding against its banks. Ailing showed me the parts that were safe, the shallows and the still pools where rocks slowed the river's flow. We beat the laundry there, shirts and shifts slapping against stones made shiny by tallow soap. When it was dried and ready to be returned, Ailing would slip dried lavender in between the folded material, so that her customers were surprised by its heady scent when they shook out their fresh, clean clothes. She did it for me too. I found dried lavender in my apron pockets and under the bolster in my bed. I grew up with its fragrance all around me. It was a reminder, she told me, that she was always there with me, even if I couldn't see her.

When I was no longer a child, I began to go to the river alone. Ailing was content to let me do the laundry while she tended her plants and made ointments and tinctures to put into bottles. In the summer months, once the washing was done, I would pull my skirts up to my thighs and let the rushing water run over my bare legs. Even though I was already of an age to marry, there had been no talk of a husband for me. Ailing had never been married, and I did not grow up thinking that I needed a man to complete me. I told myself that I didn't want to swap the river's cool caresses for a fat-spattered stove and an infant tugging on my skirts, which was just as well because no man from the town had so much as tried to speak to the shy woman with the white stripe of a badger in her hair.

During the summer I turned one and twenty, the mayflies returned to the river, hatching in their thousands and swarming into the air, their translucent wings bright as fireflies in the sunlight. The river shifted underneath them, a lurking, stalking thing, waiting to engulf the weak and the spent. I stood alone in the river, my feet on the soft moss that carpets the underwater stones, watching pike and bream rise slowly from the deeper waters and open their tented mouths, sucking in mayflies spinning like tiny stars on the water's surface. And what the fish didn't get, the swallows did, swooping through clouds of insects rising like steam from the river.

After a while I began to hear a single, whistling note threading through the air. It cut through the slosh and slap of the wet linens, changing its pitch, pausing and resuming, as if the mayflies danced to a strange, shrill tune. A little way upstream was an old blade mill. It had lain empty for years, but its huge waterwheel now churned through the river again. The sound was the blades of scythes, swords, and sickles screaming against the grindstone. After a while the noise stopped and a man came out of the mill. He stood on the stone bridge that arched across the river from the mill to the opposite bank, watching me. There was only a thin gauze of mayflies between me and the sight of his naked chest, bare in the sunlight. It was so disconcerting that I immediately turned my back on him, plunging a shirt into the water in a resolute manner. The river seemed suddenly agitated, pushing against the back of my legs and catching at the pulled-up hem of my skirts as if trying to take hold of me and carry me away from him. I should have let it because the river has always looked out for me but, instead, I felt compelled to turn back toward him. When I did, he smiled and tossed something into the water. The river tried desperately to snatch it away, make it disappear into the frothy currents that tumbled over the rocks, but it reemerged and continued downstream until it came to rest in the shallows near my feet. A white flower, plucked from the dogwood tree overhanging the little stone bridge.

That flower was only the first thing he sent me. Over the next few weeks, when I was working at the river's edge, I sometimes saw little baskets fashioned from reeds floating down the river. I began to expect them, hope for them, every time there was a pause in the blade mill's eerie song. First there were more flowers: wild geraniums and valerian, tiny bunches of willowherb tied with string. I ignored them all. Then he tried to tempt me with food: a fat, ripe pear, which I could hardly bear to let pass, and even a misshapen potato cake, which made me laugh out loud. After that his offerings became more obvious: a piece of hemp rope tied into a love knot, and a message written on paper that had been carefully folded. I almost bent to scoop that one from the river. I saw it coming, bouncing against the rocks, zigzagging toward me. I was desperate to know what he wanted to say to me. The paper had begun to unfold, and I could see the words, though the river spat at them and made them bleed into the paper. Then, as I stepped out toward it, the basket caught on a branch jutting out above the surface of the river and flipped over. The river claimed his words greedily, as if they had been meant for her all along.

He seemed to give up after that. The noise of his sharpening blades started up again, more strident than before, and the baskets stopped.

Eventually, though, the shrill of the blades began to soften. By the time the week was out, the sound had taken on a decidedly gentler, more conciliatory tone. I found myself casting glances up toward the blade mill in between scrubbing petticoat hems. I scanned the water constantly, searching for a basket made of reeds. Perhaps he saw me looking and felt encouraged, because the very next day he sent me something that I simply could not ignore.

It had been raining heavily overnight and the river was bloated and bad tempered, her waters murky. I was about leave, as, for all the dirt I tried to get out, the river would put back more. The mill was silent, save for the breathless rush of the waterwheel. For once, I could hear the birds trill and the bees rouse themselves from a damp slumber and lift into the breeze. I bent to pick up my laundry and, out of the corner of my eye, I saw it coming.

It was bigger, sturdier, than the other baskets and rocked slightly on the river's undulating surface. I stood up straight to see what it was. I didn't have to wait long as it sped down the swollen river. When it came near, the basket tilted and a twitching nose with white whiskers popped up over the edge, then swiftly retreated. I gasped and stepped into the shallows. Inside the basket was a tiny leveret, long ears flat in alarm, body quivering. I glanced up, outraged, and saw him standing on the bridge, already smiling because he must have known that I would not be able to let that beautiful creature pass by without rescue.

I positioned myself ready to catch hold of the basket. The leveret was no more than a tight ball of fur, dark at the roots, pale fawn at the tips. The basket was almost within touching distance when it hit a rock and spun out into deeper water. I could still reach it, but I had to go out farther into the river. I wasn't worried: I had stepped into the river so many times that I was as sure-footed as a mountain goat among the rocks and stones. But that day the river was a different creature entirely. It had a power to it that I had never experienced before, and footholds that were usually second nature to me were now submerged, hidden in swirling depths that seemed to shift under my feet. I should have turned back but, foolishly, I leaned over and tried to grab hold of the little hare.

The river suffers no fools. She simply snatched my feet away from underneath me as my hand closed over the rough weave of the basket. Suddenly, I was sitting on the slippery rocks, the leveret held aloft with one hand, clutching at the reeds near the bank with the other. Not even this indignity was enough for the river. She pummeled against my back, trying to push me off my ledge and send me tumbling downriver. A fitting punishment, in the river's eyes, for giving in to the blade grinder's games. Slowly, I felt her winning. My skirts became so heavy with water that they hung around me like lead. I felt the thin reeds slipping through my fingers and I began to be drawn off the rock.

Then a strong hand gripped my arm and pulled me back. The basket was lifted from me and placed upon the bank. The grinder's arms, tanned brown from the sun and covered with tight-curled hair, circled my waist and dragged me back to the side. As we tried to get up the bank we slipped in the mud and fell upon the grass, lying there, panting, our bodies already intertwined with little effort on the grinder's part.

"That wasn't meant to happen," he said, propping himself up on his elbow, laughing.

I wanted to shout at him, beat his bare chest with my fists and tell him that I could have drowned, that it was cruel to misuse an animal like that, but he was staring at me so intently that the words got lost in his dark, moleskin eyes.

"You're even more beautiful close up," he said.

No man had ever spoken to me like that, and my only instinct was to look away. It was then that I caught sight of the basket. I had assumed that the leveret would be long gone, but she was still there. Even though she was now rescued and perfectly free, she just sat there, caught in the blade grinder's gaze.

She didn't even try to run away.

I should have known that a love affair that began with the mayflies could never last. We were as doomed as they were, destined to have only a moment together.

He told me he had taken over the old blade mill that summer. He lived above the waterwheel in a house built in layers, every floor an afterthought, jettying above the one below, each with its own lattice window and little pitched roof. It was built so precariously that the whole structure looked as if it might topple into the river at any moment. I swear I went inside only to dry my skirts. I only went up to the little room above the waterwheel to see how the wheel worked, and I only stayed there longer than I should have because I was so seduced by its sound: the creaking of the wood, the calming rhythm of the turning wheel lifting and releasing, the pulsing rush of the water.

It seems obvious now, but, back then, I never noticed that the baskets only ever appeared on Tuesdays and Fridays. All the other days of the week the blades sharpened against the grindstone without interruption. It also didn't occur to me that men too young to be widowers do not often live in higgledy-piggledy houses all on their own. They need someone to sweep the floors and polish the hearths. When they set down their sharp-bladed knives, there must be potato cakes on the table waiting for them.

Tuesdays and Fridays are market days, the days the wives of butchers and bakers and, most certainly, blade grinders put on their boots and mantles and leave the house to go shopping. The day I saw the leveret floating down the river was a Friday but, unbeknownst to the blade grinder, his wife would never reach the market that day. Granted, she left soon after breakfast, in her usual fashion, and took her familiar route through the woods and down the hill, but at the midpoint between the mill and the market, she encountered a problem. The heavy rains had caused the river to breach its banks and part of the wooden bridge had been swept away, which just goes to show that there was no end to what the river was prepared to do to keep me from that man. With no other way to get over the river, the grinder's wife had to abandon her trip to the market and return, quite unexpectedly from the grinder's perspective, to the mill.

If her suspicions were raised by the unusual sight of another woman's skirts laid out over the side of the stone bridge, they were horribly confirmed when she came inside and marched up to the little room above the waterwheel. Had the wheel been quieter, we might have heard the determined thud of her boots coming up the stairs but, as it was, there were no sounds in that room save our own breath and the river's constant whisper of a cautionary tale that went entirely unheeded.

There is nothing more emasculating for a man than a wife who has caught him doing that which he should not. No more did the grinder walk out onto the stone bridge, six foot tall and broad as an ox, ablaze with lustful confidence. Instead, from that day on, he slunk to heel like an obedient pup and kept his nose to the grindstone every day of the week.

And I carried on with my laundry because that was what I had to do. I certainly didn't expect any more gifts or messages, so I was shocked when I saw a reed basket bobbing along the water. I told myself to ignore it, but then something glinted in the sunlight, which made me think that there was a trinket, or perhaps even a ring, inside. Despite everything that had happened, I was still thrilled by the thought that there might be love coming down the river from that mill. I stumbled into the water to get it before it passed, but as soon as I touched it, my blood ran cold.

Inside was a knife, sharpened to a flawless edge.

When I looked up toward the mill, it was not the grinder who stood on the stone bridge watching me, but his wife. Her arms were folded across her chest, and there was an unforgiving set to her jaw.

Boróka is so immersed in her reading that she doesn't realize she is not alone in the countess's privy chambers. When she comes to the end of the passage her senses return to the library; the tick-tock of the golden clock, the musty-sweet smell of row upon row of old books, and . . . something else.

A male voice, low and caressing, and then a woman's. Boróka snaps the book shut. The voices are coming from the countess's bedchamber, and the man's voice is growing louder, as if he is approaching the door. She hears the click of a doorknob turning and springs up from the stool. As the door to the bedchamber opens, Boróka reaches the table. Just as she lifts the rosewood box and tosses the book inside, someone is coming out, and as she closes the lid, he turns around to face her.

"And what is this?" says Ficzkó, walking toward her.

Boróka sweeps her hand over the box's lid. "I'm dusting," she says.

He laughs. "Dusting? But why would you be dusting *inside* the box?"

"I wasn't."

"You were. I saw you close the lid. It looked to me like you were snooping, not dusting." Ficzkó looks down to where Boróka's hand is still placed firmly on top of the box. "Show me," he demands.

Boróka keeps her hand on the box. Attack seems the best form of defense. "Tell me what you were doing in the countess's bedchamber," she says.

He enjoys this question. Nothing pleases him more than when someone catches him trying to come and go from the countess's chamber without notice. "It is not for you to ask," he replies, and yet, he wants her to.

"You should not be in there. What would Dorka say?"

"Nothing, once she realizes that I am there at the countess's invitation."

"Why would she want you in there?"

Sweet girl, he thinks, so naive.

"Sometimes the countess succumbs to . . . melancholia," Ficzkó replies. "I console her, distract her from her worries, that is all."

Ficzkó holds her gaze. He waits for the information to settle and take root. The countess expects discretion, but what can he do when he has been caught red-handed, just like the goose-girl has been.

"Open the box," he says, his voice serpentine, as if it might slither under the lid itself.

"No."

Ficzkó laughs. "But you are already caught. You cannot stand there all day guarding a box. As soon as you run off to peel a potato or darn a sock, I will see what you're hiding." Ficzkó's expression becomes grave. "The countess will be so disappointed when she hears you have been prying into her personal affairs. She has some affection for you, I believe, though I know not why."

There is nothing Boróka can do but take her hand away. Ficzkó's glance, before he opens the box, is triumphant. He likes it when the serving girls do as he tells them, especially this one. He had hoped that she might thank him for returning that silly wooden ornament, but no, she remained as aloof as always, never so much as glancing in his direction. She must think herself above him, with her visits to the gynaeceum and delusions of being a countess, even if only in a painting.

His self-satisfied smile soon fades when he lifts the lid. He clenches his jaw in unmasked fury. "Do not play with me, goose-girl," he spits. "I am not an enemy you would wish to have."

But Boróka is already laughing. She tries to stop but she can't, so she presses the back of her hand against her mouth and snorts against it.

Inside the box is an elaborate feather duster, made with elegant, black-tipped eagle feathers.

That night, in the turret room, Boróka turns over on their pallet and whispers to Suzanna.

"Something strange happened today."

Suzanna is drowsy. "Hmm?" she says.

"There is a box in the countess's library. Whenever I open it there is a book inside, yet when others open it the book isn't there."

"What of it? Someone has taken the book out." Suzanna doesn't open her eyes, so as not to encourage this line of conversation.

"No, it has *disappeared*," insists Boróka. "Or perhaps only I can see it. Then, today, it turned into a feather duster."

Suzanna thinks she must be dreaming, or at least she wishes she was. Her days are hard. She scrubs and she cleans. She mends and she sews. But, above all, she prickles under Ilona's flinty gaze. She braces for the sting of a slap across her skin whenever she drops a stitch and cowers from the pinch of Ilona's bony fingers every time her mistress inspects her work, as it is always found lacking. She lives from one tick of Ilona's clock to the next, always on edge, always in fear. At night she is exhausted and sleeps like the hogs her mother kept back home, snoring and twitching, till she has to wake at dawn. It is Boróka—who barely has to lift a finger, unless it is to tighten the strap of her velvet shoes—who can afford the luxury of lying awake at night thinking about boxes and dusters.

Suzanna sighs and opens her eyes. "The duster must have been in the box already." She is surprised Boróka has not thought of this. Plainly, one does not learn common sense at the gynaeceum.

"It wasn't, I would have seen it when I looked inside."

"Then it must be some black magic of the countess's," says Suzanna, pulling the coverlet up to her chin. "You have not told me what you have seen her do."

"That is because there is nothing to tell, Suzanna. I have never seen the countess be anything but kind to the girls." She pauses, thinking of Judit. "Well, most of the girls," she clarifies. "She can be strict, but usually only when she is trying to teach them something."

"Humph," says Suzanna, rolling over.

"I have told you what I can. Now will you do something for me?" Boróka asks Suzanna's back.

"Mmm?" says Suzanna. She will agree to anything if it means Boróka will be quiet.

"Open the box," she says. "I want to know what you see when you look inside."

Chapter 15

MELANCHOLIA

The girls wait, but the countess does not arrive. She is late, very late. Not the entitled tardiness of her appointments with Valentino, but an entrenched absence that, seemingly, has no end. Yet they cannot leave until they are dismissed, so they sit waiting in the privy chambers for their missing mistress.

Chattering is frowned upon, so they look out the windows, pick at their nails, and, occasionally, whisper guarded words to each other: *Where is she?* and *What can be wrong with her?* They wonder if Dorka was even correct when she told them that the gynaeceum was to resume now that the sickness has passed.

Boróka stares at the door to the library thinking about the box, wondering how to get Suzanna to the library to look inside it. Then someone catches her eye: the girl sitting to her left in the same place in which she has always sat. Almost. One chair is gone, of course. One girl has not returned, so the chairs have been arranged slightly differently, spread out to occupy the space she left behind.

Boróka turns her face toward her. Normally, she would not presume to look this girl in the eye. She would lower her gaze, offer her the subtle deference she expects, but things have changed now, surely. They are both altered since that August day. Boróka is no longer the upstart serving girl; she is the nurse companion, the one who held her hand and spoke words of comfort. The one who wiped the sweat from her brow and the vomit from her mouth. And the girl is changed too. Gaunt now, her luminescence faded. Boróka chooses not to lower her head. Instead, she smiles. It's a bold, warm expression that acknowledges their connection, a shared experience that runs deeper than the supposed nobility, or otherwise, of their blood. It is a smile that says they are friends.

Despite the fact that she is looking right at her, Orsolya does not appear to see her. Her gaze simply floats over Boróka as it might her own chamber pot: something unavoidable, but not to be acknowledged. Boróka's smile disappears. She is no longer thinking of new friendship, just beginning; she is prickling with bitter thoughts. She is wounded that the girl who clasped her hand and thanked her for looking after her now will not offer her even a smile in return. Before she turns away, Boróka stares hard at Orsolya and gives her a look that says, *I wish you had died instead of Judit.*

Dorka comes in. "My lady countess is indisposed today," she says, her voice brisk. When the girls don't move, she becomes impatient. "Don't sit there gawping," she tells them, "get along with you." She flaps her arms to chivvy them, herd them out of the privy chambers like goats. Boróka lingers behind to put away the chairs. As she stacks one on top of the other, Dorka approaches.

"You are to go to the library," she says. "The countess is waiting for you."

Boróka nods, but before she can walk away Dorka grabs her. "Say nothing of what you see there," she hisses, digging her fingers so hard into Boróka's arm she yelps.

The countess is at her writing desk, though she is not writing. Crumpled pieces of paper litter its beautiful marquetry surface and a thin stream of ink trickles from an overturned bottle, dripping onto the carpet, bleeding into the patterns and flowers. The ink is not just on the carpet; it is on the countess herself, on her hands and the cuffs of her gown. There are streaks of it on her cheeks where it looks like she has clawed at her face with her fingers. Her eyes are red-rimmed and tearful. When she tries to collect the scattered papers, Boróka sees that her hands are shaking.

All etiquette is forgotten. Boróka rushes toward her, crouches down beside her. "Oh, mistress," she whispers.

The countess swallows, takes a ragged breath. "Boróka," she says, trying to keep her voice steady and the tears at bay, "I wish you to help me, please."

"Anything, my lady."

"Can you write?"

"Yes."

"I had thought so." The countess manages a weak smile. "Anyone who knows the verse of Hans Sachs can surely put pen to paper. I need to write a letter, but, as you can see, I've got myself into a mess." The countess indicates the desktop with trembling hands that she seems ashamed of, appalled by, even. She snatches them away, interlaces her fingers, and presses her hands into her lap to still them. "Every time I try to write, I cannot seem to control the pen. The ink goes everywhere, my words look . . . like *spiders*." The countess's voice is riven with distress. She wrings her hands in her lap. "I don't understand it. I am blessed with such a neat and steady hand!"

"Come." Boróka places her hands on the countess's shoulders and gently guides her up from the desk. "Why don't you sit on the settee and I will tidy this."

The countess obliges, meek as a child.

"Who is the letter for, my lady?" Boróka asks as she clears the desk.

The countess sniffs, a little more composed. "It is to Balázs Kisfaludi, my deputy sheriff in Vas County. There is an old woman in the town of Tokorcs whose home has been vandalized. Two cows and a chicken have been stolen."

Boróka stops wiping the desk with her apron. Surely this is not what has been causing the countess such upset.

"But this is quite a trivial matter, my lady. Can it not wait until you feel calmer?"

"Trivial? A defenseless woman who has faulted no one being taken advantage of in this way? No, that is not trivial, it is abhorrent. This woman has petitioned us for assistance and we will help her. Those responsible shall be punished, I will make sure of it."

"I understand, my lady. My only thought was to compose yourself first. The letter can wait a day, can it not?"

"No, it cannot." The countess rises from the settee, pulling herself up to her full height. "It is my job to protect the people on my estates and resolve their disputes."

The countess walks back over to the desk where Boróka is now seated with fresh ink and paper. The countess wipes her face with a handkerchief, smooths the hair from her brow. She looks delicate yet resolute. Perhaps *sprezzatura* is not so much making things look easy, thinks Boróka, as a front. A pretense. It is putting on a mask, no matter how you are feeling.

"*May God grant you many blessings, your grace,*" the countess dictates in a clear voice. "*We bring this matter to you on behalf of the old woman of Tokorcs.*"

Partway through describing the woman's plight, the countess loses her train of thought. "*The petitioner has lost two cows and a . . . a . . .*"

"Chicken?" offers Boróka.

But the countess has turned and is looking out the window. She stares at the fields and vineyards beyond the castle walls, at the hamlets settled like snowfall in the valleys. It is almost as if she is looking for someone, guarding against attack. When she turns back around the old woman of Tokorcs appears to have been forgotten.

"Do you know who György Thurzó is?" she says.

Boróka almost begins to write the question down before she realizes it is meant for her.

"No, my lady," she says, putting down the quill.

"He is the new count palatine of Hungary," she says. "My husband fought alongside him, when they led the Habsburg campaign against the Turks, and showed him great loyalty. When Count Nádasdy fell ill with a terrible sickness, it was to Thurzó he wrote to formally entrust his widow and heirs to his generous protection, should the unthinkable happen. As it turned out, my husband wrote that letter the day before he died. He knew how vulnerable we would be, you see. Me, a widow, and his only son but six years old." The countess gives a bitter laugh. "So much for deathbed promises. Almost as soon as he was appointed palatine, he moved against me."

Boróka stays silent. She is not expected to answer, nor does she want to tell the countess that these matters are already spoken of by the servants. That rumors jump from one to the next, like lice.

The countess comes over to the desk, places both hands on the smooth marquetry. "Earlier this year he told András of Keresztúr to *make inquiries of reliable witnesses*. And who were these *reliable witnesses*? My girls? No! Serfs, that's who. Peasants who would not be allowed through the stable doors. They have never even been inside my castle, let alone to the gynaeceum, yet they presume to know what goes on here!"

"What did they say?"

The countess's fierce stare wavers. She abruptly pushes herself up off the desk and turns around. "Just that they saw nothing themselves but *heard* this, or *heard* that. Hearsay, the lot of it!"

"Heard what, my lady?" Boróka is almost whispering. A countess is like a sleeping cat and should generally be left well alone, not prodded or nudged.

The countess scans the rows of books as if all the secrets of the world were contained in their yellowing pages. "That I have set aside my reverence for God and man and cruelly murdered numerous girls in varied and ingenious ways." The countess swings back around to give Boróka a vehement stare. "But of course they did! They were told before they opened their mouths that they would be fined sixteen marks if they dared to deviate from the *pure truth*. Sixteen marks is a lot for a peasant to lose, Boróka. No wonder these 'witnesses' were careful to make sure that their *pure truth* was the exact truth the palatine was hoping for!" The countess draws in a deep breath. "But you must have heard about all this, I'm sure."

Boróka hesitates. She cannot lie to her mistress, yet she feels she wants to protect her from an entirely candid account of the terrible things that people say about her. "I heard that the priests were concerned, my lady," she says carefully. "I believe they said that there were an unusual number of dead girls being carried out of your castles for burial."

The countess sighs, exasperated. "I give work to so many young girls in my castles and estates that it's inevitable that God takes some of them each year. I wish there was no plague, no sickness, no death, but that is not the world we live in. You know that better than anyone, Boróka. You saw how sick Orsolya was."

Boróka nods. "And Judit."

The countess sighs heavily. "Yes, Judit," she says, as if frustrated that the girl still has the power to annoy her from beyond the grave. "They are asking questions again because this time a highborn girl died. No matter that other girls died of this same affliction. The deaths of servants, howsoever caused, are a sin against God, not a crime in law. Not a crime for which *I*"—she flattens her hand against her chest—"could be held accountable."

"Then you must tell the palatine that Judit died of a pox."

"He will not listen, Boróka." Instinctively, the countess brings her hand up to her throat and touches the amulet Dori Majorosné gave her. Her fingers are trembling again.

"But you are Countess Báthory, the Lady Widow Nádasdy. How can he say a word against you?"

In answer, the countess simply holds her hands palms up. "Because of all this," she says. "My wealth. My lands and fortresses that stretch all the way from the east to the southwest of this kingdom. Things that the count palatine does not think should be left in the hands of a woman."

"That cannot be allowed," says Boróka, outraged. "King Matthias will not permit the most noble woman in Hungary to be treated like that."

"Will he not?" The countess begins to laugh. It's a shrill, wild sound that spirals up to the ceiling and seems to hang there, like smoke. "Almost everyone owes me money, and King Matthias owes me most of all. If the king can make a case against me then I could be executed. The crown treasury would not have to repay its substantial debt to me and all the rest of my property would automatically cede to the crown." She pauses, takes a resigned breath. "Now do you think King Matthias will help me?"

Boróka is silent. The golden clock measures out the pause. *Memento mori*, it reminds them with every jolting creep of its needle.

"Surely your son will protect you, my lady?"

"Pál is still only twelve years old and much influenced by his tutor. That Imre Megyeri is too clever for his own good. My husband appointed him, on his deathbed, to be Pál's mentor and guardian because he is Pál's cousin and the Nádasdy family's representative in parliament. I do not doubt that Megyeri's loyalty to the Nádasdys is beyond question, that he would protect my son with his life; but he shows no fealty to me, a Báthory."

"Your sons-in-law, then, mistress. They must want to uphold the Báthory name?"

"They circle like dogs around me, Boróka, hoping to snatch the spoils of my downfall themselves. Count Drugeth only married Katalin in January, yet he is already impatient to see some of the great wealth he married into. I'm sure he finds it quite tedious that I am still alive at fifty years old! Think of it, Boróka, an aging widow managing her castles and estates as well as any man! A woman, past her usefulness bearing children, refusing to disappear! They consider me an affront to the natural order!"

The countess walks over to the window again. "You know," she says, looking down at the orchard leaves, already shades of red and orange, "sometimes I think about that English queen Anne Boleyn. One minute she was the king's sweetheart, the next she was a witch, a whore who fornicated with her own brother." She turns back to Boróka and gives her a tremulous look. "It frightens me what lengths men will go to once a woman becomes . . . inconvenient."

Once the letter is finished the countess retires to her bedchamber with an instruction that she is not to be disturbed. Her daughter Anna Zrínyi is coming to visit soon, and she must try to rally before then. Boróka is left to take the letter to the stable master for dispatch. As she leaves, she catches sight of the rosewood box. Who will miss it if she takes it for a moment? The countess is resting and Valentino is not here. If she finds Suzanna straight after going to the stables, the box could be back before the golden clock chimes again.

Suzanna is picking her way across the courtyard. It would not do to get mud on her hem now, not when she is so nearly there, and with not a hair out of place. She is on her way back to the east room, having been sent to her turret to change by a darkly furious Ilona Jó. Her apron was grubby and her coif was as wonky as her stitches. If she takes no pride in her appearance, then how can she take pride in her work? Or did she think that Ilona would not notice the shameful spatters of yesterday's stew? The poor girl is as rigid and white as her newly starched apron as she steps carefully over the cobbles. Well, it's not *her* apron, of course, it's Boróka's. There was no point looking for a perfectly pressed, stain-free, carefully mended apron on her own side of the bed.

"Suzanna!"

Sweet Jesu! She almost slips on the shiny stones out of fright. Boróka has jumped out at her like a kitten stalking a feather.

"On my mother's life," exclaims Suzanna, clutching her chest, "what possesses you?"

"Did I startle you? You're so jumpy these days."

You would be jumpy too, thinks Suzanna, if you had Ilona Jó waiting for you. "What is it?" she says, impatient.

"I have the box," says Boróka.

Suzanna lets out a little puff of exasperation. "I can do nothing now, I need to get back to my sewing or Ilona will make lace out of my fingers."

"It will only take a moment. *Please*, Suzanna, have a quick look inside." Boróka gives her friend an impassioned look. Then her eyes drop down from her face.

"Is that my apron?"

"Give me the box," says Suzanna, quickly.

Boróka hands it to Suzanna, still looking suspiciously at the apron. Suzanna turns the key and looks inside.

"Well," says Boróka, her voice full of anticipation.

"I see eight stockings with holes in them."

"Do you?"

"No! That's what's waiting for me in the east room while you make me do this nonsense." Suzanna reaches into the box. "There's only this inside." She holds up a book, bound in dark red vellum. Boróka inhales sharply.

"But that's what I see in there."

"Is it?" says Suzanna, sarcastic. "How very strange."

"Open it," insists Boróka. "Tell me if there's anything written inside."

Suzanna sighs but sets the box down on the cobbles. With both hands free, she opens the book.

Unlike some other places, the free royal town of Trenčín has a school. The sons of merchants, shopkeepers, and barber-surgeons jostle and fidget on benches in a drafty stone building that sits in the shadow of a fortress first built by Marcus Aurelius. Occasionally, a bright boy from a village farther afield might be privileged enough to attend, but not the fourth daughter of an impoverished pigkeeper. Suzanna stares at the marks on the page, but for her they hold no meaning. She knows they are words, of course, but they are just shapes and patterns, which tell her little more than the swirl of a shell or the stripes on the courtyard cat.

"Ssss," she attempts, because the first letter of what is written is the same as the first letter of her own name. The landlord's son scratched it out for her in the dirt with a stick, and the barrows and gilts came to sniff at it with curious snouts. It was easy to remember because the shape and the sound match. *S* for snake, *S* for Suzanna. He had taught her all the letters of her name and the numbers one to ten before her mother noticed what he was doing and chased him away with a broom.

"May I see?" asks Boróka gently.

Suzanna hands her the book and Boróka flicks through the pages. At first she doesn't understand what she's reading, but then, with a feeling of dread, she begins to make sense of it.

"What does it say?" asks Suzanna, interested herself now.

"It's a list of women and what seems to be when, where, and how they died."

Suzanna gasps. "It's her," she says. "It's a list of all the girls the countess has killed. For goodness' sake, Boróka, why did you take it?" Suzanna thrusts the book away from her, as if it were capable of murder itself. "Put it back, I beg you, put it back now!"

"Hush, Suzanna, it cannot be that. Look here, some of these women are from far away."

But Suzanna snaps the book shut herself. "It's a book of death, and I want no part of it," she says, her eyes wide and fearful.

Then she turns and runs toward the east room, hobnail boots ringing on the cobblestones.

"Where have you been?"

Ilona's voice is like a caress, the soft slide of a cat against her calf.

"I . . . I had to stop by the kitchen to . . ." Suzanna is finding it hard to speak. Her run from the courtyard was no distance, yet she cannot catch her breath at all. The knowledge of those murdered girls is coursing through her, mingling with the fear that Ilona always instills. She closes her eyes to think, but the strange shapes from the pages of the book are imprinted on her eyelids.

"But you were not in the kitchen."

Suzanna's eyes flick open. Ilona has stepped toward her and is now so close Suzanna can see the crop of hairs on the edges of her chin that catch the light. "Silly girl," says Ilona, "I could see you from the window gossiping with your friend when there is work to be done."

"I'm sorry, mistress." Suzanna is resigned. She cannot argue against the truth, plainly observed. Nor can she bear to look Ilona in the face, so she glances past her to the other girls. None of them are looking up, but she knows they are listening because their hands have stopped sewing. "I will get my needle right now."

"No need." Ilona's voice is as silky as the stockings she makes her darn. "I have one for you here."

Suzanna looks down and sees the needle in Ilona's hand, but it is not one she could use for stockings. Instead, it is thick enough to seam a leather boot. The sight of it makes Suzanna step back, but Ilona is quicker than she looks. She grabs Suzanna's jaw in her bony hand. The strange thing is, Suzanna doesn't even try to pull away. She stands there, a terrified statue of herself, as Ilona brings the needle up to her lip and jabs it into her skin. Ilona lets go of the girl and watches as she sinks down to her knees, cradling the needle still sticking out of her lip with trembling hands. When Suzanna pulls it out blood runs down her chin, drips onto her lap.

Ilona tuts and shakes her head. "You have dirtied your apron again," she says.

Chapter 16

DORKA

When Dorka was a child she found a field mouse in the grass behind her house. It was a tiny thing, with pale pink paws and eyes as dark and round as blackberry drupelets. Apart from its quivering whiskers, it wasn't moving at all, as if perfect stillness rendered it invisible. But Dorka could see it. She saw that it was frightened and alone. She saw that the fur on its back was damp and matted from where it had been clamped in the jaws of a half-hearted predator. Probably the fat cat next door. Just a plaything, not a meal; caught and released until the cat grew tired of such games and retired to a sunny spot on the wall. It offered as much resistance as a windfall apple when she bent down and scooped it into her hands. "Poor thing," she whispered into the little cage she had made of her curled fingers.

She put it in an old basket, with a broken tile placed on top so it couldn't get out. After some time in the basket's shady quiet the mouse began to move again, investigating every gap in the weave with a twitching nose and scrabbling up and down the wicker. Dorka knew that it was recovered enough to be released, but somehow she didn't want to set it free. She was also old enough to know that all creatures need some kind of sustenance, yet she gave it none.

The next day she found the mouse sitting at the bottom of the basket. It lifted up on its haunches when she took off the tile, sniffing at the light. Dorka crouched down by the basket, observing it. Every time the mouse tried to climb up the side of the basket she would wait for it to almost get to the top and then flick it off the wicker with her finger. This went on all morning, until the mouse grew weary and Dorka peckish. She took a handful of strawberries from the bowl on the table and ate them, one by one, letting the juice drip from her fingers onto the bottom of the basket, where the mouse sniffed frantically before the liquid sank into the surface of the wicker.

By the next day, the mouse wasn't moving at all, save the rapid suck and release of its flanks. By the day after it was as still as the day she had first seen it, and the shiny drupelet eyes were dull and glazed. Dorka picked it up by its tail and dropped it back in the grass where she had found it.

It takes a starved mouse almost three full days to die, she noted with interest.

In Čachtice Castle, eight girls are locked in the furnace house. There is no light in there among the coal, no warmth, and certainly no food or water.

Dorka didn't have many friends while she was growing up. Sometimes she would approach a group of girls playing outside and stand near them, awkward in her sister's hand-me-downs, which were too tight for Dorka's solid build. She wanted them to ask her to join in their game of ribbons, or marbles, or hops, skips, and chases, but mostly they ignored her. It seemed to Dorka that they had a secret, unspoken language that she didn't understand. Purely by dint of looks and glances exchanged among them, her petition to play was considered and dismissed. If she joined in anyway, simply thrust herself into their game of hide-and-seek, they all disappeared, like phantoms, and she found herself in a futile search behind low stone walls and inside old sheds, looking for friends that could not be found.

The girls have been in the coal house for two days already. Dorka watches over them, the most attentive of gaolers. If anyone asks what they have done to deserve such punishment, she tells them that managing the servant girls is her domain. Dorka, and only Dorka, decides what to do with them. Not even the most perfect behavior could survive such unfettered power. "A curse on anyone who lets them out," warns Dorka when the other servants try to help the girls. "May the thunder slay anyone who feeds them," she declares.

There was a boy near Dorka's village who had been born with a palsy. If he had been the child of a peasant he would likely not have lived out a week. Of necessity, a poor woman's instincts are as finely tuned as an animal's, and the weakest offspring are invariably pushed from the nest. But Jacob was born to the wife of a local landowner who had money for lemons and sweetmeats, heeled shoes and furs. She cheerfully overrode nature's more ruthless diktats and cared for the boy with as much love and attention as she did all her children. Which is to say, not very much at all, as she generally preferred card games and books to her children at the best of times. Happily, in the presence of material wealth, children can still thrive despite such benign neglect, and all the landowner's other children were hale and hearty and, often, up to no good.

Jacob, though, needed care beyond the patience, but fortunately not the means, of the landowner's wife. What she lacked in character, she could purchase with coin, so she offered payment for someone else to tend to Jacob's needs. Dorka's mother volunteered her for the job. This daughter of hers was sullen and melancholy. She was now sixteen and under her mother's feet all day, as she had neither friends nor sweetheart. Dorka was quick to point out what needed to be done, but slow to do it herself. She had neither wits nor grace, and it seemed clear that only an imbecile would pay for her company.

So Dorka earned a few groats every day sitting with Jacob. At first she was horrified. She turned her face from Jacob's dribbling rictus. She neglected to bring the cup of water to his lips quite as often as she was meant to, and she made no more than a token effort to spoon milk into his mouth. She changed his linens with revulsion, and after the first day, she vowed never to return. Her mother, however, made it plain that it was Jacob or marriage to the tanner; a great slab of a man who stank of rotting hides and lime. Mixing up vats of chicken droppings for a husband some years older than her own father did not much appeal to Dorka, so she chose Jacob. At least for as long as it might take the aging tanner to succumb to the consequences of a life lived seeped in alum and hemlock bark.

Remarkably, Dorka soon began to enjoy her work. She realized, in the quiet moments it was only her and Jacob, that she was not an underling any more, but in charge herself. Despite having little to recommend her—no education, no wealth or noble birth, and limited personal charm—in this space her word was law and there was no one to gainsay her. All her life she had been told what to do. Her older siblings pushed her around and made her do all the worst jobs. Her mother sought to direct her in everything, including what to wear (even clothes that Did Not Fit) and whom to marry. By contrast, when Dorka herself sought to influence others, she found that they were as pliable as stones in her hands. She could no more persuade the other girls to be her friends than she could make it rain. In fact, the only thing in her life she had ever had complete control over was that mouse. And now she had Jacob.

She began to call him her Little Mouse, to the delight of his mother, who was both thrilled and relieved to see him cared for by someone who had such affection for him. And Dorka certainly was delighted with her new charge. Though there was no wicker surrounding him, he could not run away. Though there was no broken tile stopping him, he could not escape. He was hers entirely, to do with as she pleased. He could neither complain nor defend himself, and she need not fear any consequences because the life of one so afflicted is not held dear. She was there simply to ease his inevitable passing, and that she certainly did.

It is not strictly true to say that Dorka had no friends. She did, in fact, have one. Only a few months after Jacob's birth, the landowner's wife surrendered to her seventh pregnancy. When the child was born, she could no more bear the tug of him at her breast than she could the sight of the landowner, so a wet nurse called Ilona was employed to suckle him.

Pity the poor landowner's wife to have her two most vulnerable children cared for by Dorka and Ilona Jó.

It is perpetual night in the coal house. Not a clear, starry night but a night fogged with dust and heavy with damp. The girls whisper to one another in the darkness until their mouths become cracked and dry, and even the solace of a kind word is not worth the breath it expends.

One of the girls is braver than the others, or perhaps more desperate. The darkness will not leave this girl alone. If she opens her eyes it presses against her eyeballs, and if she closes them it creeps around her, sighing into the back of her neck, rippling up and down her spine. She feels as if she cannot breathe, but when she gasps the darkness is like ash in her mouth. She has to get the door open before the darkness chokes her, so she thumps with her fist. "Water, Dorka, please," she begs. "Give us water or we shall die."

As it happens, Dorka had been to get a bucket of water only moments ago. She takes the key from around her waist and unlocks the coal-house door. When it swings open the girls flinch, as if the daylight itself could harm them.

"Who asked for water?" Dorka peers at the pale shapes in the gloom.

None of them speak. It is as if the devil has asked which one of them is prepared to sell their soul, a bargain each hopes the other will make.

"Well?" Dorka's voice is so forceful it makes them jump and scrabble backward. Lumps of coal roll off the coal pile and come to rest at Dorka's feet.

The girl who banged on the door feels a pointed elbow jab into her ribs. "I did," she says, reluctant now. She licks at her dry lips to ease out the words. "If you please, mistress."

Dorka nods, satisfied. "If it's water you want, then you shall have it," she says. "Come here."

The girl gets to her feet, unsteady as a newborn foal. Dorka stands to the side, and the girl walks out of the coal house, squinting in the light. It is late afternoon on a clear, cold October day. The girl wraps her arms around herself because the coal house—among the breath and living limbs of the other girls—suddenly seems warm. A chill east wind blows down through the outbuildings to greet her. It embraces her like an old friend, ruffles her hair.

Dorka picks up the pail by its metal handle. It is large and heavy, with enough water to fill all eight empty bellies. The girl eyes the water sloshing inside with distrust, as if it were a figment, capable of disappearing in the blink of an eye. Dorka supports the bottom of the pail with her other hand and raises it toward the girl's mouth. Now that the water is close, the girl cannot restrain herself. She claws at the pail to bring it closer, and she gulps and sucks greedily against the rim.

"Disgusting girl," says Dorka, abruptly pulling the pail away. "Who can share the water now that you have slobbered all over it? You will have to have it all yourself."

For a moment the girl is confused. She reaches for the pail again, but Dorka swings it up and away from her grasp. When it is high enough, she tips it over the girl's head. Precious water rushes over her hair, drips down the back of her neck. It saturates her chemise and seeps into her kirtle. The girl gasps from shock and cold. Inside the coal house, seven girls shrink into its farthest corners. If they go back far enough, stay still enough, they will become one with the coal itself, a hardened heap, noticeable to no one.

The girl draws her fingers across her face, wet with water and tears. She puts them in her mouth, sucks on them like a baby. Once, she was desperate to get out of the coal house, but now she longs for it. Longs for the darkness, even, to wrap itself around her and protect her from the cold and the wind. The sun is already sinking behind the west wall. Soon the coal house will be no darker than anywhere else.

She turns to go back inside, but Dorka grabs her. Now she has seen the girl's tears, heard her sobs, she doesn't want to stop, nor does she have to. Besides the countess, the only person who could censure her behavior is Ilona, and she is not at the castle. It rankles that Ilona will always be a notch above her just because she was a wet nurse. Suckling a child is easy—what Dorka had to do for Jacob was far harder—yet their pecking order was set even from those days. Then Ilona joined the countess's household first and forged the closest bond with her. Dorka is only there because Ilona invited her to join the castle staff, as Ilona often reminds her.

But Ilona is not here now. Dorka is in charge, and her veins fizz with cruelty unbridled.

"You're to stand here," she tells the girl. "Do not move until I say you can. Let's see if a night outside will teach you some manners."

Chapter 17

KATA

It is early morning and Kata is looking for the serving girls. She has searched in the kitchen, but there was no one there save a cook weighing out flour. When she asked him if he knew where the girls were, he shrugged and looked away. The east room was empty, and the courtyard was full of nothing but leaves, plucked from the trees and scattered over the cobbles by a mischievous squall. The castle is quiet, its rhythms suspended, as if the weather has frozen it in time, ready to be reawakened in the spring.

It is now too cold for the countess to live in Čachtice Castle, so she has retreated to the *kastély*. Her manor house is an elegant stone building with tall windows and a porticoed entrance. Its great hall and solar are warmer than the castle in the winter months, and the countess can sit out the January snows and February winds in relative comfort. Only a few of the serving girls are at the *kastély* with her. Anna Zrínyi is visiting, so the countess has sent most of the girls back up to the castle, under Dorka's watchful eye, so she can spend time in peace with her daughter.

Anna found her mother in poor spirits. She is jumpy and distracted, spooked by every bang and clatter, in a way that is most unlike the ruthlessly capable countess. Anna has suggested a trip to Piešťany to take the waters.

But for that they need serving girls to accompany them.

138

And Kata cannot find any.

She walks down to the outbuildings. The laundry house is empty; there will not be another great wash until the spring. The outhouse is now a storeroom, full of grain and orchard fruit carefully preserved in rows. She almost doesn't go as far as the coal house—what could be there in that tiny space, save lumps of dusty rock and an old shovel?—but a flash of white catches her eye, something rippling in the breeze.

The girl is propped against the coal-house wall, a sentinel standing guard over her own demise. She stood for as long as she could while Dorka, wrapped in her fur mantle, watched her, pinched her if her eyes closed or doused her again if she swooned. But then even Dorka grew chilled and hungry, and rather bored of this slow sport, so she demanded the girl take off her kirtle and stand there in her chemise. It didn't take long for her to stagger back against the coal-house wall, crumple against it, and when she did there was nothing even Dorka could do to rouse her, so she abandoned the girl for a supper of dumplings and steaming hot *paprikás* back in the castle.

Kata runs to the coal house. The girl's chemise is flapping in the breeze, the white flag of her surrender. She touches the girl's skin, though she already knows it will be cold as the coal house's stone wall. Kata's teeth clench and the sinews of her jaw tighten.

"Dorka!" she roars.

Her voice is snatched by the tail end of last night's squall and carried off toward the castle, though Dorka's ears are always deaf to any pleas. But Kata's shout did not go unheard. There is movement in the coal house, scrabbling like the room is full of mice instead of rocks. Kata stills, listening, turns her head toward the door.

A whisper, cracked as summer earth, says, "Help us, mistress, please."

Kata grabs hold of the handle of the coal-house door, rattling it in desperation long after she realizes it's locked. She knows where the key must be: hanging from Dorka's waist.

"How many of you are in there?" Kata asks the rough grain of the wooden door.

"Eight, mistress," it replies, then a pause. "No, seven."

Kata stands up. The dead girl's kirtle lies discarded on the floor. She uses it to cover her, then runs, skirts hitched up around her ankles, toward the castle.

She finds Dorka having breakfast in the kitchen: a fine white roll with plum jam and buttery eggs.

"Give it to me."

Dorka doesn't look up when Kata speaks. Instead, she pulls the fluffy roll apart with her fingers. It's so fresh a plume of steam escapes. "And good morrow to thee too," she says.

"I have not time for pleasantries when there are seven girls dying in the coal house. Give me the key, now."

Dorka takes a knife and slices it through the jam's glistening red flesh. "I'll not," she says. "They are being punished."

"Punished?" Kata is incredulous. "For what?"

"Never you mind. Disciplining the serving girls is my job, not yours," replies Dorka smoothly.

"The girl you left outside is *dead*. Did you know that?"

Dorka shrugs and bites into the roll, licks the sweet jam from her lips. "It matters not. She was a sloven, with the manners of a hog."

Kata approaches the table. She leans over and presses her fists down onto the wood. "I'll make this plain," she says, her voice measured and precise, "give me the key or, by God, I will rip it from you myself."

In an instant, Dorka has slammed her hands down on the table. Her knife clatters off the plate and the greasy pile of eggs shudders. She stands up and glares at Kata, furious. "You meddlesome wretch," she spits at her. "If you take a step toward me, I'll cut that sanctimonious tongue from your mouth."

But Kata just smiles. "As you wish," she says. "I will leave it to you to explain to your beloved countess why she has no maidservants to accompany her on her trip."

A muscle in Dorka's face twitches, her eyes narrow. "The countess sent the girls away. She has all the servants she requires with her at the *kastély*."

Kata shakes her head. "No, she does not. The countess and her daughter are preparing to depart for the spa at Piešťany. She sent me to find girls to accompany them." Kata pushes back up from the table and briskly brushes her palms together, as if ending her involvement in the matter. "I will simply have to tell her that there is not a single girl left to serve them because you have locked them all in the coal house."

Dorka sets her jaw, draws in a slow, seething breath. She studies Kata for a moment, then takes the keys hanging from her girdle and drops them on the table. Kata swipes them in one swift motion and goes to the door that opens out into the courtyard. Before she leaves she turns back to Dorka and says, "Send Ficzkó with water and a cart for that poor girl's body."

The first thing to escape from the coal house is the smell. It is both pungent and sharp. It is the fusty damp of the ground, mixed with the accumulated reek of confined humanity. Kata covers her face with her hand and steps backward, flinging open the door.

Like all imprisoned creatures suddenly free, the girls don't move. They stay hunched on the mound of coal like roosting birds, blinking in the light. They do not yet know if it is Dorka or Kata who has reeled from their stink, and the last time one of them stepped forward, she did not return. Besides, they have been trapped in the coal house for almost three days. They are blind, their bodies shrunken from lack of water. Their eyes scrape like dusty pebbles in their sockets and their joints creak like they are wooden dolls. One of them cannot sit at all and lies, delirious, on a bed of coal as if it were the softest feather mattress.

Kata comes into the coal house. She kneels by the girl lying down and takes hold of her hand, squeezing and rubbing it. "It's all right," she tells her, "you're safe now."

The girl turns her face toward Kata's, but her eyes seem sightless, as if the girl were already on the brink of another world, staring into somewhere unseen by anyone else.

"Is that you, Mother?" she whispers.

The countess is aghast. The maidservants are in a pitiable state and not one of them is able to accompany her to Piešťany.

"This should not have happened," she tells Dorka, who studies the shapes and swirls of the countess's Turkey carpet. "I knew I should not have allowed you to supervise the girls without Ilona there. You shall not have that privilege again."

Dorka smarts, visibly affronted, but the countess doesn't care. If Dorka had not been introduced by Ilona, was not her friend from years ago, then the countess would have sent her packing by now. She seems slippery, somehow. Not to be trusted in the same way as Kata and Ilona.

"There is nothing else for it," announces the countess. "Kata must come with us herself."

"Kata, my lady?" questions Dorka.

"Yes, Kata. Go and fetch her, please."

Dorka swallows, she presses her lips together and her eyes flick around the room as if looking for an answer. "Kata is . . . not well, my lady."

"Not well? What do you mean?"

"She fell down the stone steps leading to the grain store, I believe, and injured herself most horribly."

Chapter 18

ROSE HONEY

It's not unusual for the air in the *kastély's* kitchen to be tart with vinegar and rich with goose fat but, on this occasion, no one is cooking.

Boróka trickles vinegar over the wound above Kata's eye, catches the runoff with a cloth. Kata smarts from the pain and the smell, blinks furiously when a drop seeps into the creases of her eye. "I can do it," she insists.

Boróka rests a hand on the arm Kata lifts to take the vinegar from her. "Did I never tell you that my *apa* was a doctor?" she replies.

Kata tries to smile, but her lips are bee-stung. "He taught you how to treat a wound, did he?"

"In a manner of speaking," Boróka says. She doesn't tell Kata that the only wound she has actually dressed was when one of the geese was bitten by a particularly vicious squirrel.

"Don't worry, I'll tell you what to do." Kata points to some lint on the kitchen table. "You need to mix that with some honey," she tells her. "A doctor I once knew told me what type of honey is best but, I confess, I've clean forgotten what it was. I can't seem to think straight at the moment." Kata touches her fingertips to her brow, presses gently around the gash.

"Was it rose honey?" asks Boróka.

Kata looks at her, surprised. "Yes, that's it, rose honey."

"That's what my *apa* used as well," she says. "He always said the rose hips help with the healing." Boróka leaves Kata sitting at the kitchen table and goes over to the shelves. She inspects rows of preserves and pickled this and that, before she takes down a jar of honey, cracks it open, sniffs. "I think this is it," she says, walking back to Kata.

At the table, Boróka mixes a small amount of the lint with the fragrant pink-tinged honey. She applies it to the open wound while Kata braces against the stinging. "I'll be as gentle as I can," she reassures her. Once the exposed flesh is packed, Boróka covers it with fat to seal it.

"There," she says kindly, "I think it will be fine in a few weeks."

"I'm sure it will be," says Kata, managing to smile. "I haven't felt so well looked after since my mother used to rub chamomile on my skin to help me sleep. Thank you, Boróka."

"I was happy to do it," Boróka replies, and she means it. She had not realized the pleasure to be had caring for someone. József always seemed to be as tough as old leather. A little worn in places, perhaps, but always the healer, never the healed. It was almost as if he had guarded against relying on her—even pushed her away, sometimes—knowing that she would not always be with him. It was not a relationship into which she could sink and stay there forever, like having a mother might have been.

"Is there something the matter?" Kata reaches out, covers Boróka's hand with her own. The warm pressure of Kata's hand, the stroke of her thumb, feels like a glimpse of something she has never had, like when she first caught the scent of the countess's perfume, at once unfamiliar and intoxicating.

"Being with you makes me wonder what it would have felt like to have a mother."

"Oh, Boróka," says Kata, gripping her hand more tightly. "Did you have no one at all, not even an aunt or a grandmother?"

"Not that I know of. The man I call my father took me in as an orphan. He always said he could tell me nothing about my mother, but now I am beginning to wonder whether he didn't know, or didn't want to tell me."

"Why would he not tell you?"

"Only to protect me, I feel sure of that, but . . ." Her voice trails away. "I want to know about her. It's like I cannot make sense of myself until I can make sense of her. I *need* to know what happened to her."

"But if your father can't, or won't, tell you, then how will you ever know?"

Boróka pauses for a beat, says, "I found a book, and every time I open it there is a little more of a story inside. But when I read it, it doesn't feel like a made-up story. It's as if someone is trying to tell me something."

"Where did you find this book?"

"In a box in the countess's library," says Boróka, shamefaced.

Kata is stern. "You shouldn't be looking at things in the countess's privy chambers."

"I know, but I *had* to. It's like I'm meant to see what's inside."

"What's the story about?"

Boróka is silent for a moment, then: "I think it's about my mother."

"Why do you think that?"

"Because only I can see it." She pauses, casts her eyes down to the kitchen flagstones. "And because I sense that the story doesn't have a happy ending."

"Boróka, you've missed a mother all your life and I understand that her loss might mean that you see her everywhere you look, even when she is not there at all. If you want my advice, then forget this book. Try to be content with what you *do* have, like a father who loves you and, now, me as well."

Kata holds out her arms, and Boróka leans in toward her, allows herself to be comforted by Kata and her familiar, tallow-soap smell. She squeezes her back, perhaps a little too hard, as Kata winces, sucks air through her teeth.

"Oh, Kata, I'm sorry," says Boróka, releasing her. "Your face."

"I keep forgetting about it," she says, "until it hurts again."

Boróka studies her. It is hard to believe that she could have done such damage simply by falling down the steps to the grain store.

"What really happened to you?" Boróka asks quietly.

Kata's eyes slide away from hers. She gets up, begins to tidy away the honey and goose fat. "I told you," she says, "I fell."

"But—"

"Boróka, there are some things you don't understand."

"But I think I *do* understand. They did this to you, didn't they?" There is no need to even use their names; Kata knows who she means.

When Kata does not respond Boróka gets up and walks over to her. "Why does the countess tolerate them?" she demands.

Kata sighs, shakes her head. "It's complicated. She has known them a long time, especially Ilona. And it's Dorka's job to manage the staff. The countess mostly leaves her to it."

"But if she knew what they do, she would dismiss them, surely?"

"Perhaps."

Boróka feels a chill run through her. "You cannot mean that she *does* know?"

"Years ago," begins Kata, hesitant, "I asked her why she allowed such cruel people to stay in her household."

"What did she say?"

Kata walks away from her, places the rose honey carefully on the shelf. When she turns back around, her face is inscrutable. "She told me that she was scared of them herself."

Boróka is incredulous. "A countess," she says, "scared of a few brutish servants? How can that possibly be true?"

But Kata gives her no more than a slight shrug of her shoulders before she opens the kitchen window and scatters the last of the lint out into the breeze.

Chapter 19

KÁRÖRÖM

The countess loves puppets.

She loves their bright painted faces and tiny clothes, she loves their humor and antics, but most of all she loves the stories they tell. She may be the highest of mortals, but she still, like anyone else, just wants to get lost in another world.

The restorative properties of the thermal mud baths at Piešt'any have not been enough to improve her mood. Everyone has noticed that the countess is preoccupied. Most are too terrified to do anything other than keep out of her way, but Ficzkó has arranged a puppet show tonight to cheer her up. Not the crude bobbing fists of the day they met but the most elegant and sophisticated performance that money can buy, with porcelain faces and velvet clothes, limbs suspended on strings that dance a lively jig. With music, wine, and good food, he hopes it will be a much-needed diversion.

The countess, however, is in a bad mood. She did not sleep well, lying awake for much of the night thinking about Thurzó and his investigations now that he has stepped into his new role as count palatine. In the darkness, while sleep eluded her, she thought of the arrangements she would make, should the worst happen. She has already been to her castle at Sárvár and brought her jewelry and valuables safely back to Čachtice before the winter roads become impassable. All she needs to do now is write a will that leaves all her property and assets to her two daughters and son. Perhaps, with the line of inheritance clear, she will become a less appealing target. As she lay there, staring up at the canopy of rich, tasseled brocade over her four-poster bed, she realized a simple truth: If anything should happen to her the only possession among all this wealth that she would really like to keep is her wedding dress. She made a mental note to put that in her will in case, in the future, that is the only voice she has.

She finally fell back to sleep just before dawn. She batted Ilona away when she tried to wake her at the usual hour and slept on, which left her feeling groggy. It was already midmorning before she was sitting in the little closet off her bedchamber, sipping her hot cinnamon water. She heard the maidservants come in to tidy her room and make the bed. The girls chattered loudly, clanking the chamber pot and thumping the pillows, completely unaware that the countess was sitting, unseen, in the adjoining room.

"Shall we change the bedsheets," said one, "or wait till after her courses?"

"When was the last one?" the other replied.

A pause, then: "I can't think," the girl said.

The countess sits at her dressing table in her corset and petticoats, getting ready for an evening of entertainment for which she has no appetite. The mirror in front of her is exquisite— fine Venetian glass with an ornate frame of gilt and lacquered wood—but the face it reflects is not. The night's poor sleep has done her no favors. Her complexion is sallow and her eyes are underscored with purplish smudges. She takes a pot of Venetian ceruse and smears some under her eyes. The effect is disastrous. The dragging motion bunches the slack skin together, caking white makeup over the wrinkles. Every crease in her skin is now writ large. But ceruse, once applied, is difficult to remove, so she has no choice but to persevere, covering her whole face in white. When she has finished she is deathly pale, the ghost of the young woman she once was. She wants to cry, but she cannot risk the track marks of tears down these coated cheeks.

She licks traces of ceruse from her lips, tastes the vinegar and lead. Even biting them doesn't bring much color, so she reaches for a brush, swirls it around a tiny glass dish filled with cinnabar. The pigment turns her lips vermillion red. The result is startling: a face as painted as a puppet's but with none of its porcelain smoothness.

It doesn't help that she can see Boróka's reflection in the mirror as well. She is standing behind her, a pale green lustring gown draped over her arm, gently smoothing the creases in the silk with her hand. She catches her mistress's eye in the mirror, says, "You will look beautiful in this, my lady."

But the countess knows she will not, for all that it is one of her favorite gowns. For a moment she imagines it on Boróka. The countess has already given Boróka one of her old gowns to wear tonight, which—save for the length of the hem, which was a good few inches too long—looks quite well on her. They have the same long nose and high forehead. Boróka's hair is much like the countess's, only with a slight wave and a few shades lighter. Earlier that evening the countess had unexpectedly caught sight of Boróka in her own gown and, for one absurd moment, thought that she saw herself. Not as she is now, of course, but as she was when she too was on the brink of womanhood. A preposterous notion—the girl is a servant—but nonetheless, the countess is drawn to her. She is one of a handful of girls she chose to accompany her to the *kastély*. These days she is more lady's maid than serving girl, much to Dorka's ill-concealed dismay.

"The silk is so soft." Boróka is standing right behind her now, with the gown held up under her chin. She holds the material of the skirt, lets it slip through her fingers. The dress looks like it was made for her. Of course it does; it is a dress for a newlywed maiden, part of the countess's wedding trousseau. The countess looks away—the girl's careless beauty is making her eyes hurt—and sees herself again in the mirror, eyes staring wildly out from that frightful face. It is as if Boróka is taunting her deliberately, the way a smart new apron makes an old gown look all the shabbier. She is overwhelmed by the urge to rip that gorgeous lustring right out of her hands.

"Find me something else to wear," she says, her voice strung taut as a fiddle string.

"But my lady, this gown is perfect."

The countess twists around in her seat to face Boróka. "I told you to find me something else." She is snappy and irritable. Boróka looks shocked, hurriedly bunches up the gown, and takes it out of sight. The countess doesn't care that she has hurt her feelings. Boróka has everything—youth, beauty, even some learning—let her suffer in this small way. Really, sometimes the countess cannot decide if she adores the girl or despises her.

A few minutes later another maidservant comes in carrying a dove-gray damask and a lemon-yellow velvet. The countess waves her hand in the general direction of the gowns, which the girl takes to mean the yellow velvet. In fact, the countess does not much care which gown she wears; either will do. She stands wearily, allows the girl to fit the bodice over the sleeves of her chemise. After a bit of pulling and tugging, the countess is yanked suddenly and forcefully backward. Who is this cack-handed girl? she thinks. She has not seen her before, doesn't even know her name. There must be no one else to dress her because Dorka has half starved the rest. The countess inhales deeply. Patience, she tells herself, patience.

"It won't do up, my lady," says the girl in a small voice.

"Of course it does up," hisses the countess. She puts a hand on either side of her waist, presses inward and braces herself. "Try it now."

Another yank. Nothing. The gap will not close.

"Pull harder," demands the countess.

So the girl does, she pulls on the bodice as if her life depends on it. The seconds seem to stretch, along with the material, until there is a tear and a sound like an anguished squeak.

The countess swings around. "You have ripped it, you stupid thing." The girl looks stricken, braces for a slap, but the countess pulls off the bodice and flings it to the ground. "Where's Dorka?" she demands. "I cannot suffer such incompetence a moment longer."

"At the castle, gracious lady," says the girl, almost in tears.

Of course Dorka is banished, barred from the puppet show. Ostensibly this is punishment for her misdeeds but, really, the countess finds she wants Dorka around her less and less, has little desire for her irritating manner, both obsequious and overbearing. Nevertheless, the countess tuts, annoyed that the one person who could make her feel thin is nowhere near.

"Find me Ilona," says the countess. At least then she will not feel so old and ugly.

Finally, and only two hours late, she is ready. The dove-gray damask was the right choice. The gentle color does not make her face look too garish, and the material is muted enough to take plenty of what the countess still has in abundance: jewels. She slips a ring on to every finger and circles her throat with a choker of emeralds. Matching earrings hang heavy at her earlobes, and her hair is covered by a headdress of seed pearls. She blazes yet, this woman.

Now that she feels better about herself, she is more kindly disposed toward Boróka, who has slipped back into the room to retrieve the offending lemon-yellow bodice for mending. And letting out.

"Will you accompany me to the great hall to watch the show?" the countess asks by way of mild apology.

"Of course, my lady." The girl is pathetically pleased, delighted that her earlier transgressions, whatever they were, appear to have been forgiven.

Everyone at the *kastély* is permitted to watch the puppet show. The great hall is full of the countess's staff. There are the male castellans and stewards, the cellar master and stable master, and, of course, Court Master Benedek Deseö, who oversees her estate. Alongside them are the female members of the household, the seamstresses and personal attendants, senior servants like Ilona, and the countess's lady steward, Dori Majorosné, come from Myjava.

The countess likes to make an entrance. Her audience has been waiting awhile and they are restless and fidgety, but as soon as she appears there is a hush, followed by a collective obeisance. She glitters in the candlelight. Her white face and painted-on lips make her seem otherworldly, not of their kind, which, of course, she is not. She is a thing apart, an object of beauty and admiration, and as soon as she steps inside the hall, she knows that they all still know it.

All eyes are upon her. Even the gothic angels set high into the thick white walls cannot drag their stony gaze away from her. But there is one person whom she seeks out in the crowd. She needs to know that *he* is looking at her, and with the same adoration he always has. When the countess lost her husband to sickness and had to give up her son to his guardian, all in the same year, Ficzkó was there to fill the void.

She sees him; he stands out because he is staring right at her, as if transfixed. He has the look of someone blindsided by beauty, literally smacked in the face with it. Though she does not doubt that, on occasion, Ficzkó has exaggerated his devotion in order to flatter her, this reaction of his is too visceral to be feigned. She is just thinking that she will use this Venetian ceruse again when there is a movement next to her. She turns her head and sees that Boróka is right behind her, quite resplendent in that hand-me-down gown.

The puppet show is "Fortunatus and His Purse." The countess tries to pay attention to the story but the inexhaustible purse, magically replenished every time someone takes from it, just reminds her of all the people who owe her money. Still, the marionettes are beautifully crafted. They even have little moving jaws that go up and down when they speak. She watches them, tries to appreciate the skill of the puppeteer pulling the strings, but the foolish greed of Old Fortunatus's sons is so brilliantly depicted that most of the room is in fits of laughter. The puppet show was a thoughtful idea, but what Ficzkó has forgotten is that, while the countess loves puppets, she detests raucous laughter. The honking merriment of the people around her feels like it is bouncing inside her skull. And it's so hot in the great hall! Who stoked up the fires to roaring? Her face feels like it's burning, as if the carefully applied ceruse will melt and run off her face, leaving her puce and exposed before the guffawing crowd.

She stands up abruptly. She has to get some air, get away from all this terrible mirth. Court Master Deseö sees her rise and immediately goes to stop the performance, but she circles her hand in a gesture that says, *Carry on.*

The countess is gone for over an hour. When she returns to the great hall her mood is no better, but she wishes to thank the puppet master, as the fault was not his. It is clear that no one was expecting her to return until dinner is served. Most of the staff have dispersed and only a few serving girls are left, clustered around the puppet master, who is show-ing them the marionettes. They are so engrossed in the dainty, moving dolls that they do not notice the countess come back in. The girl who brought her the yellow dress has a marionette on her lap and is pulling its strings. She gives it a funny voice, which makes the other girls, and even the puppet master, laugh. She doesn't seem so inept now, this girl who destroyed one of her best bodices only a few hours ago. And what is it she is making the marionette say? Whom does it impersonate?

The countess glides up with the stealth of a cat. "And see," the girl says, already snorting with laughter, "it even *looks* like her," and with that she points to the deep lines that run from either side of the mari-onette's mouth right down to its jaw.

In that instant, the girl looks up and sees the woman of whom she is making fun. The other girls have their backs to the countess and are still giggling as the girl thrusts the marionette from her, as if it were the puppet, not her, who devised this ill-judged entertainment. All the girls are suddenly quiet. The puppeteer bends down to retrieve his marionette, regretting that he was so keen to show off to these silly creatures. The girl now sits alone. Her companions—who, only a moment ago, thought her wickedly funny—have all deserted her. She sinks to her knees on the floor.

"Your grace, I . . ." the girl begins, but the countess holds a finger up to her lips and makes a shushing sound. She cannot hear even a word more from that girl's filthy mouth.

The stewards are readying the tables for dinner. Silver plates and goblets are lined up along the length of the high table, shining in the light of the huge candelabra that flowers at its center. They will be having swan stuffed with peacock, and for that a carving knife is already laid out, its blade sharpened to perfection at the Trenčín blade mill. The countess picks it up. Anyone who knows her, even a little, would agree that she is a master of *káröröm*: Her punishments always fit the crime in a witty and clever way. They are both cruel and ingenious. There was the girl who stole a gold piece and had it heated to scorching and pressed into her palm. There was the greedy girl who accompanied the countess on a carriage trip who was told to hold the warm potato cakes. She couldn't resist eating one, so the others were heated to burning and forced into her mouth. And, of course, there was poor Miss Modl, who was told to dress up as an unmarried virgin and attend to tables during a festival, as there were not enough actual maidens to do it. When Miss Modl protested that she was a married woman, a mother no less, and begged not to be made to dress up as a maid, the countess became enraged and paraded Miss Modl around the castle carrying a log as if it were a baby suckling at her exposed breast.

So, what to do now? This girl has insulted her. She should have slapped her when she pulled on her bodice as if she were yanking weeds from the kitchen garden, but she didn't. She showed her patience and forgiveness, and in return, this wretch has humiliated her. Still, she supposes that a girl who has lived barely more than a dozen years simply takes her perfect skin for granted. She needs to know what it feels like to look in the mirror and be horrified by what she sees, and who better than the countess to educate her?

The countess walks toward the girl. She cowers, crouched on the floor with her hands already poised to protect her face. The countess tells her to stand up, and she does, tears spilling from her eyes, tiny glass beads in the candlelight rolling down cheeks that, for now, are as flawlessly smooth as the plucked swan feathers that will decorate their evening meal. She takes the girl's chin in her hand. How she sobs, this child. She is making quite a commotion, but no one is looking at them. Instead, they have become engrossed in polishing the pewter, or have slipped away into the kitchen to fetch another pitcher of water, though there are already four on the table. And what objection could they raise? The countess owns this girl's flesh as much as she owns that of the roasted fowl.

The countess wrinkles her nose. Soon a revolting mix of snot and spit and tears will drip into her palm. She touches the knife to the corner of the girl's mouth. She knows what she will do: She will score the girl's skin from mouth to chin, on either side. Then she will have lines like a marionette herself, and every time she catches sight of her scarred reflection, she will be reminded that a puppet should dare open its mouth only when its master pulls the strings.

The countess presses the knife against the girl's skin. It is as if all the evening's humiliations, the petty annoyances and disappointments, are concentrated at its very tip. She feels a kind of blind rage, not just because of the pathetic creature clasped in her hand, but because of literally everyone and everything. The knife is so sharp that even slight pressure pierces the flesh, causes a red bead to well beneath the blade.

The sight of blood, freely flowing, is so peculiarly shocking that the countess hesitates, pulls back the knife. In that moment of pause, she suddenly feels something else far more acutely than rage. Fatigue. Overwhelming, bone-aching tiredness. All she really wants is to be completely alone. To be out of these ridiculous clothes and in her bed. She pushes the girl away from her and lets her crumple, gasping with relief, to the floor.

Chapter 20

Dutiful Love

If she didn't know better, Boróka might think that one of the puppets had been left behind: a deflated, dejected thing sitting slumped in a chair, alone in the now empty great hall. She has to walk past him; there is no other way back from the kitchen to the countess's privy chambers. He is staring fixedly at the fire, as if its animated flickering were even more entrancing than the puppet show he arranged at such cost, and to such little avail. At the whisper of her skirts over the flagstones, he looks up.

She feels she ought to say something to him. "I enjoyed 'Fortunatus and His Purse,'" she says as she draws level. "Thank you for organizing it."

He glowers at her, thinks she cannot mean it. "It was a disaster," he says, casting his gaze back to the hearth.

She steps closer to him, unsure. Since she joined the countess's household, Boróka has found Ficzkó to be like the fire itself. Often, she has felt the desire to draw near, but has always ended up stepping back, singed.

"Did you not hear the laughter?" she asks him. "Everyone found it most entertaining."

He looks up at her again, searches her face for sarcasm, finds none. "Not everyone," he replies flatly. "*She* did not enjoy it, and that is all that matters."

156

"Do not let that concern you. She was in a bleak mood from the beginning. Nothing you could have done would have pleased her."

"It is my job to please her, in all ways and in all things."

"No one can do that for anyone."

He looks away from her. She disconcerts him in that dress. When she walked into the great hall wearing the countess's gown, with seed pearls in her hair, he was unable to take his eyes off her. No matter that he sensed the countess watching him, black eyes owlish in that flat white face. Foolish of him, really. All his efforts that evening were as nothing in the face of a few moments too long spent staring at a serving girl made incandescent by the candlelight.

"Only someone who has never loved deeply could say such a thing," he tells her. He sees her smart, but he doesn't care. It rankles that she doesn't know how it feels to want to be everything to another person; it shows she cannot feel about him the way he might like her to.

She takes another step toward him, close enough now to reach out and touch him. He wonders that she is not scared of him, like the other girls are. Well, some are scared, others are fascinated. He sees them watching him while he works in the courtyard, hears their whispers and giggles when he strips down to his shirtsleeves. There is only one explanation for the difference: It depends whom they see. If Ficzkó draws their gaze, then they fawn and simper, but Stefan is not quite so appealing. He is sharp-tongued and ham-fisted. He lurches around the place with sweat on his brow and dirt under his fingernails. No wonder people are repulsed by him. He stares hard at her, asks her with his eyes, *Whom do you see?*

"True love is not so one-sided," she says.

"It is when you love a countess."

"Then that is dutiful love."

"I have never known any other kind," he tells her.

"Nor I," she says.

The way she is looking at him makes Ficzkó wonder whether the same void exists in them both. An emptiness, yet to be filled. Ficzkó feels the impulse to stand up, to align himself completely with this girl whose skin is marmoreal in the firelight, whose hair holds the seed pearls like a sky full of stars. Just to be close to her, that is all he wants. But he cannot get up. Stefan has a strange weight to him. He stays put, sprawled in his chair, twisting his wine goblet around in his fingers. Obstinate.

She collects herself, the moment is gone. "I bid you good night," she says.

Ficzkó presses on the pewter stem of the goblet so hard the knuckle of his thumb blanches. He feels such loathing for Stefan that he can barely stop himself from flinging the goblet against the wall, just to hear the clang of metal on stone, to see the wine spatter like blood over the floor. She turns away from him and it is only then that he allows himself to look at her freely, to sweep his gaze all over her: from the back of the neck he has never touched but imagines to be downy-soft, to the feet he cannot see but remembers bare and speckled with straw. If Ficzkó had a voice then he would call her back, ask her to do no more than sit with him awhile, but Stefan is already talking. He slings words at her because she is already leaving him, so the only thing left to do is to make sure that he pushes her away completely.

"I'm sorry about your friend," he says, with a strange edge to his voice.

Her steps slow.

"I happened to be there when Mistress Kata fell down the steps." He sucks air through his teeth. "Very nasty."

She doesn't look back, just carries on walking.

Chapter 21

WINTER'S WITCH

Boróka is staring at the countess. She is taking shape in layers, each one built up gradually from painstaking brushstrokes, overlaid with translucent glaze. Boróka's understanding of her mistress is much like the portrait itself. Everything she observes, their every interaction, layered one over the other, like oil paint. And once a stain is there, especially if it is dark, it is impossible to remove.

Boróka thinks of Kata, of the maidservant she saw sitting in the kitchen after the puppet show with a bloodied linen pressed to her face, being offered hot water and honey by a concerned steward. The woman in the portrait stares mildly back at her, clutching the key that proclaims her *the perfect mistress of her household*. Her expression is still empty, as if she were indifferent to the opinion of those around her. She does what she does because she can.

The portrait has been moved with them to the *kastély* in the hope that it can be finished over the winter. But it cannot be rushed. Every layer of paint, of glaze, has to be left to dry over many days. If it is not, the image of this woman, built up so carefully, over so long, will simply crack.

Boróka turns her face away from her. There is no point staring at it because a painting, no matter how nuanced, will not tell her who this woman really is.

The painting's setting has yet to be reassembled, but the clock is there, the table, and the same Turkey rug. Even the chopines are there, but Boróka no longer wants to step into the countess's shoes. At first she thinks that the rosewood box is missing, but then she sees it on a shelf above the table. She takes it down, unlocks it.

The same book is inside, but when she opens it the list of names is gone. Instead, the story she has been reading continues.

It was everything Ailing had feared might happen. I could no more keep my swelling belly from her than I could hide it from the grinder's wife, who stood in the middle of the little stone bridge like a full-busted ship's figurehead, observing the fruits of her husband's inconstancy growing ever larger with a kind of grim satisfaction.

Soon it became too cold to wash clothes in the river. The winter of 1595 was fierce: Buildings collapsed under the weight of snow, livestock had nothing to drink because the water froze in the troughs and wells. The ground was hard and unyielding as stone, and ice lay over the compacted fields like a mirror, reflecting the farmers' misery back at them. Everyone longed for spring, but by March it still hadn't come. When the wheat could not be planted, they began to fear for the autumn harvest. And where there is fear, there is blame.

Only rumors flourished that winter. They took hold with a grip as unrelenting as the cold itself. It was Winter's Witch, they said, refusing to leave. The preparations for the spring festival began with a kind of desperate intensity. This year it was even more vital to banish Marzanna, the goddess of winter, plague, and death. On the fourth Sunday in Lent, they clothed the Marzanna doll in an old bridesmaid's dress and draped strings of beads around her thick straw neck. The women and girls found pieces of ribbon with which to adorn her so she could go prettily to her death, then they paraded her through the bitter streets, singing defiant songs to the lingering cold.

The puddles and water barrels, the troughs and wells, were still partly frozen, but they dunked her in each one nonetheless, thrusting her face—gaudy with red cheeks and a painted smile—through the glassy surface and into the icy water below. Once the Marzanna doll was well and truly drenched, they took her to the river to drown. Before they tossed her in, they tore her clothes, made her shabby and wretched, then set her ablaze and flung her high into the air to land in a river swollen with snowmelt. It's bad luck to look back at a Marzanna doll, but had anyone done so, they would have seen her floating on the surface of the water for a moment, a ragged, smoldering nest of straw, before the river spun her away and claimed her charred dress and cracked clay beads as spoils.

A brutal end to winter. Except that, this time, the winter refused to leave.

The people of the town awoke the next morning and searched the sky for the pale light of spring. They stood outside to see if the harsh air blew milder and they pressed their heels into the hard earth to see if it now yielded. When spring could not be seen, or felt, or even tasted in the air, they retreated to sit inside by their fires and brood darkly on their misfortunes.

That same day, an itinerant merchant arrived in the town. He had traveled up from the Danubian lowlands where, he told them, the forest glades were lush and green. The marshes flowed freely and were already scattered with wild garlic. Why, the townsfolk asked themselves, had spring come everywhere else but here? There could be only one explanation, and that was that Winter's Witch was still among them.

Whispers of witchcraft begin with a simple dispute, usually one involving someone with a big mouth and a vengeful heart. In my case, it was the grinder's wife.

It was easy for her to suggest that Winter's Witch must surely be marked by frost and snow, that she would be easy to identify because there would be something strange about her. Like a shock of white hair, for instance, inexplicably running through the dark. And if that person had always been thought aloof, well, now they knew why. If she lived in a household of women, that was odd enough on its own, but if one of those women dabbled in herbs and potions,

then it was downright suspicious. And, just in case they needed
proof positive, she had only to mention that nothing marks out a
witch more than sexual impropriety. They are whores, copulating
with the devil himself. If they wanted to find their Winter's Witch,
then they need look no further than the woman with the bastard
newborn.

My daughter had been born in February when the snows were
still too deep to call anyone to help. But Ailing had seen babies born
before, and we had no need of a midwife to meddle and gossip. I
called my baby Angéla because she was my angel. I had seven weeks
to hold her, to feed her, to marvel at the perfect softness of her skin,
before they came for me.

The grinder's wife led the women of the village up the street,
following the same path as the Marzanna doll days before. This time
they would not leave the fate of the village to a straw effigy. They
would banish the actual witch herself. The clay beads were the same,
hung like a noose around my neck and used to yank me outside. I
stood barefoot in the market square while they pinned ribbons to my
clothes, tawdry colors that fluttered gaily in the brisk March wind.
When they twisted me around, my feet slid in the mud and slush,
which surely meant that the ice was melting. Spring was coming, but
they chose to be blind to its approach.

Then I heard someone screaming, "Give me the baby," over and
over, and I realized that it was Ailing. I turned my head and saw
her, one arm outstretched toward me, the other caught and held
by the man who sweeps the floor of the nave every Sunday after
church. It was man's work now, this witch business. It was only
then that it even occurred to me that I had Angéla pressed to my
chest, shielding her with my arms, while in return her presence
gave me warmth. I tried to hand her to Ailing, but they dragged her
away, still screaming and clawing at the nave sweeper's face. I had
never seen her wild like that. They treated her harshly, but that
was because she was almost as guilty as me. We had tainted each
other: she, me, with her independence and knowledge of healing;

and me, her, with ... well, nothing so noble or useful, just reckless, foolhardy lust. I pressed my face into the folds of the shawl around my daughter and inhaled deeply. It was faint, but I could smell the lavender, dried and preserved from the summer before. Then I felt a hand at my back, shoving me forward. So began my final walk down to the river.

Centuries of tradition drowning the Marzanna doll every spring could not compete with what was happening now. The straggle of excited girls who accompanied the doll was nothing compared to the crowds that followed me. Everyone came out to finally see off Winter's Witch. The baker, who had handed me my daily loaf for as long as I could remember. The chandler, who had asked Ailing for a remedy for his rheumy eyes not a week before. Even the seamstress, who often asked me to wash the clothes she mended and tipped me an extra groat if I brought them back the next day. Yet none of this mattered. The fabric of my life had been as easy to tear apart as the shreds of ribbon stuck on my clothes.

The grinder's wife set off toward the river. Walking beside her was the local notary: the man in charge of convenient justice, swiftly implemented. As I stumbled behind him I kept my eyes on the stockings visible beneath his woolen culottes. I recognized the stain on one, had slapped it against the river's soapy rocks many times.

My baby didn't even wake up until the first time they dunked me. What it is to feel so safe against your mother's chest that such palpable hatred can pass unnoticed. The water was like ice in my eyes and fire in my throat. I thought I would drown right there, with my head submerged in a water trough next to a startled cow. When they pulled me up my lungs clutched at the precious air while my stomach contracted, and I fell to my knees, choking on water and vomit and my own slick terror. It was then that Angéla began to wail. I shushed her, rocked her, tried to dab the spatters of water from her head. It was a ludicrous notion, but I somehow thought that they wouldn't hurt her if she didn't cry.

"Maybe we should take the child," a man said, his voice uncertain, but I shielded Angéla all the more. I would never abandon my baby as my mother had abandoned me.

"No, leave it be," replied a woman. "The fruit of her womb is as guilty as she." I think it was the weaver's wife who spoke; I recognized the shrill sanctimony in her voice from the day she berated me for soaking her white chemise in the same bucket as an overskirt dyed with madder.

The trough in the market square was followed by a barrel outside the tavern, with its lingering yeasty smell. Soon we were on the edge of town, where no one lives except the reeking tanner. There is plenty of water there, to soak the rotting hides and wash away the lye. I was almost grateful that my eyes started stinging; it made me blind to their leering, twisted faces. I was glad my ears were ringing; I was deaf to their taunts and mocking catcalls. My world had narrowed to placing my feet, frozen numb, one in front of the other, in time with the deafening beating of my heart. And I clung to Angéla, felt the distress vibrating through her with every cry. Heartbreaking as it was, it reminded me that we were still alive.

Beyond the town, the final walk down to the river is through meadows thick with comfrey and primrose in the summer. I had followed the dirt path so many times that it seemed to lead me down itself. By the time we were through the last copse of trees, my eyes had cleared and I saw the river. She was restless, churning fretfully against the banks. Her waters seemed troubled, a bleak, murky gray.

The notary reached the bank first and stood close to the edge. He began a speech, brimming with rectitude and moral condemnation, and the river spat at him until he frowned at his wet boots and stepped away. I suppose the good people of my town were too busy listening to him to notice that, in the days since the drowning of the Marzanna doll, purple irises had pushed up along the riverbank. I suppose his strident tones drowned out the sweet sound of the blackbird and the song thrush.

While he was talking I looked upstream, toward the blade mill, and it occurred to me how short the distance from there to here. I almost thought the grinder might be standing on the stone bridge; that somehow, in the midst of all this, a basket might come bobbing down the river with something in it that could save me. But there was no one, and the mill was silent, almost as if abashed.

The notary finished his speech with a flourish. The grinder's wife nodded her approval and the townspeople clustered forward as if they were all part of the same spreading stain. Then one of the men yanked on my sleeve, pulled my chemise down off my shoulder. Until then, I suppose I had thought that they wouldn't actually do it. I expected to be dunked and humiliated, to be made humble and contrite for all the many ways I had transgressed; but torn, burned, and drowned like a straw doll, without even a chance to speak to my innocence? Surely, even the most spiteful of women scorned would not want that?

"'Tis a shame for the infant," someone said.

The notary glanced down at Angéla, a muscle in his jaw working. She was a dilemma, indeed. On the one hand, it was his job to rid the town of its witch, and everybody knows that witches are like a tumorous disease and must be exorcised completely, with no part left behind. But then, who would want the blood of a child, in only its second month of life, on his hands? So he came to a compromise, something that got the job done but with an element of mercy and compassion that he could remind himself of in the years to come.

"We will not burn them first," he said.

In the end, I gave my daughter to someone I knew would keep her safe. The river. She took her from my arms as I sank. She brought her back to the surface as the breath left my body so that she could be reborn into a world without me in it. Then she carried her away from the blade mill, the murderous mob, and all the other things that could do her harm.

It might have been that the river's good intentions were in vain—she could not keep the child forever, after all—but a little way downstream a man was waiting. He was a man of learning, a doctor. He did not believe that if he reached into the river to save her, his hand would wither, like the rest of the town did. Instead, he waded out into the rushing water and braced himself against the river's grief and fury until she brought the baby right into his outstretched arms. *I will keep her safe,* he promised the river as he lifted her out. Then he used his own warm breath to revive her, and in that way he gave her life as surely as I had myself, seven weeks before.

I wished I could have told him that she was called Ángéla, but he plucked her from the water a nameless foundling. Over the course of a few tumbling yards my daughter had lost everything, including her name. The doctor had to think of a new one so, like me, he simply called her what she was to him. Not "angel" this time, but "stranger."

The river has always been my friend, and we live together still. I am liminal, neither dead nor alive, residing forever in the element of my own demise. I spend my days tending my hair with a fishbone comb, ruminating on my untimely death. My hair is loose and unbraided because I belong to no man. Yet men still desire me. When I see one pass by, I sing to him. My songs are always sad, about lost loves and missed opportunity, but nonetheless they draw the men to me because there is nothing so enchanting as a singing *rusalka.* Then we begin to dance together, and we keep on dancing even when he begs me to stop. When he can dance no more, I laugh as he dies in my arms.

One day I will go back to the blade mill and sit by the churning waterwheel, waiting for the grinder to stop his work and walk out onto the little stone bridge. While I wait, I will think about what mischief I can make for these lucky humans with their precious lives. If the grinder found me pleasing years ago, drubbing laundry in the river, he will find me irresistible now: naked, with my pale greenish hair falling over my shoulders. Yes, I will dance with the grinder yet, I know it, because revenge is the only way the drowned dead can ever be at peace.

All around Boróka is the noise of people approaching, doors opening and closing, instructions delivered—*do this, do that, put this here*—but it is deadened by the noise in her head. Her mind races, her thoughts tangle like yarn.

The voices are becoming louder. She hears someone say, "By winter's end I should like the jewels, the furs, and the gold to be packed. In the spring, when the roads are passable, we can send them to my cousin in Transylvania."

With a jolt she realizes it is the countess and quickly puts the book back into the box just before she walks in. The countess looks hard at Boróka. "What are you doing in here?" she asks. "You look like you have seen a ghost."

It is as if Boróka is seeing the woman in front of her for the first time. She studies her face intently, as if she will find answers in the precise arch of her nose or the set of her eyes.

"Well?"

Boróka opens her mouth but finds she cannot speak. How does she begin to find the words?

The countess turns to Kata, who is with her. "Why has the cat got her tongue?" she asks, impatient.

"I know not, my lady."

The sound of Kata's voice breaks the spell.

"Forgive me, mistresses," Boróka says, dropping into a curtsy.

The countess frowns, but she is clearly preoccupied with other things. "I want my most precious items locked away before my lord palatine brings the king and Megyeri here at Christmastide, do you hear?"

"Yes, mistress," says Kata.

"The less they see, the less they will covet, that is my thinking," the countess says, with the trace of a sly smile. Then: "Are you still here?"

Boróka startles, collects herself. "I was just leaving," she says, as she picks up the box and goes to put it back on the shelf.

The countess's eyes narrow. "What are you doing with that?"

Boróka stares down at the casket. "Is it yours, my lady?"

"Everything's mine," says the countess flatly.

The box begins to feel heavy in Boróka's hands. She almost wishes she had never opened it. "I was reading, my lady," replies Boróka. The countess always encourages expanding the mind through reading.

"Reading what?" The countess's voice is both suspicious and impatient. Ever since she heard about Thurzó's impending visit she has been tense and irritable. She looks for threat everywhere, sees betrayal around every corner.

"I found a book in the casket, my lady."

"*Found a book?*" the countess repeats. "You cannot just happen upon a book in a locked casket. What exactly were you looking for? Jewels, money?"

Boróka gasps. "Nothing, your grace! Forgive me, please. I opened it when I was helping with the portrait. I only sought to pass the time."

The countess looks more weary than angry. "What is this book?" she says.

Boróka feels Kata's eyes bore into her, but what choice has she than to carry on?

"In truth, I don't know what it is, but I feel as if it was written just for me."

"Is it the gooseherd's almanac?" quips the countess.

"No, mistress. It is the story of a girl," Boróka begins, but the countess is already staring out the window. Her mind wanders back to Thurzó and the fact that he plans to visit her in December. Boróka pauses, presses on. "She was of noble birth and had a baby, unmarried, at the age of just thirteen."

The countess is perfectly still. "A commonplace tale," she says quietly, her eyes still at the window.

"She gave the baby away," continues Boróka. "It was taken in by a woman called Ailing. When the baby grew up she washed clothes in the river until she was seduced herself, by a blade grinder."

The countess looks back at Boróka, raises an eyebrow. "Goodness. What happens then?"

"She has her own baby, a girl, but then she's accused of witchcraft and drowned by the people of the town she lived in."

The countess purses her lips. "I see this is a sad story. What happened to the infant?"

"She was saved from the river by a doctor."

"Well, I am glad to hear it." The countess is suddenly brisk. "Kata," she says, "tell Court Master Deseö to bring the chests of florins up from the caves."

"My lady," interrupts Boróka, "I beg your indulgence to finish the story."

The countess sighs. "Who wrote this book?"

"The drowned woman, mistress."

"Impossible," says the countess.

"She's a *rusalka* now."

"Ah, I see. So it is a fairy tale, then?"

"Perhaps," says Boróka.

The countess laughs. "No, not *perhaps*. If the book is about a *rusalka* it must be folklore!"

Boróka glances down at the box in her hands. "There was no *once upon a time* about this story, my lady. It had real details: places, names, dates." She pauses, swallows hard. "The father of the drowned woman was called Ladislav Bende. He worked in a manor house in Trnava."

The countess seems to contemplate Boróka for an age before she says, "What is it you want from me?"

Boróka shakes her head. "Nothing, gracious lady."

"Then why are you saying these things?" She is rounding on her now, fixing her with the same malevolent gaze that scrutinized Judit in the gynaeceum.

Boróka sinks to her knees, clutches the box in her lap. "I am only saying what I read in the book, mistress, nothing more."

"You did not read that in a book!" the countess retorts, her eyes blazing. "Who has told you to say these things?"

"No one, my lady!" Boróka is crying now, tears running freely down her cheeks.

Kata steps forward, rests a hand on her mistress's arm. "Please, your grace, she is just a child and she knows nothing of what she speaks. She should arouse your pity, not your anger."

The countess shrugs off Kata's hand.

"I spoke to you as an equal," she says to Boróka. "I confided in you, and you repay me with this nonsense!"

Boróka shakes her head. "I have only ever wanted to serve the will of your grace."

"I used to believe that was true," says the countess, circling around her. "I thought that there was something special about you." The countess gives a short, mirthless laugh. "I am well aware that people wonder why a countess considers four lowly servants her closest confidantes! But I can tell you the answer to that, Boróka, and you should learn from it: discretion, *absolute* discretion. They hear nothing, see nothing, and say nothing! It is rare that I find someone I can truly trust, but when I do, I do not care if she is washerwoman, wet nurse, or witch!" The countess pauses, takes a ragged breath. "So many people seek to slander me, spread the most abhorrent lies about me, and there is little I can do about them, but I refuse to be betrayed by those closest to me. Do you hear? I refuse!"

Kata tries again to calm the countess. "Be sure that it is really the girl who angers you and not—"

The countess swings around to face her. "Thurzó? Megyeri?" She almost looks as if she will break down, but she composes herself and gestures for Boróka to get up. "You are right, Kata, I am allowing those wretched men to unsettle me." She gives Boróka a rather grim smile. "I have need of a diversion and I have always enjoyed a fairy tale. Perhaps I should read the *rusalka*'s story for myself? Then we will know where the goose-girl gets her tattletale from. Kata, open the casket."

Kata looks almost startled. For a moment she eyes the box warily, as if to open it would be to unleash something that could never be put back. "Of course, my lady," she mumbles, then walks over to the rosewood box.

Boróka offers it up to her and watches as Kata places her fingers on either side of the lid and slowly lifts it up. Even the countess seems tense beside her, as if all the evils of the world might suddenly spill out.

The countess's eyes widen. "I knew it," she whispers, triumphant, "there is no book!"

And, indeed, there is not. Nonetheless, Kata stands rigid in front of the empty casket, staring into it so intently that, surely, she sees something that they do not. Then she inhales deeply and closes her eyes, as if she has caught hold of something and doesn't ever want to let it go.

A moment later, the whole room is filled with the powdery scent of lavender.

Part III

Winter

Chapter 22

The One to Whom the Herbs and Flowers Talk

The countess's bath is scalding hot. Plumes of steam rise into chilly air that even the roaring fires of the countess's great chamber cannot properly heat. The bitter weather started on the high peaks of the White Carpathians and crept slowly downward. It's now Christmas Eve and the first snowfall already clings to the dense branches of the black pines. Shards of ice have begun to form at the edges of the rivers. They reach into the water like fingers, clutching at its incessant flow, bringing the world to a wintery pause.

"Tsk, not yet, my lady. You will burn yourself."

The countess is poised to step into her bath, one foot on the little stool, her crimson velvet robe already slipping from her shoulders. Dori Majorosné kneels by the bathtub, a basket of herbs in her lap. Snip, snip, go her scissors as fragments of sweet chamomile fall upon the water's surface and eddy away. Dori dips a fingertip into the bathwater, swirls it around. "A few moments more," she reassures her mistress, "and it will be cool enough for us to begin."

The countess sighs and steps off the stool, but she is glad that her forest witch is so exacting. They must get this right. The consequences, should they fail, are too great.

Dori is singing to herself, or perhaps muttering. Her chants always sound as if she is speaking in tongues. The countess neither knows, nor cares, what she is saying. She only hopes that it works. Dori finishes her incantation and picks a sprig of lemon balm from her basket. The countess draws in a long breath, her lungs filling with citrus-scented steam. Next Dori takes a piece of ginger and rubs it against the back of a clamshell until pieces of it peel away and drop into the water. She sits back on her heels, satisfied. "It's ready, mistress," she says.

The countess steps back onto the stool and dips a toe into the water. It's still very hot, but that is necessary for the charm to work. Without heat, the required essences cannot be extracted. She shrugs the robe from her shoulders, lets it fall to the floor. Dori offers her an arm for balance as she steps into the bathtub and settles herself gradually into the fragrant water.

Dori takes a linen cloth, dips it, squeezes it. She bathes her mistress as she might a child, with love and infinite care. She wipes her brow and around her ears and neck. She lifts the countess's arm and drips water onto her skin, watching it run in rivulets over the delicate hairs, the scattering of moles, the tiny scar from when the countess fell from her horse into a hawthorn bush. She knows every inch of her. The spiced air is intoxicating; the ginger is like fire in Dori's lungs and the lemon balm is making her head spin. The steam is so thick it shrouds them, shields them from view, allows them to pretend that no one else exists. She bends down, gently kisses the countess's outstretched arm, tastes her wet, lemony skin.

Dori draws the linen across her mistress's chest, lingers over the nub that breaks the surface like a pink pearl. The countess sighs and leans back, settles farther into her bath. Dori's hand drifts down to where the water is deeper, darker, scattered with cinnamon bark that churns in the rhythmic currents her hand makes. The water seems to glow as it moves, as if with some strange fluence. This is what her potion needs, thinks Dori: the right combination of herbs and spices and the very essence of the countess herself.

An hour later—and after the countess has had a good long soak—the cook is standing in front of an earthenware jar full of liquid. He peers at it, sniffs it, asks the forest witch what it is. "Never you mind," she tells him. "Just make sure that it is used to make the dough for the cake that will be served tonight, when the lord palatine comes to dinner."

Dori dims the room. It is barely four in the afternoon, but she only needs to snuff out a couple of candles in their sconces to plunge the room into darkness, for the winter equinox has passed and the days are at their shortest. The countess sits at her card table looking at a grayish cake. The dough was plaited and formed into a circle before it was baked. At its center is a thin, transparent wafer. The countess picks up the special cake that she and Dori have made and peers through the wafer. It is a window into the future, a scrying glass.

"Chant the spell," Dori instructs.

"Make me invisible," she implores the cake. "Protect me from my enemies."

She stares hard at the wafer's mottled surface. Something about the way it reflects the firelight gives it a strange depth. Dori's potent herbs seem to linger in her lungs and still course around her body. Or is it something else that makes her heart feel like a moth in her chest, something that does not sit well with her fifty years of unquestioned privilege? Fear? She stares hard into her scrying glass. Just the concentration, the minute focus, is enough to distort her vision. She begins to see things. They appear in the shadows the flickering fire makes, they take shape on the wafer's undulating surface. She sees them, she really does. "Tell me, tell me," she urges the scrying glass. "Reveal to me those who would do me harm."

And then the shades of the wafer shift and darken. A thick, curling beard takes shape, luxuriant as a winter bear's fur. She thinks she knows the proud nose that thrusts above it, those nostrils with their pronounced flare, but it is only when the eyes appear that she is certain. They observe her with the same hooded stare they always have, and an expression that suggests his vast power almost bores him.

The countess begins to cry. She cannot help it. The tears roll down her cheeks, and her shoulders shake with the force of her distress. Dori circles her arms around her to quell the trembling, rests her cheek on her beloved mistress's hair.

"Protect me, protect me," the countess begs the scrying glass.

She stays like that for a full hour—muttering her spells and desperately searching for whatever the wafer might reveal—until the palatine and his men arrive.

Chapter 23

UNKNOWN AND
MYSTERIOUS CAUSES

You would not know to look at her that the countess has been crying. She sits at the head of the high table in a silk gown, such a dark shade of purple it seems almost black. Her back is straight and her movements, as she eats and drinks and engages with her guests, are steady and graceful. Tonight, there is no Venetian ceruse, no gaudy jewels; just the countess in plain damask, with strings of opaline pearls at her wrists and throat.

György Thurzó, the count palatine, did not come alone. He brought with him King Matthias himself and Imre Megyeri, her son's tutor. Megyeri the Red, they call him. His beard is the same russet shade as a fox tail, and as bushy as the palatine's own. He eats doggedly, spearing his food as if it were still alive on his plate. There is grouse and veal for dinner, plates of loach and fogas baked with parsley and dill. The palatine is known for his love of rich food, but tonight he is restrained. It is the last day of advent and overindulgence is frowned upon, but, even so, he seems distracted, merely picks at his plate as if he has a great matter on his mind.

"How does your daughter now she is married?" asks the countess to put him at his ease. The countess attended his daughter's wedding to Baron Jakusith de Orbova three years before, back in the time she and Thurzó still called each other "cousin." In truth, the pleasantries are tiresome—the endless inquiring after relatives, Megyeri's plat-itudes about her son's progress, the cloying compliments—but it is something through which they all have to wade, sickly as treacle, be-fore they can talk about that for which they really came.

Thurzó winces as if he's in physical pain. Perhaps he is; he suffers from the disease of kings, and the wine has likely inflamed him in some way. Or perhaps the distaste he feels is unrelated to the meal.

"Very well, I thank you," he replies, but his voice is curt. In the moment of silence that follows, Thurzó leans back in his chair, inhales deeply, sets his jaw. "Madam," he says.

The countess's stomach contracts. He has not yet said anything of consequence but just the tone of his voice causes the fish to stick in her throat. She puts down her fork, awaits the inevitable.

"You are aware, I believe, of the investigations that have been car-ried out."

Investigations. The serfs rounded up, like sheep, who all repeat the same thing, as if they were children rote-learning in a classroom. "I am indeed, your grace," she says, keeping her voice level. She gestures to the stewards to clear the table. Everyone has finished eating and she wishes the servants gone now that the conversation has taken this turn.

The palatine nods. Megyeri flashes him a look, while the king sits silent, always an observer of the messy work undertaken on his behalf. Even in the carriage on the way there, these men could not agree on their approach to this delicate task. The issue is not as straightforward as an errant countess with a predilection for brutality; it is as complex as the situation of the Kingdom of Hungary itself. Behind the outrage these men share in relation to the unspeakable crimes against female blood are constantly shifting allegiances, religious differences, and the endless jostle for money and power. But, for now, they have set aside their differ-ences so they can face down the termagant as one. The palatine waits for the last dish to be carried out, waves away a refill for his goblet of wine.

"This December my castellan has recorded the testimonies of forty villagers, under the strictest of oaths. His findings concur with those of my notary, András of Keresztúr, earlier this year. The evidence against you continues to mount, Lady Nádasdy." He takes care to use her dead husband's name, though she refused to take it when they married. In this small way, he diminishes her.

"You will understand, then, that matters cannot . . ." Thurzó pauses, picking his words as carefully as he might the candied fruits that decorate the high table. "Go on," he finishes, rather weakly.

"Go on?" The countess raises an eyebrow. She will not lend him her eloquence, find for him the words he seeks.

"It suits you ill to pretend, madam," cuts in Megyeri, impatient. "You know full well of what we speak. *Murder*"—Megyeri relishes the word as if it were as flavorsome as the veal—"*torture*, and of maidens, the most innocent of young souls."

The countess gives him an impassive look. "It is my prerogative to govern my staff how I see fit. You have no right to interfere."

"This matter has gone beyond that, as well you know."

The king leans forward. He is wearing a dark green brocaded dolman, its sleeves slashed with midnight-blue silk. As he moves in the light of the candelabra he shimmers like a peacock. "We cannot tolerate the death of noble girls," he says.

"We speak of Judit Vasváry, of course," says Thurzó.

The countess's breath quickens. Under the table her hands seize her skirts, scrunching fistfuls of plum silk, squeezing them tight until she feels able to speak. "Judit died of a plague. I have said as much on many occasions. There was a serious outbreak in the castle at the end of the summer."

The men exchange glances. "One witness described three bodies in one coffin," says Megyeri. "Your households are most *unfortunate* when it comes to pestilence."

"That is not true! I do everything I can to save them but I cannot stop a pox from spreading, as much as I would like to. The outbreak has not even completely subsided. Another girl died of the same thing only a week ago!"

Thurzó cannot stop his lip from curling into a sneer. "*Another* girl has died of last summer's plague, has she? Mistress, does that sound likely, even to your ears?"

The countess pauses. When Dorka had told her of the maidservant's death, she had not thought to question it, but now she can think only of those girls Kata told her she found in the furnace house, their wasted limbs and parched mouths. The trickle of distrust she has begun to feel about Dorka flows through her more strongly.

"Well, that is the truth, my lord," she replies, a little uncertain.

Thurzó leans back in his chair, regards her intently. "Pastor Ponikenus and Reverend Zacharias suggest a different *truth*."

"Lutherans both!" she exclaims, slamming her palms down on the table, making her bracelets clatter. "They fulminate against me at every opportunity."

"You cannot suggest that these men of God decry your sins just because you are a Calvinist?"

"I do," insists the countess.

"But nine maidens buried in one night, madam? And all dead of the same *unknown and mysterious causes?* What say you to that?"

"Who in their right mind would murder girls and then take the bodies to a priest to bury?"

Thurzó's mouth gapes for a moment. He sits up, flusters a little. "They were buried with undue haste; you cannot gainsay that."

"I do not," she says, her voice forceful, impatient with these fools. "*All* bodies should be buried quickly, especially during an epidemic, to guard against contagion and panic." The countess is breathing heavily. She tries to control herself, marshal her thoughts. The way to deal with these men is with logic and facts. She needs to present them with hard evidence that even they cannot deny.

"Your graces," she says, sounding a little more measured, "I would remind you of the voluntary deposition lodged by the widow Hernath."

Thurzó wrinkles his brow. "Deposition?" he says vaguely.

"Yes!" insists the countess, that forceful edge creeping back. "I accompanied the gentlewoman Hernath to the Vasvár-Szombathely county court. There she stated under oath that her daughter, who was in my service, died of natural causes. She was perfectly clear in her deposition that the marks on her daughter's body were due to disease, not violence, and that I was wholly innocent of her death."

Silence around the table. Both the king and Megyeri look to Thurzó to respond. He shifts in his seat, rotates the stem of his goblet in his fingers. "I know of no such deposition. When was it filed?"

"The August just passed. I remember it clearly," says the countess.

"I will follow this up with the Vasvár-Szombathely county court," he tells her. "I can do no more."

"Oh, but you can," she exclaims. "You can stop this outrageous persecution of me!"

"Whatever it is you desire, you would do well to adopt a less hysterical tone, madam!"

The countess tilts up her chin, regards Thurzó with flashing eyes. "'Tis your voice raised," she replies, with all the hauteur she can muster.

Megyeri holds up his hands to return calm to the table. "It serves no one to bicker like children. Instead, we must try to find a resolution to all of this. That is why we are here."

"Indeed," replies the countess, doing her very best to appear calm. "We must all take a moment to let our tempers settle. Perhaps we should have the next course?" The countess rises, and a moment later a steward appears.

"Bring in the cake," she says.

The king regards his plate with knitted brow. "What manner of cake is this?"

"It is something we have prepared especially for you, your grace," the countess replies.

He picks it up, breaks it open along the plaited join. The exposed crumb is grayish but nicely risen. He gives it a cautious sniff. "Cinnamon?"

"Yes, and ginger, along with a blend of other . . . ingredients."

"I like it," says Megyeri, his mouth full.

The king prods the springy crumb with his finger, pinches out a morsel, tastes it. "Well, I do not care for it," he says, putting the cake back down on his plate.

"It is an excellent digestive," encourages the countess.

Thurzó breaks his own piece in half. "I will have some," he says. "I have need of a purge." He yanks at the crust with his teeth, chews gamely for a while, and swallows. "It's rather good," he says, nodding.

The king picks up his own serving again. He observes Thurzó and Megyeri eating, then tentatively puts the cake in his mouth. He eats like a stray dog, watchful, skittish.

"Will you not have some?" Megyeri asks the countess.

She shakes her head. "I have not the appetite these days," she says.

Thurzó looks up at her. "Things change as we grow old. We cannot enjoy the things we once did, is that not true? I wonder, madam, whether the answer to all this is for you to just . . . retire. Gracefully."

"Retire, My Lord Palatine? Whatever do you mean?"

"A convent, Lady Nádasdy, that is my meaning. Somewhere you may live out your days simply, with time to reflect on your sins and repent."

"You would confine me to a nunnery?" The countess is incredulous, cannot stop from raising her voice again. She, the highest lady in all the land, stripped of her wealth, her fine clothes, her freedom, and consigned to a life of paucity and prayer?

"In no wise will I agree to that!" she says.

"Madam." Thurzó's voice is grave. He puts down his food and steeples his hands together, peers at her over his interlaced fingers. "You would do well to consider the alternative."

Thurzó's gaze is penetrating. It is making her prickle. She feels it again, that creep of heat up her neck and over her face. She wishes he would not stare at her so intently; her cheeks must look like ripening tomatoes. Damn this room full of flames and warmth. Damn her heavy gown and woolen petticoats. And damn these men.

"I do not think the Vasváry family will consider a convent sufficient punishment," interjects the king, "nor will any other right-thinking noble." The richness of his brocade in the candlelight, the gossamer weave of his silk, lends him a kind of glittering malevolence. "Madam, you should know that, in my view, the only just penalty for your crimes can be death."

A percussion of fear begins somewhere deep inside the countess. It seeps into her blood and pulses through every limb. She reaches for some water, wills her hand not to tremble, begs her body not to betray her. She sips slowly, concentrating on the smooth feel of the silver goblet, the coolness of the water.

"I can see," she says, setting down the cup, "that a nunnery is not the outcome that would suit *you*, your grace. I wonder, when will the treasury be repaying its debt to me? Or would severing my head from my body be a less costly solution for the royal treasury?"

"Speaking of money," replies the king, "I hear you are secretly financing Gábor Báthory's rebellion against the Habsburgs. He has formed a new alliance with the Turks, has he not?"

The countess smiles with understanding, gives a slow nod. "You fear what might happen to the Habsburgs' hold over Hungary if challenged by the combined forces of Gábor Báthory in Transylvania and the Ottoman Empire."

"There was no one more loyal to the Habsburg cause than your husband, madam," says the king.

"Oh indeed, he was admirably loyal," she replies. "That is, until you withheld the ransoms due to him for Turkish prisoners and the imperial treasury refused to pay back all the money he had lent it."

Thurzó looks affronted. "Count Nádasdy is revered as a war hero in Vienna. He would turn in his grave to hear you say such things," he says.

The countess turns her gaze toward Thurzó, looks at him long and hard before she speaks. "How dare you even speak my husband's name," she hisses. "You rode into battle alongside him, flank to flank. He trusted you with his life and then, on his deathbed, with ours. He named you my protector! Whose betrayal would cut him deepest, do you think? Mine or *yours*?"

Something passes across Thurzó's face then, an expression so fleeting it is gone almost as soon as it appeared. If she wrong-footed him at all, there is no sign of it now. His expression is steely, the set of his features resolute. "I *am* protecting Count Nádasdy's heir," he says. "It's just that, on this occasion, it's from his own mother who seems intent on destroying his family's good name."

She flinches, she cannot help it. It is as if Thurzó has slapped her. Anything, she could take, but not the suggestion that her own children have suffered because of her. "And where is my son?" she retorts. "If you are so sure that you act in his name, then why not bring him tonight? Let him witness what you say about his mother for himself."

Thurzó shakes his head, almost sorrowful. "I would spare you that humiliation, at least, madam."

He wounds her more with his pity than with his accusations. She wants to hurt him in return, belittle and unman him. "You should be glad," she says, "that my husband did not live to see you become the king's cat's-paw."

"Better that than a murderer," Thurzó counters.

"Or a traitor," says the king.

"We must have a mind for the rest of the family in all this, your grace," says Thurzó. "Counts Zrínyi and Drugeth, married to the lady's daughters. If the charge were treason, and the harshest penalty applied, they would forfeit their inheritance, and they are innocent in this matter."

The king shifts in his seat. This is not the outcome he desires. He wants a trial, a guilty verdict, and the crown's swift confiscation of the shrew's assets. But he has to tread carefully. His rule in Hungary depends on the support of its most powerful families, not least the Nádasdys, the Zrínyis, and the Drugeths. He is well aware that, for many of them, the Habsburgs' only advantage is that they are not the Ottoman Turks. So he allows them a degree of autonomy, permits them to be Lutherans and Calvinists. He relies on Thurzó, his palatine, to represent him, to mediate between him and these volatile, fractious nobles, all of whom have egos, and a desire for wealth and power, to rival his own. For now, he knows he would be wise to simply bide his time.

"I wish no injustice to the Nádasdy heir," he says magnanimously.

At the mention of Pál, they all instinctively look at Megyeri, who has much to gain from his pupil's continued prosperity. But Megyeri is in no position to speak. He is hunched in his chair, arms clutching his stomach. Now that they are all silent, they can hear his low groans. He seems to be afflicted by a stomach gripe, of unknown and mysterious cause.

"Megyeri," says Thurzó, concerned, "what ails you?"

The king turns pale. "I knew it!" he exclaims. "We are poisoned, all!"

Megyeri belches into the tawny bristles of his beard. He grimaces, as if someone were twisting his insides, and rises a little off his seat. "Agghhh," he exhales, looking somewhat relieved.

Then the countess does something quite shocking: She laughs. Not the kind of modest titter of which she would ordinarily approve, but unrestrained howls from the pit of her belly. And once she has started, she cannot stop. Who knew that there was such freedom in unbridled laughter, such sweet release?

The king is appalled. "She cackles like a crone," he says, beckoning to his footman. "Ready the carriage, I feel *most* unwell."

The king rises and Thurzó does likewise, pulling Megyeri to his feet, still doubled over and beginning to sweat profusely.

Before they leave Thurzó looks down at the countess. "I know not what has happened to you, madam," he says. "You used to be such an enchanting creature."

But this just makes the countess snort all the more, and her mirth does not subside until after they have gone, when the wild laughter turns to sobs.

Three days later, on December 27, 1610, formal charges against the countess are filed by order of the crown.

Chapter 24

PAPER FLOWERS

Boróka is so engrossed that she does not hear the door as it opens. She sits alone at a table, surrounded by sheets of paper dyed the palest shades of rose madder and bright fustic yellows. She cuts carefully, tiny scraps of paper drifting like blossom onto the floor. She unfolds the shape and wraps the very tips of the paper around the scissor blades to make the petals curl, then forms it into a cone, dripping beeswax onto the join so that it stays in place.

The table is already strewn with flowers. There are dahlias and poppies, simple white daisies and morning glories in rich indigo shades. The beauty of midwinter is that any flower at all is possible, but right now, Boróka is making a rose. She folds another piece of paper, once, twice, thrice, into a V, then rounds the end for the petal shape, snips away a hole at the other end. When she unfolds it, she has the outer layer of petals into which she will slot all the other petal cones she has made. This is her favorite part, when all the work comes together into something beautiful.

Had he come in earlier she might have noticed him straightaway, but, as it is, she is too busy making sure that the wax glue drops directly into the middle of the cones without mess or dribbles, that the palest pink shades are on the outside, deepening to a blushing center. By the time she finally looks up, he has been watching her for a minute or more.

The sight of him makes her jump. The wire she is feeding through the finished rose pricks her finger, makes her drop it onto the table. As she tries to stop it rolling off onto the floor, she knocks the scissors to the ground so that everything is suddenly all a-clatter.

"I didn't mean to startle you," Ficzkó says.

And yet, she thinks he did.

"I have much to do," she replies.

"So I see."

He saunters over to the table, picks up the paper rose. "You're good at this," he says, rolling the wire stem between his fingers. "The flowers the other girls make look like colored cow pats."

She tuts away his compliment, snatches back the rose from his fingers. The wire needs to be pulled fully through before the wax sets, which gives her sufficient excuse to ignore him. She concentrates on her work, but she cannot stop him watching her. His gaze is almost palpable, as if he is touching her skin. After a moment, he pulls out a chair and sits down beside her.

Boróka sighs in frustration. "What is it you want?"

"Only to help you," he says.

Boróka stares hard at him. His expression is as ambiguous as his blue-green eyes. She purses her lips, unsure, then slides a piece of paper, dyed with greenweed, toward him. "You can make some leaves," she says.

Ficzkó smiles, amused. "No, I didn't mean that."

"What, then?" There is a note of desperation in her voice. There have been many times over the last few weeks that she has looked up to find him watching her, occasions when she has thought herself alone only for him to seemingly happen upon her. Though he has done nothing, said nothing, his very presence makes her heart beat faster, heightens all her senses. She eyes the door, wonders whether, if she bolted, she could reach it first.

"The countess will have no need of decorations this Christmastide," he says, his voice flat.

"Then I know not why I have been told to make them."

Even as she says the words, she knows they aren't strictly true. She does know, or at least suspects, that she has fallen out of the countess's favor. In fact, the closest she has come to the countess since the confrontation about the box was when she held her lemon-yellow bodice in her hands and mended it. She is no longer part of the countess's circle, attending to her person. Instead, it feels as if jobs are being created for her, invented to keep her busy, keep her away. *Just make some decorations for twelfth night*, Dorka had told her, even though they surely have all the paper flowers they could ever need.

"Boróka . . ."

The sound of her own name—the way he says it—makes her hands still. She cannot think of a time he has used it before. It sounds almost improper coming from him, as intimate as a sweet nothing in her ear. She sets down the rose, forces herself to turn toward him. Winter sunlight trickles through the lattice windows and falls upon his face. She looks from one eye to the other, both shades of a water meadow in the sunlight.

"You must leave the *kastély*," Ficzkó tells her, "go back up to the castle. Tonight, if you can."

"Why?"

"Do not ask, just do as I say."

Boróka's eyes narrow. She doesn't trust him. She remembers the time she was in the outhouse, how he accosted her, how frightened she felt. She remembers how he glowered in front of the fire after the puppet show, how he taunted her with what had happened to Kata. The castle is a different place without the countess in residence. A girl would be vulnerable there, all but alone in the deep midwinter.

"I cannot leave the *kastély* unless I am dismissed." She picks up the rose again, begins to adjust the precise curves of its petals.

"Boróka, listen to me, please."

She almost wishes he would go back to calling her goose-girl. It had a more flippant sound to it, made it easier to pay no heed to his words. When she keeps her eyes on the rose, he reaches out to gently take it from her. As he does, his hand brushes over her fingers. She is surprised how warm they are when the fires can barely keep the cold at bay, how soft the skin is on hands that chop and saw and heave.

"You *must* go." He sets the rose down on the table. She keeps staring at it until he takes her chin in his hand and tilts her face toward him. "They are coming for the countess," he says.

"Who?"

"Thurzó and Megyeri. The countess has spies everywhere. She knows they have filed charges against her and are already on their way."

"When will they get here?" Boróka tries to keep the fear from her voice.

"It's two days' ride from Bratislava, so tomorrow, perhaps."

"Who else knows of this?"

"Just myself and Court Master Deseö. You must tell no one."

"But why should *I* leave?"

There is a flicker of something in Ficzkó's expression: sadness, perhaps, or regret. "Do you think that they will take just her? They need evidence, confessions from those closest to her."

Boróka's breath catches in her throat. She knows little of courts and law, but she does know that confessions are not often freely given. But she has been part of the household for only a few months. Surely, she would not be considered the countess's intimate compared to Dorka, Ilona Jó, and . . . She pauses, looks up at Ficzkó.

"What of yourself?" she whispers. "Will you not leave?"

Ficzkó smiles, no more than a resigned lift of his lips. "And go where? The countess is all I have known from when I was five years old. I'll not ever leave her."

Boróka's mind is racing. It cannot be that they will all just wait for the palatine and his men to arrive. "The countess must escape," she insists. "She could go to Gábor Báthory in Transylvania. He is her cousin, he will help her."

Ficzkó shakes his head. "It is no coincidence that they have chosen to do this now, in midwinter. Christmastide, no less. It's deliberate, designed so that she *cannot* flee. The roads east to Transylvania are impassable. It will take time even for word of her arrest to spread, and that will delay anyone coming to her aid. This is why I say to you: Go to the castle and stay there until they have taken her."

Boróka swallows, parts her lips, but finds there are no words there.

Ficzkó turns his attention to the greenweed paper. "I have never made paper flowers," he says, then falls silent. Boróka is waiting for him to leave, but he doesn't move. It is as if he has something more to say but cannot get the words out. After a moment spent studying the paper's whorls and fibers, he says, "If you will permit me, I should like to stay with you awhile." He slides the paper across the table to her. "Perhaps you could show me how to make the leaves?"

"Why did you warn me?" she asks him, still unsure.

Ficzkó lifts his eyes to hers. "I would not wish you to come to any harm," he says.

Chapter 25

Plumes and Swagger

The countess raises her hands high in the air and claps them to-gether. "Dance," she says.

The *kastély*'s great hall is illuminated by the light of a hundred tiny candles. They are nestled on holly wreaths, gravid with red berries, and set among the evergreen boughs that adorn the mantelpieces and frame the doorways. And in this candlelight, strings of glass beads sparkle, paper flowers bloom.

The countess's face is flushed and her eyes are bright. In the corner of the hall a group of musicians play fiddles, flutes, and lutes as if their lives depended on it. The countess twirls so fast she feels giddy, her skirts rippling and fanning out around her. She is wearing the pale green lustring from her wedding trousseau. And why not? Who knows when she will ever get to wear it again?

The countess rests her hand on the back of a chair, catches her breath.

"Ficzkó," she says, beckoning to him, "why do you not dance?"

Ficzkó walks over to his mistress. The gentle light of a hundred candles is forgiving. He sees her almost as she was years ago: at once wicked and kind, mischievous, still the most beautiful woman he has ever seen. "Forgive me," he says, "I cannot."

The countess gives him a sly smile. "I know what will persuade you," she says. "Boróka, it is my pleasure that you should dance with Ficzkó."

The music takes a more sedate turn. Ficzkó steps up to Boróka and offers her his upturned palm. In return, she rests just the tips of her fingers on his hand. When she steps toward him, he says, "Why didn't you go to the castle?"

Boróka looks him in the eye, as the dance requires. The next beat, she turns her body away from him, but they are still connected by their locked gaze and the slightest touch of their hands.

"A goose does not flee when the fox comes near," she says.

Beyond the warmth and vitality of the great hall, the world is a different place. It has started to snow. Fat flakes catch on the watchman's bearskin hat as he patrols the *kastély*'s outer walls. A huge white Komondor paces beside him, its corded coat hanging heavy over its eyes, swishing around its paws, like petticoats.

The snow is too late. Had it come a few hours earlier it would have delayed the steady progress of the men on horseback who wind their way up toward Čachtice. As it is, Thurzó, Megyeri, and the armed escort that trudges behind them have made good time in the clear night. They are the king's men, after all, propelled onward by their own rectitude, all plumes and swagger.

The countess is trying to remember something. Not the gist—that is not good enough—but the exact words. "*God help, little cloud,*" she murmurs, for no one can hear her above the music and the slippered feet that leap and tap over the floor. "*Send eighty cats from beyond the mountains.*" No, it wasn't eighty, it was ninety. Why can't she remember? She thought she knew the words of Dori's bewitching charm, but now that she desperately needs it, the words are as easy to grasp as egg white. She looks toward the door. All is not lost, for any minute her steward will return, the one she has sent to Myjava to write down the words of the charm, *precisely* as Dori speaks them, and bring them to her, on pain of beheading if he gets it wrong. She can do nothing but wait for him to get back. In the meantime, there is one bit that she does remember. "*Gather those ninety cats and send them away to bite*

King Matthias's heart, to bite my lord palatine's heart, and let them eat the heart of the Red Megyeri so that Erzsébet Báthory may come to no harm." These are the words she whispers, over and over, as her household dances around her with fin de siècle abandon.

Soon the snow is as thick and haphazard as fireflies in the night sky. It blinds the watchman to the approach of the king's men, but he feels the Komondor pull against its leash, tilting its muzzle toward the road that approaches the manor house. The watchman strains to listen, tries to catch the sound of boots and hooves and panted breath in the muffled night. Then the Komondor begins to bark, a deep throaty growl that answers the clink of approaching armor, the thud of pikestaffs on the earth.

It is almost seven o'clock, and the countess is about to have dinner. She sits at the head of the high table with the handful of noble girls she has brought with her to the *kastély*. Orsolya is there, along with a few others. The senior servants, stewards, and bailiffs are permitted to dine in the same room, albeit at a separate table. Boróka is on her way out of the great hall. As she passes the fireplace she bends to pick up a fallen paper rose and replace it carefully on the mantel. The countess feels a small stab of guilt. She has barely acknowledged the girl after her silly nonsense about the *rusalka*. For every spy she has herself, she knows there are two more lurking in her own household. It is her job to distinguish loyalty from self-interest, genuine adoration from sycophancy. She really had thought that Boróka could be counted among those who would never betray her, but the girl is full of strange fairy tales, and the countess knows that such stories do not always have happy endings.

But this is not a night for suspicion and grievances. "You may stay, Boróka," she calls out, while flicking her hand over the chair to her left, which tells the girl about to sit on it that she had better not.

The countess has little appetite. She does not touch the oysters placed in front of her, nor the wine poured into the silver goblet. She eyes the door nervously. She still believes that at any moment her steward will appear, clutching a word-perfect transcription of Dori's spell, and that Thurzó may yet be repelled by force of magic alone. She drags her eyes away. She is still the Countess Báthory, she reminds herself. She must be gracious and smile as she presides over her table. She is all things to all people: mother, mistress of her household, and sovereign overlord. Let none of them know how her heart drums, that fear is like a vise around her throat. It is her duty to appear as if her mastery of the world is the same as it has always been, even as it collapses around her. It is *sprezzatura*. It is what she was born to do.

There is cheer in the warm light of the flickering candles. There is familiarity in the Christmastide decorations: the same pretty things, in the same places, year on year. And there is comfort in having her people around her. She watches Dorka at the servants' table, chiding Ficzkó for some transgression or other. She sees Ilona Jó observing them, eyebrow raised; and Kata, sweet Kata, trying to intervene. And she turns to look at Boróka, a girl she never knew existed a year ago, who now sits right beside her. Then she closes her eyes a moment, lets it all wash over her, be a balm for what is to come.

When the palatine and his men push through the *kastély*'s wooden doors, the watchman's heart is heavy, but not as heavy as his pockets, which are now full of coin. Once inside, the soldiers bleed through the building. In minutes they are down every corridor, in every room. When they burst into the great hall they are met, not with resistance, but with gently playing music, the smell of rich dishes spiced with cumin and caraway, festive decorations, and the honey-sweet scent of burning beeswax.

Thurzó strides to the front of his men; it is easy to be brave when he is met with only a woman sitting at her table. The lute's delicate strains falter and die. The whole household is silent, shocked by the intrusion and the icy midwinter air that barrels in with them.

The countess places both palms on the table, inhales, then pushes herself up to standing. "My Lord Palatine," she says.

Thurzó walks toward her, spurred boots jangling. In the warmth of the great hall, the snow dusting his beard and wolfskin cape begins to shrivel. "Widow Nádasdy," he replies, and with those two words he strips her of everything. The countess's hands are still touching the table. The palatine cannot see her fingers flex, the skin around her joints blanch.

"I know not why you have been so heavy-handed, your grace," she says calmly. "You only had to knock."

"Mistress," says Thurzó, "you are indeed a bloodthirsty female. In the name of King Matthias II, I arrest you for your crimes: namely, the torture and murder of countless girls, all of them most innocent."

"You are making a grave mistake," she replies, her voice now ringing clear in the silent room. "My allies will not allow you to do this."

There is a flash of something in Thurzó's eyes that, in a kinder man, might have been pity. He turns to his men. "Take her," he says.

Two soldiers march toward the countess. They come to stand on either side of her, and each grab hold of an arm. "I will *not* be manhandled," she spits at them, wrenching her arms free. The countess, it seems, has swagger of her own. The soldiers look to Thurzó, who gives a slight nod of his head. She is right, of course: Whatever the circumstances, she must not be mauled like a common cutpurse. The soldiers stand aside.

She will not allow them to touch her, prefers to walk alone, but as she steps out around her chair there is a problem with the heel of her satin slipper. It seems to simply give way, so that her legs wobble beneath her and she lurches over to the side. For an awful moment she thinks she will fall, but then Boróka is there, one hand under her elbow, the other around her waist. "Courage, gracious lady," she whispers into her ear, "courage."

Megyeri, who appears to have recovered from his recent malady, stands by the servants' table. "Who is the one they call Dorka?" he says.

Dorka blinks at him. "Who would wish to know, sir?" she replies, sounding almost coquettish.

"So it is you, then," says Megyeri.

Thurzó joins him. "I know of all her familiars," he says. "That one there was the wet nurse." He points at Ilona Jó, who merely stares back at him. "And there is another, the lad who is her jack-of-all-trades."

Megyeri sniggers. "So I have heard. Which one is he?"

Immediately, Ficzkó stands. "It is my honor to serve the lady," he says.

"Arrest them all," instructs Thurzó.

Dorka gasps. "You cannot mean it, my lord!" she says, but the soldiers are already upon her. She wriggles out of their grasp and throws herself at Thurzó's feet. She clutches at the fine wool of his culottes, grabs the fur trim of his cape, kisses it, over and over. "Mercy, your grace, I beg you! What have I to do with my mistress's sins? I am just an old woman. I have only ever done what I was told, nothing more. Please!"

Thurzó looks down at her with complete revulsion. He jerks his leg, as if she were an annoying dog. The metal spur of his boot stabs her, makes her yelp.

"Get this hag off me," he says to his men through gritted teeth.

A soldier pulls her up, while two others take hold of Ilona and Ficzkó. Soon they are all standing together, heavily guarded.

"There is a fourth intimate," says Megyeri. "Another female."

Thurzó nods. "A laundry maid or some such." He looks around him and his eyes alight on Boróka, who stands next to the countess, supporting her arm. "Perhaps it is the one that still clings to her now."

"Yes!" screeches Dorka. She reaches out a trembling finger and points it at Boróka, her eyes wild. "Indeed, sir, you are right. She's the one. That girl has done plenty of laundry!"

"She seems a little young," says Megyeri, dubious.

"The boy is not much older," replies Thurzó, glancing back at Ficzkó.

Ficzkó scoffs loudly. "Do not bother with her," he says, indicating Boróka. "They call her goose-girl because she is good for nothing except tending geese."

"Take her anyway," says Thurzó to his men, "we must have all four accomplices."

There is the scrape of a chair sliding across flagstones. "I am the fourth you seek," says Kata, rising.

Thurzó and Megyeri exchange glances. "We do not need five," says Megyeri.

"*She's* the washerwoman," confirms Dorka, jerking her head toward Kata because her arms are now pinned by guards. "And not one of us is closer to the countess than she. The things I could tell you about them, sir, really."

Ilona gives Dorka a furious look, hisses at her to be quiet, but Dorka ignores her. "Spare me, gracious lord, and I will tell you!"

"You will have every opportunity to tell me what you know," says Thurzó darkly, "do not doubt that."

Dorka looks stricken. "Please, your grace," she whimpers, but Thurzó has already turned away.

"Arrest the old washerwoman," he says, "the young one is of no consequence."

The countess slips her arm away from Boróka's. She knows it is time to leave and would not have the girl try to go with her.

"My lady, tell me what I can do to help you," pleads Boróka.

The countess looks at her blankly. What can a child do to help her now? Then she remembers something. "Ask Thurzó if he has found the deposition from the widow Hernath," she whispers, before a soldier silences her with a glare.

Thurzó is pacing back through his men. "Take Widow Nádasdy up to the castle," he says, "and lock the others in the cellars for questioning."

"You've forgotten that witch from Myjava!" Dorka screeches after him, but he is already through the door and pulling on his gloves, feeling the first surge of relief, the exhilaration of a job well done.

Outside, some of his men are waiting. Their hands are full—not of weapons, but of spades, forks, and shovels. He nods at them from the manor's porticoed entrance.

"Start digging," he says.

Not one hour later a horse gallops up the road toward the *kastély*. Its rider furiously urges it on, pressing in his spurs, until they are through the outer stone walls. He swings down from his horse almost before it has come to a halt and grabs a leather pouch from the saddlebag. The Komondor whines with pleasure and leaps up at him as he approaches, trying to lick the steward's face. "Not now," he says, quickly running his fingers through the thick cords of its coat, "I have something important to give the countess."

The steward stops, suddenly noticing that the *kastély*'s grounds are alight with torches and bonfires. He hears the thud and scrape of shovels being driven into the frozen earth, sees the watchman sitting idly by a burning brazier, warming his hands.

"You're too late, my friend," the watchman says, shaking his head. "Too late."

Chapter 26

BETWEEN STONES

M arta is sure that it is one of hers. As soon as they pulled back the shroud and fragments of chamomile and lavender fell to the floor, she knew. If she were closer, she would look at her eyes. There were no florins for this common girl, so she had put two flat pebbles on her eyelids instead, from her own collection of Interesting Things. She remembers the stones had strange spirals in them that had made the girl look as if she were seeing something amazing. It had made Marta smile to think that she would stay looking astonished forever.

The pebbles are probably gone now: lost, or stolen by someone who found them as curious as she. She will not try to get nearer to look. There are too many people here. Not just from the castle and the *kastély*, but from the village and the nearby hamlets as well. In fact, *everyone* seems to be here: scullions to shepherds, butchers to book-keepers. Everyone except the countess. She's nowhere to be seen.

There is a man standing next to the girl's body. Marta doesn't know who he is, but he has curly whiskers on his face and fire in his eyes. He gestures to the dead girl. *Look upon her*, he tells the crowd.

Marta feels sorry for the girl. You would have thought that after a life spent at the beck and call of the rich, they would let her rest in peace now. But no, she is still pandering to their whims and de-mands. She wants to cover up her nakedness, shield her blue-white skin from their gaze. At least she is not long dead and the cold weather has slowed her decay. She does not lie before them reeking and sup-purating.

Behold the bruises, this bushy-faced man is saying, *the lacerations and wounds*. Marta doesn't need to look. She knows what the girl looked like when she wrapped her in the shroud, the pustules that populated her body like mushrooms. The man struts around the corpse, to her feet. *See the rope marks from torture and restraint*. Marta feels bad now. Was it wrong to tie the girl's wrists and feet? It's just that the boy preferred it that way, found the bodies easier to carry if their limbs were not falling about or sticking awkwardly out. She didn't think she was torturing her. And as for restraint, well, nothing is more important than making sure the dead do not climb right out of their graves. Though that doesn't seem to have worried this particular man, who has yanked the poor girl from her resting place like he was pulling up a turnip.

But the crowd seems very angry. They gasp and jeer. They shake their heads in dismay. Marta starts to twist her apron tie round and round her finger. Will they find out that it was she who did this to the girl? Her stomach seems to drop in her belly. She knows what they do to people who hurt other people. The men behind her want a better look at the naked dead girl. She finds herself jostled forward when all she wants to do is get out. She looks around the great hall, in case she could slip away, but there is a guard at every door. Viewing the girl's corpse is compulsory.

The man addressing the crowd has a loud, booming voice. *You can see her sins with your own eyes*, he is telling them. Marta begins to whimper. Her apron is wound so tight her fingertips are turning puce. Kata will help Marta, she thinks, so she lifts herself on her tiptoes, searching the crowd for her. She cannot see her, but she does see something else, something she hadn't noticed before. Behind the corpse is another girl, alive, but with the skin of one arm as raw as a flayed rabbit. Marta's heart begins to pound. "But it wasn't Marta's fault," she mutters, shaking her head.

The rich man steps toward the injured girl. He takes her uninjured arm gently, solicitously, and guides her to stand in front of the crowd.

See here, he says. *I found another victim of torture in the kitchen, surely only hours from death.*

There is a voice inside Marta's head. *Picsa!* it says. She really *is* a stupid woman, but she didn't mean to hurt the girl; she was trying to carry too much at once, trying to get all her jobs done quickly and not be *lazy* and *stupid*, like Dorka says she is. She shouldn't have been carrying hot fat in a pot without a lid, but the girl really did come out of nowhere, laughing and chatting and not looking where she was going.

Marta feels sick. That man does not seem kind; she doesn't like how he shouts and swishes his cape around him as he struts in front of the crowd. He stops and turns to face them directly, takes a deep breath, as if gathering himself for what he is about to say. *In my capacity as the highest legal authority in the Kingdom of Hungary, I, the lord palatine, will pass sentence on the perpetrator of these outrages against the female sex.*

Marta had no idea how important this man is. Her breath is coming in short gasps, and the blood pulsing in her ears is so loud that she can hardly hear what he is saying. And yet, she *must* listen so she can know what will happen to her.

Last night, I surprised the Countess Erzsébet Báthory, Lady Nádasdy, in the very act of murder. The innocent serving maid who died at her hands was only one of many, and the butchery that you see before you has been practiced for years. I have imprisoned Widow Nádasdy between stones, and she will remain imprisoned in her own castle in perpetuity.

Marta is confused; she didn't even know the countess had a castle in Perpetuity. But she does know that she should own up, tell the Highest Legal Authority in the Kingdom of Hungary that it was she who did those awful things. The crowd is clapping and cheering now. The Highest Legal Authority looks very pleased with himself. What to do, she wonders, unraveling her apron tie and winding it over again, what to do? She tries to think, but the press of people, the noise, the commotion, is too much, so she sinks down, squatting on her haunches, presses her palms to her ears.

Boróka knows it doesn't make sense to go to see the palatine alone. She witnessed the macabre spectacle that he put on that morning, along with everyone else. She needs something of her own with which to confront him. Something irrefutable. A voice from the grave, almost. Even though the unfortunate girl Thurzó displayed could not speak, there are those who can.

She stands watching them now. They are concerned, these noble girls. They wonder what will happen to them now that they have lost the patronage of such a high-ranking lady. They worry that their mistress's disgrace will have harmed their marriage prospects. They huddle together, like birds, and twitter about their misfortunes.

When Boróka approaches, the girls do not stop talking. How can they? The day's events have been shocking, quite thrillingly so. They have more to talk about than ever before.

"Forgive me," says Boróka, by way of interruption.

They seem not to have heard her. They are eating the leftover puddings that should have been served last night. One of them is talking, and the others lean forward on their elbows to listen, popping custard tarts into their open, scandalized mouths. *I have heard*, the girl is telling them, *that the countess has been walled up completely, with nothing but a small slit left to give her food and for her to pass out her—*

"Forgive me," says Boróka again, louder.

The girl speaking purses her lips. "What is it?" she says.

"I need someone to help me, please."

She sighs. She is very busy, after all. "What with?"

"Some of you had the same affliction as Judit last summer. I need one of you to come with me to speak to the lord palatine, if you please. I want you to tell him that you were ill, that Judit was ill too, and that the countess played no part in her death."

The girls exchange glances. "But we do not know that," one says, giving a small shrug of her shoulders.

"But you do!" exclaims Boróka. "You have known the countess for months, years perhaps. When has she ever harmed any of you?"

Despite their interest in the castle's current affairs only moments ago, all the girls now seem preoccupied by their nails, which some are inspecting, or the ends of their hair, which others rub between their fingers as if they suddenly consider them worryingly dry.

"It is a shame we cannot ask Judit that question," says the girl who spoke.

"Why do you say that?"

"I never noticed that Judit was ill. None of us did. Did you?"

Boróka opens her mouth, about to say *of course*, then she stops. She didn't actually see Judit when they brought her down to the dungeons. She was with Orsolya, and she heard only the ominous sounds of her incarceration, the clanging doors, the footsteps echoing down the stone corridors. "She would not have been brought down to the dungeons unless she was sick," she says instead.

The girl shakes her head. "The palatine told us that the countess has special places in her castle, heavily guarded, where she takes the girls to be tortured. How do we know whether Judit was brought down to the dungeons to be cured or murdered?"

"Because the countess has only ever sought to help you all," says Boróka, desperate, "as well you know."

"All *I* know is that one moment Judit upset the countess and the next she was dead," insists the girl.

"She even *told* Judit she would kill her," says another. "We all heard her."

Boróka is incredulous. "She was annoyed with her! You cannot think that she really meant that she would dance with Judit's corpse and play bowls with her severed head?"

Boróka suddenly feels both furious and tearful. What would the prospects of these girls be without the countess? They consider themselves *noble*, yet they could not dance, nor play the lute, nor discuss anything with any degree of insight or learning before they came to the gynaeceum. They owe everything to the countess, yet they do nothing but sit around picking over her misfortunes like a chicken carcass.

"Why don't you speak to the palatine yourself?" asks one of the girls.

Boróka gives her a grim smile. "Because the word of a maidservant does not carry the same weight as the word of the nobility. This is all because *Judit* died. The palatine is accusing the countess of killing highborn girls, so we need a noble girl to say it's not true. So, I ask you again, which of you will come with me to help her?"

Nothing but silence. Boróka feels weary, defeated. "The countess would be disappointed," she says. "You are her favorite girls, the ones she chose to come with her to the *kastély*. You were all so talkative in the gynaeceum, yet now, when she desperately needs someone to speak out on her behalf, you seem to have quite lost your tongues."

Boróka turns to leave, as she can do no more, but as she reaches the door one of them stands, brushes pastry crumbs from her skirt.

"I will come with you," says Orsolya.

Now that his work at Čachtice is done, they find Thurzó about to leave for his castle at Bytča. He is keen to be off but will always find time to talk to any girl who wishes to tell him what went on in the household of that most bloodthirsty female.

He smiles at them benignly so that they are not too intimidated by his greatness. "Tell me," he says, looking at Orsolya, as she is much the finer dressed and therefore should be better able to articulate her thoughts in a way of which he can make some sense.

"Your grace," says Orsolya, with a quick curtsy. "We wish to talk to you about the countess."

"Of course you do. A most terrible business, I must say. But you are safe from harm now." He gives them another smile, one that he hopes is reassuring.

"In the great hall this morning you showed us the body of a young girl. She had marks on her which you said the countess inflicted."

Thurzó nods. "I am sorry for that, but the people had to see her crimes for themselves. Did it upset you?" His eyes are already flicking to the clock on the mantel. He should be away, he cannot spend his time playing nursemaid to squeamish girls.

"It's not that," says Orsolya, shaking her head. "I wanted to tell you that I have those marks on my body too." She lifts her arm, pushes up the sleeve of her chemise. The raw pustules have healed, but the ghosts of them remain, silvery-white circles on her skin.

Thurzó scowls. "They are not the same. Not at all." He has already decided that these maids will be of no use to him and he now needs to extricate himself.

"Mine have healed," says Orsolya, "but, before, they were like the other girl's. I was very sick, I almost . . ." She goes quiet, glances at Boróka.

Boróka clears her throat. "What we are trying to tell you, your grace, is that the girl you, um . . . *unearthed*, died of natural causes. She was not killed by the countess."

Thurzó takes a deep breath, searches again for the smile that came so easily moments ago. "I understand that it is difficult for innocents such as yourselves to comprehend that these bestial acts could be committed by anyone, let alone a *woman*, and a countess no less! It's natural for you to try to find other explanations, rather than accept the grim truth, but you really must try to understand. And please, do not worry. I have the matter entirely in hand."

Thurzó picks up some papers from the desk and shuffles them. In truth, all the papers he needs are already in his leather wallet, but he hopes this will be enough to encourage the girls to leave.

"I cannot believe it of her, your grace," says Orsolya, suddenly emphatic. "You describe her as 'bestial' but her intelligence, her eloquence, suggest otherwise."

Thurzó gives her a hard stare. "The nightingale is still the bird of darkness and mourning, even though its song is sweet."

"Then the countess must, indeed, be a master of *sprezzatura*," says Orsolya wryly.

The palatine cannot help but laugh. "Oh, she is most certainly a master of that!" He puts down the papers, steps around the desk to stand in front of Orsolya. "*Sprezzatura* is as much *deceit* as anything else, you foolish girl. It is simply appearing to be that which you are not. It is deception, mere trickery! The countess has played the part of the cultured benefactor for so long she probably even believes it herself, but that is *not* who she is. Behind the facade she is truly a monster, a sadist, a murderer, and I will bring her to account for it!"

Boróka's head is spinning. All her memories and impressions of the countess are churning in her mind. They blur and meld together, until the countess is a confused, murky mess. She wants to leave, to run down the corridors until she can find somewhere to be alone to unpick the thoughts in her head. But she made a promise, and she will not leave until she has done what the countess asked her to do. "Your grace, I wish to ask you if you have located the deposition made by the widow Hernath."

Thurzó turns a steely gaze on Boróka. "What know you of this?"

"Nothing, except that the countess should like to know if you have managed to locate a copy of it."

He peers at the girl more closely. Now that he inspects her, he can see that she is the same wretch who attached herself to Mistress Nádasdy the night before. He should have arrested her along with the other familiars when he had the chance. He worries, now, that she will make trouble for him.

"No such deposition exists," he says, his voice perfunctory. "I have checked with the county court and they have no record of this woman Hernath."

He makes to leave. He has wasted far too much time with these girls as it is. But they are sweet-faced, the both of them, and so young that his kindly heart makes him pause.

"I see you are vexed, but you need not be. You are both safe now, I assure you. This terrible violence against female blood is at an end."

But in fact, as Thurzó well knows, it is just beginning.

Chapter 27

A Better Man

She knows where they took him. On the night of the countess's arrest, the palatine's guards had taken the prisoners outside and she had watched, along with the rest of the household, as the countess was loaded into a cart to be taken up to the high castle. Somehow, as the countess's cart drew away, her eyes had not followed it up the hill. Instead, they had stayed fixed on him.

She saw them separate him from Dorka and Ilona and push him roughly through the thickening snow. She flinched herself when he stumbled and fell to his knees, his hands bound, unable to break his fall. She was almost relieved when he disappeared through the small outside door that leads down to the cellars.

He has been there a night and a day now. The cellar door is guarded constantly, but she knows that the cellars stretch all the way under the *kastély*'s kitchen. Inside the pantry are steps that lead down to a storeroom, full of grain in the winter and ripening cheese in the summer. Set into the wall of the storeroom is a grille that allows air to circulate between the cellars and storeroom. She sits beside it now, whispering his name.

At first she hears nothing save the sounds of dinner being prepared in the kitchen beyond the pantry's closed door. She leans forward, speaks again. "Ficzkó," she says, her voice louder, more insistent.

There is a rustling in the gloomy recesses of the cellar. Shuffling steps, then a clang as something is kicked over. She tenses, holds her breath, but the kitchen above her is busy with the endless cycle of food preparation that never stops in a household like this. She has a candle with her, so she brings it up to the grille, lets its soft light spill over into the unlit cellar. He walks toward the light, crouches down beside it, squinting until he can make her out.

"What are you doing here?" he says, his voice raspy with concern and disuse. "Away with you, Boróka."

"I have brought you something to eat," she says, handing him a small packet, covered in muslin, through the metal bars.

He eyes it for a moment, then takes it gratefully. "I meant what I said: If they find you here, you will end up this side of the grille."

She shakes her head, refusing to go. "You tried to warn me," she tells him. "And now I will do what I can to help you."

He gives her a bitter look. "And do you see that I was right?"

She cannot meet his eye, doesn't want to think about what lies in store for him next.

"Is there anything you need? I will bring it for you."

"But I have all I could ever need," he says, gesturing grandly around him. "A stone ledge to lie on, a pot to piss in. I am king of my own castle at last." His sarcastic smile soon fades and his voice becomes serious. "You should be doing what you can to help the countess, not wasting your time on me."

"Should I?" she says, her voice quiet.

His lips curl. "So even you doubt her now?"

"No! I mean . . ." Her voice trails off, disappears into the darkness like the candlelight. "I don't know what to think," she whispers.

He stares at her, both eyes now murky, brackish pools. "About whom?" he says carefully.

She shifts a little, adjusts her position on the hard storeroom floor. Before she speaks, she swallows because her mouth feels suddenly dry. "What did you do, Ficzkó?"

"What does it matter now? Guilty or innocent, there is no way out of this for me."

"It matters to me," she says.

Deep inside him, something stirs. It touches him that, even now, she is still trying to work out who he really is. He wants to tell her, but he isn't sure he knows the answer himself.

"Did you hurt those girls?" she insists. "Did you hurt Kata?"

Somewhere in the dark corners of the cellar a monster rears its head. It is the most frightening thing Ficzkó has had to deal with his whole life. More terrifying than the father who turned against him in his first few weeks of life, or the puppeteer's swinging fists. It is himself, the things of which he is capable. It is *Stefan*, watching him, wondering what he will say next.

"You don't understand what it was like to grow up in Čachtice," Ficzkó says. "They controlled me, made me do things . . ."

Over in the corner, Stefan gets up and moves closer. He squats down on a cask of wine in front of Ficzkó, leans forward and rests his elbows on his knees.

"Who," says Boróka, "the countess?"

Ficzkó shakes his head. "No, Dorka and Ilona Jó."

At this, Stefan throws back his head and laughs out loud. *Oh, come on*, he says. *You cannot tell her you were controlled by a couple of old women!*

Ficzkó glares at him, his breath now coming fast with rage.

"Ficzkó?" says Boróka. "What is it?"

"Nothing," he says, "I'm just tired." Ficzkó has slept little, and eaten even less; no wonder the dark plays tricks on him.

"When I was younger," he begins, "no more than a boy, Dorka would make the girls stand naked in front of me and tell me to slap them."

Behind the grille, Boróka is silent. Then: "Did you do it?" she asks.

"No," he says vehemently, "I refused."

Stefan scoffs, gives Ficzkó a look that says, *That's it, blame it all on me.*

Ficzkó drags his gaze back to Boróka. She grounds him. Even the hatched image of her behind the metal bars is something to which to cling, a vision of what might have been. "They wanted me to hurt the girls," he tells her. "Sometimes they could not do it themselves; they were too old, too weak, to beat them." Ficzkó's voice begins to crack. Something about the grille between them, Boróka pale in the candle-light in her white chemise, reminds him of a confessional. He wants to tell her everything, be absolved, but Stefan shakes his head, presses a finger to his lips.

Ficzkó clenches his jaw. "You do not tell me what to do," he spits into the darkness.

But Stefan just shrugs. *Go ahead, then, tell her. See what she thinks of you then.*

"What are you saying?" asks Boróka, confused.

"I—" There is so much he wants to say to her that it has all wedged in his throat. He cannot speak, can hardly breathe.

You see, whispers Stefan, *you cannot tell her. That's because you are disgusting. If she really knew you, she wouldn't be sitting there now. She would have abandoned you, like your mother did. No one could blame them: You are . . . despicable.*

Ficzkó is staring into the darkness, a look of desperate fury on his face. He pulls back his leg and kicks out suddenly at the wine cask in front of him, sending it clattering against the wall.

Boróka gasps, scrambles to her knees. "Ficzkó, no! The guards will hear."

When Ficzkó turns back toward her there are tears streaming down his cheeks. "Do you think that I am evil?" he asks her.

Boróka leans forward, presses her hands against the bars. "No," she breathes, "no."

He moves toward her then, reaches for her through the bars. She offers up her hands readily, wants to touch him.

Her skin feels as soft as he remembered it from when she stroked his face in the outhouse. It makes him imagine a world in which there is nothing to stop him being with her: no iron bars, no Stefan. "I think," he says, drawing her hand toward him, pressing it against his chest, "if I could have known you sooner, then I would have been a better man."

If she could, Boróka would hold him, kiss away his tears. She desperately wishes the grille were not there; yet, at the same time, she is glad of it. She knows now that broad-shouldered blade grinders should be treated with caution, that capering men with harvest-blond hair should be avoided. Who knows what trouble a beautiful boy, with eyes the color of water meadows in the sun, might have caused?

Chapter 28

PHANTOMS

There is a gap under the outbuilding's locked door. It turns from hazy gray to a bright, white strip before it fades again and disappears. Dorka has watched it do this twice over, so she knows it must now be New Year's Eve, and on New Year's Day they will move them all to the gaol at Bytča.

She knows what will happen to her once she is there. She has had two days to think about it, imagine it happening. Night has fallen and the dank room in which she is being held is pitch black. Nonetheless, she can make out the outlines of things she knows are there. The landscape of boxes and barrels, ladders and tools, has been revealed to her on two occasions when the door swung open and she was given some basic nourishment. But the last time that happened was hours ago. Since then, she has had nothing but wild thoughts to sustain her.

It is the noises she cannot stand. The rustling and scampering. The squeaking and chattering. The slap of feet, no bigger than a fingernail, over the chill stone floor. The whip of a scaly tail. Earlier that day she made a mistake. She was so hungry by the time they finally brought her food that she forced the bread into her mouth, spooned in the whey with such speed that it smeared around her mouth and dribbled down her chin. She lay down after that, exhausted. She must have nodded off, because she didn't notice the quivering nose that sniffed her face, the whiskers that were like butterfly wings over her skin. But she noticed the teeth when they pierced her lip. She screamed and flung the creature off her, but now she cannot rest, cannot allow herself to close her eyes. She sits hunched on a pile of sackcloth, hugging her knees, eyes darting around the darkness, ears straining for the scrabble of claws up the wall behind her.

Every so often she hears things. A thread of something in the air that sounds like Ilona screaming. Her fear tells her that it must be the sound of Ilona's agony, as her shoulders pop from their sockets on the strappado, but when she tries to pin the sound down it becomes the winter wind, whistling through the manor gardens.

She sees things too. Impossible things like the flash of a white chemise flapping in a brisk October breeze and the splash of blood from an opened vein. The shadows become the phantoms of her past and peer at her through the gloom, with eyes as dark and round as blackberry drupelets.

Dorka is thinking about the kitchen at Čachtice Castle. So many times she would come down in the morning to find the storage sacks shredded and the vegetables gnawed or stolen. She tried everything to stop them, including putting the sacks in wooden casks or earthenware jars, but the rats gnawed through everything. It was quite astonishing to see the destruction that a hungry rat could cause: any material at all bitten, shredded, clawed.

She shudders. She can almost feel it on her naked belly already. She imagines the touch of its feet as it runs around the perimeter of the upturned cage that traps it against her skin as she lies outstretched. It would just tickle at first while it sniffed out this new enclosure, but it wouldn't be long before she felt the sharp scratch of its claws once it became impatient to be free. Then they would set a fire smoldering on top of the cage and the rat would sense the smoke and heat and become frantic. How much harder it would be to gnaw though a metal cage than dig down, through the loose, yielding flesh of an old woman.

Terror, pure as rainwater, sluices through her. She cries out, tries to reason with the pitch night. *I will tell you everything*, she pleads, *there is no need to hurt me.*

Not even the shrill wind replies.

Then she realizes that there is someone who can help her. Someone she has tried not to think about for a very long time. But she needs him now, desperately. She clambers to her knees—awkwardly, her joints creaking and protesting—clasps her fingers together, and bends her head.

Hours later, that is where the new year finds her, kneeling in the dark on some dirty sackcloth, praying to a god who will not listen.

Chapter 29

ET TORTURA

With its whitewashed walls, Bytča Castle blends into the landscape of snow and frozen water meadows like an Arctic fox. Its corner bastions, curved and smooth, are topped with green turrets that pierce the wintery sky, like treetops. Next to it is the wedding palace Thurzó had built for the lavish marriages of his daughters. Its frescos of all things flowering and fertile—plants, animals, maidens—suggest a fruitfulness that is hard to imagine on this, the first day of January.

Inside Bytča Castle itself is a school, a library, an archive, and a pharmacy. It is a center of learning, of culture and enlightenment—everywhere, that is, except its prison, which is quite as godforsaken as any other.

The cell where Ficzkó sits in chains smells both damp and ferrous. His short, shallow breaths draw in air thick with mold and sharp with sweat. It tastes metallic in his open mouth, as if he is inhaling the remnants of blood shed long ago. In front of him a man is laying out the tools of his trade, carefully, precisely. A vise, a spiked collar, pincers, and finger screws. He draws out the flail, lifts its chains with his palm, sees how the pointed barbs glitter like tiny stars. He is the magister torturarum, trained to extract abominations from the conscience with the practiced ease of a tooth-puller.

But there is no rush. At first the instruments do the work without any effort on his part. Just their presence is often enough. If not, their cool touch when laid on the skin can loosen a confession as if it were a boil, perfectly ready to burst forth. Ficzkó, however, stays silent, save for the quick rasp of his breath. No matter; the magister has time to warm his subject to the task. He begins with an easy question, something to get the boy talking.

"What is your name?"

Of all the people he has been in his life—János, Ficzkó, Stefan— Ficzkó's not entirely sure who sits there now. The irons, heavy around his wrists, remind him of the boy he once was. He feels them cut into his skin, they seem to burn like his father's shovel. But he is Ficzkó, of course, devoted servant to a benevolent mistress, a boy on the brink of falling in love. And yet, he also knows that only Stefan can truly answer the questions the magister will ask.

The magister lets out a slow breath. He fears this will not be easy. The boy's tongue needs to be loosened by tomorrow, when he and the old crones will be interrogated by the palatine's examining magistrates. He lays out the flail alongside his other instruments. "You are very young," he tells Ficzkó, in a voice that is almost kind. "No doubt you did only what she told you to do."

Ficzkó looks up at the man addressing him. He is the *hóhér*— "executioner"—a word Thurzó now uses to describe the countess.

"I would have done anything for her," replies Ficzkó.

The magister nods. "I understand. What did she make you do?"

"Nothing." Ficzkó's voice is clear. It rings around the gloomy cell, brightens it like candlelight. "Everything I did for her, with her, I wanted to do."

The magister knows from experience that going around in circles serves no one, and besides, he is paid a fixed sum for every instrument applied. Ficzkó's foot is already inside the boot. The magister torturarum has only to turn the crank to earn his money.

"How many girls did Widow Nádasdy murder?" he asks.

Ficzkó tries not to look, but his gaze has a weight of its own. His eyeballs swivel down as if they were made of lead and he stares at the magister's hand, watching, fascinated, as the fingers curl around the crank.

"None, I swear it," he says, but his voice sounds helpless.

The pain, when it comes, makes him feel like the skin on his calf is splitting open. He is cleaving apart again, becoming separate people. Someone is screaming now, begging for mercy. He wishes Stefan would shut up, blubbering and squealing like a stuck pig. Ficzkó would never tell the magister anything, but Stefan is not nearly as brave. Soon he will tell the magister whatever he wants to hear, just to make the pain stop.

Ficzkó cannot bear to watch, so he turns his back on this most abhorrent part of himself and retreats as far into his mind as he can go, to that place where all he can hear is the sound of his mother's voice, all he can smell is bacon scraps and wholesome cabbage soup, and all he can see is paper flowers, strewn everywhere.

Chapter 30

ELEVEN QUESTIONS

The scrivener holds his pen up to the light, such as it is. This January is particularly bleak. When the dawn comes it brings with it an ashen, reluctant, sky, which lingers only as long as it has to. He needs to work quickly, get everything down before the need for a candle burns through his profit for the job.

He rotates the pen in his fingers, checks the trim of the nib. No, this will not do. If ever there was a document that had to be perfectly transcribed, this is it. He picks up his penknife with his other hand, flicks up the blade. A curl of quill peels off the nib, then another and another, until the desk is scattered with shavings as thin and translucent as a bee's wings. One more, he thinks, rounding off the tip to perfection, then he plunges it into the pot of hot sand over the fireplace, to harden it before he's tempted to tinker with it further.

He's using a swan quill. The bird's flight feather, from its right wing, arcs perfectly over his own right hand as he settles himself at his desk. He pulls his notes toward him. Broadly, he can remember what the witness said anyway. It was only an hour ago that he sat quietly in the corner of the room, scribbling down the gist of the boy's responses to the examining magistrate's questions. He inspects the nib. It has cooled quickly in the midwinter air, so he dips it into the inkwell.

Every new pen needs to be tested first. Even the slightest error in its cut and shape can result in a scratchy, uneven flow, or blotches and thick, clumsy-looking letters. He takes a sheet of parchment and touches the nib to it. The magistrate was clear that he had to use good-quality goat parchment, not paper. This is a record that will exist in perpetuity. He is momentarily thrilled to think that the very words he is writing now could be read for hundreds of years to come. He begins, holding his breath as the letters emerge, allowing himself a smile when he sees that they are fluid and smooth.

> This is the confession of persons of low rank against Mistress Nádasdy, Erzsébet Báthory, on the second of January 1611 in the county town of Bytča where an assembly was held. First János Újváry, otherwise known as Ficzkó, gave the following confession to the questions in order.

He exhales, glances anxiously at the light. There are eleven questions in all and the transcript needs to be copied before the next interrogation. But he need not write out literally *everything* the witness said, surely? There was a bit of to-ing and fro-ing about some of the questions, he recalls. Hardly surprising, as the boy was in a sorry state. At least the first question is quick.

> First: How long has he lived with the lady, and how did he come to her court?
> Answer: Sixteen years, if not longer, he lived with the lady, having been brought to Čachtice by Mistress Deak, taken there by force.

A strange start to a life, the scrivener thinks. The boy looks barely more than sixteen now, but then torture can do that. It shrinks you, diminishes you. He looked like a street urchin when he was answering the questions, the kind of waif you might see begging in a market square. He almost wishes they'd asked him what he meant by "taken there by force," as it was a curious thing to say. Still, if they had, there would be more to write, and he wouldn't want that.

Second: From that time hence, how many girls and women had been killed?
Answer: He doesn't know about any women, but of girls he knows thirty-seven while he was with her. He buried five in a pit, two in a small garden, and one under a drain. Two were taken into the church by night and they were buried there. They were taken there from the castle because that is where they were killed. Mistress Dorka killed them.

Only yesterday he had been writing a letter on behalf of a disgruntled farmer whose neighbor's cattle were grazing on his fields. It seems bizarre to have gone from that to this, a tale as diabolical as any he has heard before. His pen catches on the word *killed*, making the nib twitch. He pushes on. Neither he nor his pen are allowed to balk at the words it is their job to write.

Third: Who were they that she had killed and where were they from?
Answer: He does not know whose daughters they were.

The scrivener has a daughter himself. As he replenishes his pen in the inkwell, he makes a mental note to hold her close when he finally gets home.

Fourth: In what ways were these same women and girls enticed and brought to the castle?
Answer: Six times he himself, with Mistress Dorka, went to look for girls, and the girls were promised that they would either marry a merchant or that they would be brought somewhere to work as a servingwoman. Mistress Ilona also brought enough. Kata never brought any but merely buried those whom Dorka had killed.

He shudders. There was a time, when his daughter was about thirteen, that his wife wanted her to find a position at Čachtice, but he refused to allow it. The girl has a fine mind and a steady hand. He is quite convinced she has the skill and patience to be a scrivener herself. A female scribe is not such a rare beast, despite what his wife says.

Fifth: By what torture and what manner did they kill these poor
unfortunates?
Answer: They tied the arms of the girls with Viennese cord, like the color
of death their hands were. They were beaten on the flat of the hands and
the soles of the feet—as many as five hundred blows.

Here he has to set down his pen. Instinctively, he crosses himself,
as if evil flowed through his pen with the ink itself. He is not a super-
stitious man—on the contrary, he is a scrivener notary and works with
words and facts and logic—but there must be the devil at work here.
Perhaps it is time to take a break. He eyes the bread and cheese by
his desk. It seems a meager repast when the task is so demanding, but
he should eat something, for this afternoon he will note the women's
evidence. He bites off a piece of bread, but it feels thick and heavy in
his mouth, so he pushes the plate away.

Sixth: Who assisted in the killing and torturing?
Answer: There is a lady who is known as Mistress Ilona, the wife of
the bald coachman, who also tortured maids. She pricked them with a
needle if the lace was not tight. If they didn't take off their hair covering,
if they did not start the fire, if they did not lay the apron straight: They
were immediately taken by the old women and tortured to death. The old
women burned them with the fire iron and she herself stuck pins into
the mouth, the nose, and the chin of the girls. If their needlework was
not completed by ten o'clock in the evening, so they were brought into the
torture chamber. The Sittkey girl was punished because she stole a pear.

Instead of moving on to the next question, he finds himself rereada-
ing that last sentence. By this point in the witness's evidence, there
had been quite some discussion as to whom, exactly, the witness was
referring. Was it the countess, or Mistress Dorka? He found it hard
to follow, especially as they had started early, and he had not yet had
so much as a glass of ale to fortify himself. He has to confess that he
lost track a little of who was saying or doing what. He pulls his notes

toward him and rereads them carefully. They are no help. The third-person pronoun is the same whether he has noted the actions of a man, a woman, or a dog. This lack of clarity is not his fault. He prides himself on being a craftsman of words, but he can use only the tools the language gives him.

If the examining magistrate were anyone other than Theodore Syrmiensis he would not worry so much, but Syrmiensis is a very exacting man, not to mention a great personal friend of Thurzó's. The evidence must be entirely . . . *clear*. Ever since he started writing he has had a niggling thought: What if Syrmiensis is displeased with the transcript he produces? What if he refuses to pay him for the work? He is on his fourth sheet of expensive parchment already, every page now covered in his laborious hand. He cannot risk it all being for nothing.

The scrivener takes hold of his penknife again. With the tip of the blade he is able to scrape off the surface layer of the parchment. As he does, the word *punished* is erased, letter by letter. True, his notes do say *punished*, but "punished" could mean anything, and what mistress is not allowed to punish a thieving servant? He blows on the page, brushes away the fragments; *killed*, he writes instead, albeit a little stretched to fill the space. There, it's much clearer now.

> Seventh: Where did they bury the dead bodies? Who hid the bodies and where were they taken?
> Answer: The old woman hid and buried the girls here in Čachtice. He, the accused, helped to bury four of them, accompanied by singing. When the old women killed one of the girls, the mistress gave them presents. She herself tore the faces and other parts of the bodies of these girls and pricked them under their nails. After that, the tortured girl was taken into the frost-covered field and splashed with water by the old women. She herself also poured water over the girl, who froze and died.

Who is *she*? he wonders. In his notes, he has used the word *asszony*, as he would when referring to any married woman, but now that he comes to interpret them, he realizes that it is unclear whether the witness was referring to Erzsébet Báthory, Mistress Dorka, or, indeed, another woman. He has added *herself* in a few places, for emphasis, where he thinks the witness must surely have meant the disgraced countess.

Eighth: Did the woman herself torture them and what did she do when she had them killed?
Answer: When she herself did not torture, she took them to the old women, who put them in the coal storage for a week without food. If someone secretly gave them food, that person would be immediately punished.

Again, a woeful lack of clarity, which rankles with his rather precise nature. He wishes the magistrate had pressed the witness on this point rather than let him go off on a tangent about the old women again. Still, they don't have much time for this investigation, and all that really matters is that they have the confession. Its detail is not as important as the weight it adds to the body of evidence, overall. Besides, the boy was flagging by that point. He struggled so much to get the words out that the scrivener had almost walked over and given him a sip of water himself. It seemed the least that could be done for him.

Ninth: In what sort of places were the poor ones tortured and killed?
Answer: At Bekov they were tortured in the chamber next to the wash-kitchen. In Sárvár they were torturing in the inner part of the castle where no one was allowed to go. In Keresztúr they were torturing in the privy, and at Čachtice they were torturing inside the furnace house. When they were on a journey, at that time she herself tortured in the carriage. She was beating them and pinching and pricking the girls' mouths with a needle.

The scrivener interlaces his fingers and bends them inside out, sighing with the intensity of the stretch. Recently, he has noticed that his fingers are beginning to look like twigs, knobbly and angular. It is almost as if they are molding themselves around his quill, as a vine grows around a trunk. He cannot help a rueful smile coming to his lips. One day he will be so welded to his pen that they will have to bury him holding it.

Tenth: Who, of important people, knew or saw the deeds of the lady? Answer: Court Master Benedek Deseő knew best over the others, but he, the accused, did not hear the gentleman say anything about it. It was also common knowledge among the servants. There was also a person called Ironhead Stefan, now beyond the Danube, who recently left the lady's service. He was aware of everything—much better informed than the witness himself—and he had been playing freely with the woman. This man had carried more to be buried, but the witness does not know whither.

The scrivener frowns. He has no idea who this Stefan is. He has just appeared, suddenly, yet seems to have been very involved. Perhaps . . . too involved? When the witness had said that this man had been *playing freely* with the woman, the scrivener had paused his note taking, quite taken aback. Did he mean that he . . . No, he cannot articulate the thought, even in his own head. Surely the countess was not . . . Or was she? It is a very strange comment, and impossible to interpret, so it is just as well that he is there only to make a record of the statement. He has set out what the witness said, verbatim, and whether he meant that this man literally played children's games with the countess (personally, he finds the thought unlikely) or whether he meant something else entirely, well, that is for others to ponder.

In truth, he is quite relieved that the witness did not elaborate on the widow's indiscretions. Unpalatable as the facts of this case are, at least he does not have to write out pages and pages of lurid whoredom. In his experience, allegations against women tended to fall into three categories—he finds himself actually ticking them off on his fingers (it's a little odd, but he spends a lot of time alone): infanticide, witchcraft, and sexual impropriety. Mass murder is most unusual but, he supposes, it would be hard to countenance the typical weaknesses of her sex in a widow of fifty.

Eleventh: For how long were they aware of the woman's terrible deeds?
Answer: Even when the master was alive she had been torturing girls,
but in those days she did not kill them as she now did. Then later the
lady became more cruel. Something like a pretzel was kept in a box,
with a mirror in the middle, before which she prayed for two hours.
Dori Majorosné, the Mistress of Myjava, prepared some water and at
about four o'clock brought this water for the woman to bathe herself in.
The water, along with other mixtures, was blended in a washtub where
something was put into it. They baked a sort of bread which they wanted
the king, my lord palatine, and also Imre Megyeri to eat and, thus, poison
them. But these lords recognized this enchantment and moved against the
woman, because as they ate from the first baking, they complained of their
stomachs, and she then did not dare arrange the second baking.

There, finished, and it is only just midday (as far as he can tell from
the position of what must be the sun in that turbulent sky). He cracks
the bones of his hands again, resetting them, ready for the afternoon's
work. He must wait for the ink to dry before he stacks the pages together, so he sits there a moment rereading the words. Strange, given
the nature of the crimes, that the longest passage he had to write was
about a pretzel. Still, the references to witchcraft were almost inevitable and, now, something like treason to boot. He wonders what
Syrmiensis will think of the confession, whether he has what he needs.
One thing the scrivener is sure of, though, is that the boy gave them
everything. He was broken completely, mind and body. At the end of
the interrogation, they had to carry him out. The scrivener tried not
to look—it saddened him to see a young man so pitiful. Almost as an
afterthought, he dips his nib once more and makes the appropriate
marginalia to the confession: *et tortura*.

Chapter 31

LET THE MASTER ANSWER

Ilona Jó wishes that Dorka would stop talking. Fear has made her garrulous. Loose words tumble out of her like dislodged stones scattering down a hillside. Ilona sees every one as dangerous. Once they are out, they cannot be controlled and the momentum they gain will trip them all up. At least Kata is quiet. She has always been one to keep her own counsel.

"How long have you lived with the lady, and how did you come to her court?" the examining magistrate asks Dorka in an attempt to focus her ramblings on the eleven questions through which they have to get.

"Mistress Ilona lured me to the castle with beautiful words," she replies, blinking like an ingénue. "She told me that I would be taken on by the countess's daughter Lady Drugeth."

Ilona tries not to listen to her. It would have been better, she thinks, if they had been interrogated separately, like Ficzkó. At least then they would not have had to sit and listen to each other's petty betrayals and to have former friends witness their own. The whole procedure reminds Ilona of the tale of the blind men and the pig. Four blind men were each given sticks and put into a pen with a pig. Each man was told that if he could kill the pig, he could eat it. So they all set about trying to kill the pig, while the people of the town stood around enjoying the spectacle. The four blind men are now busy beating one another with the sticks, while the pig—representing any hope of freedom—sits in the corner watching them.

The examining magistrate moves on to the second question, which Ilona is to answer first: "How many girls has she killed?"

Ilona shrugs, says she doesn't know. The magistrate stares hard at her. "She has killed enough," she says, avoiding his gaze.

"Thirty-six," responds Dorka, sounding quite emphatic.

"I was the washerwoman," says Kata. "I do not know how many."

Theodore Syrmiensis does not like Kata's answer. He glances from left to right at the magistrates who sit either side of him, Kaspar Bájaky and Kaspar Kardoss. Syrmiensis asks Kata if he should bring back the magister torturarum?

Kata visibly contracts, like an oyster, shucked. The *hóhér* has written himself into all their bodies. He is in every pop and crack of their joints, every opening of their skin. When they speak, he sighs through every word.

"It could be fifty that the lady killed," she says, her voice devoid of any emotion. The magistrate gives the scribe a quick nod as if to say, *Make sure you make a note of that.*

But first, Syrmiensis needs to be clear on the basics: Who did what, to whom?

"Ficzkó would slap the girls' faces whenever he was told to," Ilona says. "Dorka cut the girls' flesh with pincers."

Dorka's face turns an indignant red. "For shame," she says, glaring at Ilona. "This lady knows well enough that I was *ordered* to hurt those poor girls so." She gives Syrmiensis a pleading look. "What could I have done, sir? Me, a lowly servant, told to commit such shameful acts by my exalted mistress?"

Syrmiensis's face remains impassive. Dorka turns to Kata, tries to point at her, but she winces and takes back her arm, cradling it. "What about her?" Dorka whines like a child who doesn't want to take the blame. "When the girls died, she dragged their bodies into the wheat pit!"

"Do not dare point your finger at me," Kata spits at her. "If my crime was to give the girls some kind of burial, then I own my guilt. What should I have done, left them to rot? But I never hurt them, though you tried to make me, Dorka, many times." Kata turns, furious, to the magistrate. "I was beaten myself when I refused to do it. I once spent a whole month in bed because of the beating I suffered!"

Syrmiensis holds up his hands. He needs to focus the confessants on the bestial acts of the lady herself, not allow them to bicker with each other. "But did the woman herself torture the girls?" he insists.

Ilona answers first. "The lady heated a key and burned the hand of a girl," she says.

That is not nearly enough for Syrmiensis. "Go on," he urges.

"She also did the same with coins when the girls were found with them and did not give them to the lady."

Syrmiensis's expression is pinched, as if frustrated to have his time wasted by such trivialities. "Knives," he says, "pincers, tongs: What of these things?"

Ilona thinks for a moment. There was a knife, she remembers. Right after the ridiculous puppet show the boy arranged. Perhaps the magistrate wants to hear about that?

"I did see the lady hold a knife to a girl's face once," she tells him.

Syrmiensis nods, encouraging her. This is exactly what he wants to hear.

"She was quite furious with the girl, I know not why."

"She lost her temper often, I believe," Syrmiensis clarifies for her.

Ilona shrugs. "I have never met a noble who didn't. Keeping your temper is a skill only the lower orders are obliged to master."

Syrmiensis tuts, impatient. "Did she murder the girl?"

Ilona shakes her head, no.

"Mutilate her, then?"

"There was blood," recalls Ilona, "but . . ."

"But what?"

"Something stopped her from cutting the girl. She just pushed her away in the end."

Syrmiensis draws in a slow breath. "It appears that you are not yet *ready* to make a full confession," he tells Ilona carefully. "Am I right? In which case, the *hóhér* clearly has further work to do."

Ilona shifts in her seat. It is impossible to get comfortable after what happened the day before. The pain lingers, crouches next to her like the gargoyles on the castle walls. She cannot go back to the *hóhér*. Whatever will happen in the future, she cannot go back to that.

"I . . ." she begins. "I did not recall correctly. It was hard to see what she did because there was so much blood. She maimed the girl, yes. Cut her face with the knife, flayed her like a rabbit." Is that enough? she wonders, searching Syrmiensis's face. She realizes now that there is no way out. Not one of them will ever get that pig. The best she can do is give them what they want and get it all over and done with as soon as possible.

"What else?" asks Syrmiensis.

Ilona takes a resigned breath. "She stripped them naked and made them stand before her," she says, her voice monotone, as if she were recounting the precise sequence of crossing and twisting for one of her lace patterns. "There was so much blood that it saturated the lady's clothes so she had to change. It covered the walls and was so thick on the floor that cinders had to be spread to soak it all up."

Syrmiensis's eyes widen and his tongue slides over his lips, as if he could taste the blood himself.

Dorka sees exactly what Ilona is doing: She is trying to turn herself into the helpful one! No, Dorka will not have it. Ever since she was looking after Jacob, and Ilona came to suckle the new baby of the landowner's wife all those years ago, Dorka has suspected that Ilona considers herself above her. It was Ilona who knew the countess first, Ilona who was wet nurse to her children, Ilona who had the lady's ear in all matters. It was as if Dorka were no better than an inconsequential servant. But Dorka knows this isn't true. The countess *loves* her. Beneath the conventions of rank and status that dictate their every move, there is real friendship, not that Ilona would ever give her credit for it. It almost feels as if Dorka has had to compete with Ilona for everything—their mistress's affections, the highest status in the lady's household—and she competes with her still. Dorka is convinced that at least one of them will be set free. There is simply no need to execute them all. The boy has no hope, of course, but a woman can expect more lenient treatment. What is the advantage of her sex, after all, if not that?

But Dorka, Ilona, and Kata are all women, and all in their later years. She will not be freed because she is more pathetic than Ilona or Kata but because she has been the most forthcoming. She doesn't like the fact that the lips of the typically taciturn Ilona are loosening. Thurzó must read the confessions and know that only Dorka delivered everything she promised. And more.

"Sir, I should like to tell you something," she begins.

Syrmiensis swivels his eyes toward her, drawn by the insistent sound of her voice. "Go on," he says.

"Once, at Čachtice, the lady was sick a-bed and too ill to punish the girls. She told me to bring one to her bedside." Dorka pauses, aware that the room has gone quiet. All that can be heard is the scratching of the scribe's pen as he catches up with her words. "The lady reached up from her sickbed and grabbed hold of the girl, then bit lumps of flesh from her face and shoulders with her own teeth."

Dorka sits back, quite breathless. Even she is not quite sure where that came from, but she is pleased to see the scribe scribbling furiously and the magistrate's nod of grim satisfaction. She glances at her follow accomplices. Surely, she thinks with a sense of triumph, not one of them will be able to do any better than that.

It takes only another hour to hear the confessants' answers to all eleven questions. When they are finished, the scrivener leans back in his chair and inhales deeply. Interesting that none of the women mentioned Stefan Ironhead, despite his supposed intimate involvement. Who Stefan is or, indeed, if he exists at all is a mystery that will likely never be solved. Otherwise, the weight of evidence seems chillingly clear. Such was the witnesses' consistency that, for many questions, he will only have to write *Declares as the others said*, rather than copy out all that tedious detail again. And if it is still slightly unclear which acts belonged to the countess herself and which to her devilish servants, then it no longer matters. Their guilt is her guilt. *Respondeat superior*, reads his marginalia. Let the master answer.

Chapter 32

Paragon of Evil

Taking care not to splash the sheets of paper with hot cinnamon water, Boróka makes her way up the winding stone steps. She carries writing materials, beeswax candles, and the countess's favorite breakfast. As she nears the top, it occurs to her that it was not so long ago that she stood for the first time under the kitchen's vaulted ceiling while Dorka told her that she was too lowly to bring the countess her morning refreshments. But now there are none of the countess's most trusted servants left to do it. The corridors do not ring with Dorka's admonishments. Ilona does not silently glide into view, ready to anticipate her mistress's every whim. There is no lingering smell of sandalwood or lavender in the washhouse to tell her that Kata had been there moments before. There is only Boróka, her arms full of whatever comforts she can find to give to a woman who now thinks a pen and paper as precious as the emeralds that once circled her throat.

Contrary to what is being said down in the *kastély*, the countess is not still imprisoned in the dungeons or bricked up in a turret. She is, in fact, confined to modest apartments in the castle, and the only thing that gives away her drastic change of circumstances is the armed guard who bars Boróka's way.

"I bring essential supplies for the countess," she tells him, offering up the potage of honey and brandied figs for inspection. He glances at it, frowns, lets her through.

It is still early, but the countess is already up. She stands at the window gazing out, not over the orchards but at a bleak, northerly landscape.

"I brought you the things you wanted, my lady," says Boróka, setting the paper and a bottle of ink on a small desk near the window. "And some breakfast," she adds. "I wasn't sure if those attending you would know what you like."

The countess turns and Boróka hands her the hot cinnamon water. Without saying anything, the countess cups it in her hands, bends her head, and inhales the warm, spicy scent that lifts from the surface. "I'll put the potage on the table for you, my lady," Boróka says. "Is there anything else you need?"

Boróka turns back to her mistress. Perhaps it is the mist of steam, but the countess's eyes seem to glisten. Boróka becomes brisk, thinks what Dorka might say to distract her. "I'll stoke up the fire for you," she says. "It's cold as a fish in here." This way Boróka is able to politely turn her back on her mistress. If the countess is tearful, Boróka doesn't want to see it. She needs her to be as indomitable as always, because that is the only way in which Boróka can hold herself together.

"Sweet Boróka," she hears the countess begin, but Boróka just pokes robustly at the logs in the fire, lets their spitting, crackling response save her from hearing the strongest woman she knows sound so vulnerable. "There," she says, standing up and dusting fragments of ash from her hands, "you should be warmer in no time."

The cinnamon water must have fortified her, as the countess's cheeks are pink. "Do you know what they did to me?" she asks.

Boróka suspects she does know. As soon as Thurzó had left, the *kastély* was invaded again, by rumors.

"No, mistress," says Boróka, to spare her feelings.

"They followed me up the hill," she says. "On the night I was arrested, the townsfolk gathered behind me *gloating* as I was led up to the castle. They were mocking me, calling out despicable things. These people whom I have tried to defend and protect." She swings around to point to her desk, slopping cinnamon water over the lip of her cup.

"How many times have I penned letters for them about their stolen chickens or unwed daughters? But they care not a groat for any of that. It was as if they delight in my misfortunes!"

It would not help matters to suggest to the countess that she is not as popular among the townsfolk as she might think. Instead, Boróka says, "It serves no purpose to think on that now."

"No, it does not, yet I am haunted by it. Whenever I close my eyes, all I can see is their leering faces." The countess's voice sounds splintered. It suggests the countess herself is feeling just as brittle.

"What news of Ilona and Kata?" she asks.

"Still in Bytča," Boróka responds, "awaiting trial."

"And Ficzkó the same?"

"Yes."

The countess does not ask after Dorka and nor does Boróka expect her to. She saw the look of disgust on the countess's face when Dorka prostrated herself at Thurzó's feet, as quick to turn her colors as a ptarmigan in winter.

"Have they . . . *interrogated* them?"

Boróka nods.

"How wretched," whispers the countess bitterly. What now of her servants' *absolute discretion?* Who can manage to *see nothing, hear nothing, and say nothing* when it is the magister torturarum who is asking?

"Madam, you need someone to support you." Without her confidantes, whom does the countess have to comfort her? Boróka thinks quickly. "Your daughter Anna," she ventures, "or a priest, perhaps?"

She soon wishes she had not suggested a priest. The countess inhales sharply and her eyes flash with the same indignation Boróka has seen so often before. Though she braces for the outburst, Boróka is relieved to see her mistress reinvigorated.

"They have already sent me that treacherous Lutheran Ponikenus!" she exclaims. "He came on New Year's Eve, with Reverend Zacharias, when they held me in my own dungeons, would you believe? They claimed they had come to console me with prayers and to *protect me from temptation.*" The way the countess labors the last words makes

Boróka flinch. There is only one temptation to which a woman who has lost everything might succumb. "But I told them that *they* were the reason for my grievous imprisonment. All this began with the lies they preached against me! I told them they would die for it, along with Megyeri, no doubt, when the uprising begins."

"Uprising, my lady?"

"Indeed." The countess nods vigorously. "East of the Tisza an uprising will start and they will be here as soon as the weather allows. I am expecting my cousin in Transylvania to take revenge for the terrible injustice done to me."

The countess sinks down onto a chair at the table as if exhausted by the battles raging in her head. "The priests denied being the cause of my troubles, of course. They tried to give me a prayer book, but I refused it. Instead, I told them to look upon me and judge for themselves what sinful soul might be inside this paragon of evil!"

Boróka crouches down beside her mistress. "What care you for what these reverend lords think? You must look to the future and how to clear your name."

"And how do you think I can do that?" The countess turns and gives her an incredulous stare. "I have been arrested and imprisoned, with no formal summons and no trial. I have asked for the opportunity to speak for myself in court, as is my God-given right, but Thurzó will not allow it. How can it be that he accuses me of such heinous crimes, yet denies me the chance to defend my honor?"

Boróka responds with silence to a question she cannot answer. The countess looks away. "The others have confessed, I am sure," she says quietly.

Boróka nods.

"I do not blame them, you know," she says. Then her face hardens. "Except Dorka. I most certainly do blame her. She indulged her proclivities at my expense and is as culpable in all this as Thurzó and Megyeri."

"She will have to answer for herself at the trial, as they all will," says Boróka.

"When is it?"

"The seventh of January."

The countess scoffs. "How remarkable that they are able to arrange a full trial immediately after Christmastide with only a few days' notice. Why, it is almost as if they had the whole thing planned!"

The door opens, and the guard tells Boróka she must leave. For a brief moment, the countess looks bereft. "Oh, my lady," says Boróka, taking hold of the countess's hand. "How I hate to leave you alone."

The countess rallies, forces herself to smile. "But I am not alone," she says. "Hans Sachs is with me, and Niccolò Machiavelli." She plucks her hand from Boróka's and stands up. "Look," she says, striding over to her desk and picking up a copy of *Orlando Furioso*, "here is Ariosto. They have allowed me to keep some books, at least, so you see, I am in quite wonderful company."

"I fear they are not enough, mistress."

"Ah, but you forget that I also have my words! The one thing that even Thurzó cannot take from me." The countess sits down at the desk, still clutching Ariosto to her chest. "If they will not let me speak, then I shall write. I will send as many letters as it takes to force Thurzó to allow me a fair trial."

Chapter 33

BRIDLE THY TONGUE, WOMAN

Marta counts the men she can see in front of her. She does it slowly, focusing on something about each as she does so. *One*, the man with eyebrows like the black caterpillars she finds hidden in dandelion greens; *two*, the man wearing a dolman the same bright orange as the exposed flesh of the winter squash she peels for the cook; *three*, the man who twitches like the courtyard cat, asleep in the sunshine. She does it because it calms her, helps her to find glimpses of her familiar life in this strange place.

When she gets to ten, she stops. There are no more numbers left, so she has to start over at one again. By the time she has counted every man, she has used all the numbers twice over. That means there are ten-twice-over men in the jury.

They have told her that they want to ask her some questions. She is not in any trouble herself, they explained. But Marta cannot stop thinking about the Highest Legal Authority, how he raged and swirled his cloak around him, like a wizard from the stories that Kata has told her. What if she doesn't give the correct answers to the questions they will ask? What if she cannot even get the words out?

That is why it's very important to concentrate. There is a man—Závodsky, the "prosecutor," he said he was—who is telling the jury that *the lord palatine has acted to protect the goodly and the innocent*

239

and bring the widow Nádasdy's inhuman crimes to an end. He had gone, this prosecutor says, *in the company of the knight Imre Megyeri and the lord palatine to Čachtice, where he surprised Countess Báthory in the act of torturing her victims. One girl was already dead and two others were nearby, dying.*

Strange, thinks Marta, because at the very moment these men burst into the great hall, Marta had been sent in to help with the main course. She screws her eyes shut, tries to bring the scene back to life. She can remember the salty, fishy smell of the oyster shells she cleared away, heaped like autumn leaves on the platter. Then there was the spicy tingle on her tongue when she dipped her finger into the *paprikás* and sucked it, to taste the dish, before she set it on the servants' table. She stares hard into the memory; no, there are definitely no dead or dying girls there. In fact, all she sees now are the pretty paper flowers, but when she tries to look closely at them they are blown off the mantelpiece by a chill breeze and trampled by boots with jangling spurs.

The prosecutor is reading something out. Marta was trying so hard to remember the night the men came that she didn't hear him say what it was, but it seems to be a list of questions about killing girls, along with answers that make her want to close her ears. Závodsky takes the topmost sheet of parchment and slots it behind the rest. *Next,* he says, *is the confession of Dorottya Szentes.*

Marta doesn't want to look at her, but she can't help it, because she is sitting right in front of her. Every so often Dorka tries to catch her eye, gives her a pleading smile, which only makes her feel uneasy because Dorka never usually looks at her like that. Marta shifts her eyes to Kata instead, sitting in between Dorka and the boy. She adds the smile Kata gives her to her list of Reassuringly Familiar Things.

Once the prosecutor has read out all the confessions, he asks Dorka, Ficzkó, Kata, and Ilona if they have anything further to add. They all reply, with varying degrees of indignation or resignation, that they were forced to do what they did.

Marta's palms are beginning to feel slippery. Her hand creeps toward her apron tie and she loops her forefinger around the string.

While the prosecutor speaks she circles her finger around, so that the tie draws tighter and tighter. It must be soon, she thinks.

There, he said it: her name. It's time for her to get up. She feels lofty when she stands, as if she were the figure atop a weather vane, spinning, giddy, in the wind. She wants to squat down to safety on the floor, creep up to the witness chair like a spider, but she knows she must not. It seems like a throne to her, with its high back and scrolled arms. Surely, the likes of her should not be sitting on it, yet, in a moment, there she is, lowering herself down. The upholstered seat feels both wonderful and wrong, like the sweet taste of an apple strudel she once stole from the kitchen.

The prosecutor approaches her. Under her skirts, where no one can see it, she twists her apron string once more around her finger. The pain anchors her, lessens the spinning sensation in her head. The prosecutor wants her to tell the ten-twice-over men sitting in the room who she is and what she does at Čachtice. As if any of them should pay any mind to a scullion! At least the questions are easy, and a simple nod the only answer required. She cannot look at the prosecutor directly, so she fixes her eyes on the collar of his shirt. Something tugs at the corner of her vision. It's Dorka again, sitting bolt upright and blinking at her, expectant as a dog hoping for a scrap.

"Tell me," says the prosecutor, "did you ever see any dead girls while you worked at Čachtice?"

Marta has never had a mother, at least, not one she can remember. Or a father, for that matter. But that doesn't mean she doesn't know right from wrong. She always tells the truth. Well, not *always*. Admittedly, when the cook noticed that apple strudel was missing and asked her if she knew anything about it, she shook her head without looking up from the boiled turnips she was mashing. But, apart from that, she says what she believes to be true.

"Well?" The prosecutor's voice sounds impatient. It makes Marta's jaw tense, as if he were about to strike her. How will the words get out now?

Marta nods. It is enough of a yes for the prosecutor, who nods back, pleased.

"Had the girls been tortured?"

Marta shakes her head, no.

The prosecutor frowns. "But there were marks on the bodies, correct?"

Marta tries to find the word. It is in there, somewhere, she just needs to get it out. She looks at Kata, who gives her the tiniest nod of encouragement.

"S-sick," she says.

"Sick?"

The juryman in the orange dolman sighs, exasperated. "This woman is a half-wit," he says. "We shall be here all day, and there are twelve more witnesses to hear."

The prosecutor ignores him and presses on. "Did the countess murder the girls?"

Marta shakes her head. More men in the jury start to murmur and rustle. To Marta, they are like one shifting, malevolent creature.

"But she was there, was she not, with the dying girls?"

Marta thinks hard. She remembers the noble girl in the dungeons, the one whose skin was so shiny smooth she looked like her own tomb effigy when they laid her on the examination table. After that she was under the table with a bowl full of blood. Did the satin slippers she saw belong to the countess? She can't think who else's they could have been. No, they *must* have been the countess's because she remembers she heard her say that she was fond of the girl.

Marta nods. She's clear now that the answer to that question is yes.

The prosecutor flashes a triumphant glance at the jury. "Have the scribe note that the witness nodded her agreement to the fact that the countess was there with the dying girls." He turns back to Marta. "Did the countess touch the girl?"

Marta thinks hard. She must have, because at one point the forest witch became quite agitated and told her to leave the girl alone. Marta nods, yes.

"As part of our investigations in relation to the cruel deeds of Mistress Nádasdy we heard evidence from a witness called János Sl'uka, who said that he was sent to obtain poisons from the pharmacist at Trnava.

He told us that the poison purchased was antimony and that the pharmacist, Dr. Martin, had asked him why such a large quantity was needed, because it could kill many people. Did the countess, or any of her accomplices, ever poison the girls with antimony?"

Marta would be the first to admit that she understands little of the world. She is, as the juryman said, a half-wit, every bit the *picsa* that Dorka so often called her. Nevertheless, she has always wondered how antimony could be considered a medicine given its unpleasant effects. But her job was not to decide on the treatment, only to sift through the shit to find the expensive pellet so it could be reused. But is it *poison?* She doesn't know. Is that even what the man asked? Does he want to know whether antimony is a poison, or whether the countess gave it to the girls? She can't even remember, so she screws her eyes shut and twirls the apron string around her finger, pulls it tight.

"Were the girls given antimony?" the prosecutor insists.

Marta opens one eye, a tiny bit. That makes it simpler. Yes, Marta nods.

The prosecutor turns to the jury. "This witness has confirmed that the girls were indeed poisoned by the countess with antimony."

Despite her cushioned seat, Marta is beginning to feel uncomfortable. She must have misunderstood what she is doing here. She had thought that it was the four accomplices who were on trial, but the questions make her feel like it is the countess who is being judged. Marta looks around nervously. Does that mean that the countess is here, watching her somewhere in the crowd? She shifts around in her seat. She has spent her whole life completely invisible to countesses and Highest Legal Authorities. Why are they all so interested in her now? The thought that any of them would turn their lofty gaze toward her makes her squirm like a worm in plain sight of the owl. She glances at Kata for reassurance but sees that her smile is gone. She casts about for something else that feels even the slightest bit comforting, finds nothing. She doesn't think that the countess *is* actually watching her, yet she feels she must say *something*, because what the prosecutor said is not really what she meant.

"I," she says. Stops. Starts again. "I—"

"You . . . what?" says the prosecutor.

"I told you," shouts out the juryman the color of winter squash, "she's a simpleton."

She cannot find the words. In desperation she looks at Kata again and is appalled to see swollen teardrops brim at her eyelids and roll down her cheeks. Kata lifts her hands toward her face, but her wrists are in shackles that grate and clink. She bends her cheek to the back of her hand and manages to wipe away a tear.

Marta feels panic seeping through her bones, like the January cold when she has to sleep on the kitchen flagstones. Kata must be upset with her, or she wouldn't be crying. Kata has never, ever been angry with her before. Well, she was a little annoyed about the apple strudel, but she never would have taken one if she'd known Kata made them! And anyway, it wasn't really Marta's fault; Kata's strudels are simply irresistible—the whole castle finds them so. Marta begins to rise, lifting herself off this ridiculous chair on which she should never have sat. She wants to creep away and never have to look at Kata's sad face again. What more can they want with her, anyway, when she is getting it all so wrong?

"Sit down," says the prosecutor, his voice low and growly. Marta freezes, lowers herself back down. She winds the apron string again, but it doesn't even hurt any more, it's just numb. She unwinds it all, waits for the blood to bring the pain back.

"Now to the accomplices," says the prosecutor. "Which of the four you see before you murdered the girls?"

Dorka shoots up from her seat, unable to contain herself any longer. "Little Marta," she pleads, "was I not always kind to you? Did I not feed you? Take care of you? Help me now, little one, help me!"

Dorka is pushed back onto her seat by a guard.

"You may point, if you wish," the prosecutor tells Marta.

Marta's arm feels heavy. It is as hard to lift as the huge poker that leans against the fireplace in the *kástely*'s great hall. Yet lift it she does, though it wavers and shakes a little. She turns her head, so that she can see her only out of the very corner of her eye, then points directly at Dorka.

"Good," says the prosecutor. "Let the scribe note that the witness implicated Dorottya Szentes."

"She did not!" Dorka exclaims. "She was pointing at her!" Dorka swivels and jabs at Kata, so far as her shackled wrists will allow.

The prosecutor tuts and sighs. "Was it this one?" he asks, pointing at Dorka.

Marta winces, nods.

"She cannot be believed," shrieks Dorka, standing again. "The girl is dumb and softheaded, as the good juryman said!"

"Bridle thy tongue, woman!" the prosecutor says. "You have had your chance to speak."

Dorka sits back down, panting with rage and distress. "You ugly moth," she spits at Marta, once she has caught her breath.

"What about this one?" asks the prosecutor, pointing at Ilona Jó.

Marta shrugs. She was never allowed to do anything so refined as sewing.

"And this one?"

Ficzkó sits slumped in his chair, staring at the floor. His foot is stretched out in front of him and his shackled wrists rest between his thighs. When the prosecutor stands over him, only his eyes move, flicking up to his outstretched hand, before rolling down again as if even that were more effort than he can bear. Marta feels a pang of something. It emerges as pity but then hardens into something else, like a bead of blood clotting. She thinks how *carefully* she prepared the girls' bodies for their final journey, and how *carelessly* he dropped them into the ground; but that is not the same as murdering them himself. Marta should know: She has to mop up all kinds of messes, but that doesn't mean she *made* the mess.

Marta shrugs.

The prosecutor glances again at the jury before he steps in front of Kata and points at her. "This one?" he says, sounding a little weary.

Marta cannot leave this to chance. She needs to say something, make her answer absolutely clear. She closes her eyes, inhales deeply. When she forces her eyes open again, it is as if someone is staring right back at her. On the prosecutor's outstretched finger is a large ring. It is inlaid with a polished stone that has the same strange spiral as the pebbles she put on the eyes of the dead girl the Highest Legal Authority dug up. She seems to lock eyes with it, as if the dead girl were staring at her now, still astonished. *Why do you not say something to help your friend?*

Marta shakes her head, dislodges the words.

"N-not Kata," she manages to say.

Chapter 34

PROTECTOR OF
THE GOODLY AND
THE INNOCENT

In his offices at Bytča, Thurzó feels a creep of satisfaction. He picks up the papers in his hands, feels the weight of the evidence for himself. He is preparing a report to go to the king. He has confessions from all four of the countess's intimates, signed by the examining magistrates, and now their trial is underway. Theodore Syrmiensis is a good and loyal friend, he thinks, as he casts his eye over the document he prepared on the second of January, as chief magistrate. Also present are the signatures of Kaspar Bájaky and Kaspar Kardoss, both Thurzó's employees at Bytča. He makes a note to remember them for future promotions.

It would not do for Thurzó to be present at the accomplices' trial himself. This is a fully independent judicial process, after all. He merely made the case to answer; it is for others to determine the guilt, or otherwise, of the accused and the appropriate sentence. Still, he is certain that Závodsky is doing a rigorous job. He is Thurzó's secretary, and the attention to detail he brings to that role is second to none. He saw him briefly when they took lunch together. Apart from the scullion, who barely spoke a word, the evidence seems to be progressing in a most pleasing manner. One witness, György Kubanovich, has testified that he saw the corpse of the last murdered girl, covered in blue welts and burn marks, carried out in a trough while the Lady Nádasdy was being taken into custody, a fact confirmed by the four witnesses who followed him. Ladislas Centalovich has sworn to seeing injuries on girls still alive; and Tamás Zima has stated that two female servants of the lady were buried in the cemetery in Čachtice, with a third buried at Leszetice, specifically because the preacher at Čachtice challenged the murder. Nine witnesses so far, all strikingly consistent in their evidence.

Thurzó frowns, rubs his thumb and forefinger over the soft bristles of his beard. Although the evidence is compelling, it is vital that it be presented to the king in the best possible light. Of course, everyone is well aware how confessions are properly and lawfully extracted but, nonetheless, he wishes the scrivener had not written *et tortura* so prominently on the transcripts. He doubts he will use this scribe again. His copy is littered with annoying marginalia, when the man's only task was to write down what the witnesses said, word for word, without comments or observations of his own, whether on the state of the witnesses or the performance of his pen! Thurzó resolves to make additional clean copies of the evidence, both for the king and his own archives here at Bytča. In the meantime, he can resolve this current issue himself. He picks up his quill, dips it in ink, then strikes out the words *et tortura*.

She will not survive this, he thinks, as he gathers up the papers. For a moment, he allows himself to wonder what Ferenc Nádasdy would say if he could read the case he has put together to bring down his wife. It is only a fleeting thought, a momentary niggle that he easily dispels. His job is to grease the wheels for the king in Hungary, to smooth the ruffled feathers of disgruntled nobles. To that extent, he is more peacemaker than perpetrator. He knows that his old comrade in arms would understand that it was only right to sacrifice the Báthory wife in favor of the Nádasdy heirs.

And if he benefits himself, so be it. He unlocks his desk drawer and takes out the secret letters Count Zrínyi has written him. The first is dated December 17, 1610, almost two weeks before Thurzó stormed into Čachtice Castle and surprised the Lady Nádasdy in the very act of murder. He reads it again, to remind himself how delicate this matter is.

> I desire a peaceful conclusion to the affair and I hope that Lady Nádasdy will remain in that place in peace, and that the treasury will not confiscate the estates, but most importantly for the whole family that the gravest punishment, the loss of the fortune and the losing of one's head, shall not be applied. In truth, your lordship must remember our agreement. When we spoke face to face at that time we came to no agreement concerning the estates; and now you wish to divide those estates, but I am not prepared for that to be done. I am myself related to the family; therefore I want my portion, both on this side and on the far side of the Danube too.

Thurzó smiles to himself: How Count Zrínyi's entitled tone has changed by his most recent letter, the one he wrote knowing that the king had instructed Thurzó to immediately summon Lady Nádasdy to answer to her crimes. He reads this one too, just to make sure he has not misunderstood Count Zrínyi's intentions.

> In view of Mistress Nádasdy's terrible deeds, I must confess that, regarding a penalty, you have chosen the lesser of two evils. The judgment of your grace served us for the better, because it has preserved our honor and shielded us from too great a shame. When, in your letters, you made known to us the will of his royal majesty including punishment by horrible, judicial torture, we, her relatives, felt that we must all die of disgrace. But your grace, as a benevolent and truly loving brother, willing to prevent these shameful things from coming about, found the right solution whereby

she should be imprisoned forever. For your benevolence and
brotherliness we would desire to serve you until our death,
and we will do our utmost to show our gratitude to you.
Lifelong will I repay you.

Thurzó leans back in his chair, inhales deeply. *Lifelong will I repay
you.* There is no mistaking what that means. It will all be worth it in
the end.

Thurzó decides to walk past the courthouse to check that proceedings
have recommenced in a timely fashion. He soon wishes he had not, as
outside he sees the two girls who accosted him when he tried to leave
the lady's manor house. He sets his hat at an angle, tries to pretend he
hasn't noticed them.

"My Lord Palatine," says one, "a moment, sir, please."

Her voice is annoyingly pleading. And loud. People are looking,
and he doesn't want to appear anything other than the protector of
the goodly and the innocent that he has set himself up to be; so he
stops, forces himself to turn toward them.

How extraordinary! The girl drops to her knees at his feet. And it's
not even the common one. It is the noble girl who touches her hands
to his boots, an unlikely suppliant in such good-quality damask.

"Your grace," she says, tilting her pleasing oval face up to look at
him. "We have heard that the court hears evidence about the Countess Báthory today and have come to beg you to allow us to speak on
her behalf."

He sets his jaw. Not this again. He allowed the court hearing to
be public because he thought it could only help for as many people
as possible to be aware of the lady's terrible crimes. The less welcome
consequence of this is that it stirs up the zealots who insist on protesting her innocence.

"The witness schedule is already in place," he mutters, trying to
step around her.

"But, sir, we have important evidence that the court should hear."

Now the other one speaks, moving around from his flank to block his path. Really, these girls are like wolves hunting in pairs!

"What evidence?" he says, gritting his teeth.

"We have lived at Čachtice and attended the gynaeceum. We never saw the countess kill any girls."

"There is no time for more witnesses," he says, then presses on, the spurs on his boots jangling resolutely.

"But what about the marks?" says the noble girl. She is standing now, running alongside him with the sleeve of her mantle pulled up most indiscreetly. "I can tell the court that they were caused by disease, not torture."

"The fact that you are pockmarked tells us nothing about Widow Nádasdy," he tells her, rather unkindly.

"Why do you not let the countess speak herself?" asks the other. "She has the right to go on trial and defend herself."

At this he stops dead. The girls don't realize immediately, so both skitter on a few steps before they stop, turn around. In that moment, he takes a very deep breath.

"You have no idea of what you speak." He exhales each word, releasing both the breath and the irritation building inside him. "I have done everything I can to *prevent* Widow Nádasdy being made to stand trial. You think I do her a disservice but, in fact, I act only out of respect and love, both for her late husband and—yes, I admit it—even for her. If she stands trial the Nádasdy name will be publicly shamed. Her children will be disgraced and her sons-in-law along with them." He fixes the girls with an intense stare, rather enjoys the shock he sees in their eyes. "Even if you care nothing for them, think for a moment what will happen to the countess herself. She will almost certainly be convicted, in which case the *only* punishment can be death. By preventing a trial, I do not seek to silence her, but to protect her."

He is breathless by the time he finishes, surprised by the strength of his feelings. He has almost managed to forget that Erzsébet Báthory was ever anything more to him than that bestial woman. The girls are silent. He gives the noble girl a curt nod to signify their parting and is relieved when they both step aside.

As he passes the courtroom window he sees Závodsky on his feet again, addressing the jury. It is almost over, he reassures himself. Nine witnesses already examined and four more to hear this afternoon. Then the proceedings against the accomplices will be at an end.

Surely, now, there can be no surprises?

Chapter 35

THE TENTH WITNESS

The girl lays her hand on the Bible. "I swear," she says in a loud, clear voice.

Boróka and Orsolya jostle to see who the girl is. Tales of numerous murdered virgins attract people like raw meat attracts dogs, and the courthouse is heaving. They have had to go up some steps to the gallery and are pushing themselves toward the front. If Thurzó will not allow them to give evidence in the countess's defense, then the next best thing they can do is listen to what is being said about her and take that knowledge back to Čachtice.

"Forgive me," says Orsolya when she accidentally treads on a man's shoe. He glares at her but allows her to move in front of him. Rank has the power of Moses to part the waters. All Boróka has to do is follow in Orsolya's wake.

"I am a servant at Čachtice Castle," the girl is saying.

"Tell the court your name," replies Závodsky.

Boróka is almost at the balustrade. Orsolya shuffles to the side to make space and she steps forward, looks down upon the court below. The movement in the gallery makes the girl giving evidence look up, and for a brief moment she locks eyes with Boróka before she turns back to the prosecutor.

"My name is Suzanna," she says.

Boróka's hands close over the balustrade's top rail. She feels the need to steady herself. She has not seen Suzanna in weeks. She was not chosen to accompany the countess to the *kastély*, and when Boróka has been at Čachtice she has not seen her. The court settles, quiet now, and Boróka becomes aware of the strength of her heart beating and the words in her head accompanying its rhythm: *Why her, why her?*

"Tell the court which of the accused is known to you."

Suzanna turns toward the four accomplices. When her eyes settle on Ilona it is hard to tell if Suzanna looks horrified or thrilled. "All of them," she says, "but I worked mainly for Mistress Ilona Jó."

The prosecutor nods. "What did she have you do?"

"She made me sew, though I know not why, as I can sew about as well as a chicken makes honey."

Some of the men on the jury chuckle. Suzanna, with her building indignation and wispy wheat-ear hair, makes for an engaging witness.

"Did she ever mistreat you?"

Suzanna raises her hand to her mouth, touches the tip of her finger to her lip. "Yes, Mistress Ilona stuck a needle in my lip when I did not do the work."

Ilona has been almost silent throughout these proceedings. Unlike Dorka, she simply refuses to provide them all with the entertainment of watching her blundering blindly around after that elusive pig. Instead, she keeps herself to herself because she knows that the outcome of this farce is already set. There is no point debasing herself by protesting, explaining, or begging. However, even she cannot sit by and listen to a useless, ignorant, lazy chit like this girl speak ill of her.

"She lied," Ilona says.

The prosecutor swivels around to face her. "What did you say?"

"I pricked her because she lied to me, not because she didn't do the work. You may want to remember that when you listen to whatever else she has to say."

For a moment the prosecutor is wrong-footed. He gapes at her, says, "It is not for a prisoner to tell the court what to think. You have had your chance to speak, now we shall hear the witnesses." He turns back to Suzanna. "Were any girls murdered at Čachtice?"

"Many."

"Who murdered them?"

"The countess. Everyone from the cook to the court master knew it was she. Why, the screams from the gynaeceum could be heard for miles around." Suzanna's cheeks are flushed pink. She avoids the hard stare that Boróka is trying to pin on her from the gallery by looking only at the prosecutor, who nods back at her in support.

"And who helped the countess murder the girls?"

"These four," says Suzanna, indicating the little row of accomplices. "They killed the girls."

"Very good," says Závodsky. "And was each as culpable as the other?"

Suzanna pauses, contemplates a moment. "The boy was mainly a girl catcher, sent out to steal the girls and bring them back to the castle."

"He did not kill the girls?"

Suzanna shrugs. "I know not, but if the countess was the executioner then Dorka and Ilona were her willing henchmen."

"And what about Kata Beneczky?"

Boróka's grip on the top rail tightens. What does Suzanna know of Kata? She has barely had anything to do with her since the great wash. What makes her think she is able to pass judgment on her now? *If you condemn her, they will kill her,* she tries to tell Suzanna with an impassioned look. She must have connected with her somehow because Suzanna's eyes slide up to hers. Her chest rises as she inhales deeply and says, "Kata was far milder and gentler. She was merciful and brought food in secret to the martyred dead."

Relief makes Boróka lean against the balustrade. She cannot see Kata's face from where she is standing, but there is a shift to the set of her shoulders, a loosening of the coil of her body.

"Thank you," says Závodsky by way of dismissal, but Suzanna doesn't move. She remains in the witness chair, gripping its scrolled arms.

"There is something else," she says.

Závodsky glances at the courthouse window. Outside it is beginning to darken, and they still have three more witnesses to get through. He already has what he needs from this girl. It is the *quantity* of evidence that is important, not its length or detail. Now he needs as many people as possible to confirm the same thing.

"It's about the countess," says Suzanna.

He glances back at his witness. "Well?"

"She kept a book."

Závodsky sighs. There are two key skills to examining a witness. Most certainly, the first is to be able to loosen the tongues of the unforthcoming, but the other is to quell the enthusiasm of those who enjoy their role a little too much; the ones who, having briefly experienced an importance above their station in life, are reluctant to relinquish it. He suspects this girl is an example of the latter.

"A book, you say?" he asks, but his voice holds no real interest.

Suzanna nods. "It was a book of the murdered dead."

The court ruffles like a bird disturbed. Incredulous whispers start to rise from the crowd, forcing Závodsky to raise his voice to make himself heard. "Tell us about this book," he says.

Suzanna sits bolt upright. There is not a soul in the courtroom who is not listening to her now. "It belonged to the countess," she says. "It was in a rosewood box in her library."

"You opened it?"

"The key was always kept in the lock."

"What was inside?"

"A book, a kind of ledger."

"Well, what was in it?"

"A list of girls' names," says the girl, "and alongside each one was how she died."

Even Závodsky's jaw has slackened in disbelief. "You saw this book?"

"I did," confirms Suzanna.

"She cannot even read!" Boróka's voice drops from the gallery into a court shocked into silence. Závodsky glares up at her. Having been handed this startling revelation, he is reluctant to let it go on such a technicality.

"I could see it was a list of names, plain enough," says Suzanna. "It was in the countess's own hand, a record of all the girls she murdered, and how she did it."

"How many names were there?" Závodsky asks.

Suzanna lifts her eyes to the gallery, queen for a fleeting moment on that make-believe throne.

"Hundreds," she replies.

Chapter 36

PRIVY AND PURPOSEFUL
ACCOMPLICES

It is a surprise when the sentences are handed down immediately.
Dorka can't take in what is happening. She expected the jury
to at least discuss what they had heard. While the last three witnesses
spoke, she spent the time imagining Závodsky making the point that
she alone of the accused has been consistently helpful. In her mind's
eye, she saw the good men of the jury nodding and murmuring their as-
sent. The reality is that the evidence against her has been no more than
finger pointing by disgruntled lackeys, who plainly resented her for
the disciplined way in which she managed the countess's household.
The jury are all men of a certain quality. She feels sure that they will
understand that a robust work ethic never garners popularity among
servants.

Perhaps they simply know this already without the need to draw
the proceedings out. Certainly, the guilt of the others is clear. It was
annoying, and surprising, to hear how reluctant the witnesses were to
implicate Kata, whom she and Ilona have always known to be slippery
as an eel. No matter, they have both made it clear in their confessions
that Kata was the countess's most intimate and culpable companion.
Her death will be enough. It is a fact, plain and simple, that an example can be made of just one of them. It's not often she is thankful to
be an old woman, but this is one of those times. The least valued and

most insignificant members of society are the ones who can be quietly released.

Dorka inhales and whistles out a slow breath. In a few moments, this could all be over. She dares to wonder, What will she do when she is released? She still believes that she secured her freedom the moment she threw herself at Thurzó's feet. Survival is simply a case of picking the right side, at the right moment. She had nothing to do with Judit's death, and what does anyone care for a pricked seamstress or trodden-on scullion? She tries to catch the prosecutor's eye as he stands to pronounce sentence. She even offers him a hopeful smile, just in case. It is never too late for mercy, whatever is written on the paper he holds. It is never too late to turn the hand of fate.

The lady has committed terrible crimes against the female blood and in this Dorka, Ilona, and Ficzkó were privy and purposeful accomplices.

Dorka's lungs empty but somehow the next breath doesn't come. If her body is perfectly still, if her lungs don't draw air and her heart doesn't beat, the world will stop now, right at this moment.

All the accused before the court, in the confessions that they made voluntarily and also under torture, prove beyond doubt the guilt of the accused which surpasses the imagination in the many murders and slaughter and specific tortures and cruelty and all kinds of evil.

If a moment ago the world was still, now it has speeded up. The words are spilling out like water from a leaky bucket. She cannot stop them, no matter what she does, she cannot.

And as these most serious crimes should be matched by the severest punishments, we have determined and we hereby decree that regarding firstly Ilona Jó Nagy and secondly Dorottya Szentes, as those most implicated in the bloody crimes, the sentence is that all the fingers of their hands, which they steeped in Christian blood and which are the instruments of murder, shall be torn out by the executioner with iron tongs, after which they shall be placed alive on the fire.

Shock, pure and muffling as snow, envelops her. They cannot mean to burn her like a common witch? No, this is *not* what will happen. It is simply the sentence required by their confessions. It is for show, in the same way that this whole trial is for show. Afterward, when the paperwork is complete and everyone has gone home to their warm fires, it will be quietly forgotten. Never implemented. She has only to keep faith, to keep breathing. In, then out.

As concerns János Ficzkó, his guilt and punishment is alleviated by his youth and his lesser participation in the crimes. He is therefore sentenced to lose his head; only his dead body will be placed on the fire with the two other condemned persons. As concerns Katalin Beneczky, Ficzkó stated that she had not participated in these affairs and she cannot be condemned solely on the basis of the confessions of Dorka and Ilona; therefore she shall be kept in close confinement until her guilt may be determined.

Her ears are playing tricks on her. Terror is conjuring demons again, causing her to hear things that are not true. *Cannot* be true. Dorka, not Kata, is the one to be spared. She didn't listen closely enough. In, then out. This is not real; it is a rat scuttling in a pitch-black outhouse; it is the flash of a white chemise.

Ilona shifts in the seat next to her, clanking like a spectre in her chains. "What time will I die?" she says.

It doesn't take long for Ilona's question to be answered. It is almost as if the faggots were already piled high in anticipation of the prosecutor's decision, almost as if the first whiff of woodsmoke were already winding down the valley. The punishment is to be carried out immediately: a fitting conclusion to a legal process marked by its brutal efficiency, the swiftness of its justice.

The last time the accomplices all stand together is outside the courthouse. Here, Kata is taken back to the public gaol to languish with the whores and thieves and debtors. The other three are put into a waiting cart to jolt and trundle their way to the meadowland by the river, where the public executions are held.

It is already dark on this January afternoon, so a torchbearer walks in front of the cart. The bitter breeze catches the flames, blows the smoke back over the cart, where it stings the accomplices' nostrils, catches in their throats. Dorka starts to cough, then sob. She cannot get her breath back. Already she gasps for clean air, blinks the soot from her eyes, and the flames are not yet upon her. She gulps desperately at the night sky, as if she could store it in her lungs to protect her.

"Stop it," Ilona hisses. "Where is your dignity?" But Dorka cannot stop. She shakes with cold and terror, she whimpers like a child lost in the dark.

The *hóhér* is waiting. He stands by the chair that will restrain the women, heating his iron tongs in the fire. As they approach, he is a black silhouette against the flaming pyre, a faceless apparition. Dorka will not get out of the cart. She balks like a stubborn mule until they drag her down, and even then, her legs will not carry her and she sinks down into the mud and snow. Ilona steps over her, leaves her behind, and does not look back. She has already decided that she wants to go first. That way she will not have to view a rehearsal of her own death, experience the terror twice over.

Crowds have gathered. The fire illuminates their awful, excited faces. Ilona looks behind them, out toward the wild hills of the Carpathians. She senses him in the fresh breeze that cuts through the smoke; she sees him in the infinite blackness of the mountains. Dorka fears death because she has no one waiting for her, but Ilona does. She has her son; she knows that they can finally pick up where they left off; that she will, at last, be able to be a proper mother—nobody's stand-in, nobody's surrogate. Though the flames will burn her, turn her body to ash, it is her son who will truly melt her. He will take the stone woman she has become and bring her to life again.

They sit her down, and as the straps tighten around her, Ilona suddenly wonders what will happen to her clock. She would have liked to have bequeathed it to someone, feels a passing sadness when she realizes she has not a single loved one to whom to leave it. The soft leather of the executioner's glove closes over her hand. He seems not to know where to apply the tongs. Ilona's fingers are bent at odd angles, her knuckles protrude like the knots of trees. Ilona almost wants to laugh.

Take these painful fingers, she thinks, they are useless anyway, quite incapable of gripping even a spoon, let alone all the implements of torture she is supposed to have wielded.

There is a thin, wailing scream that she knows is not her own. Dorka cannot even leave her to her own death in peace. She ignores her friend's pitiful cries, closes her eyes to the spiteful brightness of the pyre, shuts out the press of the tongs into her flesh. In the distance, the town clock begins to strike. Its chimes pace her beating heart, slow her ragged breath.

Ficzkó tells Stefan that he needs to decide how he is going to die. Will it be like Ilona, silent until the first pull of the tongs, who seemed to welcome death by drawing the burning smoke deep into her lungs? Or will it be like Dorka, begging and pleading till the last, squirming and squealing until she fainted when the first finger parted from her body? Ficzkó already knows the answer. Stefan would die in the same way that he lived: a coward in the shadows, never owning up to anything, never standing up for anything.

It would be the easiest thing in the world to let Stefan die now, for him to experience the thud of the blade against his neck and the slump of his useless body, but when they call for him, somehow it is Ficzkó who steps up to the executioner. If he really is to die, then at least he will die standing in his own shoes. He will leave them all behind: János the changeling, Stefan the lumbering gravedigger, even Ficzkó, the boy who might have been a better man. For the last moment of his life, he can be the person he always wanted to be: someone brave, unafraid. Going to his death as no one but himself.

Part IV

Spring

Chapter 37

SUNDRY WITCHES

Were you going to leave without saying goodbye?"

Suzanna looks up from where she is packing her things into a cloth bag. "I didn't know if you wanted me to," she replies warily.

Boróka steps into the little turret room she and Suzanna used to share. It is almost empty now, devoid of the imprint of either one of them save for a few of Suzanna's possessions strewn over the straw pallet on which they'd slept.

"What you did was wrong," Boróka says, her voice quiet.

Suzanna stands up to face her, juts out her chin. "I spoke only the truth."

"Hundreds of girls? You don't really believe that's true."

"It was true enough. I saw the list of the dead for myself."

"But you didn't. You shut the book before we had a chance to look at it properly."

"Indeed I did, and you should not have made me open it in the first place."

Suzanna turns away from her and walks over to a little table beneath the window. With her back to Boróka she slides something into her bag. The way she tries to shield it from view makes Boróka step forward to see what it is. It looked like a pair of leather slippers disappeared into the bag's open mouth. A good woolen petticoat follows it and then, sneakily, as if Boróka might not even notice, a silver goblet.

"But those things are not yours!" Boróka exclaims.

Suzanna swings around, pulls the bag's drawstring tight. "They most certainly are."

"You cannot afford them!"

"You think I stole them, don't you?"

With the countess locked away and her most trusted servants dead, the castle has become a different place. It still functions—there are cooks and cleaners, people to tend the gardens and do the laundry—but its rhythms are without animation, just the mechanical dance of a marionette. All the once watchful eyes are now blind to laziness, incompetence, and petty pilfering.

"Then where did you get them?" Boróka says, not accusing, just asking.

Suzanna is silent for a moment, clutching the bag to her chest. "If you must know, the lord palatine's wife gave them to me."

Boróka stares at Suzanna, stunned. "Lady Czobor?" she says eventually. "You cannot mean it. How do you even know her? Why would she give you such fine . . ." Boróka pauses. "Oh, Suzanna, no," she whispers.

Suzanna is defiant. "I have done nothing wrong."

"Nothing wrong? You have been pretending to be part of the countess's household while, all along, you have been in the pay of Lady Czobor."

"It wasn't like that."

"Then tell me how it was."

"I already told you what happened. My mother did sell me, but not to the countess, to Lady Czobor. I was to find work at the castle and tell her what went on there. That was all I had to do."

"And in return Lady Czobor gave you nice clothes and silver? But only if you told her what she wanted to hear, I suppose."

"You are just jealous because now it's me, instead of you, who is the favorite of a rich and noble lady! Where is your countess now, eh? Disgraced. Bricked up in a room, never to see the light of day again. Lady Czobor was *kind* to me. She cared about me. She treated me like I was some*body*, not some*thing* she found on the bottom of her shoe, like Ilona did. Like my own mother did. Like even you did, sometimes." Suzanna's breath comes fast as she glares at Boróka. "For the first time in my life, I felt like I was doing something well for a change."

Boróka shakes her head in distaste. "You even made me tell you what I had seen. I feel like you made me spy on her myself."

Suzanna shrugs. "Well, like you said, there was nothing to tell."

"You must take back what you said to the court about the countess's book and the hundreds of murdered girls."

"For what purpose? It's done now."

"No, it is not. You are wrong about the countess. She is not bricked up in a room waiting to die, she is trying to clear her name. She has begun a letter-writing campaign to ensure she has the right to a proper trial."

"Well, good luck to her with that."

"*Suzanna*, you said something to the prosecutor that wasn't true!"

"I saw what I saw."

Boróka realizes it is futile to argue with her. She looks around the turret, thinks of all the moments she shared here with a girl she never really knew. Her eyes alight on the straw pallet, where they whispered together in the night, now strewn with things Suzanna doesn't want anymore: her old apron, still stained with blood from her pierced lip; a broken blocking board; and . . .

Boróka gasps, turns to Suzanna with a look of astonishment on her face.

"My goose!"

"Oh," says Suzanna, the color blanching from her face. "Yes."

"You had it all along!" says Boróka, her astonishment turning to anger.

"No! I found it only now while I was packing. It was, um . . . under the mattress."

"It was *not* under the mattress," says Boróka, furious. "I looked there."

Suzanna sighs. There is nothing to be gained now by lying. "It was the factotum," she says. "He found it in the outhouse."

"Ficzkó?" Boróka breathes.

Suzanna nods. "He gave it to me ages ago and asked me to give it back to you. He wanted me to tell you that he was sorry."

Boróka bends to pick up the goose. She folds her hand around its smooth body, strokes the worn groove of its neck with her thumb. After a moment she brings it up to her lips, closes her eyes. She didn't go with the crowds to watch Ficzkó die. She wanted to remember him out in the courtyard, turning his face to the breeze and sitting next to her in the winter sunlight, making paper flowers. It is hard for her to believe that something that had just begun is already gone. She cannot help but ask herself whether things could have turned out differently. If she'd known about the goose, could she have helped him to be a better man?

Boróka opens her eyes, stares hard at Suzanna. "You knew what this goose meant to me," she says, fighting back tears that she knows are not shed for the goose.

Suzanna shrugs. "I'm sorry, I forgot to tell you. It was hard to remember anything with Ilona around."

Boróka takes a deep breath. "If you are really sorry, then there is something that you can do for me."

Suzanna's eyes flick up to hers, wary now. "What?"

"I want you to look in the box again."

"Never!"

"You owe me this much, surely!"

It is only then that Suzanna notices that Boróka has brought something with her. Her eyes widen as Boróka slips a bag off her shoulder and takes out the rosewood box.

"Get that thing away from me!"

"Open it, Suzanna. There has been such tragedy all around us. I need to make some sense of it all. I need to know what the list really is so I can try to help the countess. Let me read it again and I can prove to you that you were wrong."

"I will not. It's cursed." Suzanna doesn't want to even look at the box, but she cannot help herself. Its six-petaled rosette is like a round unblinking eye, staring back at her from the lid.

"It's not as if Ilona or Dorka are here to punish you. Even the countess is locked away. Nothing can happen to you now."

"There is no purpose to this." Suzanna's voice is pleading. "Even if I were wrong, what good can it do to know that now?"

"It's not just that," Boróka insists. "I think I know what the list is. I am hoping that it will give me answers to things I desperately want to know. Please, Suzanna, this is your chance to make things right."

Suzanna looks pained, but she reaches out and places her hands on either side of the lid. "This is the last time, Boróka. I don't ever want to open this box again. Promise me you won't ask me."

Boróka nods, and so Suzanna lifts the lid. She searches Suzanna's face for an indication of what she sees, but it is a mask of reluctant distaste, as if she were peering into a chamber pot.

"What's inside?"

Suzanna reaches into the box and takes out the oxblood book. "This again," she says, holding it up.

Boróka puts the box down on the mattress. "Open it," she says, coming around to stand by Suzanna's shoulder.

Suzanna holds the book, arms outstretched, as if it were a honeycomb covered in bees. She doesn't want to touch the pages, so she lets it fall open against her palms.

Boróka sucks in her breath. "It's the same," she says. "Can I take it?"

Suzanna nods eagerly and lets Boróka lift the book from her hands. Once she is free of it, she cannot help but wipe her hands on her skirt.

Boróka cradles the book carefully. She knows she may never see what is written there again, knows Suzanna could snatch the book away at any moment, so she starts at the beginning. Something deep in the pit of her stomach contracts when she sees the title: *Sundry Witches*. And then the names begin, the date each woman died and the place and manner of her passing.

"It's all the women who have been executed as witches," whispers Boróka.

Suzanna too is staring at the pages. Occasional letters reveal themselves to her. There are snakes in many of the words, circles and lines with dots on top that remind her of little candles. "How do you know for sure?"

"I don't," replies Boróka, "not yet."

Boróka flicks through the pages, looking for the end of the list. When she sees it, she stops, smooths out the page. "I was right," she breathes.

"Show me."

"Look at the very last entry," Boróka tells her. "You know your numbers, don't you?"

Suzanna nods.

"See, here's the date: *twenty-fourth of January, 1611.* That's almost a month after the countess was imprisoned, so it cannot be anything to do with her. And see here, the name."

"What does it say?"

Boróka swallows, tries to keep the sadness from her voice. *"Dori Majorosné."*

"Did they execute her?"

Boróka nods. She remembers that she was the one to have to tell the countess that they had burned her beloved companion, that they had taken Dori to the meadows outside Bytča and, without even a trial, set her alight. "But Dori never harmed any girls," the countess had whispered when Boróka told her. "There were no allegations against her, no evidence, no confessions. Her only crime was to have loved and served me." It wasn't something she'd ever been able to say about Dorka or Ilona.

"So you see," Boróka says, "this cannot be a list of girls the countess has murdered."

Suzanna looks shamefaced, then fearful. "Do you see these names when you open the box?"

"No, I don't."

"Then why do I see them?"

"I don't know. The box seems to show whoever opens it something that is significant to them. It tells you something about yourself. Maybe, when you see this list, it's a warning."

Suzanna's eyes are round and anxious. "About what?"

"The dangers of ill-thought-out words and the consequences they can have, perhaps? All these women died because of lies, or rumors or half-truths."

Suzanna drops her gaze to the floor. She is silent for a while, then says, "Please close the book."

"I will," replies Boróka, "but first I want to find out the answer to a question I have had all my life. Will you let me?"

Suzanna nods and Boróka begins to flip backward through the pages. Time reverses until she is back in the previous century. When she gets to 1595, the year of her birth, she stops, scans down the page. January was a busy month. Perhaps the new year did not bring the good fortune for which people wished, so they looked for someone to blame, lit the burning faggots to warm their hands through the bleak midwinter. February was almost as bad: seven sundry witches murdered. Then March. Boróka hardly realizes she is holding her breath, so focused is she on what she is reading. There is an entry for the twenty-third of March. József never knew what day she was born, so he chose the day of the first spring saint, February the fourteenth, as her birthday. Whatever her actual birthday, Boróka would have been a few weeks old on the twenty-third of March, a babe in arms. *Drowned, in the market town of Trenčín,* the entry reads. She reaches out her finger, strokes it over her mother's name, knowing this is the closest she will ever get to touching her again: *Erzsébet Beneczky.*

Chapter 38

THE PALATINE'S WIFE

Boróka has requested that Valentino finish the portrait.

He was reluctant at first. He has enough experience working for the nobility to know that the richer his client, the harder it is to get his bill paid in the best of times. What hope has he of receiving the agreed sum from a woman between stones? It is ludicrous, a waste of his time; better he paint more baronesses, and their yappy pets, than sit here completing something that is no more now than the picture of a young servant. And yet . . . when she asked him, he agreed. So there he sits, applying the last brushstrokes to a face already perfect. If he could draw out the moment of the portrait's completion, he would. If he could stave off adding the final touches of light to her eyes, the last strand of hair across her forehead, he would. That way, he could look upon her forever. She would be his, captured, just as surely as her image on the canvas.

But, of course, he knows he will have to let her go. He steals a glance at her, smiles to himself at the poised way she stands in her chopines, no longer the trembling fawn. The look of her, the way she sometimes glances at him down her long nose, has all the dignity of the countess herself, though hers is a gentler countenance. The portrait barely pretends to be the countess now, but yet it *is* her. It's the glimpses of her that he got on the rare occasions she smiled, the times she revealed to him someone far . . . simpler, more carefree. But it is not the likeness of a girl either. It is a young woman with a ring of state on her finger and pearls at her throat, entirely sure of herself and the power she holds. He has painted Boróka, not with lust in his heart, but admiration, perhaps even envy; it seems to him that the key she clasps in her hand is the key to all the world.

She is smiling at him now, that same quirk of understanding they shared almost a year ago. "Surely, it is done, sir?"

He nods, puts down his brush. "Yes," he has to agree, "the portrait is finished."

Boróka slips the countess's ring from her finger, unclasps the pearls. Now that Valentino's work is done she can return them to the countess. She lifts the golden clock off the rosewood box. The countess will be pleased to have something so elegant to help her measure out the time while she petitions the palatine for a proper trial. Boróka cannot imagine what the countess's days are like now, shut away in a room with only the ghosts of her former friends for company. And if Dorka, Ficzkó, or Ilona do ever appear to her in an unguarded moment, Boróka wonders what she might say to them. Does she beg them to forgive her because they were only ever pawns in a bigger game against her, or does she rail against them for the part their foolish cruelty played in her downfall?

Valentino has already gone. His departure was brisk: no more than a click of his heels and a nod of his head. She would have liked to take his hand, had he offered it. It would have meant something to her to touch the hand that looks as thick and broad as a farmer's, yet paints with the grace of an angel. For all his creative agonies—the false starts, the times he was paralyzed by the fear of failure—Valentino's portrait of the countess is luminous. She hopes the countess herself will see it someday. No, she corrects herself, she *will* see it. She *must* see it.

Boróka is stepping out of her chopines when the door to the countess's library opens. A woman walks in, bringing an air of entitlement wafting in with her, like perfume. When she catches sight of Boróka she stops dead. The color blanches from her face and she stares at her, slack-jawed, for a second before she recovers herself.

"Why, for a moment I thought you were . . ." she begins. Then: "A foolish thought," she chides herself, before she turns away and begins to look over the countess's bookshelves.

But who are *you*? wonders Boróka as she watches her lose interest in the books and swivel around to inspect the countess's marquetry desk. She picks up a silver pen holder, rotates it in her fingers, puts it down.

"Where does Widow Nádasdy keep her jewels?"

"Who would wish to know, mistress?"

"Don't question me. Where are they?"

Boróka is mutely defiant. The woman strides over and squares up to her, her cheeks the same indignant pink as her gown. "I am Lady Czobor, the lord palatine's wife, and I insist you tell me where Widow Nádasdy keeps her jewels."

She is young, thinks Boróka, to be the palatine's wife: perhaps only thirty. No doubt she hopes the countess's jewelry will suit well her smooth skin and slender neck.

"Perhaps I should call the guards, my lady," says Boróka, "and they can tell you?"

Lady Czobor laughs: a harsh, scratchy sound that makes Boróka feel like she is being rubbed with salt. "The guards are already forcing open the treasury, at my command. Soon I shall have all the money and trinkets I please. I only thought that some of the countess's favorite items might be here, in her privy chambers."

Lady Czobor waves her hand around in an indifferent manner, but her eyes are hawkish. They dart everywhere, as if testing the thickness of the velvet curtains, the weight of the candlesticks, with just a glance. Inevitably, they are soon drawn to the pearls, the beautiful golden clock.

"Like these, for instance," she says, picking up the string of pearls by their clasp. She lowers them slowly into her open hand, so that they coil in her palm like the swirl of an iridescent shell. She drops the countess's ring on top and clasps them tightly. "I shall need somewhere to put these things," she says, looking around. Her eyes settle on the rosewood box. "Open that old casket for me," she instructs Boróka.

Boróka doesn't move. "I will not," she says, her voice barely louder than the clink of gold against pearl in Lady Czobor's hand.

"You certainly will," says Lady Czobor, narrowing her eyes.

Boróka straightens. Even without the chopines, she stands taller than she ever has before. "No, mistress, I will not."

Lady Czobor hisses out a breath, but she says nothing. Instead, she slaps the pearls, clattering, down onto the table and pinches the key of the rosewood box between her finger and thumb. She twists it. She jiggles it. She even yanks on it, but it will not turn.

"Is the lock stuck, my lady?" asks Boróka, barely suppressing a smile.

Lady Czobor rises slowly and faces Boróka. "Yes, I see now," she says, nodding eagerly, "*this* is where she keeps the best jewels. You think you are making a fool out of me, but I shall not rest until this box is opened!"

Lady Czobor swirls around and begins to search the room. Over by the window is a walnut cabinet with a large fruit bowl on top, which Lady Czobor strides toward. The fruit the countess once picked over is long gone, but the little fruit knife remains. Lady Czobor grabs it, flicks up the blade. With a smug glance at Boróka, she returns to the rosewood box and squats down until it is at eye level. She pokes the blade at the box, trying to insert it into the join between box and lid. She tuts and mutters as the sharp knife makes tiny pits in the wood as she jabs and winkles. Then the blade engages in the slim gap and Lady Czobor forces it in farther with a grunt.

Once it is firmly wedged, she stands back up and closes her fingers around the knife handle. She leans over it and bears down, using her body weight to increase the pressure. For a moment it is a battle of wills between knife and box, and it almost looks as if the knife will snap in half before the lock gives, but then the wood splinters. Lady Czobor turns to Boróka, gleeful. "Now we shall see what the countess has for me," she says, her eyes glittering.

Lady Czobor takes the corners of the lid delicately between finger and thumb and lifts it up. At first, she looks perplexed. She squints at the box as if she must be missing something, leans right over it and peers down into its infinite darkness. Then she flinches and wrinkles her nose. There is a strange smell, something earthy and dank, like old cauliflowers. She opens her mouth to draw a complaining breath, to berate the girl watching her for making her go to such trouble to open a musty old casket; then something jumps straight into her gaping maw.

Lady Czobor rears up, gagging. She tastes it in her mouth, slightly bitter. Her tongue slips over its skin, both textured and slimy. Its pointy little bones press against the insides of her cheeks as it squirms in her mouth. As soon as she can manage to manipulate it, she spits it out. Her eyes search frantically for it. Where is it? *What* is it? Then she catches sight of the inside of the casket and her eyes widen in horror. The box is a seething mass of river frogs. They climb over one another, creeping with slender, webbed limbs toward the edge of the box. She is transfixed, appalled, yet she cannot move. The frogs begin to leap out and land, wetly, on her face and clothes. There are hundreds of them, jumping into her hair, crawling through it with strange three-fingered hands. Lady Czobor starts to claw at her own skin; she rips the jeweled combs from her hair and drags her nails through the sticky strands, trying to pull the frogs out. The floor seems somehow wet and slippery, covered in silt and mud. She staggers back, her heeled shoes slipping on rotting river reeds. She falls and sits there, gasping and spluttering on the floor, while the frogs hop onto her skirts and blink at her with their bulbous, watery eyes until she covers her face with her hands and screams into her open palms.

She screams until her throat is hoarse. She screams until she has no breath left. Then, when she can scream no more, she takes her hands from her face and opens her eyes. Nothing: just her hair combs lying on the woolen pile of the Turkey rug and the ticking of the golden clock. She casts about, searching for her tormentors, but all she sees is her own reflection in the mirror above the mantelpiece, face scratched red, hair wild as a banshee.

She looks up at Boróka, her mouth moving uselessly, forming sound-less words. Boróka steps toward her, offers her a hand to help her up.

"Did you not like what you saw in the box, mistress?" she says.

Chapter 39

Homecoming

Marta is inside the oven. She quite enjoys the womblike feel of it surrounding her while she works, the meaty smells of long-ago dinners that linger like ghosts. She dips her brush into the pail of water and begins to scrub. The fat has dripped and burned so many times it's turned tarry and will not shift. She takes a little knife and scrapes at the spit, smiles when she sees the shiny metal emerging from under the sticky layers. She cannot even remember when it was last cleaned properly. There is time, now, to get around to jobs like these; a pause in the entertaining of nobles and the hosting of lavish dinners; an end to the countess as mistress of her household, dining on oysters, baked starlings, and tiny custard tarts.

A noise in the kitchen makes Marta jump. She finds she cannot stop doing this. She tries to tell herself she is safe now, but every bang makes her cower, anticipating the thud of Dorka's boot. Every time she makes a mistake she still braces, waiting for the impatient slap of her hand. Though the bully is dead, her legacy survives, as hard to get rid of as the baked-on grease of a thousand roasted meats.

Marta listens from inside her red-brick shell. It's quiet now; she must have imagined it. She goes back to scrubbing and scraping, squatting in the ashes of the castle's former life.

"Marta?"

If Marta didn't know better, she might have thought that someone called her name. But it cannot be; there is hardly anyone left at the castle, and among those who remain she is a nameless scullion. It must be the wind whistling down the chimney. *Ugly moth*, it sometimes whispers to her, as it chills the back of her neck.

"Are you there, Marta?"

Marta is stock-still, her hand dipped inside the cold water of the bucket, though her heart is beating fast. They *did* kill her, didn't they? It's just that Marta wasn't there to see Dorka actually tossed onto the burning faggots. Or could it be that Satan saved her from the flames and she stands there now, in the kitchen, as vicious and dissatisfied as she always was? Marta wraps her wet hands around her shins and buries her face in her knees, fearing the swipe of a scorched, fingerless hand.

"What are you doing in the oven?" The voice—right beside her now—is too singsong to be Dorka's, the tone too kind, but nonetheless, Marta refuses to unfurl.

"It's only me, you silly woodlouse," says the voice. Then someone strokes her cheek, tucks a strand of hair behind her ear.

They say you can always tell a washerwoman from her hands: the scent of lavender and lye that never seems to fade, the flaky roughness of skin too often submerged. Marta *knows* who this is; she feels it, hears it, smells it, but she still doesn't dare open her eyes, because eyes can't play tricks the way other senses can. If this woman isn't real, she will vanish in a blink and then even the hope of her will be gone and Marta will be all alone again, sitting in a greasy oven.

"I tell you what," says the woman, her footsteps retreating into the kitchen, "if you come out of the oven, we can make something nice to eat. I seem to recall you're quite fond of apple strudel?"

Marta snorts. Only Kata would remember that. She lifts her head, sees her standing by the kitchen table. Marta slithers out of the oven, reborn, and runs into Kata's outstretched arms, covers her in kisses and ash.

Boróka overhears that Kata is back while wiping dust off the countess's bookshelves. Servants are gossiping in the corridor, wondering quite how she managed to escape. The shock of the news makes her teeter on the little stool and she has to place her hands on the row of spines, for balance. She jumps down and goes, straightaway, to find her.

There is a delicious smell coming from the kitchen: buttery, with the freshness of apples and the warmth of cinnamon. It's so familiar that it announces Kata's presence like a herald's proclamation.

"Apple strudel?" asks Boróka eagerly, coming into the kitchen.

Kata breaks into a smile as she walks over to embrace her tightly. Boróka buries her face into Kata's shoulder, staying there, in the woolen softness of her kirtle, for some moments. She has so many questions she hardly knows where to begin. When she lifts her face up to Kata's, she starts with the obvious, saying, in a hushed and awed tone, "How did you escape?"

Kata laughs. "I didn't escape, they released me. I think the authorities got to the point where they didn't know what to do with me. There wasn't enough evidence to convict me so I became just another mouth to feed. After a respectable time had passed, they let me go."

Boróka steps away from Kata and looks at her properly. Her face is gaunt, the skin sallow as parchment. She cannot imagine that Kata was fed much in prison at all. She reaches out her hand, touches Kata's cheek. "I'm so pleased to see you," she says.

"And I you," replies Kata, clasping her hand. "I'm even glad to be back at Čachtice, though I find it much changed." Kata's voice quiets with the last words, sounding more somber, almost grim. "How does the countess? They will not allow me to see her."

"She does the best she can, writing letters and the like."

"She's good at that," she says, smiling, then she squeezes Boróka's hand. "Thank you for staying with her when so many others deserted her. She will take heart from that, Boróka. You were ever a favorite of hers."

Questions bubble up inside Boróka. "Kata," she begins, but Kata has turned away, sniffing the air.

"I think the strudel's ready," she says. "What do you think, Marta?"

Boróka hadn't even noticed Marta, but she sees her now, eyeing

Boróka with a slightly reproachful gaze that suggests she wants to share neither Kata nor the strudel.

Boróka keeps back her questions while they eat the strudel. They don't speak about Kata's imprisonment or the trial. Kata seems only to want to talk about ordinary things, like whether anyone ordered any wood ash and lye for the spring great wash and how the bees fared over winter. It's as if she wants to step back into her old life and immerse herself in it, like a soothing bath that washes away all that has gone before. Boróka suspects that it will not be as easy as that. Kata's body seems awkward somehow; her movements are stilted, lacking their previous grace and ease. When she takes the plates over to the sink, Boróka sees that she limps a little.

Marta notices it too. When Kata picks up the empty pail to get some water for washing, she immediately takes it from her and slips out the kitchen door. Kata sighs, grateful, and comes to sit back down next to Boróka. "What's on your mind?" she asks.

"Why do you ask?"

"I don't know, you seem jittery, as if there is something you want to talk about."

Boróka thought she had been able to hide the turmoil of her thoughts, at least for as long as it took them to eat an apple strudel.

"It's the rosewood box," she says.

Kata nods slowly. "It might be better if you stopped looking in the box. Have you ever thought about that?"

"But how can I? Every time it's opened I find out something more about myself."

"Do you? How do you know that what you see is even about you?"

"The doctor who saved the *rusalka*'s baby from the river gave her a name that means 'stranger.' That's what Boróka—*Borbála*—means."

Kata sighs. "Think of all the girls who are called Erzsébet or Anna. It doesn't prove anything."

Boróka stares hard at Kata. "All my life I've never really known who I was or where I came from. I was just a motherless girl named for the geese. I need to know who my mother is."

"Why do you think that I can help you?"

"At the gynaeceum the countess said that something had happened to her when she was younger and that God had punished her for it for the next ten years by denying her a child . . . or, should I say, *another* child."

Kata's face darkens. "Boróka, be careful what you suggest," she warns. "Even locked away, the countess is a formidable force for someone like you."

"That's why I have never said anything about this before, but when Suzanna looked in the box she saw a list of women executed as witches. My mother's name was in there—or at least the name of the woman I think is my mother. Her surname was Beneczky."

Kata's eyes slip away from hers. She stares down at the table, studying a whorl in the wood, before she draws in a slow breath. "Erzsébet Beneczky?" she says.

"Yes, Erzsébet."

"I cannot tell you for sure whether Erzsébet Beneczky was your mother, Boróka," says Kata carefully.

Boróka's heart is beating fast, but she tries to keep her voice level. "Then tell me what you can. Please, Kata."

Kata sighs. "It all seems so long ago now. I was working at the manor house in Trnava when the countess arrived, aged thirteen, betrothed to Ferenc Nádasdy. There were few girls her own age around so she sought me out, kept me company while I worked. That summer it was not as if she were a countess and I a laundry maid. Instead, we became friends. She has been like that all her life. I mean, how many countesses count among their closest confidantes a washerwoman, a wet nurse, and a servant?"

Boróka nods. What Kata says is true, but the countess's choice of friends now seems ill judged to the point of foolish.

"I know what you're thinking," says Kata, "but you have to remember that the countess was brought up knowing that she could do precisely as she pleased. She believes herself to be untouchable, beyond reproach, whatever she does." Kata glances out the kitchen window, as if she could see the countess locked away in the farthest reaches of the castle. "I suspect she still thinks that, even now."

Kata looks back at Boróka, almost mischievous. "It certainly made her hard to control when she was younger. If she wanted to climb on a horse and ride off somewhere, she would. If she wanted to stay out late in the summer evenings, then no one could find her. I suspect her new mother-in-law despaired of her, but the marriage contract was already made. Then she met Ladislav Bende. No one knows what really happened; certainly she never spoke of it to me. All I know is that by the time the autumn came I began to see less and less of her, then nothing at all. The following March I was asked if I would take in an infant."

"The countess's baby?"

"Perhaps. There were rumors, of course, but we never knew for sure. If it *was* the countess's child, then I like to think that she asked them to give it to me, rather than anyone else."

"But you were an unmarried maid yourself?"

"Yes, but I was no countess. They gave me money for the baby's food and keep, so I didn't have to wash clothes for a few years. And I was glad to take her." Kata smiles, a wide grin that creeps over her face, giving her the look of the old Kata, before prison sucked the life out of her. "She was such a lovely child. Serious, solemn, but so clever and engaging."

"But Erzsébet Beneczky called her mother Ailing."

Kata chuckles. "Yes, she did call me Ailing. I tried to teach her my name, Kat-a-lin, but she was so young she could barely manage it. Somehow 'a-lin' became Ailing. I liked it; it seemed right that I was someone different to her than I was to anyone else."

Boróka releases a breath. "What happened to her?"

Kata leans back and looks to the ceiling as if the answer were written on the smooth stones of the vaulted roof. "I have gone over this in my mind so many times," she says, "wondering if what happened were somehow my fault."

"How could it have been?"

"I kept her away from everyone; I was fiercely protective of her because of her past. Perhaps, if I had allowed her to mix with people more, they might have accepted her. But she didn't want to, you know. She found them strange, and threatening, and so they found her strange in return. It made her . . . *vulnerable*, as well that blade grinder knew, I believe." Kata's face is suddenly hard, her jaw flexed. "And as for his wife"—she folds her arms across her chest—"shame on her for what she did to a girl who never even knew how she wronged her."

"She was just a hurt and jealous wife, Kata. It should not have been so easy to persuade the townsfolk to harm her."

Kata leans forward, touches her fingers to her temples. "This is where it is all my fault," she whispers.

Boróka reaches out a hand, rests it on Kata's shoulder. "*She* didn't think it was your fault."

Kata looks up, tearful. "But it *was*. In the years I didn't have to wash clothes, I turned to plants and remedies. I made medicines that even the town doctor relied on. But a woman alone will never be left to her herbs in peace. They had already begun to talk about me, *accuse me*; what Erzsébet did gave them an excuse to come for us."

"But you survived?"

"Yes, I did," she says, a little bitterly. "I believe they fully intended to drown me next, except . . ." Kata's eyes meet Boróka's, and there is humor in them. "They didn't realize that I had an influential friend. There wasn't much the notary could do when a messenger arrived from Čachtice telling him Countess Báthory had urgent need of a washerwoman." She sits back, lifts her hands to indicate her surroundings. "And I have been here ever since. Whether the countess kept me with her out of friendship or because of what I did for her child, I know not."

Boróka is silent, letting what Kata has said seep through her.

Then Kata says, "I'm sorry I cannot tell you if Erzsébet Beneczky was your mother. For all I knew she was drowned, and her baby along with her. I never dared go back to Trenčín again."

Boróka's mind is racing. She hears the countess's voice in her head: *Why would the doctor take you in?*

"Rose honey," says Boróka.

Kata looks perplexed. "What are you talking about?"

"You told me to treat your wound with rose honey because that's what *József* would have used."

"József." Kata says his name as if she could taste it. "Yes, József."

"József was my father, the man who took me in. This doctor you talk about, the one who used your herbs and potions, was József too."

Kata stares at her. "József was our only friend," she says, after a few moments have passed. "He never listened to the lies people said about us. It doesn't surprise me that he was waiting by the river for you, that he would want to do that for you. For *us*."

Boróka leans toward Kata, reaches for her. "He sent me back to you, I feel sure of it. He let Dorka take me because he knew they had taken you here. I was always meant to find my way back to you."

Kata takes Boróka's hand, smiles. "Dear József," she says.

There is a noise in the courtyard, shuffling steps and the clank of a pail set down on the step. Marta is back.

Boróka grips Kata's hand more tightly. "The countess," she says. "How can I ask her if my mother was her daughter?"

Kata glances quickly at the opening door.

"Why don't you ask her to open the box?"

Chapter 40

THE IDEAL COURTIER

The golden clock looks ridiculously opulent in the countess's re-
duced surroundings, but the countess herself is gracious.

"I am glad to have it," she insists to Boróka. "It will be most useful
when . . ."

Her voice trails off. It is hard to think what use a clock could be to
her now. She is not allowed to leave her chambers. Her food arrives
when it arrives, just like the sun rises when it rises, and the countess
has as much influence over one as the other, clock or no.

"Well, it's beautiful to look at, is it not? I shall pass many an en-
joyable hour watching its clever mechanism, and winding it up shall
occupy my idle hands."

Boróka's guts twist with pity. What does the countess do all day?
She cannot just read and sew, surely? She glances over to the desk.
There is not even any evidence of a letter in progress, as if the countess
has run out of pleas and demands, or the inclination to make them,
falling, as they do, on deaf ears. For a brief, terrible moment, Boróka
wonders who received the worst fate, the countess or her accomplices.

"And I brought you these," says Boróka in a deliberately bright
voice, taking out the countess's ring and pearls. Lady Czobor seemed
not to want them after all, when she, rather hurriedly, departed the
countess's privy chambers.

"Thank you," says the countess. She holds them up, inspects them. "I had forgotten how fine they are. I hope that useless painter did them justice."

Boróka laughs. "You do him a disservice, my lady. His portrait depicts them most ably. Not only them, but you too."

"Really? But is it"—the countess touches her hand to her neck—"*accurate?*"

"You will not be disappointed when you see it, I assure you. I shall speak to the guards and see if they will allow someone to bring it up for you."

"Thank you, I should like to see it. And tell Court Master Deseö to make sure the man is promptly paid."

Boróka nods her agreement. The countess leans forward and peers into Boróka's bag. "What else have you got in there?"

Boróka swallows hard. "This, my lady," she says, taking out the rosewood box.

The countess looks first surprised, then a little cross. "What makes you think I want that?"

Boróka places the box carefully on the table. She has spent almost a year with the countess, and she has been quite terrified of her for most of that time. But the woman who was once a force of nature is now a little spent, a storm that has almost blown itself out. If she cannot speak freely now, when can she?

"Mistress, there is more magic in this box than anything you summoned with Dori Majorosné."

"I saw no 'magic' when Kata opened it," she replies, a little peevish. "Not even that book you spoke of."

"Then perhaps it is time to look inside the box yourself."

"Why would I want to do that?"

"Because it will connect you to your daughter."

"My daughter?" The countess scoffs. "Anna is still able to visit me."

Boróka shakes her head. "Not Anna, my lady."

"Katalin also visits, when she can."

"I am talking about your *firstborn* daughter," says Boróka, her voice barely more than a whisper. "The one you had when you were thirteen. The one you called Erzsébet."

The countess purses her lips, but she looks more sad than angry. "Boróka, these stories have to stop."

"I don't believe it is a story, my lady."

"Based on what? A fairy tale in a book?"

Boróka sinks to her knees in front of the countess, dragged down by the weight of her own expectations. "*Your* daughter, Erzsébet, was *my* mother, I am almost certain of it. That was what the box was trying to tell me."

The countess shakes her head. "The box told you nothing, Boróka. You saw your mother's story in the box because that was what you *wanted* to see. We all have such a box. When Thurzó looks inside his, he sees a *bestial woman;* and when the king opens his"—she pauses, arcs her hands to suggest a plume—"all manner of riches spill out."

"Open the box yourself, my lady," whispers Boróka. "Erzsébet will show you something that connects you both, I know she will. I beg you to open the box, please!"

For a long moment the countess looks at Boróka, then she lifts her hand and reaches for the box. It almost looks as if she will open it but, instead, she rests her fingertips on top of its polished lid.

"I will not open the box," she tells Boróka gently.

Boróka gasps, tries to stop the tears that threaten to overwhelm her.

"The reason I won't open it, Boróka, is because I do not have to."

Boróka stares up at her, not understanding.

"Come." The countess offers her a hand, raises her up. "I do not need a box to tell me that you are as a daughter to me. I know it already from the love you have shown me. These past few months I have seen my own family turn against me. Anna and Katalin are most beloved, but they are their husbands' wives before they are my daughters now. What does it matter that they are of my blood when Lords Zrínyi and Drugeth are intent on destroying me? I have seen my most trusted friends accuse me, but you"—the countess lifts a hand to Boróka's cheek—"you have been there for me like no one else."

Boróka covers the countess's hand with her own. The tears have come anyway. They roll down her cheeks and dampen the countess's hand when she turns her face to kiss her fingers.

"Do you see, Boróka?" the countess insists. "Do you understand that I don't care what is or isn't inside that box?"

Boróka nods, blinks at the countess with tearful eyes.

"And now I have something I would like you to do for me," she says, taking back her hand and walking over to a trunk in the corner. The countess bends down and lifts the lid, takes something out, carefully, with both hands. When she turns back around, Boróka sees that she has in her hands the green lustring dress she was wearing the night she was arrested. She walks back over to Boróka, offers it up to her.

"I have no use for this now and, anyway, it is a dress for a young woman. It should be worn by someone who deserves it, someone who"—and here the countess cannot help but smile—"possesses all the virtues of the ideal courtier."

Boróka nods her agreement. One by one, all the noble girls left the castle after the countess was arrested. Far from helping their marriage prospects, any association with the countess was now a source of shame, tainting their reputations. None stayed to even speak out in her defense. Except one.

"Orsolya, my lady," says Boróka. "You are right: She *has* shown herself to be the ideal courtier. I will give it to her."

"No," says the countess, letting the silk slip from her own arms onto Boróka's, "you will keep it for yourself. I cannot think of anyone more noble than you."

"What are you doing with that dress?"

Orsolya is in the courtyard cutting sweet bay from a bush in the kitchen garden. The countess's arrest has leveled them all. Nobles now cut herbs and servants hold silk dresses in their hands.

"The countess gave it to me," says Boróka, still breathless, disbelieving.

"You lucky thing," says Orsolya, only a little envious. "It really is beautiful."

"I hope I get a chance to wear it," says Boróka, and both instinctively look up to the diamond-leaded panes of the countess's empty chambers. There seems little hope now of music and laughter and dancing.

"How long will you stay here?" Boróka asks.

Orsolya laughs. "A while. My mother prefers to keep me out of sight until my scars have faded and she can try to find a husband for me."

"That will not be hard," says Boróka kindly.

Orsolya brushes away the compliment. "The scars don't bother me. I feel grateful to be alive."

Boróka nods. "Do you ever wonder why you survived and Judit didn't?"

Orsolya studies her with eyes that are deep and unfathomable. "I *know* why," she says softly. "The witch saved me. She was there that night in the dungeons when you came to sit with me. Do you remember? I shall always be thankful for her magic."

Boróka remembers the amulets heaped around Orsolya's neck, the bloodstone, the charms. "Oh, Orsolya," she says, overcome with sadness, "did you not know? They burned Dori Majorosné in January."

But Orsolya gives her a strange smile. "Not that witch," she says, and she looks out across the courtyard to where Kata—the one who always escapes, always survives—is in the orchard, scattering wildflower seeds onto the ground, breathing new life into the cold earth.

Once Boróka left, the sound of the clock became deafening in the absolute quiet of the countess's chamber. She doesn't know when she will next see a living soul, yet, somehow, she doesn't feel completely alone. There is a presence beside her, something impossible to ignore. She glances at the rosewood box, looks away again. She rises and walks over to her desk but cannot bring herself to sit down and write another letter when all her others remain unanswered. She tries to recall when Anna and Katalin said they would visit next but cannot remember. Now that she thinks on it, she doesn't know when she will see any of her children again. She is so tired she feels as if she could lie down and sleep for a hundred years, like a princess in a fairy tale, but even sleep offers her no refuge. She has strange dreams in which she cannot breathe and wakes up gasping.

She wanders over to the window, but the view is too familiar to offer her any distraction. The days are lengthening, the landscape changing. The hills are already green, dotted with the young of livestock. Though she cannot see them, she knows the water meadows must be full of wild garlic. In her mind, she steps into the Váh Valley, inhales the scent of the marsh marigolds that cover its banks, reaches out to catch the bulrush seeds floating in the breeze. But she cannot stay there for long. Something is calling to her.

She walks back to the table and stands in front of the box. Really, there is no reason not to open it, no evil that could be unleashed that is not already abroad. And if a void opens up that threatens to engulf her, no matter, she would gladly step into it. The lock is damaged, so she has only to lift the lid. It comes up smoothly, almost as if it is opening by itself. She stares down into the box. Such an inconsequential thing she sees: a piece of cream linen edged with lace, a swaddling cloth for a highborn baby.

She gathers it up and holds it against her cheek, feels that the material is soft and fine. She breathes in, deeply. The smell of it makes her body ache. It is sweet and milky. It is as familiar as her own self, yet also the scent of something new, just beginning. It is comfort and connection, both something lost and something found. It is as if her whole life were caught between the threads, her memories stitched into every seam.

Author's Note

Guinness World Records describes Countess Erzsébet Báthory as the most prolific female serial killer of all time; she is alleged to have murdered more than six hundred girls. However, the only evidence for this shocking number comes from a young servant, described only as "Szuzanna," who testified during the accomplices' trial that she had heard that someone called Jakob Szilvassy had seen a list of 650 dead girls, in the countess's own hand, kept in a special box. The box was never produced and nor was Jakob Szilvassy called at the time to confirm, or deny, Szuzanna's astonishing claim.

This is just one of many myths that have grown up around this most sensationalized of women. She is best known for bathing in her young victims' blood to preserve her youth. However, this was never one of the contemporaneous allegations against her, and there is no mention of it in any of the trial testimonies or witness evidence. The story was likely created, some two hundred years after her death, when the sealed documents relating to the proceedings against the countess were opened. She seems to have been this person ever since, constantly evolving into an ever more diabolical character with every book and film that depicted her as a murderous vampire.

I have tried to remain largely true to original sources when describing the countess's arrest and the trial of her accomplices. In this regard, and in relation to many details about the countess and the place and time she lived in, the work of Tony Thorne in his book *Countess*

Dracula: The Life and Times of Elisabeth Bathory, the Blood Countess has been invaluable. (Any mistakes or misunderstandings being entirely my own, of course.)

Very little information about the accomplices exists. But where details are known (facts mentioned in their confessions, for example), I have used these as the basis on which to build their fictionalized backstory and inform their relationship with the countess. The accomplices' terrible final sentences are recorded in the trial judgement, as is the fact that Kata was spared execution because she was kinder than the others.

There was one further "accomplice," a servant called Anna Darvolya, who was said to be the most brutal and was heavily implicated by Dorka and Ilona in their evidence, which was highly convenient as she had died the year before. I left Anna Darvolya out of this novel simply because she was already dead by the time the events took place, and because I felt it would confuse matters to include reference to another character with a similar sounding name to many others. Similarly, the countess's forest witch was actually called Erzsi Majorosné.

The portrait described in this novel is based on Tony Thorne's discussion in *Countess Dracula* of the portraits of the countess that might exist, including one ascribed to "Valentino" which appears to show a young girl, not a woman of the age that the countess would have been. In having Boróka pose for the portrait, I suggest a fictional explanation of why this might have been the case.

It was Báthory's Austrian biographer, R. A. von Elsberg, who, in 1894, described the countess's relationship with Ladislav Bende and their subsequent child. Like so many of the other stories and legends surrounding the countess, it is impossible to prove, or disprove, this part of her biography, but the manor in Trnava did exist and, apparently, records show Ladislav Bende lived there. No more is known about the child than that it was a girl and she was given to a local to be brought up in one of the surrounding hamlets.

The proceedings against the countess were not limited to the events in this book. They spanned years, with further witness statements being taken in 1611, including one from Jakob Szilvassy in which he never mentioned the mysterious box or list of names Szuzanna had given evidence about.

The king continued to agitate for a trial, which would allow Báthory's lands and property to cede to him following her conviction and execution; Thurzó and the countess's sons-in-law resisted this, preferring her wealth to be quietly distributed among themselves. The countess was never afforded the opportunity to give her own evidence or defend herself, and nor was the deposition filed by the widow Hernath in her support ever referred to in any of the proceedings.

There is evidence that Thurzó plundered the countess's estates after her arrest to such an extent that in 1612 the chief justice of Hungary wrote to Thurzó and demanded that he hand back all the goods and monies which had been taken from Čachtice by his wife.

Of course, I am not the only person to be skeptical about the countess's guilt. The Hungarian judge, Dr. Irma Szádeczky-Kardoss, declared the proceedings against Báthory and her accomplices to be a "show trial . . . riddled with serious violations of the justice process of the time." I have attempted to provide a flavor of the summary nature of the proceedings, but more detail can be found in Dr. Szádeczky-Kardoss's *The Bloody Countess? An Examination of the Life and Trial of Erzsébet Báthory*, English translation by Lujza Nehrebeczky.

A few years after her incarceration, in 1614, the countess complained to her guards of having cold hands. The next morning, she was dead, at the age of fifty-four.

Use of Translated Text

Much of what we know about the proceedings against Countess Báthory and her accomplices comes from the original seventeenth-century Hungarian trial transcripts and various extant letters passing between key individuals at the time. This novel is a work of fiction; however, I have used the actual transcripts of the accomplices' confessions, witness evidence, and the trial judgment, along with various letters, in an attempt to portray the historical events in this book in a reasonably authentic way. A number of different translations of these documents exist, but I have used those contained in Tony Thorne's book, *Countess Dracula: The Life and Times of Elisabeth Bathory, the Blood Countess* and Kimberly Craft's books, *Infamous Lady: The True Story of Countess Erzsébet Báthory* and *The Private Letters of Countess Erzsébet Báthory*. Because this is a novel, I have felt free to cherry-pick and rephrase those translations at will, and this book in no way seeks to literally represent any individual or what they might have said.

I have relied particularly on translations of the following documents, and Thorne's discussion of them, found in *Countess Dracula*:

- Ficzkó's confession (*"Et Tortura"* and "Eleven Questions").
- The confessions of Ilona, Kata, and Dorka ("Let the Master Answer").
- Letter from the Vicar of Čachtice, Jan Ponikenus to his superior, Elias Láni, dated January 1, 1611 ("The Gynaeceum,"

"The One to Whom the Herbs and Flowers Talk," "Unknown and Mysterious Causes," "Plumes and Swagger," and "Paragon of Evil").

- Letter dated February 16, 1612, from Count Zsigmond Forgách, the chief justice of Hungary, to Thurzó ("The Palatine's Wife").
- Letters dated December 17, 1610, and February 12, 1611, from Count Zrínyi to Thurzó ("Protector of the Goodly and the Innocent").
- The court transcripts of the hearing of January 7, 1611, and the judgment handed down ("Bridle Thy Tongue, Woman," "Protector of the Goodly and the Innocent," "The Tenth Witness," and "Privy and Purposeful Accomplices").
- Translation, interpretation, and discussion of the word *Káröröm* and its fascinating meaning (*"Káröröm"*).
- Details of the portraits that might be of Báthory and the meaning of the objects portrayed ("Keys, Clocks, and Pearls").

I would like to credit Kimberly Craft's translation of Countess Báthory's letter to György Bánffy on February 3, 1606, in *Infamous Lady* for the opening epigraph and her translation of the countess's January 19, 1609, letter to Balázs Kisfaludi about the plight of the woman from Tokorcs ("Melancholia") in *The Private Letters of Countess Erzsébet Báthory*.

Any mistakes, misunderstandings, or artistic licenses in relation to interpreting these texts are entirely my own.

Acknowledgments

Thank you to the agent dream team, Jenny Bent and Juliet Mushens, for finding this book the perfect home with Harper Perennial, and for their support with everything else, from covers to titles and more.

I was struck by the wonderful enthusiasm of Amy Baker and the Harper Perennial team from our first video call. Thank you for bringing your energy and skill to the whole publishing process. Particular thanks to Millicent Bennett for her editorial vision and for being completely right about the prologue.

Turning a computer file into a fully fledged book requires so much work from so many different people. Huge thanks, therefore, to Liz Velez and the Harper Perennial marketing and publicity teams, particularly Megan Looney and Rachel Molland, to Alissa Dinallo for the stunning cover, and to Bob Castillo for an incredibly thorough copy edit.

Finally, thank you to my mother, Sandra, to whom this book is dedicated, for five decades of love and care, and to my children for being themselves.

About the Author

Sonia Velton has been a solicitor in Hong Kong, a Robert Schuman Scholar in Luxembourg, and spent eight years as an expat mother of three in Dubai. She now lives in Kent, England. She is the author of *Blackberry and Wild Rose*—which was short-listed for the Lucy Cavendish Fiction Prize, long-listed for the Historical Writers Association Debut Crown Award, and has been optioned for film—and *The Image of Her*, a literary thriller.